THE VICTOR
AND
THE VANQUISHED

BY
MARK WILDYR

HERNDON, VA

THE VICTOR
AND
THE VANQUISHED

BY

MARK WILDYR

STARbooks

KENDOCK, VA

Herndon, VA

Herndon, VA

CONTENTS

PROLOGUE

Approaching sleep had begun to blur images of the two of us skinny dipping in the creek until a familiar voice, thick with alcohol, came out of the darkness.

"Hey, where the fuck are you pansies?"

I lay in my bedroll feigning sleep as a familiar figure staggered out of the dark forest and wove its uncertain way across the moonlit clearing, bringing the sharp, tangy smell of beer along with it.

"How you girls doing?" The man tripped over his own feet and almost stumbled into the little lean-to we'd built.

"We ain't girls. And be quiet," my companion said in a hushed voice. "You'll wake him up."

"Fuck him. Let'm sleep. You'n me's gonna get it on."

My heart thudding wildly, I opened my eyes a squint and saw the man snatch the blanket off my friend.

"Don't! He might wake up. Please, not with him here."

"Shit, he's not dumb. He knows what you are. Hell, you probably had his cock, too."

The man swayed as he stripped off his shirt and dropped his pants. He wasn't wearing shorts, and his thing jutted out in front of him as if reaching for the stars before he knelt astride my friend. The man shoved his hips forward and almost fell. He was sweating, although the night was cool.

"That's it. Suck my cock like a good little pussy." He hunched his powerful hips. Soon, he was panting and groaning like he was about to get it, but then he pulled out, threw the long legs atop his shoulders and prodded the exposed crack. He shoved hard and then rocked forward so his butt rode high in the air. His naked cheeks dimpled in the moonlight as he thrust in and out of the smooth buns. He mumbled and picked up speed – and urgency.

At last, he gave a lunge and reared up until his head struck the top of the lean-to. "Take it, you fairy. Take my cum, you fucking queer. Ungh!" Panting from his exertions and the force of his ejaculation, he snarled, "You like that, don't you, faggot? You like my big cock up your ass better'n his little prick, I'll bet."

"Please don't wake him. We didn't do anything."

His seed spent, the man jerked out and stood, his long cock sagging like a piece of bark peeling from a tree trunk. "I oughta make you lick it clean."

Instead, he picked up his clothes and reeled away, pausing to cleanse himself in the creek before stumbling noisily down the path. When he was gone, the night grew quiet – unnaturally so. The nocturnal creatures had gone

1

silent. A quarter moon hid behind a bank of clouds. Even Big Beaver, normally a noisy stream, seemed muted. The scent of honeysuckle wafted in on a silent breeze. The odor was so thick I could almost taste it.

I watched, fascinated by the silhouette of my companion's dick pulsing above his stomach, bobbing down onto his belly, and then rearing back up again. It was almost as big as the man's had been.

"You awake?" The whisper was barely audible.

I didn't answer. I didn't even breathe. My thing throbbed against my britches so hard it hurt, but I didn't dare move.

2

CHAPTER 1

The Native American Settlement of Rolling Hills

"Wilam!" Matthew called from the sidelines.

I waved him off and got set as the pitcher sent a fastball over the plate. Hitchcock, a chubbo whose belly moved slower than his hips, whipped thin air – with the bat and the belly. I rolled my shoulders and pounded the glove with a fist to loosen up, hoping my brother would go away. I didn't get a chance to play ball with the other guys very often, and I didn't want to be pulled off the field. Besides, I'd really come down to the tribal rec center to find James, but he wasn't around. I planned to go looking for him pretty soon.

"William Greyhorse!" Matthew yelled. "Hey, man, you need to get your butt home."

"Not now."

"Okay, but don't say I didn't warn you. The old man's on a rip-snorter, and he sent me to get you."

I spotted the kid whose glove I'd borrowed and motioned him over. Then I ran to catch up with my brother and fell into step beside him, which wasn't easy. Matthew'd turned twenty-one this summer. Now he could get into the bars over in Mapleton without sneaking around, but it also meant he stood six-one and had legs to match. They ate up the ground a lot faster than mine. I was a little better than five-nine but considerably short of five-ten. I'd already accepted the fact I was the runt of the family. My dad was an even six feet. Something I'd never match.

"What's going on?" I was panting because he hadn't shortened his stride for me like he usually did. A bad sign.

"We're leaving."

"What do you mean?" I asked between gasps.

"Just that. We're leaving. Got almost everything packed. We're pulling out soon's we get home."

"Why? What happened?"

I asked the question from long experience. This wouldn't be the first time my dad – or my mom, for that matter – got drunk and pulled something so bad we had to pick up and leave. We'd already moved half a dozen times, always ending up back on the reservation after a period of exile. That's why I was eighteen and still had another year to go in high school. Or that's what I told myself, anyway. I think it was probably true.

"Old man got in a fight last night ... or maybe it was this morning. Cut up Brewster Whitetail pretty bad."

"Drunk?"

Matthew's laugh was almost a snarl. "Both of them."

"Kill him?"

"No, but it's bad."

"Where'd it happen?"

"Not on the rez, thank God. Else the FBI'd chase us all over hell and gone."

"How come the cops didn't pick him up?"

"Him and his buddies were partying out in the boondocks somewhere. He hightailed it home while the others took Brewster to the hospital. The cops'll be along soon enough. That's why he's in a hurry."

"Where're we going?"

"Dunno. He got some money from Uncle Dulce. Said something about New Mexico."

Our place was a rundown affair sitting right at the eastern edge of the little settlement of Rolling Hills. The big barn behind it was usually empty except for junk. Now, our twenty-year-old pickup was hidden in the middle of it, half loaded with our belongings. The truck had been black once, but the Bondo smeared all over it rendered the vehicle two-toned. Black and gray usually looked pretty good together, but not on a beat-up Dodge half-ton. The barn already smelled of rubber, gasoline, and burned motor oil.

Dad lurched out the back door loaded down with his hunting rifle and fishing tackle. He was sweaty and wild-eyed from his drinking, but he didn't seem drunk. Cutting up a man must have sobered him some.

"Where the hell you been?"

"Rec center." When speaking to my father, I kept my answers as brief as possible.

"Well, get your ass in gear. We're out of here in ten minutes."

I headed for the room I shared with my sisters, Nola and little Junie. There wasn't much I wanted to salvage except for my carving knives – and my clothes, for all they were worth. Mostly Matthew's hand-me-downs cut to size.

My knives were something else. Because I never knew when Mom would pass out for the day or when Dad would come home mad dog drunk, I was practically house-bound all summer on account of the girls. During the school year, I'd rush home as soon as class was over. I whittled to keep busy while I was stuck at home. Got pretty good at it, too. I made all the toys the girls ever had, including their dolls.

The last couple of Christmases I'd even sold a few carvings. I put the little money I made right back into better knives. Mom said it was a waste of good money buying up different carving knives, but if it was, it was the only wasting I ever did. I never bought candy or soda pop like the other guys. Sometimes, I got sweets for Nola and little Junie with money I made from doing quick chores around town or selling a carving.

I liked to whittle animals mostly, but I did a head of Nola once that looked pretty much like her. Or at least the way she looked when I carved it a couple of years back. Never been able to capture little Junie, though. It always came out bland like a baby's face. Nola said that's because Junie had a bland baby's face, even if she was walking around and jabbering hard enough to raise a dust devil.

I passed Mom in the living room. She was folding some sheets and towels and looked sober. Tired but sober. Her cheeks were sorta mashed in – you know, sunken. She'd been over at Uncle Dulce's and Aunt Aurora's last night, and she usually didn't drink around her youngest sister's family. They were born-again people. That was why I'd been able to get away for a ball game down at the rec center this morning.

Nola, thirteen and big enough to know what was going on, seemed scared. Little Junie wasn't yet three, and she just looked excited. Of course, every day was an adventure to her. She was a happy baby except when my dad was in the house raising hell.

"Wilam!" she yelled when I came through the door. She called me that because she couldn't pronounce William when she first started talking. The rest of the family fell into the habit of using that label, and pretty soon I was Wilam to the whole reservation. I patted Junie on the head and gave her a kiss on the cheek before rushing to our room and slinging my things into plastic grocery bags.

We abandoned all of the furniture; it was mostly junk, anyway. That left enough room in the bed of the pickup for the girls and me. Matthew kicked over the motor and made straight for the Mini-Mart at the south end of the reservation for gas and food to take on the road. Dad and Mom went inside while he filled the tank and a couple of Jerry cans.

I bailed out of the bed of the pickup when I spotted James walking down the road on those long legs of his. I knew he'd seen me, but he veered off around behind the store. I found him sitting at a little picnic table they put back there for customers.

"I heard," he said.

"Yeah, looks like the Greyhorse family's off and running again. Man, I get tired of it. I wish we'd just settle down somewhere."

He didn't have an answer for my wishes, so we went quiet. Loblolly pines flooded the clearing with the sharp smell of resin. Somewhere a woodpecker tapped out a message only he understood. It got a little awkward after a minute. I put it down to the way our camping trip had ended. When I woke up the next morning, he'd been asleep, so I went down to the creek to wash up. By the time I came back, he'd cleared out. Truth be told, I was a little relieved at the time, but James was a friend from way back, and we needed to fix things.

"I've been looking for you. Why've you been so scarce?" I asked.

"Me? I've been around."

"I usually see you every day. It's been three days since we camped out on the Beaver. How come you haven't been around?"

"Busy." He blew it off.

"Where'd you disappear to that morning?"

5

"Had things to do. Thought you went on home, anyway."

"You knew I didn't. My blankets were still there. I just went to clean up in the creek."

He shrugged. I sat down on the table across from him. Finally, he said something I didn't catch.

"What?" I looked over at him. He had on his usual blue jeans, gray muscle shirt, and home-stitched buckskin moccasins. He'd worn those moccasins ever since his feet quit growing. He looked good. That thought was off and running before I could grab hold and pull it back.

"You was awake, wasn't you?"

"What do you mean?" I played dumb.

He looked at me funny, but I guess he accepted my lie. "I wish you had been. Awake, I mean. It'd be easier."

"What'd be easier?"

"Letting you know how I feel ... about you."

"I know how you feel. We're friends. We're about the only friends each other has."

"Yeah. I guess." His fingertip traced a set of initials carved into the rough oak table. "We're both loners."

"Just a couple of oddballs." Why the hell had I said that?

"You're just different because you act like the man of the family and take care of your sisters" There was bitterness in his voice. "Me, I'm a certified oddball."

"That's trash talk, James."

"Okay, here's some more. I wish it had been you the other night. I've been wanting to do it with you for a long time, but I was scared to let you know." His voice faltered. "Every ... every other guy on the rez who don't have a girl for the night comes knocking, and I do whatever they want. I do it even when I don't like them. You never came around like that, so I just kept my mouth shut, afraid of chasing off my best friend."

I sat there with my mouth open and my cheeks flaming.

He fixed me with dark, haunted eyes. "Go ahead, say it."

"S ... say what?" I stuttered.

"Whatever you're thinking. Call me a queer or a faggot. Tell me you don't want anything to do with me anymore. Or tell me it's okay, and we're still friends. Or tell me you've been wanting us to do it, too."

"Why're you saying this to me?" I swatted at a wasp buzzing around my head. It circled once more and then flew away.

He shrugged and glanced off into the trees over my shoulder. "Because ... because I like you. I thought you liked me, too."

My face felt hot. "I do, you know that. But ... but ...."

"Yeah, but not like that."

"I don't know. Maybe I do. Or could. But we're leaving. Going away. Probably forever."

6

"No, you'll comeback someday. I know you're leaving for right now. I wouldn't of got up the nerve to tell you if you wasn't." He looked at me again. "You're taking off in a few minutes, so I can't chase you away. I can say anything I want."

"Okay. Now that's out of the way, is there anything else?" Where'd that stupid question come from?

"Just that you're the best-looking guy around. That your're fun and a good friend. That I want to touch you and do things with you." He shut up for a moment while he studied those initials enshrined in the picnic table. "That's all there is, except ...." He swallowed hard. "Well, except to say I'll wait for you if you ask me to. I won't get with anyone else as long as I know you're coming back for me someday. I can do it. I know I can."

A shiver went down my back, and my thing started to get stiff in my pants. I couldn't get my voice past my throat.

His puppy dog look changed to one of anguish. He dropped his gaze to the table again. "That's okay, I understand. I gotta let you know something, Wilam. No matter what happens, I gotta say it." He lifted his head and met my eyes. "I love you, man."

I'd have said something to that, all right, but I don't know what because right then Matthew poked his head around the building. My brother's glance swept James and then fixed on me.

"Come on, Pissant. The old man's ready to go."

I shoved both hands deep into my pockets and turned to walk away. At the corner, I glanced over my shoulder. James looked like a guy facing the gallows. In a way, maybe he was. We were a band without a tradition of respect for Two Spirits like some tribes had. I guess we acted more like white folks when it came to people who were different. You know, gays they called them when they wanted to be polite. Queers, when they didn't.

My heart gave a sudden lurch. It was almost like I was abandoning him, leaving him alone and exposed to all the predators who cursed him by day and sought him out by night. With a lump in my throat, I rushed to help little Junie into the bed of the pickup, breaking the invisible tether that connected us.

CHAPTER 2

As we sped south on the blacktop, I lay on some of our things in the back of the pickup and wouldn't talk to anyone. Not even Junie's cute tricks could get me out of my blue funk. I kept thinking of James back at the store. Of course, I'd heard the stories about him. How he didn't like sports or hunting or roughhousing. How he looked at guys in a way that made them queasy.

He used to hang around our place all the time, but lately my mom didn't even try to hide the way she felt about him. When my old man, Woodrow – his friends and drinking buddies called him Woodie – came home, he'd chase James off by shouting curses and slinging rocks at him. James wouldn't show his face if the pickup was parked beside the house.

We pulled off into a roadside park sometime before nightfall and ate some of the bread and lunch meat we'd brought with us. Actually, with the potato chips and pickles and sodas and things, it was probably a better meal than we'd had in a while. I always liked baloney. Liked the way it smelled and how it felt on my tongue, and the taste, too, of course.

My brother'd done most of the driving because the old man was suffering from a hangover, and that was a dangerous time for everyone. It was all right if he passed out, but if he was conscious, he made sure everyone shared his pain. Mom wasn't doing too good either. I couldn't tell if it was a dry drunk or her way of isolating herself from the rest of us. Anyway, it was up to me to make sure Nola and little Junie were tucked into their blankets in the bed of the truck that night.

I had trouble sleeping even though I was tired. I kept thinking of James and what he'd said and what he wanted to do with me. My thing got hard again. I put my hand down on it, but with the girls in the truck with me, all I could do was turn over on my side and try to ignore it. It took an awful lot of ignoring.

I remembered another camp-out with James on the Beaver a few years back. We weren't more than fifteen, and that was before they started saying things about him. After we'd eaten scraps of fried beef slapped between slices of light bread, we sat around our little campfire and talked in the dark. We'd opened up and revealed things we probably wouldn't have in another time or place. I told him some of the bad stuff my dad had done and how I felt about things.

He'd let me know how it was with him and his mom. His dad and both his brothers were gone, lost in a bad wreck that took them all at one time. Two uncles and a cousin died in the same accident. James Longhunter was one of the few kids on the rez who didn't have a male relative he could look up to. Unless you counted me, that is. Mine was living and breathing, but he was dead to me. That night, like it was bound to happen, the subject had turned to girls.

"You like them?" James had asked.

"Sure. You?"

"They're all right, but I ain't sure they're worth all the trouble."

I thought that one over. My dad put my mom through all kinds of hell, but sometimes she gave it back to him when she had a hangover or didn't like the way things were going. Matthew was always sniffing around one girl or the other. I tried to act grown up about it.

"Piece of ass is worth a little trouble."

"You know that for fact? You ever had any?"

"I guess not," I admitted. I hadn't expected him to call me on it.

"You guess not? Seems like that's something you oughta know for sure."

"Mary Pilgrim felt my thing in the coat closet at school."

"Mary feels all the boys' pricks."

"She ever feel you up?"

"Tried it."

"You ever … you know, done it to a girl."

He shook his head. "Uh uh." Then he got real quiet for a second, and I was scared about what he was going to say next. "Don't know if I want to."

"Why not? Man's gotta get a little relief," That sounded more like Matthew than me.

"There's other ways to take care of that."

"Like what?" Right away I wished I could call those words back.

"Like doing it to yourself or with a good friend. You know, a special friend."

I'd been guilty of the first, so I scooted over to the second and started babbling. "With a friend? A friend's not built like a girl. Well … uh … unless the friend was a girl. But then, she'd be a girl, and that's not what you meant." I ground to a halt and shut up. I was glad it was dark, so he couldn't see me blushing.

Suddenly uncomfortable around my best friend, I stood up and stretched. That wasn't the smartest thing to do because my cock had got hard, and by the firelight, I could see where he was looking. Ashamed, I rolled up in my blankets with my back to him. After that, he went off to take a piss or something and didn't come back for a long time. When he did, he spread his bedroll on the other side of the fire.

Had he been thinking those things about me way back then? Inside my head I heard his voice. "I love you, man."

I shivered in the dark night. Nobody'd ever said that to me before – except little Junie.

# # # # #

10

Matthew had been right; it was New Mexico. Three days after we left the reservation, we ended up in Albuquerque. Dad moved us in with somebody he knew in a little apartment in what they called the Southeast Heights. There are lots of nice neighborhoods in the Southeast Heights, but ours was nothing but apartments and more apartments in a place called the War Zone. That pretty well described it. People moved in and out all the time. You went to bed with one neighbor, and woke up the next morning with a different one. Lots of drinking and stealing and trouble of all kinds. It was a rough place for raising two girls.

The apartment was in a red brick duplex that looked good from the outside but was pretty beat-up on the inside. The Tolliver family, that was Dad's friends, lived in the place's one bedroom, and we crowded into the living room, sleeping on blankets on the floor. After a month of this, Tolliver'd had enough, so my dad found us an even more rundown apartment in an even worse area a little to the south.

If the place we left was the War Zone, this was the Combat Area. We didn't have any furniture to take with us except for what we could borrow or what we found stacked beside the overflowing dumpsters. That was where everybody abandoned junk too big to fit in the metal containers. Sometimes it looked like a tornado had ripped away a house and left broken furniture scattered all over the place.

Mom got on food stamps and some kind of welfare, but even so, things were worse than on the reservation. I didn't dare go anywhere because of fear for the girls. But now, it wasn't just Mom and Dad I had to worry about; it was the neighbors, too.

When school started, I about fretted myself sick over little Junie being home alone with Mom. At noontime, I'd run all the way to the apartment to make sure she had something to eat. Then at last bell, I'd rush back again because by that time Nola was home from school, and she was getting big enough to attract boys. There were lots of them around, swaggering like they were something special, wearing their pants so low on the hips their ass cheeks showed through their underwear. Trying to look and sound meaner than the next guy seemed to be a way of life around there.

# # # # #

My nineteenth birthday passed without anybody taking notice except Nola and little Junie. They did the best they could without money to spend on presents, but the little bag they made out of denim from a worn-out pair of jeans was exactly what I needed to hold my whittling knives. At least they cared.

A week later, Matthew surprised me by showing up on the schoolyard one afternoon and claiming he needed my help with something. He'd already checked up on the girls, and they were okay. After he said it wouldn't take but a few minutes, I went with him.

He took me to a place about four blocks from our apartment, which was where his latest girlfriend, Myra Henderson, lived. There was another girl there, too, one a little younger than Myra, maybe even younger than me. She was kinda pretty in a hard sort of way. Anyway, Matthew said happy birthday, put my hand in hers, and shoved us toward the bedroom.

"You didn't tell me he's so cute." The girl giggled and pushed me through the door. "My name's Lottie."

"William." I automatically fed her my name. "What ... what ...."

"Isn't that sweet. Matt took you by surprise."

"Matt? Oh, you mean Matthew. Uh ... yeah ... surprise."

"Me, too, 'cause you're way better looking than what he said. Sorta sexy, too." She threw her arms loosely around my shoulders and put her round little forehead right between my eyes. "I'm your birthday present, Billie Boy."

"Uh ... my name's William. What do you mean?"

"I mean what do you like, honey?" One thin arm snaked its way to my chest, paused, and then wandered south. In a second, her fingers were on my thing, massaging it through my britches. I glanced over at the door and was glad to see she'd closed it.

"Feels interesting." She giggled again.

After the shock wore off, my cock began to grow. The rest of me froze up, but that thing crawled around like it was looking for a way out. Lottie rubbed a little more, and then she pulled my shirt out of my pants and inserted her little hand. After she did that, it grew a lot faster.

Before I knew it, she had my shirt off and my pants down around my ankles. Then she pushed me over on the bed and knelt on my legs. By then, my thing was as hard as it was ever going to get. She played with me a little, bending over to kiss the tip and lick it once or twice. Then she stripped off her own clothes. She had little pointed tits that didn't turn me on, but she was cute in the face, if you could get around all the paint she wore. Her hips were nice and round.

Lottie made such a big deal out of fitting a rubber over my thing that I about lost it. When it was the way she wanted, she raised her ass and sat down on me. She had a little trouble getting it all in, not that I was so big, but she hadn't put on any lubrication to grease things up. When I was finally inside her, she raised up on me once, sat back down, and I came.

"Unggggggh," I moaned, giving a couple of pathetic little wiggles with my hips.

"Did Willie come already? Must have been a long time since your last piece."

That was all the sympathy she had, apparently, because she got right up, swiped herself with a tissue, and started dressing. That's when it came to me Matthew had paid good money for me to get a piece of ass, and I'd messed it up something terrible.

I was lying there on my back wearing only socks – two on my feet and one on my shriveled up thing – when she reached for the doorknob.

"Wait! Let me get dressed first." I stood up and started to tug on my pants when she walked up behind me and ran her hands over my back and buttocks.

"You know, you really are sexy. It's not fair you coming so quick and all. Get on the bed and let Lottie work on you some more."

That was absolutely the last thing I wanted – except for Matthew knowing he'd wasted his money. Since I didn't know how to stop the second without doing the first, I lay back and let Lottie go to work.

This time, she *had* to work. My old thing had just performed, and no matter how miserable a showing, it wasn't interested in tackling the chore again. After she sucked around on my tits and my navel and kissed me all over, the reluctant warrior finally came alive.

She got over on her back and pulled me on top of her. That felt a whole lot better, and I think maybe I got her to pop her nuts – or whatever girls have – at least once before I spilled out into my rubber again.

Getting dressed was awkward. Embarrassing, I guess you could say. No, more like mortifying. Still, it was all worth it on seeing Matthew's shit-eating grin when I came out of the bedroom.

"How was it, bro?"

"Prime!" I gave Lottie's thin shoulders a squeeze. "Thanks, honey," I pecked her on the cheek.

"Anytime, good looking." She played the game for me. "That was goo-od. You can do it for me anytime."

I couldn't get out of there fast enough, and I knew for damned sure I wasn't going to do that for her again anytime soon. Like never. The only thing that made it worth doing in the first place was Matthew thought enough of his little brother to fix him up.

# # # # #

Life settled into a routine of sorts. Albuquerque was an okay place once you got away from the War Zone. It was spread out a lot, so it looked bigger than it was. The main drag was this really long street called Central Avenue that ran from the foothills on the east down through the Rio Grande Valley, where it hooked up with I-40 and scooted on up Nine Mile Hill to the mesa on the west.

A big mountain called Sandia Crest sat right at the eastern edge of town, and some smaller ones named the Manzanos lay directly south of it. Somebody told me Sandia meant watermelon, and Manzano was Mexican for apple. The names sorta fit.

The oldest part of town was down in the valley where some families came south from a place called Bernalillo – they pronounce it with a "yo," even though there wasn't a "y" in it – and established the Villa – another "y"

13

when there wasn't one – de Alburquerque. I guess they made a mistake in the spelling, because there's one less "r" in the name now. They called that part "Old Town." Those original settlers were Spanish people, and there were still a lot of them here. I'd never met any of them before, and they sorta made me understand how the white folks felt about a lot of us Indians running around Mapleton.

They took some getting used to, but I learned some everyday words in Spanish and got along with them okay. In fact, I liked them. They didn't always think like white folks, which they call Anglos around here, and that was refreshing.

# # # # #

I came home after school one day and found Nola trying to get my mom into bed. She'd passed out from drinking, and the two girls had managed to drag her into the bedroom. I lifted her up on the bed, feeling how thin and bony she was. The old man came in right about then, yelling for Cora. Cora's my mom.

I met him in the living room. "She's asleep right now."

"Passed out, you mean. Where is she?" He elbowed me aside without waiting for an answer.

My father's darker than I am, sort of a nutmeg color, but you could see he'd been a good-looking man at one time. That was before the drinking bloated him and put a hard cast to his features. Matthew and I called him the "old man," but he was only thirty-eight or so. He married my mom when he was seventeen because she was pregnant with Matthew.

When he discovered Mom was in the bedroom, he marched in there and stripped off his shirt before closing the door behind him. "Wake up, Cora!" he roared. "Wake up, you damned cunt."

I heard him trying to slap her awake. I sure wished Matthew was here. Dad was around two hundred and had me by fifty pounds. Not only that, he was a brawler. My brother was more his size. One day, I'd have to take him on, but right now my sisters needed my protection more than Mom. I grabbed some things for a sandwich and got my whittling knives, telling them we were going on a picnic. We were almost out of sight before my old man came to the front door in his shorts, yelling for Nola to come back.

I pushed her ahead of me down the sidewalk and went straight to the neighborhood park where there'd be some people around. It took a few minutes for the girls to loosen up and pretend they were having a good time. Junie wanted to go to the public swimming pool about a quarter mile up the street, but we didn't have any suits. Of course, she was a baby and could have played in the water in her underwear if she hadn't had a big tear in the ass-end of her panties.

After I spent some time pushing the girls in the swings and weighing down one end of the teeter-totter, they settled down. I did some carving while

Junie took a nap in Nola's arms. I whittled each of them a beaver, wishing I had some paint to do them up right.

After two hours, I risked going back to the apartment. The girls stood outside on the sidewalk while I went in to check things out. The front screen door squeaked like a cat with its tail in a rocker, but the old man was passed out naked on one side of the bed. Mom was still zonked on the other side. He had undressed her, and it looked like dried cum was smeared all over her. Ashamed, I covered her with a sheet and stood looking down at the helpless man sprawled on the bed before me. I wanted to take after him with my carving knives; instead, I closed the bedroom door and brought the girls inside.

From long, painful experience, they knew enough to go about their business without making noise. I found something to patch Junie's underwear and spent an hour trying to sew it on so it wouldn't fall off the first time she put them on. Then Nola and I went through the drawer they shared in the old bureau in the corner and patched every other piece of clothing that needed it.

CHAPTER 3

There were a bunch of Mexican kids at my school. One, named Enrique Marquez – Enrique was their way of saying Henry – hadn't been here in America too long, so he was having trouble keeping up. He found out I liked to whittle when I brought some of my carvings to the school's crafts display. After that, he started going out of his way to speak to me. At first, it was only "Hello" or "How's it going?"

One day between classes, he showed me some pieces he'd carved. They were mostly Mexican things like burros and sombreros – stuff like that. They were pretty good though. We talked a little about how we worked and got friendly enough for him to go along with me one afternoon to check on my sisters after school. The girls were okay, so we sat outside the front door on some plastic milk crates and whittled together.

"You like it here?" I asked as we worked.

"Yeah, but wish I do better in school. My English, y'know." He spoke in a kind of singsong that reminded me of some of the old folks back on the rez.

"You speak it as good as me."

"I do okay with talking, but reading – not so good."

So I started working with him on his lessons. Tutoring, the English teacher called it when she learned I was helping out. His grades started picking up, but the funny thing was – mine did, too. Not only that, but when I started correcting his English, my talking started getting a whole lot better. I'd gotten lazy about saying things sloppy. It didn't seem like such a big deal around home, but when I took on the chore of helping Enrique, that put some kind of obligation on me to do better.

He returned the favor by taking me down to the New Mexico State Fairgrounds where they had this big flea market every weekend except in September when the fair's on. He introduced me to a bluff, red-faced Anglo named Ben Ames who had a booth there. Actually, it was just a couple of card tables shoved together with lots of doodads on them – mostly glass, but some wood. Ben sometimes bought Enrique's carvings.

"Show him your stuff," Enrique said after they'd finished dickering over his work.

I hauled out a balsa wood whitetail deer with long, delicate legs from the grocery sack I'd brought along.

Ames examined the carving carefully, turning it over in his hands several times. He seemed to like it all right, but his expression never changed.

"Okay, what else you got?" He looked at the bristly porcupine I handed over, but barely glanced at the other three pieces. "You always work in balsa?"

I shrugged. "Sometimes pine or oak. Whatever I can get my hands on."

"Mmmm."

What was that supposed to mean?

"I'll give you three for the deer and two and a half for each of the others."

"O ... okay. Can I bring you some more pieces?"

"Sure. Don't guarantee to buy them. Depends on how your stuff moves. Bring me something in a harder wood, next time. My customers prefer that. Some of them can't tell the difference between stained balsa wood and walnut, but some of them can. What'd you say you name was?"

"William. William Greyhorse."

"You Indian? What's your tribe?"

"Yes sir. I'm Pinoan."

"Never heard of them. Course, that's not surprising. I guess y'all got four or five hundred tribes, and nobody knows any of them except for big ones like Navajos and 'Paches."

"We're a little band from up north of here."

"Okay, bring me some more of your work, and maybe we can do business."

Enrique and I left the fairgrounds and headed down Louisiana, me with thirteen dollar bills burning my pocket. For the first time since coming to Albuquerque, I had a little money.

My buddy peeled away on business of his own before we got back home, leaving me on an emotional low. My sudden affluence didn't do me much good. I couldn't let on to my folks I had any money. I'd give it to them if they'd spend it on food and clothes and rent, but it'd just go down a bottle for one or the other of them. My dad drank with Tolliver and a couple of others; Mom didn't need any drinking buddies. She mostly drank by herself.

I bought Nola a jacket for three dollars at the thrift store and claimed somebody'd left it on the schoolyard. My old man didn't give a damn if I stole something, but he would have been on me in a minute for making an honest dollar and not turning it over to him.

After Ben Ames bought the next bunch of pieces – even though they were still balsa wood – I bought little Junie some clothes, claiming I did errands at the thrift shop to pay for them. One day when we didn't have any food in the place, I bought some staples and didn't tell them anything. Nobody bothered to ask, so I kept it up. Soon, I was the only one bringing in groceries. Matthew helped out some, but he wasn't around most of the time.

I started whittling hard, and Ben took everything I brought him. My knives were good enough by now, but I invested in better wood, the hard kind that wouldn't break the first time it got a hard knock. That almost backfired on me because different woods take different techniques, and I had to learn all over again. Still, at three and four dollars for the hardwood pieces, I was

18

bringing in a pretty steady income. I never spent any of the money on myself – except for the supply of wood I needed. Everything I didn't spend on the girls or for food, I hid in a hollow behind a baseboard I pried loose. I made sure Nola knew about it in case something happened to me, but I didn't tell anybody else.

Before long, there was a nice little sum hiding there – some twenties, four or five tens, and a few fives – more money than I'd ever seen before. I was scheming on how to buy the girls Christmas gifts without tipping my hand when I came home to find Matthew waiting for me.

"Man, where'd you get all that money?"

My heart sank right down into my shoes. "What money?"

"The old man found your stash."

I let out a cuss word. "Did he take it all?"

"What do you think?"

"Is he in there now?"

"With that kind of loot? Don't talk crazy. He's down at the bar. Mom talked him out of twenty dollars for groceries, but she already spent it on booze."

I started to brush past Matthew, but he stopped me with a hand on my arm. "Two hundred dollars, Pissant. He thinks you stole it."

"Don't you?"

He shook his head. "No, my little brother doesn't steal. Not even coats and clothes for his sisters. Or food for the family. I figure you're selling your carvings."

"Yeah. Found a guy who buys them from me."

"Down at the flea market, right?"

I looked up at him. "How'd you know?"

"Me and Myra were over there roaming around one weekend, and I saw this guy with a lot of wood stuff. I thought I'd tell you about him, but I started looking at some of the pieces and recognized a couple of things."

"Yeah, Enrique took me to him."

"You know, I admire the way you handled things. That was pretty smart doling it out for groceries. If you'd spent the money on yourself, the old man would have noticed. By the way, he won't take after you because he thinks you stole it, but he'll probably tear you a new one for not handing it over."

"I don't give a damn. Let him do his worst. How'd he find it, anyway?"

"Little Junie."

"Aw, shit." I remembered the last time I added money to the stash. I'd turned around and saw the baby standing there watching me. I made some lame-assed comment about fixing a loose baseboard, but she was a curious little cuss and took to pulling on it. It was bad luck the old man was there when she managed to tear it off.

"At first, he figured the people in the apartment before us left it behind," Matthew said. "He finally figured out it was yours when Junie kept saying, 'Wilam.' Sorry, man. You got any money left?"

"Not if he found it. I don't carry any on me."

"I can spare a twenty."

He'd been working on a construction crew for the past couple of months, but he was living over at Myra's place, and most of his paycheck went to support the two of them. Knowing how much he liked to hit the bottle, I was surprised he held onto the job. He wasn't as bad as Dad or Mom, but I tried to warn him he was on a slippery slope. Every time I did, he'd just get his back up and claim he wasn't a sot and never would be.

I shrugged away his offer. "Thanks, but I'll be okay. I've got some stuff I can take to the flea market. If they don't sell, I'll let you know. You know, for grocery money."

We slapped hands, and I don't ever remember feeling as close to Matthew as I did right then. Not even when he bought me a piece of tail. I watched him walk out of sight around the corner heading for his girlfriend's place, and then I went inside. Little Junie let out a whoop and ran for me, yelling "Wilam" like she always did. I picked her up and gave her a buzz on the cheek. No use holding it against her. She was too little to know what she'd done.

Half the baseboards were ripped out in the living room from where my dad had rooted around trying to find another hidey-hole. There wasn't one, of course. Nola, sitting on the couch sewing up a hole in her favorite skirt, wouldn't meet my eyes. It was her way of letting me know she was feeling bad for me. I went over and patted her on the head to ease things up.

"Don't do that." She aimed an elbow at me. She didn't mean it. She just didn't know how to handle my loss. I flicked her on the ear, and she stabbed at me with a needle.

"Mom!" she called. It was a feeble yell. She wasn't really asking for help. I gave her a smile, and she couldn't resist giving up a little one in return.

Mom was at the kitchen table with a bottle of whiskey clasped in both hands. There wasn't a glass in sight; she'd been drinking straight from the bottle. I went in and kissed her on top of the head. She looked startled like she hadn't even noticed I'd come in. She stared up me, but her eyes weren't focused. She looked like she wanted to ask me something but couldn't remember what it was. I knew what it was, all right. She wanted to ask for some more money. I just eased the bottle out of her hands and put it in the sink.

The basin and the counters were clear of dirty dishes. Nola was responsible for that. My little sister, coming up on fourteen, was more of a homemaker than our mother. Cora looked like somebody's grandmother, and she was only somewhere in her thirties. She'd had Matthew when she was sixteen, but I wasn't up to figuring out how old that made her right then.

20

# # # # #

I thought I was handling things pretty well, you know, like a grown-up, but when I heard the pickup screech to a halt at the curb outside the door sometime after midnight, I turned into a scared little kid. I cowered in my covers on a pallet beside the sofa. The old man hit the door like a hurricane. He flipped on the lights and looked around, bleary-eyed. I could smell him from clear across the room. I pretended to be asleep, but he headed straight for me.

"Wilam." He tore off my blankets. "I need some more money."

"I ain't got any more. You took it all."

My English grammar usually went to hell when I was under stress, and being scared of this unpredictable bastard was big-time stress. Strands of black hair stood out in all directions, the streaks of gray in it looking like snakes twisting in the darkness. If he'd braided his hair like he usually did before leaving this morning, it'd come undone – or some doxy had taken it out. Frantic black eyes with a fevered shine moved restlessly. The two-inch scar under his right eye from a childhood knife fight was livid, a sure sign of rage.

"Don't gimme that shit. Gimme the money. I got people waiting on me."

"I don't have any more. You took it all." If I said it enough times, maybe he'd believe me.

He grabbed me by the hair and dragged me out of my bedroll. He had me standing up in my undershorts in front of the girls before I knew what was happening.

"Then, by God, go steal some more. I need it."

He was just ranting. He thought I stole it, all right, but he knew I couldn't go find any money right then.

He slapped me with the back of his hand. The blow whipped my head around. My hands flew up to protect my face, and he got me hard in the belly. I went over onto the floor trying to suck air. Quicker than a snake, he had his belt off and started whaling on me. My back. My legs. My buttocks. Still winded, I huddled there protecting my belly and took it. Through my pain, I could hear Nola sobbing and Junie crying aloud.

When he turned on them, I grabbed him around the legs, but I was too weak to do anything but hold on. He tripped, and that refocused his fury on me. I don't know when he quit hitting me. The next thing I remembered was Nola bathing my face with a cool cloth. When I opened my eyes, she lifted my head and fed me a sip of water.

"Are you all right?" The voice surprised us. Mom stood across the room with a tattered old housecoat clutched around her.

"No, he's not all right!" Nola shrieked. "He's beat to a pulp."

"It's … it's all right," I muttered, trying to muster a smile. "I'll be okay. We all need to get some sleep. Uh … where is he?"

21

"He left," Nola said. "I hope he never comes back."

"Don't say that, honey. He's your father. He didn't mean it, son." Mom's wheedling voice set my nerves on edge. "He won't even remember it when he sobers up. Everything will be all right."

Lord, how many times had I heard that tired old line? It wouldn't be so bad if Dad just whipped me and let it go at that, but when he started hitting, he got to liking it so much he forgot to stop.

"Everything will be all right?" Nola yelled, setting little Junie to crying again. Mom just looked confused. "Stop making excuses for him. He's a monster. Go get the police. Wilam needs help."

Mom's eyes widened. She shook a step backward. "Police? Why would I go for the police?"

"All right, I will." Nola stood her ground.

"No, honey." I clutched my sister's arm. "I'm … okay. It's just bruises." I swallowed my pain. "Mom, go on back to bed. Nola, settle Junie down. Okay?"

After everything was more or less calm, I lay on my blankets flexing my arms and legs. Nothing seemed to be broken, but my back burned and smarted. The blanket scratched more than it ought to. My legs cramped and my breath felt hot. When I couldn't stand it any longer, I went into the bathroom and sat in the tub, letting the cold shower drench me. It was a quarter of an hour before the sting from the cuts and bruises faded and my nerves settled down enough to relax the cramps in my legs.

I didn't get much sleep after that. I kept listening for the old man to return and wondering how I was going to get through my classes at school when the sun came up.

CHAPTER 4

The next morning, every step, every movement was painful. At times it felt like something or the other was going to snap or fall off. When I sat down in homeroom, I almost let out a groan. I managed to meet all my classes that day, but when the coach wanted me to suit out in shorts for PE, I had to play sick. Hell, I was sick.

"What's ailing you, Greyhorse?" Coach Gibbins was a broad-shouldered man who was still in good shape even if he was coming up on forty.

"All over. I'm sick, Coach."

He looked at me so hard I knew he'd figured out my problem. I thought for a minute he was going to make me strip anyway, and if he saw my bruises, he'd call the cops. It was child abuse, pure and simple. Unless it wasn't – you know, because I was nineteen now. Still, the authorities might raise a stink, and my old man would never forgive that. This probably wasn't the first time Coach had run into this situation because he nodded and sent me walking around the track in my street clothes.

I was surprised Matthew kept my secret, but apparently he had. The old man remained convinced I'd stolen the money, and if that's what he thought, so much the better. The truth was, I'd never stolen anything in my life. After hours of hard work and several cut fingers, I sold some more carvings and started hoarding another little bit of savings. This time, I spent at least half of what I made on food and things for the girls. As a result, we started eating a hell of a lot better, and my sisters looked presentable.

# # # # #

Enrique went with a little Chiquita named Elena, and he kept after me until I let her fix me up with this girl at school named Karen Sue. A week or so after I met her, Matthew agreed to keep my sisters over at his place one evening, so we could take Karen Sue and Elena to a picture show. I don't even remember the name of the movie because I paid a lot more attention to Karen Sue ... and to Enrique ... than I did the film. He sure knew how to handle women. He threw his arm over Elena's shoulders as casual as all get-out the minute he sat down. Before long, they were twisted around one another and smooching.

I was so retarded about things like that it was embarrassing. All I could manage was an arm around Karen Sue's shoulders, which wasn't all that great because I was still sore from the beating a couple of weeks ago. When she leaned into me, it set my ribs to hurting, but I put up with it anyway.

Before that picture show was over, Enrique had his hand in Elena's crotch and down the neck of her blouse and just about everywhere else. I know she felt his thing at least once. Emboldened, I made it all the way up to holding

Karen Sue's hand. That was after the arm around her shoulders started aching. It was so numb I couldn't even feel her hand for the first five minutes.

After the movie, we went to a fast food joint where they made real good burgers. I'd seriously depleted my savings account buying those movie tickets and feeding Karen Sue and me, but I kept remembering what James had said about wondering if girls were worth all the effort. I needed to find out for myself. I didn't credit the Lottie thing because that was just paid stuff. Karen Sue was a nice girl. By that I mean, she was well behaved and had a pleasant personality. Blonde and kind of plump, she wasn't as talkative as Elena. Of course, most people weren't chatterboxes like Enrique's girlfriend.

# # # # #

Enrique and I whittled for two more weeks to make enough money for another double date. By the time we were ready, the old man had been missing for three days, so I felt comfortable slipping Nola a twenty, so she could take Mom and Junie to the thrift shop for some clothes. For good measure, I gave her another ten to buy hamburgers afterward.

We made the early show because we had to take a city bus all the way up San Mateo to a theater where it only cost a couple of dollars for a ticket. After the film, Enrique wanted to go back to my apartment since his family was at his place. Figuring Mom and the girls had probably left by now, I agreed to give it a try.

I started having second thoughts on the long bus ride back to Central Avenue, but Enrique kept egging me on, so we stuck to the plan. They waited in the alley while I checked the apartment to make sure the coast was clear. As soon as we were inside, I was ashamed of the way the place looked. It wasn't dirty or anything; Nola made sure of that. But there wasn't a single stick of decent furniture in the apartment. It looked like trash lived there. That was the first time that thought ever crossed my mind.

Nobody else was worried about it, and within two minutes, Enrique was down on my bedroll beside the couch, kissing and hugging and feeling Elena up. He wanted to go to the bedroom, but his using Mom's bed to fuck didn't feel right. I guess it wasn't any worse than screwing her on my blankets, but that's what he did.

He got her hot and bothered and then just slipped his pants and underpants down around his ankles and crawled right on. The sight of his bare butt flashing his dark rosebud as he pumped away did something to me. I started pawing Karen Sue up on the couch, and she didn't seem to mind. When things got serious, she wanted to know if I had any protection. I scrounged up a rubber in the bedroom, prayed the old man wouldn't miss it, and scurried back to Karen Sue. She looked chubbier without any clothes on, but right then it seemed more important to use the rubber than to worry about her weight.

Although I wasn't comfortable doing this with another couple in the room, I still managed to get my latex-covered thing inserted where it was supposed to go and set about beating Karen Sue with my hips. She gave a little moan or two, making me think she was enjoying it. I kind of was, but I was more bent on getting it over with than anything else. When I popped, I jerked right out of her because I was afraid the rubber would come off. I wasn't about to go hunting for it up there.

I turned around to get my clothes and found a naked Enrique and Elena sitting against the far wall watching us like paying spectators at a ball game. I covered myself real quick, but not before they got a good look. My cheeks went to burning – all four of them. I was more worried about them seeing the fading marks the old man had left on me than them gawking at my privates.

We'd no sooner got dressed than I heard little Junie right outside the door complaining about something. It was way past her bedtime, and she sounded cranky. Mom and my sisters trouped in and hauled up short when they saw Enrique and the two girls. I said something about them coming over after a movie, but I was just babbling stuff that didn't make a whole lot of sense. Nobody seemed to notice, except maybe Nola. Enrique and Elena volunteered to see Karen Sue got home all right, and then everyone scooted out and down the sidewalk. It was probably my imagination, but the whole apartment smelled funky.

Junie diverted everyone's attention by showing off her new pink canvas shoes with little bunnies painted on the sides. Nola sought my approval of a thrift shop sweater. I gave it to her with a big grin. Even Mom had bought something – a handbag. It was tiny and pretty and totally useless. She'd probably never even carry it anywhere. Nonetheless, it made her happy for the moment. All it would take to spoil the mood was for my dad to come home, but by the time we all went to bed, he hadn't shown – for the fourth night in a row. That wasn't unusual. He was a binge drinker.

When I rolled up in my blankets that night, it bothered me the only clear image I held in my mind about the whole evening was of a naked Enrique on top of Elena. I could still see his brown butt, his slender hips, the impossibly narrow waist, and the way his back flared out and got broader all the way up to his shoulders. He had good shoulders.

# # # # #

I only caught glimpses of Enrique at school for the next couple of days. On Friday, he hunted me up between classes and did some leering about screwing the girls. What he really wanted was to brag about getting Elena a couple more times. If that was true, he must not have done it right because it was clear she was pissed at him.

He claimed he didn't know what'd got into her, but whatever it was, she stayed mad at him all through the next week. Right about this same time, I heard around school that I was going steady with Karen Sue. That was news to me, but I was okay with it. I'd never gone steady with anyone before – and wasn't sure I was now.

Enrique hung around me more than usual after Elena started acting up. He'd come over after school, and we'd find a shady spot outside the apartment where we could sit and whittle. I'd found a big piece of cottonwood root and was doing something different with it. Usually, when I whittled – say a dog, for instance – it would just be the animal standing on four legs. This big piece of wood seemed to call for something more. It was turning into a kitten playing with a ball of twine. This time, I used the bottom of the wood for a pedestal. The twine rested on the floor; the cat stood before it, shoulders lowered, butt high, tail twisted to one side. One paw was raised and reached for the ball. Enrique said it was going to be the best thing I'd ever done. It was taking too long, but it was fun watching it emerge right out of that knot of wood.

A couple of Fridays later, he came around again, so I knew Elena was still giving him the business. The old man had shown up earlier in the week, slept off a humongous hangover, and was off on a tear again. Nola wanted to take Junie to a kiddie movie, so I gave her some money and told her to take Mom with them. Maybe that would keep my mother from drinking for the weekend. Enrique and I whittled until we got tired of it, and then ended up on the sofa talking about school and sports and things. I wasn't much into sports, but he liked to follow all of our school's teams, although soccer was the only thing that really turned him on.

"Elena's still pissed, huh?"

"She just make Enrique suffer."

"What for?"

"For being a man," he said. "Women do that."

I snorted. "A man? How old are you, Enrique?"

That pissed him off. Apparently, you didn't question a Mexican's masculinity. "Old enough to tear off a piece. Hell, you seen me do it right there on the floor."

"All I saw was your butt pumping up and down. Did you know I could see your hole sometimes when you did that?"

"Yeah, well, I seen yours, too." He added the kicker. "Elena seen your cock and balls, ya know."

I felt my ears go red, but I kept my mouth shut. What was there to say?

"I think mine's bigger'n yours."

"Your what? Oh." I flushed some more. "Well, what's the big deal about that?"

"How come you ain't giving it to Karen Sue no more?"

"Who says I'm not?"

"She says it. She giving up on you, man."

"What do you mean?"

26

"She going out with that Armstrong guy. Told Elena he got the biggest cock she ever seen. That's the straight stuff, man. That's what she said."

The straight stuff was okay with me. I'd lost interest since that night on the couch, but I couldn't say that to Enrique.

"I saw it in PE one day," he went on. "You know, the Armstrong dude's cock. No lie. It's big. Lots bigger'n yours."

"Who cares?"

"Sound like Karen Sue do." He paused. "Mine's bigger'n yours, *tambien.*"

I shoulda just left it alone, but I came back at him with about the dumbest thing in the world. "Is not." Damnation, we sounded like thirteen-year-olds.

He reached for his fly. "Prove it."

"Aw ...."

He stood and ripped open his trousers. His erection was obvious beneath his shorts. My old thing crawled around in my pants, but I just sat there gawking. Then his hand was pulling at my belt.

I pushed him away, but I stood and let him tug my jeans down over my hips. The sound of a key in the lock threw me into a panic. I jerked my pants up while Enrique fumbled with his fly. Then we both stood like deer caught in the headlights as Matthew opened the door and stepped inside. He hesitated a moment before coming on into the room.

"Hey, guys. What's up?"

"Nothing," Enrique mumbled. He collected his knife and the carving he'd worked on earlier and almost ran out the door.

Matthew frowned after him. "What was that all about?"

"His girlfriend broke up with him, and he was telling me about it. Guess it embarrassed him some." My voice sounded false to me. "What're you doing here?"

"I left a couple of shirts for Nola to mend. Need to pick them up, and then I'm gone."

Five minutes later, he left me puzzling over what had almost happened. It reminded me of my last conversation with James.

I left the apartment and restlessly prowled the small park where Enrique and his buddies sometimes hung out. I'm not sure why I went looking for him right then, and I don't guess I'll ever know. He was nowhere to be found.

27

CHAPTER 5

When I saw Enrique at school Monday, he acted as if nothing had happened, so I played it that way, too. I ran into Karen Sue, who was friendly enough, but she couldn't wait to let me know she was dating someone else. She also found a way to let me know it was my own fault for ignoring her. Girls don't like to be ignored.

The old man suddenly started hanging around the place more than usual, and that meant he was lying low for some reason or the other. I scooted home right after school every afternoon to make sure the girls were all right. On Wednesday, I came home to find him tearing out the baseboards, looking for more money. Well, he wouldn't find any. It was hidden outside in a can. I'd rather take my chances with unknown thieves than with my father.

As soon as I came through the door, he turned on me. "Where you got it, boy? I need some money. Give it to me."

I raised my hands, palms up. "I don't have any. You cleaned me out a month ago."

"Don't shit me, kid. You got some more, and I want it. Do I have to beat it out of you?"

My gorge began to rise, but I held onto my temper. He wasn't drunk, so now wasn't the time to challenge him. Besides, I wasn't up for another beating ... not quite yet.

"Look, all I've got is two dollars. I can give you that, but I don't have any more."

"Where you stealing it, boy? Maybe I can help out."

"I don't know how to convince you I don't steal, Dad." Placate the son of a bitch. Crawl if you have to. "I find jobs at the thrift store once in a while, but they don't have anything for me right now. I collect cans and sell them. And sometimes, I find other things in the dumpster I can peddle."

"Go check it out."

"I already did. I go dumpster diving on the way to school and on the way home."

"How come I don't believe you, you scrawny little bastard? I don't even believe you come outta my seed. You did, you'd be a grown man now out making a living, not a sniveling little snot-nose hiding in the schoolhouse."

I swallowed hard and willed my fists not to clench. "I'm who I am. Can't be anybody else."

"Get the fuck out of here and go find me some money."

Rather than have a fight, I went out of sight down the street and came back a few minutes later. He considered taking a swing at me when I handed him the five singles I'd had in my pocket, claiming I'd found some cans up the street and sold them. That didn't placate him much, but fortunately, he settled for cussing me out and making threats. He was too eager to make a run for the liquor store with the five dollars to take time to whip me again. As he charged out the door, I swore by everything holy that alcohol would never get its hooks into me like it had my parents.

# # # # #

Life would have been so much simpler if I could go out and get a part-time job, but I was afraid to leave Nola and little Junie alone. One of the neighbor boys was already sniffing around Nola. He was a couple of years older than she was, and although my sister was usually pretty levelheaded, she thought this kid was aces. He was pretty decent for this part of town. Even so, I could see the danger lying deep down in him. I gave up the idea of a job and kept on whittling.

Ben Ames down at the flea market bought all my work even during the winter when the crowds were down. I guess he sold all of my pieces because every time I took him new ones, there wouldn't be any of the old ones left. I wondered what he would think about the kitten and the ball of twine when I finished it. It was slow work, so I put it aside from time to time to take on smaller jobs I could finish in a hurry. That cat was the hardest thing I'd ever tackled, but I was learning something with every cut I made.

# # # # #

One Saturday, Mom, Nola, and Junie went with a neighbor lady and her family to the park on a picnic. They'd invited me to go along, but I figured to take advantage of some rare free time. Ms. Chisholm was a nice lady, sorta pretty for somebody in her forties. She didn't have a husband so far as I knew. Still, she didn't look beat-down like so many people in the Combat Area. She was strict with her kids, so I felt easy about the girls going with her. She'd keep a sharp eye on everyone. Mom, bless her heart, would just sit and talk and let Ms. Chisholm do all the baby-sitting.

Since Enrique wasn't around, I walked down to this great little park behind the big hospital on Central near the I-25 freeway. The place was full of hills and hollows and lots and lots of trees. It was the only place I knew where I could smell pine resin and musty oak and even a few flowers that reminded me of home.

Some guys playing touch football invited me to join in. I'm not much for sports, but I can run pretty fast, so I gave it a try. In a few minutes, I'd forgotten just about everything except doing my best in the ball game. The others didn't hand off the ball to me much, but whenever I got my hands on it, I ran for all I was worth. I made a touchdown on one of the runs, too.

Ball games usually bore me, but for some reason, I didn't want this one to end. Of course, it did, and that's when I noticed this blond-headed Anglo sitting on the grass with a big pad in his hand. I eased over until I could see he was drawing pictures. Good ones, too. He was working on one of a Mexican girl about twelve or thirteen sitting with her family a few feet away, and it looked exactly like her. When he was done with it, I walked on past him and sat down on a big rock. I wished I could draw like that. He made things look so real, almost like it was a photograph, except that it wasn't. Could I do that with my knives? Maybe I'd try another bust of Nola to see if it came out any better.

"Excuse me."

Surprised, I looked up to see the artist dude. "Huh? I mean, yes, sir?"

He grinned at me. "I didn't mean to startle you. My name's Jason, and I wondered if I could sketch you?"

"Me? You want to draw me?"

"If you don't mind."

"Yeah, sure. What do I have to do?"

"Nothing. Unless you want to talk to me while I sketch. Or just ignore me if you prefer. Why don't you put your foot up on the rock and prop your forearm on your knee? Let your hand drape down, but leave it open. Don't make a fist. Yeah. Like that. Now look out into the distance."

"Do I have to be still?"

"You don't have to freeze up, but don't move around too much. Just remain in that general position."

I watched him out of the corner of my eye as he sketched. He was a little taller than me and had a good build. His features were drawn into a slight frown as he concentrated on his drawing. He worked really fast. The first thing I knew, he was ripping off one sheet and starting on another one. When he finished, he handed me some money and asked me to go over to the hotdog wagon at the edge of the park and get us something to eat.

We talked as we ate our hotdogs. I grew up in a place where it's rude to stare directly at someone, but I gave him a pretty good going over. Older than me by maybe eight or nine years, he was a good-looking guy, not pasty like a lot of artist types. Probably worked out some. I don't know what it was about him, but he was easy to talk to. I probably told him more about me than I had anybody else – ever.

I got sort of envious when I found out he made his living by drawing and painting. How great would it be to live off of my carvings? He liked this park more than any other in the city, he claimed. The hills and the trees were part of it, but he said there was always somebody interesting here to draw. I got up the nerve to ask him if he was going to be back next weekend. He said maybe, so I told him I would be, too. I trudged home thinking this was one of the best days I'd had since we moved to Albuquerque.

# # # # #

The next day, the old man came home on one of his increasingly infrequent visits. He barreled through the door drunk out of his mind early in the morning. Little Junie was still asleep on the sofa; Nola and I were just getting up. I'd just pulled on my pants.

31

"Wilam!" he roared. "Money. Where you got it hid?"

"Don't have any."

"Don't give me that shit. You always got money. Where you got it hid, you little pansy?"

I didn't want to get in a fight with him in front of the girls, and I sure wasn't going to stand there and take it this time, so I pulled the two dollars I always kept on me out of my pocket and offered them to him. He snarled and batted the bills out of my hand.

"I need more'n that by a damn sight. Go get it."

"That's all there is."

He rounded on little Junie who was awake now, her big eyes wide with fear. "Where's he got it, Junie? Where's he hide it now?"

She shook her head so hard, black curls flew everywhere. He took a step toward her, and I jumped between them. If he touched her, one of us was going to die.

"What the hell's going on? Why is the door wide open?"

I don't know why Matthew showed up right then because he never came over on Sunday, but he walked in and sized up the situation in one second flat. Matthew was as big as dad, if you don't count the bloat the old man carried, and he was in a lot better shape. He didn't threaten; he just put a gentle hand on the old man's shoulder.

"Hey, Pop. What're you doing home?"

My father turned from bully to wheedler. "Need some money, son. I know he's got some. He always has some. I need it, man. Everbody's broke, and I got to have a bottle. Need a bottle to come down easy."

It always amazed me how some drunks can come down off a high by drinking more whiskey, but somehow they can.

"Come on," my brother said. "I got a few dollars. Let's go see what we can find. Wilam don't have any money. I borrowed what he had yesterday."

With that little lie, my brother led him out of the apartment docile as a lamb. Everyone took a breath at once. Junie started to cry, and Nola went to look after her. The whole world might be cockeyed, but my two sisters were angels. Matthew was okay, too.

I peeked into the bedroom and found my mom passed out on the bed. She hadn't even removed her shoes. I eased them off her feet and tucked her in as best I could. Then, the whole situation got to me.

I'm nineteen and supposed to be a man, but I went into the bathroom, leaned against the door, and bawled like a ten-year-old. I slid down and sprawled on the floor trying to muffle my sobs. Nola knocked gently on the door and asked if I was all right. I told her I was just feeling sick, and she let it go at that.

How could anything as sweet at those two girls come out of someone like my old man? Mom was all right, not mean-boned or anything, but she didn't even own her own soul. She'd turned it over to alcohol. She could be as good a mother as anybody for a day or a week or a month, and then alcohol would come around and ask her out on a date, and she'd be gone. Thank goodness, she usually drank around the house. I'd be ashamed to go looking for her in some of the places where my old man did his boozing.

Matthew hit the bottle hard sometimes, but mostly, he was fine. He pretty much stayed at his girlfriend's place, but he wasn't the kind who'd look after Nola and Junie, anyway. He had a steady job at some construction company, so he'd taken to slipping Nola something to help with the groceries. I'd even caught him a time or two giving Mom a little money.

I completed the mental survey of the Greyhorse family and got around to me. Seed of the loins of that hateful drunk. A nineteen-year-old who hadn't even graduated high school yet. A kid who sat on the bathroom floor and blubbered out of fear and hatred and desperation. All I was good for was to pick up a dollar or two while whittling away my life. I left the bathroom and did just that. I picked up the half-finished kitten and whittled like crazy.

Little Junie came over and put her chubby finger on the figure's head. "Pretty cat, Wilam."

I flicked away moisture in the corner of my eyes. "Yes it is, sweetie. A pretty little kitten like you."

"Ball." She fingered the carved yarn.

I damned near started crying again. Nola came and got Junie to clean her up, leaving me carving and trying to recover my manhood. What was it the old man had called me? A pansy? That pretty well described William Greyhorse.

# # # # #

Wednesday, I came home after school to find cop cars all over the place. There was an ambulance there, too. Oh, God! Had something happened to the girls? If the old man had hurt them, so help me I'd kill him. Even as I made this silent pledge, they brought him out of the apartment in handcuffs and loaded him into a police cruiser. I started for him, but Matthew stepped out of the house and took hold of my arm. I guess Mom'd had the cops call him in from work.

"It's all right, Pissant." That was a hell of a pet name, but better'n some I've heard.

"What happened? Why is the ambulance here? Are the girls ...."

"They're all right. Ms. Chisholm's taking care of them right now. It's Mom. He came home drunk and they got in a fight. He roughed her up, and the neighbors called the police. She was drunk, too, and she fell. Claims she hit her head on the dresser. They're taking her to the hospital."

I watched helplessly as the ambulance pulled away without giving me a chance to look at my mother. Then one of the police cars took off with the old man inside. A few minutes later, something even worse happened. Some lady from the state came out of Ms. Chisholm's herding Nola and little Junie in front of her. Matthew and one of the cops held me back while they drove away with the girls. I begged to be allowed to take care of them, but nobody listened to me.

As the car carrying the girls disappeared, I turned on Matthew. "How come you didn't stop them? You're their brother, and you're an adult. You shoulda taken them."

"I'm at work all day. So is Myra, and you're in school."

I fought to keep tears from my eyes. "I'll quit school. Stay home. Go after them, Matthew. Bring them back to your place. I'll take care of them. I will."

"I know you would." He refused to meet my eyes. "But you have to graduate this next spring. You can't do that if you take time off to care for the girls.

"Fuck graduation. I want my sisters."

"William, you're more of a father and mother to those girls than our real parents." When he called me William, he was serious. "I know you'll hate me for this, but you have to get through school. Not just for yourself, but for them, too. You're going to end up raising them. You know that, don't you? I'll help all I can, and right now that means letting them go for a while."

He touched my arm and walked away, leaving me in the middle of the sidewalk shaking like I was having a seizure.

# # # # #

I skipped school Thursday to try and salvage my family. The people at the hospital told me Mom would recover all right. That part was easy enough, but it took all day to find out where my sisters were and convince somebody to let me talk to them on the phone. Junie was crying for me to come get her, but the lady from the state said it would be better not to visit them until they became accustomed to their environment.

Environment? To being held prisoner, she meant. She was afraid seeing me would just stir up the baby worse than my phone call already had. The girls would be returned as soon as Mom was able to take care of them again. I came close to telling her that wasn't the way it worked in the Greyhorse family, but I bit my tongue for fear she wouldn't send them home at all.

Once I knew Nola and Junie were together, I rested easier. Nola was going to start back to school the next day, so I could go talk to her before anyone carried her back to wherever they were holding her. It hurt that little Junie would probably be terrified while her sister was in class, but she'd just have to get over that. The girls would be fed and kept safe, so maybe they were better off there – wherever there was. For a little while, at least.

The apartment sure was empty, especially at night. Matthew and Myra invited me over, but I was still mad at him and wouldn't go. After a rough night, I made it to school on Friday, but I sneaked out early to go catch Nola at her middle school. She claimed she was okay, but her eyes said she wanted to come home with me. She clutched onto me so hard we got strange looks from the other kids. Then the people from the Children's Department showed up and took her away.

Still troubled by the whole incident, I went down to the flea market on Saturday morning and dickered more aggressively with Ben Ames than usual. I didn't even stop to think I might piss him off and ruin everything. The outcome was that I learned a valuable lesson. If you made something another man could make a dollar off of, you don't have to like the other guy to do business together.

That wasn't fair. Ben was a decent guy even if he did play his cards close to his chest. Still, I managed to get better prices out of him for my work, which was a good thing because I'd spent so much time on the cat there weren't many pieces to sell.

Later that morning, I hiked over to the University Medical Center where they take overflow cases from the Indian Hospital next door. Mom claimed she was better, but she looked like the walking dead. One eye was black, and her head was covered in bandages. The hair leaking out from underneath the white wrappings was more gray than black. When had that happened?

The park where I'd met that artist wasn't too far, so when I left the hospital, I hoofed it over there to see if he would show up again. There was no sign of him, but a football game was going down at one end of the park. I joined in and took out some of my frustration on the other guys. It helped me forget my family was falling apart. When our opponents started losing, the fellow who owned the ball claimed he had to go home for lunch even though it wasn't noon yet.

After the game ended, I was surprised to see Jason had arrived and was sketching a woman sitting on a blanket, playing with her baby. When he finished the drawing, he said hello and sent me to get a couple of hamburgers from the cart at the other end of the park. He was so quiet while we ate; I knew something was bothering him.

When we finished, he licked the grease off his hands, wiped them on a napkin, and looked at me. "William, I want you to come with me."

"My family calls me Wilam." For some reason it was important for him to know that. I smiled at the look on his face and explained where the name came from.

"Okay, Wilam, I want you to come with me."

"Where are we going?"

He stared right into my eyes. "I want to take you home with me. First, I want you to take a bath, and then I want you to crawl on top of me and fuck me until you can't fuck anymore." His voice went up at the end like there was something desperate about it.

My mouth dropped open as if he'd slugged me in the face. I didn't know what to say, so I just turned around and walked off. I made it as far as a bench before my legs gave way and plopped me down on it. Maybe I should have slugged him or kept on walking or – something. I didn't; I just sat there. Out of the corner of my eye, I saw him working on a picture.

Why did he say that? I thought of James telling me something like it. How did I feel about what he'd said? Well, I knew James. I had feelings for him, even if I didn't know exactly what they were. Did that make a difference? I didn't know – not really. I sure hadn't run very far away from Jason. Why not? All of a sudden, he was there on the bench beside me. I tried not to jump.

"William, I'm sorry. I didn't have any right to do that. I know it doesn't excuse my actions, but I've never done anything so crude in my life before. I'm truly sorry for my boorish behavior. I think I would have liked having you as a friend. In every sense of the word."

"Then why did you do it?" He scared me. No, that wasn't right. My dad scared me; Jason disturbed me, and that's different. "Is … is there something about me that made you say it."

"Only that you're extremely attractive. If you're asking if you did something or said something to lead me on, the answer is no. The truth is, I'm suffering a little this morning. Someone I love very much is getting married today, and I don't want to be alone right now. I could have asked you to spend some time with me without … well, without the other."

"I will," I said in a low voice. "I'll spend some time with you if you need me to." I understood needing a friend. Heck, I needed him, too, but I didn't tell him that.

"That's very kind and forgiving of you, William, but I couldn't ask you to hang around after what I said."

Something crawled through my belly, and I think it was panic. "Then why did you put it to me like that? Why couldn't you just ask me to spend some time with you, so I could tell you I'd like to?"

He shrugged and lifted his hands in a helpless gesture. "No excuse. I really don't know why. Except that you're very handsome, and I got carried away."

"Me?" I almost looked around to make sure he wasn't talking to somebody behind me. "Was it because you thought I'd like you to say those things?"

"No. Nothing like that."

I looked directly at him and didn't see anything in his blue eyes to put me off. "Okay. I'll go with you, but only if you call me Wilam. I know what it's like to need somebody to talk to." I smiled a little. "And I know I need cleaning up. I'm kinda grungy from playing football. I can run home and wash up and meet you later. That way, I can change into some clean clothes."

"Nope, we're going to get you a new pair of jeans and a shirt. Then you can use the shower in my house."

"Do you have a real shower, or just one in a bathtub? That's what we have at home."

He laughed. "A real shower. Let's get you some new clothes and go take that shower. We'll go to a movie or something after that."

"Do you have a color TV? With one of those VCRs or whatever they call them?"

"Sure do."

"Then let's stay at your place and watch TV and movies and things."

"You've got a deal."

CHAPTER 6

We crawled into Jason's red Lexus crossover and drove to Coronado Mall up in the Northeast Heights where he bought me a pair of new jeans and a tank top at GAP. I didn't think I had the build for a tank top, but he grabbed my shoulders and turned me toward the mirror just outside the dressing room.

"Looks good to me." His eyes moved up and down my torso, giving me a goosey feeling.

My rib cage flared pretty good. Not as much as Enrique's, but it looked okay. My pecs were sort of slender, certainly not heavy like Matthew's, but they had some definition. The shirt clung to my belly nicely. Anyway, I let him buy it for me. He added some underwear and sneakers to the bill even though I said I didn't need them.

I was tempted to wear my new outfit right out of the store, but I was sweaty from playing ball. I'd wait until after the shower to put them on. Besides, I'd heard somewhere it was a low class thing to do – or maybe just immature. I didn't want Jason to think either one of those things about me.

We headed north out of the mall on Louisiana Boulevard and turned east on Comanche. There'd probably never be a Pinoan Street anywhere in the world, but the Comanche had been a powerful Plains tribe. Of course, we were distant kin to the Shoshone, and they probably had a few streets – and maybe even towns – named after them.

After a couple of miles, he turned south on a neighborhood street and pulled into the broad driveway in front of a sand-colored, stuccoed building with a black iron gate opening onto a small, shaded courtyard. He opened one of the big double doors with stained glass windows in them and invited me inside.

I walked into the front hall and stopped to gawk. The place was like something I'd only seen in pictures. The ceiling was so high I could have stood on my own shoulders and still not touched it. The hallway, or foyer as he called it, was tile, but everything else looked to be covered in thick carpet. All the colors were earth tones, but they ranged from the light sand of the West Mesa to the dark loam of the Valley to the red cliffs of northern New Mexico. Right in front of me on the wall facing the entrance was this big painting that grabbed my eye and drew me forward.

It was an oil portrait of an Indian man in a formal pose. He was probably in his twenties, a little younger than Jason. The man was hatless, and his flowing black hair had shards of light in them. The face was strong and manly, even though it was as beautiful as any woman's I'd ever seen. The open collar of his calico shirt drew the eye to an obvious Adam's apple, making me know his voice would be low and vibrate with bass tones. I moved closer and saw the name of the artist. Jason Bedford.

I glanced at the man standing at my shoulder. "You did that?"

He nodded. "Yes."

"Is it a real man or somebody ...." I didn't know how to say the rest of it.

"Yes, he's a real person, not someone I dreamed up. Although if I dreamed up someone, he'd look exactly like that."

"Wow, that's something." It was lame but the best I could come up with. I didn't dare say the picture had grabbed me right down in the vitals, but that's exactly what it had done.

"Thanks. Why don't I show you the shower?"

Reluctantly, I left the painting to follow him into the biggest bedroom I'd ever seen. It not only had a huge bed and the usual dresser and stuff, it also had a red leather recliner with a reading lamp beside it and a little writing desk in the far corner. He led me through an open archway into the bath area with its gleaming double sink and mirrors all around. I didn't see a stool. It must be hidden behind the door off to the left. An open door beside it revealed a big tub with jets for massaging tense muscles. I could have used that while I was recovering from Dad's beating.

The shower was at the end of the room behind big sliding glass doors. That bathroom area was half as big as our whole apartment. I asked Jason if he lived here all by himself.

He put down the bag from GAP. "At the moment, I do. There was someone else ... until recently."

"Is it okay if I take my time in the shower?"

"Take all the time you want. Glory in it."

He went off somewhere else, so I opened the door to the left and found the stool. I took a quick piss and went back out in the open area to strip after turning on the shower. I heard a noise and whirled to see Jason holding a big, fluffy towel. It shocked me that I was standing there in my altogether while he looked at me, but I stifled the urge to cover my groin with my hands.

"Sorry," he said. "I heard the water going and thought you were in the shower."

I shrugged. "It's okay." Still, I scooted into the shower and closed the door. The glass was pebbly – frosty, I guess they call it – so I could see his faint outline standing there for a second before he left.

I took him at his word and stayed under the water for a long time. The plumbing was new to me, but I finally figured out how to turn on the shower head at the top and another one about waist high. You could make either one or both pulse and hit you with little jolts of hot water. Great!

His soap was easy on the skin, and it smelled so good it had to be expensive. I worked up lots of lather and covered myself with suds from head to toe while I sang some old powwow songs. I soaped up and rinsed off three times. When my skin started to squeak, I shut down the water and dried off with that fluffy towel he'd left me. Then I tried on my new clothes. They fit really good, and Jason had been right – the shirt looked okay. In fact, it made me look … well, kind of mature. When I went out and found him reading in a big room off the kitchen, he agreed with me. Hunky was the way he put it.

We watched TV and CDs of movies for the rest of the day. He had a whole bunch of films for his VCR we could watch without commercials, just like at the picture show. We finished up with a great movie called ET. I laughed a lot and tried to hide it when a tear or two rolled down my cheeks. After all, I was nineteen, and a guy shouldn't bawl like a baby at that age. He laughed and leaked from the eyes without shame.

Late in the afternoon, I about panicked when he said he'd better get me home. I didn't want to go, and that kicked off some guilt for not thinking about Mom and the girls since leaving the hospital that morning. There was nothing for me back home except a dark, empty apartment, so I changed the subject and asked if he had any baloney or ham. He did, but he also has some good roast beef, and after I finished a thick sandwich of that, I turned to him.

"Can I stay with you tonight?" My mouth went dry as he looked at me.

"If you want. You can use the phone to call your folks, so they won't worry."

It kind of got to me that he thought I needed my parents' permission to stay out. He probably didn't know how old I was. Everyone was always saying I didn't look my age. Nobody at school knew I was older than most of them.

"No, that's okay. I'm nineteen. You know, on my own."

"Nineteen? Sorry for treating you like a kid. I'd be happy to have you spend the night. You can have your choice of a couple of bedrooms."

When we wore out the day, and it was time to go to bed, I took another shower and used one of the new toothbrushes he kept on hand for company. I came out of the bathroom with a towel wrapped around my middle and asked if I could try out his great-smelling after-shave lotion. It was tomfoolery. There wasn't a hair on my face past a few at the sideburns. I wasn't sure I'd ever need to shave.

He invited me to make myself comfortable while he took his shower. As I stood in the middle of the bedroom wondering where I was supposed to sleep, he stripped off his clothes. I couldn't help but watch. He had a good body. Those exercise machines in one of the rooms weren't just for show. He used them. His muscles were long and ropy – like James's had been.

Suddenly, his words from the park this afternoon came back to me. When the water in the shower went off, I made up my mind. I turned out the overhead lights, snapped on a lamp beside the bed, and shook off the robe he'd loaned me. I slipped under the covers of the big bed and sat up against the headboard, covered to the waist with a soft, silky sheet. I was shivering like it was cold – but it wasn't. He didn't notice me until he finished drying off with another big towel. Then he stopped dead still for a second before putting on his robe. I couldn't read his face.

"I ain't never done this before." I was so rattled I was talking like a yokel. "You'll have to tell me what to do"

He swallowed hard. "You don't have to do this. You've helped me a lot just by spending the afternoon with me."

"Did I really?"

"I can't tell you how much you helped. I haven't thought … about things but once or twice the whole day. If you hadn't been here, I would have drowned in those thoughts."

"You said something about a friend getting married. It's that guy in the portrait, isn't it?" I was sorry I'd asked when a look of pain flashed across his face.

"Yes, that's right. His name is David."

He looked so miserable, I had to try to undo the damage I'd done. "What if I want to do it with you?"

"I don't want a pity fuck, Wilam."

"I wouldn't know how to give one." I tried to get my Adam's apple to stop bobbing.

Jason looked at me for a long time before coming over to the bed. Then he slipped out of the robe he was wearing and let me get a good look at him. He had a nice, deep chest and a lean belly with some soft-looking blondish hair at his groin. His thing was long, and the hood had been cut off. I liked the way you could see his hip lines riding above his thighs. He got into bed and reached across me to snap off the lamp. I smelled the fragrance of his body lotion and felt the heat coming off his skin. It sort of turned me on.

I surprised myself. "Can we keep the light on. At least until …. You know, for a little while?"

He lay back against the headboard beside me. "Sure. We can do whatever you want. You're king of this castle tonight."

I smiled at that idea. "When you said those things to me at the park, I went over and sat down on the bench and thought about it some. When you started packing up your things, I was going to come over and tell you I would try it. You know, try what you said."

"Is that the truth?"

I remembered being surprised when he sat down beside me, but he didn't have to know that. Besides, I wasn't sure what the truth was right then. "Yeah, but then you came over to me."

"Why didn't you tell me then?"

I shrugged. "I figured you'd do the talking. And besides, I guess I was ashamed some. Maybe not ashamed, but you took me by surprise, Jason."

"I know I did. Are you ashamed now?"

I shook my head. "What … what do we do?"

"Do what you would to a girl. You've done it with a girl, haven't you?

I couldn't stifle a laugh. "Yeah, but come on."

"No, I mean it. What would you do with a girl?"

So Jason led me through it step by step. At times, I felt foolish; at times I was excited. When he touched my lips with his, I almost panicked. It wasn't all that bad, so we did it again. This time I loosened up a little. Before, he'd caught me by surprise. I didn't know guys did things like that with other guys. Especially, the tongue part.

Then he pulled me on top of him. I had a hard-on, and so did he. We lay there, pressed against one another until he pulled us down flat on the bed and opened his legs.

What does a blow job feel like? You know, to get one." I couldn't believe I'd asked that out loud.

"Haven't you ever had one?"

I shook my head. "Guys are always talking about them, but I've never had one."

"Well, we're about to correct that deficiency." He rolled me off him and started sucking on my tits. At first, I didn't like it, but then I got all tingly. He swabbed my belly button with his tongue, sending a little shock right down to my balls. Then he drew a grunt out of me by going down to my sac. He took my testicles in his mouth one-by-one and sucked gently. Then he raised my legs and licked my buttocks, moistening me down there. My thing took to throbbing something awful; just like it did when I was lying in my blankets after watching James get fucked out on the Beaver.

When he sucked my cock into his mouth, he drew a little gasp of surprise from me. He rode the shaft all the way down to my bush. I could feel his nose pressing into my belly. How did he do that? Take it all the way, I mean. I closed my eyes and spread my legs as I got goose pimples all over. I wanted to tell him to do it faster. I wanted to tell him how great it made me feel, but other than moaning when he slid up and down the whole length of my cock again, I couldn't utter a word. Afraid I'd break the spell.

Then that feeling came over me like it did when I was doing it to myself – except better. A thousand times better. A million. My balls drew up tight, and I could feel the electric shock building. I scissored my arms and legs on the bed like I was making snow angels.

"I ... I'm gonna come, Ja ... Jason," I grunted.

He just stayed down on me while I threw my hips up into the air, driving me deeper. In a minute, my nerve endings went crazy, and my pelvic contractions took over, spewing my cum into his mouth. I thought he'd come up off me then, but he stayed with me until I stopped coming. By the time it was over, I could hardly draw a breath.

Finally, he came up and wiped his mouth. "Well, how was your first blow?"

"Gr ... great," I stuttered, still trying to recover. "Like the best. Like nothing else."

"Better than your first time with a girl?"

That was kind of a touchy subject, but I admitted the blow job was better, hoping he wouldn't think bad things about me, because I was already wondering if I could get him to do it again.

"How many girls have you been with?"

"Couple." I avoided his eyes. Somehow, I felt ashamed talking about them. The times with them had seemed so cheap. So wrong.

"Have you ever been with a man before?"

That brought a smile because I could answer it honestly. "Just you."

"I'll bet you've jacked off with your buddies, though."

"Uh uh. Don't have any buddies. I just did it to myself. Well, there was one guy, but that didn't amount to anything." That's the way I felt about Enrique – he didn't amount to a thing to me.

"So you've never fucked a man?"

I thought of James, and how he'd wanted me to do it to him. "Nope. Never."

"Will you do it to me now?"

"Right now? I don't know if I can. I just blew my balls, big time."

He laughed. "As I recall, I blew your balls."

He slid down my body again until he reached my thing. He sucked it into his mouth and tongued it until it started to harden. After a minute or two, he flipped me over on top of him, and I hunched against him like I was fucking Karen Sue. He tipped me off to grab some lubricant from the table beside the bed and apply it to himself and to me. He then raised his legs, bringing his ass up toward me. I grasped my throbbing cock, put it up against his crack, and lunged. He let out a yelp, but I was all the way in, and I wasn't about to wait for anything. My balls slapped his butt.

"Is this ... the way ... you want it?" I gasped as I thrust at him.

"Yes! Do it to me. Fuck me, man. Make me forget everything except that hard cock inside me."

Talking dirty like that got to me. I stood up on my knees and hooked his legs over my elbows. I gave him everything I had. I drilled him. I pounded him. I fucked him. It took a while to get close to the edge, but when I did, I grabbed his big thing and began stroking.

"It's coming," he cried. "You're making me come."

"Do it. I wanna see you cream." Was that me yelling those things?

Jason shot all over his belly and my hand. I kept on pumping him, and he kept on coming. Then his ass muscles worked me over, and that was more than I could stand. I exploded again and shot a load into him.

Exhausted, I rolled off him onto my back. My cock wilted and flopped down on my stomach as I tried to recover. I expected my feelings to catch up with me then, but they didn't. After I jerked off, I always felt kind of dirty. When I'd done it to Lottie and Karen Sue, I could hardly wait to get away from them when it was over. I'd been embarrassed. Even worse, I'd felt a little repulsed. But I was comfortable lying here on this big bed beside Jason.

He sent me into the bathroom to clean up, and I was on my side facing away from him when he came back to bed after his own wash-up. When the light was off and we were settled in the bed, I couldn't help asking him a question.

"Did I do all right?"

"You did great."

"You're not just saying that. You know, to make me feel good"

"That was an honest answer, Wilam. You fuck like a man."

That was about as good as the orgasm. Well, almost. "Really?"

"William ... Wilam, I've been with a few men in my lifetime, and I've never been fucked so competently as you just did." He went quiet for a moment. "Except by one man."

"You mean that fellow hanging on the wall. That David?"

"Yes, that's right."

"I ought not to have asked you that. I'm sorry."

He put a hand on my arm. "It's okay. Saying it is just facing up to the facts. You know why I can talk about it? Because you're here with me. It means a lot that you saw me through a difficult time."

"It was good for me, too."

"Then we were good for each other, and that's the way it ought to be."

The room fell silent after that. I felt so easy with this man I scooted over until my butt touched his leg.

"Jason, I'm sorry if I sounded like I'm retarded or something, but I've never talked about things like this with anyone before. I'm really kind of dumb."

"Not dumb. Inexperienced. Besides, haven't you heard a lot of gays like cherries?"

I snickered. "Cherry, that's me." I moved my butt firmly against his leg. "Are we gonna do that again tomorrow?"

"We'll do it anytime you want to. Just say the word."

"Okay, but I gotta rest some before I do. What do I say when I'm ready? I wanna fuck again?"

"Maybe something a little less graphic. Something like, it's time again. Or my cherry needs rubbing."

"Yeah, I like that. My cherry needs rubbing. Uh, I didn't mean right now. I was just trying it out."

He laughed aloud. "I understand, but the next time you say it, you better mean it."

I closed my eyes, and a warm feeling settled over me as if I had found something I'd been looking for. Why I hadn't done this with James? Barely able to fend off sleep, I decided to make Jason feel good tomorrow. To be there for him. To make sure I paid attention to his needs, not just my own.

# # # # #

When I woke up the next morning, my thing was hard and I had to take a piss something awful. I had trouble doing it because it wouldn't go soft like it usually did. That might have been because I saw Jason on the other side of the bed when I got up. Had he'd seen my cock standing up and beating in the air? Probably not. I think he'd been asleep. Still, the thought of him seeing me like that was exciting. Of course, I didn't need excitement until I emptied my bladder.

After I finally got everything pissed out, I brushed my teeth and washed my face. When I went back into the bedroom, my cock got hard again because Jason was on top of the covers. I think he was just trying wake up, but the sight of him lying there on his stomach was too much for me. I crawled on the bed and pushed his legs apart with my knees. He gave a sleepy groan when I put my cock right up against his hole.

"My cherry needs rubbing," I mumbled.

This time I didn't just shove it in. I teased his pucker hole with the damp end of my cock for a minute, and then I fed it to him slowly after applying some lube. He groaned again and then arched his back, taking the last of my prick into him. I liked that. It showed he wanted me. I lay across his back, aware of my nipples against his skin, feeling the mound of his buttocks press into my groin while I fucked him slow and easy. I took my time and made it last for as long as I could before my balls started to draw up and I shot off. I know it sounds funny, but it was natural feeling.

I turned over on my back and pulled him with me. Staying inside him, I reached around and took him in my hand. I stroked his chest and belly while I beat a rhythm with my fist. He groaned contentedly and spread his legs across my thighs. Finally, he arched his back again, driving me deeper into him as he exploded all over those pretty sheets.

# # # # #

We spent the entire day with one another. We ate and read the Sunday paper, never bothering to get dressed, just staying in our robes. While he painted a little in the big room at the back of his house that he called a studio, I told him about my carvings. He asked to see some of them. After we ate lunch, I walked up to where he was sitting and stood between his legs and told him my cherry needed rubbing again. He caressed my cock a moment before taking me while it was still mostly soft. It was an incredible feeling to grow hard inside his warm mouth.

When I was really close to the edge, he suddenly stopped and put me on my back on the carpet. I thought he would go down on me again, but instead, he got astride me and sat down on my hard cock like Lottie had. I'd been intent on finishing the blow job, but this was all right, too. Last night, I'd resolved to be as good to him as he was to me, so if he wanted to get fucked, he'd get fucked.

He lifted his weight, so I could move my hips, and I beat up into him until my nerves went nuts and my juices pumped into him again. He put my hand on his hard cock, and I brought him over the edge, too. His muscles worked me over again when he came, so there was nothing to do but fuck him again to get rid of my renewed hard-on. So I rolled over on top of him and did just that.

I couldn't understand why I wasn't embarrassed or awkward or felt bad about it after we had sex. He acted just the same after we did it as before, too. I spent a lot of the afternoon looking at him and just getting pleasure from being there with him.

I didn't want to go home that night, but I knew I had to. He drove me back to the Combat Area around midnight. I was ashamed of where I lived, so I thought about having him drop me off at the park where I met him, but it was a long walk back home, and the buses weren't running. When we arrived, there was a light in the apartment, so I had him drive past and pull into a dark alley about a block or so away. I just couldn't let him go like that. I undid my pants and pulled out my thing. I saw his eyes gleam in the dark as he watched it get hard.

"Please," I said.

He didn't answer; he just leaned over and took me in his mouth. My cock was raw from the workout it'd had, but in a few minutes, I my sac shrank up, and I shot off again. He stayed down on me until I started to go soft. He let me go then and came up to look at me. I got my clothes straight, but I still didn't want to get out.

"Can we do this again?" I asked.

Sure. I'd like that."

"Can I spend tomorrow with you?"

He frowned. "You said you had to go to school."

"I'll skip."

"No you won't. If I find out you're skipping school because of me, I won't ever see you again."

I didn't like the sound of that, but it was sort of good to have somebody wanting me to do the right thing. "Okay, I won't skip. But will you be in the park next Saturday?"

"I'm not certain what this next week will be like, but I'll try. I want to talk to David, and it depends on what he says."

"I understand. Uh, do you want me to ... you know?" I made a motion with my hand.

"No, this old man's worn out. Thanks for asking."

I watched the SUV pull out of the alley and pass out of sight before walking to the apartment. The light was still on. Had the old man got out of jail already? No way I was going to be alone with that bastard. I'd sleep in the park first. Nonetheless, I squared my shoulders and marched up the sidewalk.

CHAPTER 7

Matthew was about to go back to his girlfriend's when I came through the door. "I was looking for you. Where you been, Pissant?"

I should probably have still been mad at my brother, but my great day with Jason had mellowed me. "Visiting a friend. Why were you looking for me?"

"Thought you might want to sleep over at our place tonight. I looked for you last night, too."

"No. thanks. Have you seen Mom?" I was a little ashamed I hadn't thought much about her since Saturday morning, although I had called the girls from Jason's house.

"Yeah, she's still having headaches. They probably won't let her come home for a few days yet."

"What about Dad? You know anything about where he is or what they're going to do to him?"

"They won't do anything with him until Monday. He'll probably plead guilty and get forty-five days. He'll be out in thirty. I left him a little money for butts. He'll be all right. It's not his first time in jail."

"I wasn't worried about him. I was worried about him coming home and getting in Mom's hair. She's who I worry about."

"She'll be okay."

He wasn't about to bring up the subject of the girls, so I did. "I saw Nola at school. They won't let me visit them, but I've talked to both of the girls on the phone."

"Yeah, me, too. Look, Wilam, I know you blame me for letting them be taken away, but I think they're better off where they are until Mom comes home."

"What if they decide she's not fit to take care of the girls?" A little of my anger slipped out with the question.

"Then we'll get a lawyer and do what has to be done. If they won't release them to you, I'll claim custody, and we can raise them together. Besides, Mom will still be around."

"Is that a promise?"

"Yes, it is. They're my sisters, too, you know."

"I know. It's just that you're gone so much it's almost like you aren't part of the family anymore."

"I'm part of the family, and I always will be. I've got responsibilities of my own now, just like you'll have one day. We'll get through this okay. You'll see."

"What happens when the old man comes back?"

"He'll either come back and act like a lamb for a while, or else he'll come back meaner than ever. We'll take care of it, whichever way it turns out."

I caught up on what was happening in his life. Not much, just work and going home to Myra. My brother seemed like he was going to be the man he ought to be – if he could stay away from alcohol. Myra enjoyed a drink now and then, too. I prayed it would never get its hooks into them like it had our folks.

The place was awfully quiet after he left. By the time I did the studying I'd neglected all weekend, it was two o'clock. I turned in wishing I could reach out and touch Jason on the other side of the bedroll. Or James, maybe. Or even Enrique, although I knew it would be different with him.

# # # # #

Determined to do better in school, so I could take care of the girls if it came down to that, I hit the books all the next week. Jason had shown me there was another way of life out there. Of course, I already knew it, but I'd never been exposed to it before.

I also worked harder at my carving. Jason, again. He made a good living from his painting. Why couldn't I do the same with my craft? Of course, I wasn't in the same class as Jason, but I already knew my pieces were marketable. I liked that word – marketable.

The week passed slowly, mostly because I was eager for Saturday to roll around to see if Jason showed up. I came straight home from school every afternoon, did my studying, read out of a book the English teacher recommended, and finished carving the kitten. I was so pleased with it; I got some more cottonwood roots to work on.

The only break I took was to visit Mom and spend a few minutes with Nola at the end of her school day a couple of times. She was getting used to the new situation and claimed Junie was, too, but I could see Nola missed being home.

Thursday afternoon, Matthew and I went to the hospital and picked up Mom. From there, we drove to where my sisters were being kept. Since Mom was with us, they let us visit with the girls. Nola and Junie were both disappointed when we had to leave them, but Mom wasn't in any shape to take care of them yet. We promised it wouldn't be much longer, although I'm sure every day was like a year to little Junie. By the time Matthew dropped Mom and me off at the apartment, it was clear my mother wasn't the same person she used to be. She pestered me to get her a bottle but didn't put up much of a fuss when I refused. It wasn't that she didn't hanker for the stuff. It was more like she just didn't care about much of anything.

The apartment was clean, but if it had been a pigsty she probably wouldn't have noticed. She had no energy. She took to her bed and that's where she stayed most of the time. I worried I had an invalid on my hands, but by Friday night, I was satisfied she could take care of herself if I wasn't underfoot to do it for her.

Saturday, I got up early and made sure there were enough meals in the refrigerator to hold Mom for a while. Then I struck off for the fairgrounds on foot. I wanted to hit the flea market before heading for the park – and Jason.

The hike wasn't a long one, and even though it was early, the market was busy with earlybirds already picking through the stalls. I had to wait a few minutes while Ben dealt with two hagglers. The couple walked off with two of my pieces. I sorta wished Ben had pointed me out as the craftsman who made them, but that wasn't his style.

As usual, he examined all of my stuff, setting them aside in little groups. I knew from experience that indicated what he was willing to pay for them. Then I took the cat out of the paper bag. He studied the figure for a long time, mostly leaving it on the table and looking at it from different angles. He wanted it, all right, but he was holding back for some reason. My heart dipped down into my stomach. I'd been hoping to get more money for the cat. A whole lot more. From the way he handled it, he probably knew what I was thinking. Finally, he dropped his rump into the fold up chair he sat in all day.

"William ...." He seemed to be fighting a battle with himself. He tried again. "I'm not going to buy the cat from you."

The starch went out of my spine. "Why not? Isn't it good enough?"

"It's the best work you've ever done. I'll be honest with you, son. I'd really like to take it off your hands. I could move this and any others like it within a couple of hours."

"Then why ...."

He held up a hand. "I'm not going to buy it because I couldn't do right by you. I want you to take this cat over to a friend of mine on Central. It's not far from here. His name is Horace Gresham, and he runs this place called Gresham's Indian Trading Post. Tell him I sent you."

I didn't understand, but I nodded.

Ben indicated the pieces he'd set aside. "I'll take all of these you can bring me, but you've reached another plane in your craft with the cat."

He took out the big leather wallet anchored to his belt by a chain. Someone had picked his pocket once, and he swore they weren't going to do it again. He paid me a fair price for the things he'd selected. I had some more new pieces wrapped in newspaper in the bag with the cat, but some customers walked up about that time. I could always bring them back later, so I gave him my thanks and set off down Central Avenue for Mr. Gresham's place.

I didn't know whether to be excited or disappointed because he was sending me to this Indian trader. The pieces still in my bag were bigger carvings, with mystical markings on them. One was a bear standing on his hind feet with a hollowed out place in its chest holding a faint outline of a warrior's head. I'd tried something new with paint, too. The bear was all

51

black, but I'd used a cloth to smear highlights of different colors to enhance the warrior's head and to create faint designs on the animal's upraised paws.

It was still early, and Mr. Gresham's trading post had a "Closed" sign hanging on the front door. A man was moving around inside the big place; probably the owner getting ready to open up. He noticed me standing there holding my paper sack and held up a hand. I waited while he went in the back room and returned with a set of keys. He let me in and locked the door behind us. Still too early for customers, I guess. Then why had he opened the door for me?

"I take it your name's William." He smiled. "Ben Ames called me a few minutes ago and asked me to keep an eye out for you."

"Yes sir, William Greyhorse."

"My name's Gresham. Ben said you have something you want me to see."

I nodded my head and worked some moisture into my dry mouth. "Yes, sir. I take all my pieces to Mr. Ames, but when I showed him this a few minutes ago, he sent me to you."

I placed the cat on the glass counter in front of the man. He didn't touch it at first. He just adjusted his gold-rimmed glasses and looked at it for a long time, nudging it now and then to give himself a view from another angle. He still hadn't said anything by the time he took out a magnifying glass and examined it again. This time he picked up the carving and held it close. Finally, he stood up straight and looked at me.

"Son, there's a work bench in the room back there. There's a very fine Emory cloth and a magnifying glass on the table. Use it to sand out the rough spots in some of the hollow places. I don't think it will damage the stain job. Then I want you to carve your name on the pedestal of the piece, right about here." He indicated a place near one rear paw. "Not big or crude letters, but small and dignified. Just your last name. Understand?"

"I think so."

"Come on back out here when you're finished. I'll be getting ready to open the shop."

The bench in his workroom was old but solid. It smelled of paint and varnish and wood shavings. It had seen lot of work. Not all of it was woodcarving; there were a lot of tiny grains of sand, probably grindings from some stonework. All the tools I needed hung right on the wall. I found the sanding cloth, and used the lighted magnifying glass mounted on an adjustable metal frame to examine the cat more closely. I immediately saw some places where my knives hadn't made as good a cut as I thought. It didn't take long to fix those, but carving my name on the base of the work did. When I finished, I found an old rag with some stain residue on it to take the new out of the letters I'd carved. Then I went back out into the store.

Mr. Gresham had taken the other five pieces out of my bag and lined them up on the counter. He moved the cat over to a clear space and went over it as carefully as he had the first time. That made me nervous.

At last, he put down the magnifying glass and turned to me. "What do you think this piece is worth?"

I swallowed hard and named a figure twice what Ben Ames had paid me for my best piece so far. If that got me thrown out on my ear or laughed at, so be it. Mr. Gresham fooled me; he changed the subject and asked if I lived around here.

"Yes sir. About a mile up the street."

"Do you produce much work like this? What I mean is, is this your livelihood or just a hobby?"

"Well, sorta both. I carve every day after school. It's the way I make money to help out the family."

"School? Are you at UNM or CNM?" Apparently he wasn't fooled by how young everybody said I looked.

I flushed. This was getting awfully personal, and I didn't even know how he felt about my pieces yet. "No, sir. I'm still in high school."

"How long did it take to create the cat?"

Create. I liked that. Sounded better than "made." I cleared my throat and shifted my weight to the other leg. "Too long. This was the first time I worked in cottonwood root, and I had to learn about it. I think I've got the hang of it now." I nodded to the other pieces he had lined up on the counter. "Some of those are cottonwood, and I didn't have as much trouble as I did with the cat."

"I've seen your work before. I've even bought a few of your pieces from Ben."

"Oh. Uh, thanks."

"Are you dependable, William?"

"Yes, sir. Like I said, I carve every day and take Ben some pieces almost every weekend."

"I'll tell you what, if you'll go back in the workroom and finish off these other five pieces and add your signature to them, I'm willing to buy all six."

"Yes, sir!" I oughta play it cool like Ben Ames did, but I couldn't contain myself. That was strange because I'm usually close-mouthed around people I don't know. Especially white people.

"Hold on now," he cautioned. "I'm not finished. The cat is worth the fifty dollars you're asking, but the other pieces aren't quite up to the quality of the cat. I'm going to pay you fifty for each of them, in spite of that, but there's a condition."

"What kind of condition?"

"On the condition you promise to bring me six more pieces at the same price as these."

53

"Deal!" It almost came out in a shout.

"Don't get in a hurry. I'm going to tell you what six pieces I want you to do for me. I told you I'd bought some of your work from Ben. One of them was a small head you did of a girl."

I remembered the head. It was one of my efforts to capture little Junie. It was all right, but it didn't quite look like her. No need to tell him that though.

"I want you to do six carved heads for me. But not just any six. I want one of a grandmother and grandfather. A warrior, his squaw, and one of a little boy and a little girl. All Indians. An Indian family. You don't look like a Pueblo. What are you, Plains?" I nodded. "Okay, make them Plains Indians. I want two feathers in the warrior's hair. Well, you know more about your own people than I do, so you know how to do them. What do you think? Can you do it?"

"How big?" I asked.

"I'd say about ten inches. And I want them out of walnut. It'll cost you more money for your materials, but that's why I'm willing to pay you $300 for these six pieces. I won't make my usual markup on them, but I'll make it back on the other ones. Do we have a deal?"

"You bet. When do you need them?"

"Bring me two this week. In fact, do them two at a time. Bring them in as you finish each pair. Do the heads down to the bottom of the neck. I'll take care of putting them on a pedestal. Remember to sign them. Probably on the side of the neck. An artist always signs his work. It's the way his name becomes known in the trade."

"Okay. I'll remember." An artist. He called me an artist.

I left Mr. Gresham's store with my head in the clouds and $300 and his business card in my pocket ... plus the fifty I'd made at the flea market. I'd never had that much money at one time. Wait until I told....

Who? Mom would want to buy booze with it. The old man was in jail, and he'd be the last one to tell. I'd die before he got a dime of it. The girls weren't around to lavish it on. Jason? Three hundred fifty dollars would seem like a pitiful little amount to him. Matthew? Maybe, but I was still halfway pissed at him. No. I'd keep my business to myself.

It was too early go to the park, so I took a bus all the way out Frontage road to a woodworker's supply house where I ran into a problem. It was going to be hard to come up with blocks of walnut big enough for the pieces Mr. Gresham wanted. The supply house had to special order the wood, and they couldn't promise delivery in anything short of a week.

I prepaid for my order and bought some smaller pieces to practice on. Walnut was such a beautiful wood I could hardly wait to start working with it. I added a strong magnifying glass and a small vise to my bill and settled up. Mr. Gresham had asked if I was reliable, so I borrowed the supply house's telephone to let him know I wouldn't have the wood in my hands for another week. That was the reliable thing to do. He said he understood. Then I went across the freeway to wait on a bus headed south.

On the long ride back to Central, it hit me that I'd spent $100 at the woodworker's shop. I'd never spent that much money at one time in my life. Being able to do that made me giddy, but the hole I'd made in my new nest egg sobered me up pretty fast.

Jason wasn't at the park when I got there. I didn't want to get sweaty and dirty playing ball or risk anyone stealing my stuff, so I plopped down on the bench where he'd asked me to go home with him. It was probably just my imagination, but it seemed like a special place. To me, anyway. I'd thought about doing it with him every day, but I kept my hands off myself because I wanted to be ready for him.

I waited a good half hour and was getting pretty anxious by the time his Lexus pulled off the main drag and parked in a little dirt lot across the street from the park. I went over and crawled into the passenger's seat before he even had a chance to switch off the motor.

He gave me a big grin. "Hello, handsome. What do you want to do today?"

"That's easy. My cherry needs rubbing." A little shiver went down my spine. "Until I can't do it any more."

He laughed aloud and slapped me on the leg. I caught his hand and held it there. "I mean it. I need it as much as you said you needed me last Saturday."

He rolled his eyes. "What have I created?" I moved his hand up to my crotch so he'd know I was hard and ready for him. He gave my thing a good squeeze and shifted the gears. "I think I better take care of that before it grows some more."

# # # # #

Sometimes, when you discover something new, it's disappointing the second time around. Doing it to Jason again was just as good as I remembered. The first time we did it today, I was rushed and kind of frantic. He sucked me off, and then I got on top of him while he was on his stomach and fucked him so hard I got grunts out of both of us. Somehow, I sensed he needed it hard and rough. He seemed down about something, but I wasn't going to let what was bothering him hang around long. I was going to be so good to him he just couldn't be down.

After we cleaned up, we lay in the bed and talked. He asked about my week, and I shared most of it, including the good luck I'd had with the cat.

"I guess it's wasn't a black cat," he quipped. "Seriously, that's great news. I had the feeling you were pretty good. I don't know Gresham, but I know about him. His father started the business, and he continued it when the old man died. He has a reputation for honest dealing. You're lucky this Ben Ames fellow sent you to him. Now, I've got a surprise for you."

He got out of bed and slipped on this big white robe made out of the same material as a towel. Terrycloth, he called it. He tossed a second one to me and led me into his studio. He stopped at the door and stood aside, letting me find the painting for myself.

There I was right up on his easel in the pose where I was sitting on a rock at the park and leaning on my knee. The figure – me – was finished, but he was still working on the background. I walked up to the canvas and put my arm near the painting. Jason had the flesh tone exactly right. It was me, right down to the spike of hair that sometimes stood up at the crown of my head.

"Do you like it?"

All I could do was shake my head. "Too handsome."

"Either you're modest or you don't know how good looking you are. I hate to be the one to break this to you, Wilam, but you're one hell of a handsome dude. I don't lie, and I don't paint flattering portraits. Why do you think I came on to you?"

"You said you needed someone right then."

"Right, but I didn't need just any someone. I needed a handsome, sensitive young man who wouldn't abuse me or try to take advantage of the situation. And, coincidentally, who would give me lots of good sex."

"Did I do that?"

"You gave me the great sex part, but from the way my sphincter feels right now, I'm not too sure about the abuse." He laughed at the look on my face. Jason moved to my side and clasped a hand behind my head. "You really don't know, do you? You're great in bed. You don't do things the same way every time. It's a new experience every time with you. You're gentle at times, and almost violent at times. You're considerate. You always make sure I get my share of pleasure out of our meetings. You'd be surprised at how many people are only interested in what they want and totally ignore their partner's needs."

"It's not any good unless you get something out of it, too."

He nodded. "There you have it. That's what makes you a great partner."

I grinned at him, and a look of alarm came over his face. "Oh no! My butt can't take any more. Not right now."

I pulled him to me and nuzzled his neck. "How about your mouth? Or your hand. You've never jacked me off."

"Okay, I've got enough strength left for that." He took my hand and started for the bedroom, but I stopped him. "Can we do it here, so I can look at the picture?"

Jason slipped the robe over my shoulders. "I'll watch the real you while you watch the canvas you."

It was a trip lying on the couch in his studio looking back and forth between Jason and my own image on the easel while he jerked me with one hand and stroked my belly and thighs with the other. He did it so slowly and gently my orgasm came as a surprise. All of a sudden, I started breathing in little gasps, and the contractions slipped up on me. I closed my eyes as I spilled seed all over my chest and belly. Then I changed places with him, and he watched my fist move up and down rhythmically until his eyes went out of focus. Then he gave a groan and came on both of us.

I stayed overnight with him again. I suffered a twinge of guilt at leaving Mom alone in the apartment, but it went away when he pulled me to him in bed. Sunday, Jason wanted to get out of the house, so he insisted on taking me to the mall for another set of clothes I didn't need. He also tried to give me some pocket money, but I refused it. I think he understood the way I felt because he didn't insist. It was an awkward moment, but he got us out of it by driving up Sandia Peak where he parked in a little out of the way place beside a quick running stream. He spread out a blanket and had me fuck him right out under the trees. My backside got cold from the mountain air, and I ran short of breath because of the altitude. He was doing a little more gasping than usual when he shot his jism, too. The water was cold enough to shrivel our things when we washed up.

We came down out of the mountains and drove across the Rio Grande Valley to the West Mesa. That's a huge, undeveloped place where volcanoes had built up a thick lava bed over the years. You can still see the remnants of some cones called the Five Sisters. A thick wall of lava hung over the western side of Albuquerque, looking like it froze up just before it spilled down into the valley. Right on the rim of the bluff formed by the lava flow, there are places to park where you can see the whole city that's built along the banks of the Rio Grande. To me, it was a better view than from the mountains, because the colors weren't so washed out from the altitude.

Jason didn't park there on the rim, and I understood why he sought the cover of a few straggly saplings when he spread me out over the hood of the car. He sucked me until it felt like my balls were going to come out through the end of my cock.

From there, we drove over to El Moro National Monument and saw where a lot of early travelers scratched their names on this big, monolithic rock. There were some famous names there, like Coronado and a lot of other Spanish people. Then we went to a place called the Ice Cave nearby. It was amazing because the floor of this little grotto, which was just barely below ground level, was a thick layer of blue ice that hadn't melted in hundreds and hundreds of years.

It was night before we got back to Jason's house. I was tempted to ask him if I could sleep over again, but I didn't want to leave Mom home alone for a second night in a row. My portrait wasn't finished yet, so I'd have to get it later – much later, probably. There wasn't any place I could put it where the old man wouldn't take it down and go sell it. I collected the wood and supplies I'd bought at the supply house and got into the Lexus feeling pretty good. Jason had only slipped into a blue mood a couple of times. I sneaked glimpses of him as he drove, and I could tell he was dreading being left alone for another week.

I watched him drive away after he let me off near my place. When he was out of sight, I moseyed toward the apartment. I had to move easy because my old thing was so sore from overuse that it rubbed painfully against my clothes with every step I took.

CHAPTER 8

As soon as I stepped inside the apartment, I knew something was wrong. The lights were on in every room, but I couldn't find Mom anywhere. On the edge of panic, I started next door to see if she was at Ms. Chisholm's, but I didn't have to go that far. I found her passed out in the dirt at the corner of the house.

I carried her inside and put her on the bed. She roused some and insisted she wasn't drunk. She claimed she'd fainted from a bad headache. I pretended to believe her even though the empty Old Crow bottle was right there on the kitchen table. She'd been drinking – alone again – probably for most of the weekend. I had no idea where she'd gotten the whiskey, but that didn't matter at the moment. She needed help.

I ran up the street to a pay telephone and called a taxi. It wasn't easy getting one to come down to the Combat Area that time of night, but eventually, I convinced the dispatcher this was a medical emergency. That almost backfired because he told me to call an ambulance. I didn't have any idea how much an ambulance cost, but it was bound to be a hell of a lot more than a taxi, so I claimed it wasn't that kind of emergency. In the end, a taxi showed up and took us to the UNM emergency ward.

After a long wait, a doctor came around and examined her. He decided to keep her overnight. The buses had quit running, and since I didn't want to spend any more money on a cab, I started hiking back home. By the time I cut through the University of New Mexico campus and reached Central Avenue, the cock I'd rubbed raw on Jason was bothering me so much I had trouble walking. To make matters worse, the more it chafed against my shorts, the harder it got. And the bigger it got, the more it rubbed against my clothes. I was still a good mile from home when walking didn't seem like a good idea any more. I sat down on a bus stop bench and tried to arrange my clothing so it didn't irritate my tender flesh. I'd have to wait out my erection before I could go on home. Getting to school on time tomorrow, or rather later this morning was going to be a problem anyway, and I didn't need any more delays.

"Can I help you out with that?" A man's voice surprised me.

"With what?" I looked up to see a car pulled close to the curb. A young man in his twenties was giving me the once over.

"With that." He pointed to my crotch. "That big bone looks like it's a problem; I know just how to get rid of it. You know, give you some relief."

"What are you talking about?" My face got red, and I could feel my muscles tense. I think I was shocked.

"I've gone around the block twice now, and both times you've been playing with your cock. Good-looking guy like you shouldn't do it alone. Can I play with it, too?"

"Get away from me, you fucking faggot." I got up from the bench, prepared to do battle. The man gunned his motor and pulled away from the curb with a screech.

I started on up Central wondering why I'd reacted like that. He was offering to do something I'd been doing with Jason all weekend, so why did I get my back up?

I wrestled with the puzzle as I limped home. The best I could figure, working out a relationship with a friend was okay, but trying to pick up strangers off the street just wasn't right. Of course, that didn't hold water when you considered Jason had picked me up in a public park. I was too tired to figure it all out, so when I got home, I went to bed and tried to get some sleep.

# # # # #

I slept so hard I missed my first class. Right after the last bell, I borrowed the phone in the office to call the hospital to check on Mom. They were running some more tests and wouldn't release her today. So I rushed home to start experimenting with the small walnut pieces I'd bought at the woodworker's supply house. It was good wood but unforgiving. I whittled away until one of them turned into a halfway decent little dog.

The next day I managed to come up with a cute-looking kitten curled around itself. I spent some more time working with sanding and polishing techniques using a book I'd checked out of the library. I managed a quick visit to the hospital, where they told me Mom wouldn't be released until they knew the origin of the headache problem. I promised to check with them the next day.

Wednesday, I carved the biggest piece of walnut I had left into the small figure of a girl lying on her side with her head propped up on one hand. I put her in buckskins and moccasins and dabbed just a hint of color on the fringes and the design on the moccasins. When I got through with it, I put it away out of sight. I wouldn't look at it again until tomorrow. I did that sometimes because I could see my mistakes more easily after a little time went by. I spent another lonely night since they didn't release Mom that day, either. Lord, I wished the state would send Nola and Junie back to us.

The next afternoon, I checked the carving of the girl and saw a couple of mistakes. I corrected them, refinished the piece, and put it aside. By Friday, I had four pieces I wasn't ashamed of to take Mr. Gresham. He looked them over carefully while I explained I'd made them just to get familiar with the walnut. After his examination with the magnifying glass, he bought them on the spot for twenty-five dollars each. When I asked him to check on my shipment of walnut from Woodworkers, he found it was scheduled for delivery on Monday.

That night, my world tilted again. I guess I shouldn't have been surprised. Earlier that day, Matthew had picked up Mom from the hospital, and they drove straight downtown to see my dad in jail. The news they came

back with about tore me up. The old man was pulling up stakes as soon as he
got out of jail. He was going to Arizona on the trail of some money scheme
Tolliver and a jailbird in the cell next door claimed to know about.

"I'm not going," Matthew said after he dumped the news on me. He
looked at me as if he expected me to say the same thing. In my panic, that's
exactly what I almost did.

"Mom what are you going to do?" I asked.

"Go with your dad."

Matthew and I started in on her. Why would she stay with him after
the beating he gave her? She wasn't recovered yet and might not ever be. Next
time he would probably kill her. I'm not even sure she heard us.

"Don't guess I can make you understand," she said. "You don't know
your father like I do. He's my husband, don't you see? He's my man, and I
have to stand by him. He needs me now. More than ever. Things will be all
right. Just wait. They'll be all right."

She trotted out all of the trite justifications. He wasn't a bad man; it
was the alcohol that made him do things. The women he ran around with
didn't mean anything to him. He hadn't meant to hurt her; that was an
accident. She fell. She'd probably been too hard on him. I got nauseated
listening to the tripe coming out of her mouth.

My heart turned to stone. If she was going, then Nola and Junie
would go. And if they were going, I'd have to tag along. I latched onto the
only hope I saw. It would be a couple of weeks before Dad got out of jail, and
a lot can happen in that time. Maybe the son of a bitch would kill somebody in
a fight and get his worthless ass sent away forever.

CHAPTER 9

Jason was so preoccupied the next Saturday I was afraid he was getting tired of me. That happened when people were so intense about one another, I'd heard. Burnout, they called it. I soon understood his problem – which I figured was David going off and getting married – was still eating at him. I'd never be able to stand in such a handsome man's shoes, but I could try to provide a distraction. So I did everything I could to make those next two days good ones for him. We took a shower together, and it was a real turn-on with him down on his knees sucking me off while warm water from the spray stung my nipples. I came so hard; he had to hold me up to keep me from collapsing. Like I said, intense.

After that, I got down on my knees and licked his stomach and his balls. I even licked his hard, throbbing cock, but I hesitated to put it in my mouth. He understood, and said to just make him come with my hand so he could spurt all over my chest. I did and had to hold him up. After that, we lay down in the shower and laughed and kissed while Jason said he sure was glad he'd met me, because I'd helped him through these last few weeks.

While we were lying there with the two shower sprays splattering us with warm water, I told Jason how I'd reacted to the guy who'd tried to pick me up that night.

"You really called him a fucking faggot?" Jason asked.

"Yeah. He made me mad. He didn't have any right to do that."

"No, he didn't. He didn't have any more right to proposition you than I did in the park that day. You didn't get mad and call me names."

"That was … different."

He nodded, and the pelting water dripped off his nice nose. "Yes, it was different. But do you know how?"

I swiped the spray out of my eyes and tried to see if he was joking. "Uh uh. How was it different?"

"Think about it. When I approached you – in a much more crude manner that that poor guy – you'd not been with a man. You may have thought about it, but you hadn't actually done it. Your masculinity was secure."

"My masculinity?" My voice rose an octave.

"That's right. You'd been with girls. Made a couple of conquests. You could brag with the rest of the guys. But after we spent that first weekend together, your life had changed."

"I guess that's right."

"It is. You knew why those times with women weren't entirely satisfactory."

"So you're saying I yelled 'faggot' at that guy because of me?"

He nodded. His hair was plastered close to his head, revealing the shape of his good-looking skull. "I think so. You were afraid you'd be tempted to go with him."

"I wouldn't have."

"That's not the point. You know who you are now and where your temptations lie. Women aren't a threat to you. Men are."

I leaned forward so my head was under the shower. The spray drowned out everything else while I considered what he'd said. Then I leaned back against the shower wall and shook like a dog shedding water. "That's not true. Men aren't a threat to me … you are. And I already got with you, so that means you aren't a threat, either."

"That's false logic. You're right about one part though. While I'm no threat, I am a fact of your life, no matter how permanent or how temporary, because I exposed you to the truth. You may come to thank me for that or you may come to curse me for it. Only time will tell."

"I could never curse you, Jason. You've been good to me."

"Never say never. I hope you don't. I hope you look back on this and remember me as a friend and a lover. Does that word bother you?"

"What, lover? I don't know. It's not the way I think about us."

"How do you think about us?"

That stumped me. "As special friends. Friends who can do anything or say anything we want to one another. You know, intimate things."

"That sounds like a pretty good description of lovers to me." When I got quiet, he got up and turned off the shower. Then he reached down and hauled me up. As we stood side by side at the double sink drying off with those fluffy towels of his and combing our hair, it kind of felt like he'd said. You know, that we were lovers. I got a little tingle in my gut.

"About that guy who tried to pick you up. You're going to run into more of them. You don't have to get mad, but you do have to be careful. Some guys proposition men, so they can do some old-fashioned gay bashing."

"Do you think that's what that guy wanted?" I paused in the act of straightening the part in my black hair.

Jason smiled. "No, I think he wanted just what he said he did, that hunky cock of yours. Wilam, you don't look or speak or act like a gay man. A guy's gaydar would have to be awfully sharp to pick up on you."

I didn't know exactly why, but that made me feel good. Then I remembered the night Dad beat me up. He'd called me a pussy or something like that. A queer sounding name, anyway. Did he have that gaydar stuff Jason mentioned? Did he know? Had he figured it out before I had? I shivered at the thought.

Nonetheless, as I stood there beside Jason, admiring his build and his good looks, I faced up to it – I was gay. That sounded a lot better than queer, but I told Jason I was queer for him. We laughed over that.

"I don't understand something," he said. "You're nineteen years old and one of the best-looking studs I know. Why haven't you had more experience?"

I didn't answer for a long time while I thought about his question. Finally, I turned and looked at him. Here was this good-looking, successful, sophisticated dude calling me handsome and sexy – a stud no less. I ought to be saying that to him. "I don't know. Maybe it's because I spent most of my life on the reservation."

"Don't tell me they don't have sex and sin on the reservation. There was your friend, James, for example. You said they called him the reservation queer."

"They did, and I realize now he did everything he could to let me know how he felt without just coming out and saying it. But it's a small place, and everybody knows everything about everybody else. Maybe I was just afraid I'd get caught if I showed any interest."

"So you repressed your own sexuality. The fact you were mother and father and big brother to your two little sisters probably isolated you further."

"Or maybe, I'm just a late developer." I tried to put some sarcasm in my voice, but he didn't take it that way.

"If so, man, you have sure developed. You are one hell of a lover."

My ears went red, and I didn't know what to say.

"Speaking of your sisters, when are they coming home?" Jason asked.

"Not till Mom can take care of them. Maybe sometime next week. They let me see them now, so I go over whenever I can."

"If you need help getting them home, let me know. I can give you a ride."

The weekend with Jason was great – not as frantic as the last one because when I finally went home on Sunday night, I was drained and satisfied, but I wasn't sore like the week before.

# # # # #

The wood shop delivered my walnut order on Monday, as promised, and I went right to work on Mr. Gresham's carved heads. Wednesday afternoon, I was doing the grandfather when the state woman from the Child Protection Agency brought Nola and Junie home. I was overjoyed to see them even if they made studying and carving, not to mention seeing Jason, harder.

We sat through a stern lecture from the state social worker, a woman who introduced herself as Mrs. Martinez. Mom swore she'd never let her drinking get away from her again, but it was the same old promise I'd heard for years. Mrs. Martinez had probably heard those words before, too. She had a worn, frazzled air about her that hinted she knew a bill of goods when she heard one.

As soon as she left, everyone laughed and cried from joy for an hour, but the experience had changed the girls. Especially little Junie. She wasn't the happy baby who'd left the apartment. Every once in a while, there was a fearful look in her eyes. Some of it could have been from seeing Dad hauled off in handcuffs, but most of it was remembering she'd been taken away, too. Nola was a little more independent, almost sassy. There was some resentment in her that wasn't there before.

As soon as the household settled down, I went back to work on the grandfather. Junie sat down on the floor beside my chair at the kitchen table. Nola went through the house looking for things to clean up – and didn't find much because I'd kept the place in pretty good shape. Then she came over and took a chair across the table. She caressed one of the figures with the tips of her fingers and gave me a look. She liked my work.

By Friday, I had finished the first two carved heads for Mr. Gresham. I'd given the grandmother wrinkles and a bone necklace. The grandfather had a sagging jaw line and a bear claw choker around his neck. I put highlights of white and gray in their hair, touches of ivory in the necklaces, and faint blue shadows underneath the eyes. I didn't like their blank stares, so I carved irises into the eyes and tinted them. At the last minute, I remembered to carve "Greyhorse" into the hair of each at the back of the head. Then, as was my custom, I put them away overnight.

When I took them out Saturday morning, I made a small correction and then set them side-by-side on the table. They looked pretty good. I just hoped Mr. Gresham thought so.

When I took them over later that morning, he studied them for a long time from every which direction and put them under the lighted magnifying glass back in the workroom. He noted the "Greyhorse" signature and grunted approval. He didn't find a single thing he wanted changed.

"They're good, William. They're exactly what I had in mind. When can I have the next pair?"

"Maybe by next weekend, but I'm not sure. I'm doing the warrior and his wife next, and they'll both have some feather work. Sometimes that takes longer."

"As soon as possible, but don't rush so much the quality suffers."

Mr. Gresham showed me the marble bases he was going to mount the pieces on. I redid the bottom of each one so it would fit properly. The result was really something. "Stunning," was the word he used. He pulled out a camera and took a couple of pictures of each carving and told me he'd started a book of my work. That way there would be a record of each piece, including who bought it and for how much. That gave my work a provenance, he said. Then he had to explain what a provenance was. After that, he surprised me.

"William, I know we agreed on a price of fifty dollars for each of these heads, but I consider myself a fair man. If you're going to make your living dealing with people like me, you ought to know how we operate. I won't buy anything I don't figure I can double the price on. That might sound like a lot, but it's not, because I've got to pay the rent on the shop and the lights and sales people and accountants and a whole mess of other expenses before I can take a dime out of this store. I figure to sell these carvings for $250 each. The marble bases cost me about ten apiece. I'm going to pay you $120 for each head you bring in that's of this quality. What do you say to that?"

What I wanted to do was give a war whoop, but I swallowed my joy and thought for a minute before I answered him. "Mr. Gresham, you told me about you, so I want you to know about me. I figure I do pretty good work, and it's going to get better as time goes on. I'm a fair man, myself. I want you to do a little better on my work than you do on anybody else's. I won't take more than a $100 for each of them. That way, if somebody's dickering over whether they ought to buy one of my carvings or a war bonnet or something, I know you're going to steer them to my carving."

He laughed aloud. "You're going to do fine in this business. All right, we've got a deal. You bring me the other four heads as quickly as you can, and then I'm going to tell you the next thing I want you to do for me. The holidays are coming up, and I ship all over the country. Could be we can work up a demand for a 'Greyhorse.'" He held out his hand, and I shook it, giving silent thanks to Ben Ames for sending me to this man.

Before I left the shop, I remembered Dad was coming home. It wouldn't be safe to keep so much money in the house, so I asked Mr. Gresham if he could help me set up a bank account somewhere. He sent me a few blocks up the street to a man he dealt with at his bank. The banker opened my first savings account with the $200 I had earned that day. Then I ran all the way home and brought $200 of my stash to the bank. Somehow, I felt my life had changed for the better.

The only dark cloud on my horizon was the old man getting out of jail in another week or so. If he followed his usual pattern, we'd be yanked up and moved again. That's what he always did when he got in a jam. It would be foolish not to take his intention of moving to Arizona seriously. All the way home, I racked my brain trying to figure a way to keep the girls and me here, but I couldn't come up with an idea that made sense. I was so desperate I considered picking a fight with my father, so he'd give me a beating. Then I could charge him with assault and put him away again. I held out my hands and looked at them. What if he damaged my fingers? All the dreams I had about selling Mr. Gresham an endless supply of carvings would be finished.

I clenched my fists and walked up the street as if I were approaching my own doom. At that moment, the two deposit slips in my pocket meant nothing – not even a way to escape what was surely coming.

CHAPTER 10

Jason didn't act right at the park later that morning. He told me right off the bat he wouldn't be able to spend the weekend with me. I studied his eyes, read the pain I saw there, and got up enough gumption to crawl into the cab of the SUV anyway. He gave me a long look and then drove us to his place without saying another word. I went straight to his studio, so I'd be available but out of his way. I looked at some of his recent sketches. They were wild, done in big, dark strokes. Different from anything else of his I'd seen.

He spent a long time pacing around the big room he called a den. I'd brought my knives and a half-completed wolf to show him, but it didn't seem like the time for it, so I settled down at a worktable in a corner of the studio and started whittling. At first, I was nervous and jumpy because of the mood he was in, but soon the knives and the wood worked their magic, and I was lost in my work.

When I got hungry, I fixed sandwiches out of the roast beef he always seemed to have in the refrigerator. I took one out to him and found him sitting in his recliner. The TV was on, but I don't think he was seeing or hearing any of it. He wasn't doing much of anything but suffering. I pressed the sandwich on him. He ate it without even knowing what he was swallowing. After I put everything away and cleaned up the mess I'd had made in the kitchen, I went back to the den and knelt down with my hands on his knees. It took a few seconds before his eyes focused on me.

"You want to tell me about it?" I asked. "I know how to suffer. I've done a lot of it. Maybe if we share it, the hurt won't be so hard to carry."

He touched my hair gently. "I'm sorry to be such a drag. I know you were looking forward to this visit. I just can't seem to muster any energy."

"I know. Usually by now we've rubbed the cherry at least a couple of times."

He didn't crack a smile at my pitiful attempt to lighten things, but he looked at me a long time and then started talking. He told me about meeting David in a western town a while back. Like Jason was for me, he'd been David's first.

"It only happened," Jason said, "because he'd been out on a drilling rig for six months and was stranded in this little town, broke and horny as hell. I came along at the right time, at the right place. It was magic. Especially for me, but for him a little, too. Anyway, he came into it slowly; me enthusiastically." Jason looked down at me kneeling in front of him. It felt like the first time he'd really looked at me all day. "Like you, he's a Plains Indian."

"If he'd been on a rig for six months why was he broke?" I wasn't sure what kind of rig it was, but it sounded like a way to make money.

"His mother was sick, and he'd sent it all to the hospital for her."

The way Jason told it, the meeting had changed his life. He'd been in love before, but never with a handsome young man who was basically straight. They'd kept in touch and met a few more times. After a while, they developed a relationship that seemed to satisfy them both. It was sort of a lopsided affair, because Jason was committed – not to mention head over heels in love – but David only gave a limited commitment. It was nonexclusive according to Jason.

Then David met a girl and got her pregnant. In spite of all Jason could do, David was determined to do the right thing and marry her. That was the wedding he'd talked about when I met him that day in the park – the reason he'd come on to me in the first place. Her folks didn't want her to marry an Indian and talked her into getting an abortion at the last minute. After the wedding fell apart, David had started drinking, and now he'd disappeared.

"I haven't heard from him in a week," Jason said. "I hope he's on his way here. That's why I said I couldn't spend the weekend with you."

My heart skittered all over the room as I listened to him. It fell into the pit of my stomach when he confirmed what I already knew but hadn't faced – he was crazy about another man. Not just crazy, but deeply committed. I was disappointed because I had kind of hoped it would be me. My heart went out to him because of the anguish he was going through. It bounced over to the portrait of David out in the foyer. I even felt for him.

After he finished talking, I did something I never thought I'd do. I moved forward and pressed my face into his crotch.

"You don't have …."

His voice died when my lips found the sleeping cock in his trousers. I fumbled with his fly while he sat like he was paralyzed. He was soon exposed and growing excited. I'd seen his cock before. Hell, I'd had it in my hands often enough, but I'd never really looked at it. It was bowed sort of like a banana, reaching up toward his belly. He was cut and had a big head that seemed to have two halves; at least the bottom part was sort of cloven. He let out a gasp when I took it into my mouth. He lifted his hips and allowed me to pull him free of his clothing. Then I did what he'd done for me these past three weeks. I moved up and down on him, keeping up a slight suction and twisting my tongue around the tip every time I came out to the end.

I handled it all right until he shuddered as if he was in the grip of a fit, and then his milky cum spurted out into my mouth. I wasn't prepared and about gagged. I fought my reflexes and did what he always did for me, stayed with him until his orgasm was over.

He pulled up his trousers, sprawled back in his chair like a limp dishrag, and mumbled. I had to listen hard to hear what he was saying because he was talking through his tears. "That was fantastic, Wilam. You didn't have to do that, but I'm glad you did. Thank you so much."

It did something to me to see this strong, confident man humbled like this. "You're welcome, Jason. I just hope it helped. If it did, then it was worth it." I laid my head in his lap, and he tousled my hair. We sat that way for the most part of an hour. When I realized he was asleep, I was proud I'd been able to do that for him.

I offered to stay the night, but he shook his head. I understood. What would David think if he showed up and found somebody in bed with him? Before he took me home, he spread me on the couch and did for me what I'd done for him. Even as I exploded in a tremendous orgasm, my heart contracted. He belonged to someone else, and always would, no matter how it turned out for him.

# # # # #

When I got home, I found Mom in bed, but Nola said she wasn't drinking. It was just one of those headaches. Junie was asleep on the couch, and Nola was getting ready to join her. I sat at the kitchen table and whittled half the night away before I was sleepy enough to go to crawl into my blankets.

Sunday morning, I worked on my carvings but went out in the middle of the afternoon to the pay phone and called Jason. His voice was full of hope when he came on the line.

"Sorry, it's just me," I said. "I won't tie the phone up for long, but I wanted to know how you're making it."

I'm doing all right. Thanks to you."

"Have you heard anything? You know, from David?"

"No. Nothing."

"I know you want to be alone … just in case. But I'll come over, if you want."

"I appreciate it, but …."

"I know. Is it all right if I call tomorrow after school? You know, to see if there's any news"

"That will be fine, Wilam. And thanks for understanding. Thanks a lot."

I hung up and went back to my carving with a lump in my throat. I got a lot of good work done despite suffering along with my friend.

# # # # #

Monday wasn't a good day. Matthew took Mom down to see Dad at the jail, and came back with the news I'd been dreading. The old man had decided he was going to take the family to Phoenix as soon as he got out from behind bars. That was where the scheme with some ex-jailbird was supposed to take place. Mom was still determined to go with him, which meant I'd have to go along and be responsible for Nola and Junie.

That development plus worrying about Jason wrecked my day and turned me surly. It must have been worse than I thought, because I nearly got into a fistfight in shop when this other guy kept hogging a tool I needed. That wasn't like me at all.

When the teacher caught on that I wasn't acting like the William he knew, he got in my face, demanding to know the problem. I put it down to having to move when I really didn't want to. He got this pensive look and said he was sorry. He'd seen a lot of improvement in my schoolwork. Then he said something that caught my ear.

"William, I know you're older than most of the seniors. That probably means you've been in school longer. Why don't you check in the office? You might have enough credits to graduate."

After the last class, I stopped by the principal's office and told the receptionist what the shop teacher had said. She promised to check it out and let me know tomorrow.

I went home with a lighter heart than when I'd left that morning. After I looked in on the girls, I went to the pay phone to call Jason again. I didn't want to be a pest, but I was worried about him.

"It's me," I said when he answered. He sounded sort of rushed, and I wondered if maybe I wasn't already a pest. "Sorry to bother you again, but I was worried."

"You're not bothering me. I appreciate your concern. I've heard from David. He's in Denver."

"Is he okay?"

"Yeah. He went on a bender and got thrown in jail. He's usually not a boozer, but his failed wedding and the abortion got to him. Anyway, he's in Denver, and I'm leaving now to go to the airport."

"Oh," I said. My voice got thick as I realized the implication of what he'd said. I tried to buck up. "On a rescue mission, huh? I glad he's okay. You know, other than being in jail."

"What's the matter? You don't sound right."

Me? I'm okay. But … but is there any chance I can see you? Just for a minute. I need to tell you something."

He agreed to meet me at the park in an hour but cautioned we wouldn't have much time. I went back to the apartment and made sure everything was all right, and then decided to walk to the park instead of taking a bus. Maybe I'd walk off some frustration. I still beat Jason there.

When I spotted his Lexus coming down one of the side streets, I walked toward him. He pulled up about a half a block from the park in a little vacant lot where people leave their cars on the weekend when the place is crowded.

I tried to pump some enthusiasm in my voice. "Hey man, that's great news about David. Glad he's okay."

"Thanks, Wilam." He gave me a look that said to cut the crap. "What's the problem?"

I studied my sneakers. I had on my old ones, not the new pair he'd bought me that first weekend. The toe on the right one was beginning to fray. "I probably won't be here by the time you get back from Denver." Actually, I most likely would be, because my dad didn't get out of jail until the end of this week. By then, Jason would be with David, and there wouldn't be any time for me. Might as well cut it off now.

"Why?"

"My dad's planning on moving again, and he's dragging us all along with him."

"Is he getting a better job somewhere?"

I gave a bitter laugh. "I wish. Naw, he's gotta go somewhere else for his health"

He glanced at me, so I knew he'd picked up on my meaning. "Where are you going?"

"Phoenix, probably, but it doesn't really matter." I turned in the seat and faced him. "I just wanted to see you before we left. Wanted to tell you.... Aw, it doesn't matter."

Jason touched my leg. "Yes, it does matter. What you have to say is important to me."

I swallowed a couple of times before the words would come. "That's kinda what I wanted to say to you. You're the only person I've ever met who feels like I got a right to say something or do something. You know, who wants to hear my opinion of things. You the only friend I ever had. It was important for you to know you're a friend, not just somebody to have sex with. At least, it was important to me."

"I knew that without your saying it. You've always treated me respectfully, and knowing you has meant something to me. You're a good man, and I thank you for being my friend. I just hope what we did together was good for you."

"It was. You made me feel like it was me you liked, not just my dick."

"That's about the best compliment I've ever had. But you'll find another friend. Maybe it'll be a woman or maybe it'll be a man, but you will find one. Just promise to be careful. There are a lot of people out there who'll hurt you ... hurt you physically and hurt you emotionally. Watch out for them. Don't give yourself to the first person who looks like he's interested. Promise?"

"I hear you. Can I write to you sometime?"

"Of course, you can. You have the address and you know the phone number. When you get to your new home, call me collect. If I'm not in just keep trying until you get me, okay? Or you can leave a message on the voice mail."

"What about David?"

"Trust me, David's going to know all about you. I'm as honest with him about my life as he is with me."

"So, he won't mind?"

"David handles things very well."

He leaned forward and touched my lips with his fingertips. I understood it was goodbye. I gripped his hand briefly and got out of the car. As I walked away on numb legs, I heard the motor of the Lexus kick over. I was going to miss Jason Bedford. A lot.

CHAPTER 11

Tuesday and Wednesday, I worked as hard and as long as I could, doing my homework first, and then carving far into the night. The light probably bothered my sisters as they tried to sleep, but I had to occupy my mind and my hands. I hadn't known my feelings for Jason ran so deep. I missed him in my heart, in my groin, and in my mind. My melancholy didn't seem to affect my work. The warrior's head was finished. The maiden's was coming along, and I had already blocked out the general shape of the boy and the girl.

When I got home after school Thursday, I found a note from Nola saying Mom had taken them with her to see the public defender about getting Dad out of jail. After I finished with the maiden's head, I got restless. Where was Jason? Had he gotten David out of jail yet? Were they back in Albuquerque? Most likely, he'd rented a car, and they were driving down together. That's what I'd do if I had money. I'd take a long, slow trip with my … lover. My mind stumbled over that word, so I said it out loud. It sounded better. It would sound a lot better if I was talking about my own lover. Would I ever have one?

Unhappy with the weird turn of my thoughts, I decided to walk to the little park down the street from our place. As soon as I spotted Enrique slouching along with his hands jammed in his pockets, I knew he was why I was really here. I'd been hunting for him without realizing it. He looked as bad as I felt. He saw me and waited up.

"Whas'sup?" His voice was hollow.

"Not much. What's up with you?"

"Elena, man. She dumped me. For real this time. She been flirting with this guy to get my goat, and he made his move. The dumb bitch fell for it. She's going with him now. It's over, man."

"I've got some sodas in the frig. You want one?"

"Rather have a beer."

"Out of luck. Soda's the best I can do. Nobody's home, so we can do some carving."

"Don't have my knives. Don't feel like whittling, anyway." He gave me a look. "But we can hang out at your place, and I'll take you up on something to drink."

As soon as we entered the apartment, Enrique flopped down on the couch and looked at the heads I'd finished. He examined the warrior I'd made critically. "Man, I'll bet those feathers were hard."

"Not that bad. Just slowed me down some, that's all."

"Good looking dude."

"Yeah, he's just somebody out of my head." I couldn't tell him he probably resembled the painting of David in Jason's den.

He picked up the maiden's bead and held it beside the warrior's. "He taking care of you, babe?" Then he addressed the warrior. "You giving it to her regular?"

"Come on."

"How big's his dick?"

"What?"

"If you made the rest of him, how big would you make his dick?"

I snickered but didn't answer his question. My groin tightened as he looked back and forth the between the two carvings

"Why don' you do that? Carve him a hard cock and her a nice pussy. Then you just slide him up inside her. They be a couple of love-making Indians."

He put the pieces on the table and leaned back on the sofa. "We never found out, did we? Your brother walked in on us, 'member?"

I came in from the kitchen, handed him his cola, and popped the lid on mine. "Found out what?"

"You know. Who has the biggest one?"

"Aw, Enrique, that's what kids do." Despite my words, I started to get hard.

He noticed before I could cover up. "Maybe so, but you getting a bone, dude."

"Not either. Well …."

He ran his hand down his crotch. "Me, too."

"Hey, man, I don't know when Mom will be back with the girls." I dropped down on the sofa to protect my condition from further examination.

There was a huge lump in his pants when he stood up to look out the window. Apparently he didn't care if I saw his, because he ran his fingers up and down it. "Don't see nobody. Won't take but a minute." He closed the blinds and sidled over in front of me. His groin was almost in my face. He leaned forward, forcing me back.

"Come on," he said. "Let's settle it now."

"What does it matter who's bigger, anyway?" I was tempted. Jason wasn't around for me anymore, and he'd said I'd find somebody else. Why not Enrique? Because somehow I knew it would be different with him. But does different mean bad?

He put his hand behind my head and pulled it forward until my face was in his crotch. I could feel the hard, hot flesh underneath. I jerked my head away.

"Hey man, watch it!"

"Come on, William. I'm curious. We been walking around with hard-ons. I have, anyhow. I gotta see who's biggest."

"You take yours out first." I felt about fourteen years old.

In half a second, his pants slid down over his slim hips. His brown cock bobbed right in my face. It was long, with a pronounced glans and a dark foreskin. In fact, his cock and balls were darker than the rest of him.

I pushed him aside, so I could get to my feet – inadvertently brushing his throbbing thing as I did. I pushed down my trousers, freeing my own hard cock. He turned toward me, so his shaft was right beside mine. He pumped his a couple of times and then grasped both of us in one hand. They felt hot pulsing against one another. Mine grew some more at his touch.

"Mine's bigger," he said. He was right ... in a way. He was longer, but I was much thicker around.

"It might be a little bit longer, but bigger? I don't think so."

He pumped both of us, still with the same hand. My hips gave a little twitch. "Naw," he said, "I can prod 'em deeper. You know, make them feel it way up inside."

"It's not the inches, it's the pounds." Where the hell did that stupid-ass remark come from? "They know I'm there. I fill them up to the brim."

He laughed out loud and kept pumping us simultaneously. "All right, I'm longer, and you're fatter. And we're both man enough to make them yell."

He stopped pumping, but held on tight as he looked up into my eyes. I was about a half-inch taller than he was. I could feel his heartbeat through his cock.

"You ever had a blow job?" he asked.

I was slow to answer. "Yeah."

"Elena tried it on me, but she don't know how. Don't get me wrong, it felt good, but I was sorta disappointed. Yours good?"

"Yeah. It felt good."

"Karen Sue?"

"No. We just fucked."

"You ever give one?"

I shook my head, afraid I couldn't make my lips lie. I think he saw through me.

"Me neither, but I sure would like to have one right now."

"Then go find Elena."

He shook his head. "No way. She wouldn't even give me the finger right now. How about the guy who give you yours? He do us both?"

Guy. Why did he say guy? "Uh-uh."

"Too bad. He give good head?"

"Dunno. I don't have much to compare it with." I guess that acknowledged it was a guy who did me, but at least, it sounded like it wasn't a regular thing.

He let go of me and sat down on the couch. Lifting his shirt up to reveal good pecs, he moved his hand over his chest and belly. "Man, I wish that dude was here right now. I need relief. Bad."

"Do it yourself. I don't care." I started to pull up my trousers.

"You sure you don't care? Don't pull your pants up yet. I feel like a fool being the only one with my cock hanging out. Besides, you can do it, too."

I sat down beside him. He surprised me by grabbing my cock in his left fist. His right slowly moved up and down his long prick. "Will you do it for me?"

"No way. What you think I am, anyway?"

"Just a friend. A good friend. Everybody got a special friend. You know, for when he gets all hot and bothered and there ain't no girl to do it with."

"Don't you have a special friend?"

"Not unless it's you. Look, I didn't mean nothing. I just wanted to see what it feels like."

"Are you going to do it for me?" I figured that would put an end to it.

"Maybe. Would you do it if I said I would?"

"You ever sucked anyone?"

"Nope."

"So here we are, two guys who've never sucked a cock before going to show each other how it feels? If Elena didn't do a good job, what makes you think I will?"

"I don't know." He was stroking me regularly now. I put my hand on his inner thigh near the big cock he was pumping with the other hand. He moaned and brushed me away to dip his head and touch the tip of my rigid tool with his lips. He came right back up. "Now you do it to me." He leaned back expectantly.

What the hell. He was clean. He was good-looking. Why not?

I reached over and grasped him. He shoved his hips upward, pushing himself toward me. Holding him by the root of the shaft and leaving the head exposed, I leaned down and placed my lips on his glans. I ran my tongue around the end twice before I came up.

"Wow! That feel good. Do it again."

"Uh-uh, your turn."

Slowly, he leaned down and hovered over me for a moment. Then I felt his warm mouth on the end of my prick. A second later, he was back on his side of the couch.

I took my turn, this time taking about half the glans into my mouth. Just before I came up, he clasped his hands behind my head and shoved his hips hard against me. Most of him disappeared into my mouth. I gagged and came up fighting for air.

"You son of a bitch!" I yelled, standing on my feet, fists balled, cock waving in the air.

"I'm sorry." He raised his hands in protest. "I got carried away. I won't do it again."

"Damned straight. I won't give you the chance."

"Oh man, don't quit now. Wait, I'll do it to you again. Even it up." He leaned forward and went down on half my length. Man, that did feel good. He came up and looked me in the eye. "You ever heard of a sixty-nine?" I shook my head, wishing he'd do something, grab me, lick me ... anything.

"It's where two guys lay down beside one another and suck each other off at the same time. I give it a try it if you will."

"I don't know if I trust you, Enrique."

"Don't be like that. Besides, what's to trust? I'll be doing you while you doing me."

"You mean until we come?"

"Not much point if we don't."

"You sure about this?"

"Man, I want it so bad my nuts hurt."

He moved to the floor, and I got down beside him, facing in the opposite direction. He scooted down until his head was at my groin, which put mine at his. We propped on our elbows and looked at one another.

"Both at the same time," he said. "And we gotta try to take it all. You know go all the way down on the cock."

I noticed he waited until his thing was in my mouth before he put mine in his. I got about half of him down before he took my glans in his mouth and began moving up and down me. Loosening up a little, I put one hand on his belly and found his navel. The other went down to fondle his balls. They were big and solid. This wasn't all that unpleasant, I decided, quickening my pace and moving my tongue over the end of him each time I came up for air.

He gave a little moan, so I gave him one back. After five minutes his testicles drew up. His ball sac got harder. He was still pumping my cock, but I couldn't feel his mouth on me. Then he missed a stroke, and I heard him cry out. A second later, his cum flooded my mouth. I gagged and opened my lips, letting his juices flow out of me onto his belly. For some reason, I didn't release his throbbing cock. He hunched his hips wildly, driving himself into my mouth deeper and deeper as he continued to pump cum. He'd forgotten all about doing me, and I'd been close to popping my balls, too. His head fell across my legs as the strength seemed to go out of him.

When he was through his orgasm, I lifted my head and looked at him. His long, brown torso was draped over the lower part of my body. His arms clasped my legs. Slowly, he rolled over onto his back and looked at me through brown eyes. "Man, that was something. You give good head."

I'd been about to call it quits until he said that. "You forgot something."

"Aw, man, I can't. Not after I already got my rocks off. That's gruesome."

"Enrique," I said in an even voice. "You conned me into giving you a blow job. Now you're going to pay up. You give me some good head."

79

He almost refused, but finally, he bent back over me. Just before he started, he looked at me. "At least play with me some."

As his lips slipped over my glans and his hand grasped my shaft, I smeared his come all over his cock and balls. I played with the tip until he started getting hard again, then I changed to playing with his balls. But mostly, I watched his handsome head as it bobbed up and down on me.

In truth, he jacked me off with the tip of my cock held loosely in his mouth. As soon as I started coming, he jerked his head away and let my seed splash out onto my belly. He was out the front door without washing up within a minute flat, stammering something about seeing me later. I lay there with cum drying on my chest and belly. It hadn't been bad. I'd had a decent orgasm, and Enrique couldn't go around claiming I'd blown him without admitting he'd done the same to me.

But it hadn't been like it was with Jason. Not by a long shot. Of course, Enrique Marquez was no Jason Bedford.

I cleaned up and thought over what had happened as I resumed carving the head of the boy. I'd been right. It was different with Enrique. He was strictly a hetero just looking for something different when he got cut off from his regular source of pussy. He hadn't been interested in my satisfaction, just his own. Things probably wouldn't be the same between us from now on.

The thing was, I wouldn't mind doing it with him again. Even if he just jerked me off.

CHAPTER 12

Before my dad was due home Saturday afternoon, I delivered the four pieces Mr. Gresham had ordered. As usual, he studied them a long time before reaching for his checkbook.

"You did a fine job, son. Better'n I expected. Here's your check. William, unless I'm mistaken, we're going to make some money together."

I don't have one of those stoic, unreadable Indian faces. He looked at me sharply. "What's the matter?"

"We're leaving, Mr. Gresham. I guess this will be the last stuff I bring you."

"Leaving? You mean your family's moving? Where are you going?"

I shrugged. "Probably Arizona, but I don't know for sure. I just know my dad's pulling up stakes."

"And you intend to go with him?"

He probably figured I was old enough to have a mind of my own, so I told him a little about my family situation. He adjusted the gold-framed glasses on his prominent nose and studied me through gray eyes. I had the feeling he was reading my soul and knew exactly what was going on.

"When?" he asked.

"Next few days. My dad gets ...." I broke off and cleared my throat. "When my dad gets ready, we'll go." That sounded lame, but it was the best I could do.

"Well, that's not a tragedy. We all have our family obligations, and I'm glad to see you take yours seriously. However, that doesn't mean we can't do business. I buy from artisans and craftsmen living and working all over the West. I'll show you how to box things so they won't get broken. Then you can ship them to me, and I'll mail you a check. You'll trust me to do that, won't you?"

"Yes sir." He had given me an idea. "If I keep my bank account here, can I get my money out any time I want to, or would I have to come back to do it?"

"Oh, no. You can draw on your funds from Arizona or anywhere else, for that matter. If you open an account wherever you end up, then the two banks can move funds back and forth for you."

"Then that's what I'll do, and you can just put my money in my account here."

"Sounds good to me. Don't worry, William. I like your work, so you'll continue to get orders from me. Just be sure to let me know how to reach you when you get settled."

"Thank you, Mr. Gresham. I really appreciate it."

"You're welcome. Now I want to show you something."

He reached under the counter and laid a piece of light-colored rock on the glass. "Have you ever seen this before?"

"No, sir. What is it?"

"Soapstone. It's what they call a metamorphic rock. It comes in two types. One is hard and is used to make counter tops and the like. That one is called an architectural stone. This one has a lot more talc content and is used in art, mainly for carving and sculptures. It's found all over the world in colors that range from white to greenish gray, charcoal, and dark green. This piece comes out of Vermont. Feel of it. It's got a nice soft, silky feeling."

I hefted the stone and rubbed my hand over the slick, almost soapy surface.

"See what you can do with it." He placed the soapstone in a box with several other pieces and handed it to me. Then he went over the kind of carvings he'd like me to do next, preferably in soapstone.

I thanked him and left his shop with the box under my arm and a lump in my throat. That man had done more for me than he would ever know. I blinked hard a couple of times and headed for the bank. I dithered for a while, but ended up depositing $300 of Mr. Gresham's $400 check. I took the rest in fives and tens. Harder to hide it in such small denominations, but it was easier to dole out if the old man came down on me.

As I passed through the neighborhood park on the way home, I saw Enrique sitting on a picnic table talking to a girl. I waved, and he gave me a hand-in-the-air gesture, so I kept on walking. My cock got semi-hard thinking about what we'd done the other day, but I didn't do anything about it when I got back to the apartment. I could have because everyone had gone with Matthew to pick up the old man.

Thirty minutes later, my dad hit the front door like a tornado. I hadn't realized he'd be in such a hurry to get out of town, but he was already fussing at Mom for not being all packed and ready to go. He saw me and halted in his tracks. Mom and the girls almost ran up his backside. Matthew had apparently gone back to Myra's place.

"How come you didn't come down and see me out of jail like everbody else?"

My face got red. "I figured you could find your way home without my help. Anyway, welcome home. Hope you left the jailhouse in one piece."

"Watch your tongue, you little shitass."

"Now, Woodie," my mom said.

"Don't you Woodie me, woman. He better show some respect or I'll throw him out on his ear. Maybe I oughta do it now and get it over with."

Something happened to my heart, although I wasn't sure what it was. It soared with the unexpected thought I'd be free of this bastard, but then it plunged into my belly when I realized I'd have to eat his crap for the girls' sake. He hadn't learned anything from his stretch behind bars. So what else

82

was new? He hadn't learned anything in the half a dozen previous times he'd been there, either

But maybe something had happened. For the first time, I saw confusion in those hateful black eyes. He wasn't sure what to do with me. He wanted to be rid of me, but he was smart enough to know I was the one who held the family together while he ran around and did whatever he wanted. If I wasn't here, he might have to pay someone to look after the girls.

His uncertainty humanized him, and for one second, I wondered why he treated me like he did. He didn't do it to Matthew. Of course, my brother had always been a big strapping guy, not small like me. The old man didn't harass the girls so bad, although there was that one time I figured he was calling Nola back home because he was horny, but she swore he'd never touched her like that. No, when it came down to it, he treated me more like he treated Mom. Did he have some of that gaydar Jason was talking about? Did he know how I'd turn out before I did? Before I was even interested in things like sex? Then, in a flash, his stare turned cruel again.

"All right, make yourself useful. Did you drive the pickup while I was gone?"

"Me?" I asked in surprise. "You know I don't know how to drive." I came close to blurting out I was the only kid in school who didn't.

"Maybe not, but a man would think you've got brains enough to start it from time to time so the battery don't go bad on me."

I shrugged. "I didn't know you had to do that."

Cussing, he turned around and marched back outside, yelling for Mom to bring him the keys.

It wasn't as easy getting out of town as the old man had figured. He was broke. Sure enough, the old battery in the Dodge was drained. He'd expected Toliver to stake him for whatever they had planned over in Arizona. Frankly, I was beginning to suspect there wasn't really anything in the works. Toliver and his running buddies were probably just fed up with Woodie Greyhorse and looking to get him out of their hair. Wouldn't be the first time.

I got the blame for it all. For the battery. For not handing him over a bunch of money when his buddies flaked out on him, and for whatever else would go wrong between now and then. Still, I knew he'd finagle a way to get out of town, no matter what.

The next Monday, I went to the principal's office at school to tell them we were moving to Arizona. The receptionist hadn't gotten back to me about graduating early, but when I told her I was pulling out of class, she hustled me back to the principal.

Mr. Shotty, whom all the kids called Shorty – or Snotty – behind his back, deserved the nicknames. He was a prissy little man shorter than I was. That was okay, but the way he combed thin strands of brown hair all the way

83

from one side of his scalp to the other sent shivers down my back. I probably wouldn't have noticed he was bald if he hadn't tried to hide it.

He had good news for me today though. I'd have enough credits to graduate if I successfully completed my current classes. Of course, I didn't have time for that, but he had a solution – provided I was up to it. He was willing to let me take a final test in all my classes. If I passed, I'd get my certificate. If I didn't … well, they have schools in Arizona, too.

He'd talked to all my teachers, and they'd agreed to spend a few hours after class to prepare me for the tests. Shop was no problem, the teacher just handed me a set of papers and told me to fill them out. When I did, that turned out to be the test. Coach Gibbon awarded me a grade in PE, and Homeroom and Study Hall didn't give grades. So, that left three tests I had to pass.

I didn't get much carving done that week. The old man was hanging close to the apartment, except when he was running around trying to find some money, so I had no option but to study at school. I'd go to class until final bell and then find a room where I could study for the tests, worrying about some civics or mathematics problem one minute and my sisters the next. Every time I went home, I held my breath until I saw the girls were okay.

The next Friday, I didn't attend classes. I sat in a little room off the principal's office and worked on the tests while Mr. Shotty ran in and out from time to time to see how I was doing. By noon, my armpits were damp. By the time the last bell rang, I was drenched in sweat as if I'd been outdoors mowing a lawn in the hot sun. Finally, I was finished. Now, if I'd just got enough answers right, I could move on, but I wouldn't know that until Monday.

On the way out of the building, I saw Enrique and got the feeling he'd been hanging around on purpose. He gave me a grin and a greeting.

"Heard you was leaving. That right?"

"Yeah. The old man's pulling up and heading out to Arizona."

"Arizona, huh? I got an uncle and a bunch of cousins in Phoenix."

"That's probably where we'll end up."

"You want to give me another blow before you go?"

That shocked me a little, but I came right back at him like I thought he was teasing. "You first. Then I might consider it."

He glanced around to make sure nobody was listening. "Aw, you know I don't give a good one, but you do. Interested?"

I thought about it. I thought hard about it. I remembered his dark, good-looking head bobbing up and down on me and his long, naked torso lying across my legs. I also remembered he'd acted like he was ashamed to know me afterward. I didn't need any more of that.

"No, thanks."

"Aw, come on. You know you want to."

I stared straight into his eyes. "Why would I want to? I'm like you. The only thing that counts is getting my rocks off. Not sucking on some guy's dick."

I turned around and walked away. I had to get out of there before my thing made a liar out of me. It was about halfway hard. Thank goodness, I'd emptied out my locker and my arms were full of stuff, or he'd have seen it for sure.

I got a little bit of a scare when I got home and found Dad had come up with money from somewhere. He was making noises like we were leaving first thing in the morning, but his own nature did him in. He went out that night to celebrate the move and drank up $100 of his money. Of course, that meant he took it out on me when he showed up Saturday morning.

"All right, kid," he faced me down in the living room where I was trying to work. "It's time you quit taking and give something back. You're a fucking leech, you know."

I bit my tongue to keep from smarting off. Smarting off, hell. Setting him straight was more like it. "Sorry about that, but I think I'm out of school now, so I can start helping out." I had trouble keeping my tone civil.

He blinked his bleary, red eyes a couple of times. "About fucking time, but that's for tomorrow. I need $100 now. I mean fucking today."

He was working himself up to a beating, and I didn't want to go to the principal's office on Monday all black and blue. I caved and tried to buy me some time while I was doing it.

"Look, I know where I can get $100, but I can't get it until Monday afternoon."

His eyes gleamed. "Fuck Monday. Go get it now."

"The man who'll give it to me is out of town. He won't be back until sometime Monday." When had it become so easy to lie to my father?

His mouth curled. "Man, huh. That how you get your money?"

The blood rushed through my veins. My fists balled. I took a deep breath to control myself, and then everything drained away, leaving me weak and shaking. But I couldn't let him see. I shrugged and picked up my biggest carving knife. "Man. Woman. Whatever. Monday, Dad. That's the best I can do. And $100 is all I can get, so you better not drink up any more of it."

"You little man-whore, don't tell me what to do."

I don't know if it was the knife in my hand or the fact I could get him the money that caused him to back off, but he did. He stormed out the door hurling curses behind him. I drew a long breath. I'd escaped another beating, and all it had cost me was $100. That and the fact that my father now believed I was a male prostitute. Hell, what did that matter?

CHAPTER 13

On Monday morning, Principal Shotty handed over a piece of paper proving I was now a high school graduate. It only took me thirteen years to get through the educational system, but I got it done. To tell the truth, I was pretty proud of myself. After I left the school campus, I scooted on down to the bank and withdrew another $100. Now I could give the old man his money and still have a bit of cash on me for emergencies. When I got home, nobody seemed impressed by any of my accomplishments except for coming up with some money. We left for Arizona that same afternoon.

For a while, it looked as though I was going to have to spend my stash on the road. The old Dodge broke down on the interstate in the middle of the night. We lost a couple of hours, but Dad managed to get the old girl running again. That morning, I got my first look at those cactuses everyone associates with the Old West. The saguaros, or "old men walking," had tall round, spiny boles as big as some trees with arms sticking out of them, as often as not pointing up into the sky. And like their nickname, they spread across the desert, endlessly marching over hill after hill after hill. They were something to see.

Everything in the Sonoran Desert looked as if it was made for defense, capable of biting or puncturing anyone and anything that came too close. I'd read up on the countryside at the Albuquerque Public Library and recognized some of the plants: Ocotillo, Palo Verde, cholla, and Joshua trees. The landscape of blue and purple mountains in the distance and towering thunderheads overhead impressed the hell out of me.

We pulled into Phoenix late Tuesday afternoon, and Dad promptly dumped us in a public park to go looking for a jailhouse buddy who was supposed to have a place for us to stay. He didn't give us a clue as to where he was going or when he'd be back. It was ironic that I suffered a pang of panic as my father disappeared in the pickup, leaving us alone on a tiny patch of green in an alien place. I hoped the people he was looking for were more reliable than Toliver and his bunch.

We ended up spending the night in the park. As exhausted as we were, nobody got much sleep. I don't know about anyone else, but I kept expecting the cops to show up and throw us out. No one did; however, and my father drove up around noon the next day only moderately high. He took us to an apartment that looked and smelled like the one we'd left behind in Albuquerque. Once the pickup was unloaded, he took off again, leaving the rest of us to try to put some order into our lives. Mom fretted, but I said good riddance.

The first thing the next morning, I asked around the neighborhood, found the closest school, and got Nola registered. She should have been used to getting acquainted in a new school, but the look on her face told me she hadn't got the hang of it yet. Leaving her behind was hard.

The yellow pages in a phone booth told me where to find a place called Arizona Craftsmen Supplies. I needed some wood if I was going to fill Mr. Gresham's orders. The layout of Phoenix was a mystery to me, but by asking some questions and taking a wrong bus part of the way, I finally found the supply house in a blue, corrugated metal building that must have covered half an acre. I got comfortable in my skin again by walking through the rows and rows of knives, saws, paints, cutout molds, vices, and wood. I ended up buying some walnut plus some ebony and mahogany – woods I'd never tried before. Arizona Craftsmen didn't carry soapstone, but the clerk who helped me, Carlos according to his nametag, said Maricopa Stone had the best supply of any kind of rock around these parts.

While I was there, I asked Carlos if he knew of a job opening. He wasn't much older than I was and reminded me of Enrique, except he was a lot taller. He asked a bunch of questions about woods and knives and sanders. Then he directed me to the office and told me to ask for an application. The man in the office put most of Carlos's questions to me all over again, and I guess I answered them okay, because I left there with a part-time, minimum wage job under my belt.

It was getting late in the afternoon when I finished those chores, so I caught a city bus that took me pretty close to Nola's school. I was waiting for her when the last class was dismissed. The two of us walked the rest of the way back to the apartment, even though my supply of wood and her new schoolbooks weighed us down. We both breathed sighs of relief when we found the pickup gone and Junie playing with one of the dolls I'd made her. Mom was straightening up the apartment the way she wanted it. She was sober.

# # # # #

For a while things were better. I worked hard at the supply house, putting in extra hours off the clock because I was the new man on the job. Carlos Quintana was a friendly guy and helped me get oriented to the layout of my new hometown. If I'd thought Albuquerque was spread out, Phoenix was even more so. Of course, it wasn't just one city like Albuquerque mostly was. Scottsdale and Mesa and Tempe and Glendale and Sun City and Peoria were all smashed up together, making up a metropolitan center of over 1,500,000 people.

Like New Mexico, Arizona had a lot of Indians. The ones I saw around Phoenix looked different from us. They tended to be darker with moon faces, and they were stouter – stouter all over. A lot of them were Pimas and Papagos, although I think the Papagos were in the middle of changing their names to Tohono O'odham. That was the name they called themselves before the old conquistadors came and saddled them with Spanish names.

I spent my afternoons and nights on my carving. I was beginning to get the hang of the soapstone, and by the end of the first week, I'd shipped a dozen small items to Mr. Gresham. It sounds selfish, but I was helped along because Mom was still having headaches, and drinking always made them worse. As a result, she went light on the bottle. It also helped that the old man was up to something and mostly stayed out of our hair. I never got curious over what he was doing. I didn't know his business, and I didn't want to know.

My gut ached sometimes from missing Jason, but if I kept busy I could handle it. Funny, but Enrique intruded on my thoughts a lot, as well. Mostly because I halfway regretted not taking him up on his offer the last time I saw him. I missed Matthew, too. He was never around much back in Albuquerque, but anytime he dropped in and called me Pissant, it sort of made my day. Now we never heard from him.

Then things started to go wrong. Mr. Gresham sent a deposit slip for the $350 payment for my last shipment, and getting a letter in our house that wasn't a bill or an advertisement was a novelty. My mom couldn't resist opening the letter, but frankly she couldn't make much sense of it. She left it on the table without telling me about it. Nola found it, and gave it to me, so I figured I'd survived a possible disaster. That night, bless her heart, little Junie found where I'd hidden the letter in my bedroll. She proudly brought it to me and repeated out loud what Nola had told her – it was a letter for me from a man named Gresham. The old man was home at the time, and his ears perked up right away.

"Gresham," he repeated the name. "That your friend who gives you money whenever you want it."

"He's just someone I know in Albuquerque, that's all."

He started in on me, wanting to know who Mr. Gresham was and what he was writing me about. I honestly believe he thought he could blackmail the man for messing with his son, something that had never happened. To make matters worse, I couldn't give my dad the letter to show it was nothing like that because Mr. Gresham had spelled out how much he was paying for each piece I'd sent him. Plus, it detailed a new order the trader had sent.

We almost got into a fistfight over me holding out on him, but I didn't give in. Even so, the old man got enough out of me to put two and two together and suspected I was selling those carvings I was always doing. The next day when I came home from work, the whole place had been ransacked. I lost fifty dollars I'd hidden away. Thank goodness I'd kept about two hundred dollars with me in my pocket. Worse than the money he took, he'd found my Albuquerque bankbook and knew I had over a $1,000 in the account.

"You'n me are going down to the bank and get it out. You owe me that much, you little cunt."

I swallowed the insult and resisted the impulse to tell him the money was in Albuquerque, stupid. "I won't," I said, putting as much steel in my voice as I could. "That's for emergencies."

"I got an emergency, boy. I need that money now." The greed in his eyes almost made them glow.

"Not that kind of emergency. It's for when something happens to the girls. I tell you what. I'll turn over my check from work every week for groceries, okay?" Why was I trying to reason with this man?

"Fuck the groceries. An emergency is what I say it is. I don't care how you got that money, selling your whittlings or peddling your ass or stealing it. You made it while you was under my roof, and I want it."

I lost it. "Your roof? You never paid for a roof over our heads in your life. Mom kept the roof in Albuquerque over our heads by begging the welfare people for it. I put the food on the table. You ... you put the liquor down your throat and bought loose women with it." I paused and took a breath, laughing as a giddy thought hit me. "Hell, you probably sold your ass to some of those doxies for a bottle or two, so don't throw that at me."

I'd stepped over the line. Being a drunk was one thing, being a kept man was something else. He clenched his fist and came for me. This time I fooled him. I made a fight of it. He's heavier than I am and finally managed to put me down, but I got in my licks, and he was hurting by the time it was over. My sisters screamed like they were crazy. Nola got off the couch and started pulling at his arm. He swatted her away, but she came back again. Seeing him hit Nola sent a jolt of adrenaline through me.

I bucked my hips and threw him off me. I came up swinging, catching him on one ear. He staggered, shook off the blow and swung a roundhouse, catching me on the cheek. I went down, sending the carvings I'd been working on skittering across the floor. But I wasn't out. There hadn't been much behind his blow. He was hurt or winded. He stood glaring at me for a minute before staggering out the door. I lay where I was on the floor and listened to the pickup motor grind and catch. The tires screeched as he raced away.

Mom saw I wasn't hurt in any major way and patted my arm like she hadn't done in years. Leaving me sprawled out on the floor, she went to the girls and started settling them down while I crawled to a sitting position. I understood the girls were frightened and needed her right then, but a hug would have been nice.

Shrugging it off, I went to see how many of the carvings could be salvaged. Most of them had been broken in the fight. I didn't mind so much except for one large mahogany bust of a plains warrior I'd almost finished. I had experimented with carving it at an angle, so the grain didn't run straight up and down the piece. I liked the effect, but it had sheared apart, leaving about two thirds of the head intact. The entire right side of the face from the cheekbone up was missing.

Beginning to ache a little from my battle wounds, I rooted around on the floor until I found the other piece of the bust. I tried gluing the two fragments together. That didn't work because it left an ugly crack kitty-corner down across the face. I was about to toss it away when I had an idea. I took out some of Mr. Gresham's greenish gray soapstone and laid it beside the dark wood. It made a pleasing contrast. It took some doing, but I remade the broken third of the head out of stone. When I fitted the two pieces together they looked good but not great. The next afternoon before going to work, I found a jeweler's supply house and bought some fairly heavy gauge gold and silver wire.

# # # # #

As soon as I walked into Arizona Craftsmen, Carlos let out a whistle and pointed to my cheek. The old man hadn't broken the skin, but he'd raised an obvious bruise.

"Somebody made a night of it," he said. Carlos didn't have an accent like Enrique's. He'd been born and raised in Arizona, as had his parents. He'd told me one day it was his grand folks who came across the border from Mexico back when it was easier to do.

"Yeah. Mixed it up with the wrong fellow, I guess." My joke didn't quite come off.

He must have seen something in my eyes because he let it go. Later, when we were both back in the stockroom, he brought it up again. After a little verbal dancing, I admitted my father and I had gotten into it, although I didn't tell him why.

"Hey, amigo, I catch what you're throwing. My old man never walloped on me – unless it was with a board on the britches when I needed it – but I got an uncle who beats his kids whenever he feels like it. Heavy, man."

The unexpected sympathy and understanding hit me right in the gut. I paused with a heavy box of ceramic tiles in my arms and sort of sagged against the shelf. Blinking hard to keep the moisture out of my eyes, I felt a hand on my shoulder. A warm, friendly hand. That opened up my tear ducts. I couldn't see for the next thirty seconds, and that hand stayed right where it was all that time.

"Hey, man. Don't worry about it. Family can tear a man up inside. I see it with my cousins. I just hope you got your licks in."

He took away his hand, and I wanted it back. I leaned the edge of the box against the shelf and swiped my eyes with a sleeve. "He's not hearing too good out of one of his ears." I tried to steady my voice.

"Good for you." He moved away to finish stacking whatever merchandise he'd been working on.

I watched him out of my peripheral vision. It could have been Enrique there. Physically, at least. Long and lean and whip thin. Black hair. Brown eyes. If I tried, I could imagine that dark head moving up and down on

91

me, that long, naked torso spread across my legs. I got a roaring hard-on that wouldn't go away.

I kept my back to Carlos as I worked and stayed as far away as I could without seeming like I was being unfriendly. He glanced at me a couple of times, and I figured he thought I was embarrassed because he'd seen me leaking tears.

I hurried to the apartment as soon as my shift was over to see if Dad had come home. He hadn't shown his face since we'd had our fight, but if he did, I didn't want him taking it out on Mom and the girls.

I was also anxious to try out my idea with the jeweler's wire. There was no sign of the pickup, so I took a shaky breath of relief and went inside. Mom was in the kitchen cooking stew. She didn't cook much anymore, but she sure made good stew – of any kind. She could make beef or pork or lamb work in any of her recipes, which were full of potatoes and cabbage and chili peppers and onions and I don't know what else. I swallowed hard, remembering a time when this was where she usually could be found.

After some comparison, I chose the gold wire and hammered it carefully into the crack where I'd cemented the wood and the stone together. When the smooth, gleaming band bridged the space between the two elements, I looked at it critically. It united the piece in a pleasing way. Pleasing? Hell, it looked like dynamite. Enthused by the result, I worked pieces of soapstone into the cheeks and forehead of wood to represent war paint, and identical bits of gold wire into corresponding places in the soapstone as a contrast. When I was done, I packed it carefully and sent it off to Mr. Gresham that same day. It didn't get the customary second look, but I wasn't willing to risk Dad coming home and destroying it again.

CHAPTER 14

A really fierce binge laid the old man low. Virtually incapacitated him. He hadn't come home in that condition since we got to Phoenix. Maybe me getting starch in my backbone was eating at him. He didn't have the iron grip on the family he once had. Whoa, hold up there. Better not get overconfident.

He'd be relatively harmless for the next couple of days, but when his hangover really hit, things would get ugly. I'd have to come straight home from work for the next week or so.

Excited by what I had accomplished with the warrior's head, I started to work on a young woman as a companion piece. Anchored to the apartment by my father's glowering presence, I was able to get in a lot of work on the bust. This time, I purposely split the head in two parts, doing one side in walnut and the other in soapstone, uniting them with the gold jeweler's wire. The hair, the buckskin blouse, and the necklace were done in wood.

I noticed Nola fingering my small coils of gold and silver wire one day. "Pretty, huh?"

She jerked her hand away and glanced up at me guiltily. "Yes. Pretty. They would make nice necklaces."

"How?"

"Like this." She mated the ends of a strand of each and twisted them together. They made an attractive loop. The gold shone richly; the silver gleamed brightly.

"Why don't you make yourself a necklace?"

"I couldn't do that. I wouldn't know how."

"Seems like you've made a good start."

"Maybe." She put them down and went off to do something in the kitchen.

The next day, I stopped at the jewelers' supply place and picked up some jewelry findings, a few beads of various types, and a couple of tools for cutting, crimping, and finishing pieces of jewelry. They also had a couple of books on the subject, so I bought them, too. I went to another store and got Junie a Lego set, so she could play like she was creating something, too.

When I gave the supplies to Nola after she got home that afternoon, she pooh-poohed the idea, but I noticed her reading the books later that night. The next afternoon, she started on her first piece. Junie had already halfway worn out her Lego set creating odd shapes that made no sense but kept her happy.

The old man must have caught something besides a hangover, because he took to his bed and stayed there nearly the whole week. Nola said he was easier to deal with sick than he was drunk. I was afraid it was the flu, but if it was, he didn't pass it on to anyone else.

# # # # #

At the end of the week, I got a telegram asking me to call Mr. Gresham's cellular phone number the next Saturday morning. I had to work a four-hour shift that day, but I managed to find a minute to call him before I went in. He and his wife were in town for the day and wanted to see me. We made an appointment for one o'clock at the Camelback Inn.

I boxed up the maiden's head and took it to work with me where I spent the rest of the morning torn between watching Carlos out of the corner of my eye and anticipating the meeting with Mr. Gresham. In between that, I tried to get my work done. I was building a record as a good, reliable worker and didn't want to mess that up.

I no longer looked at Carlos the same way – not since that day in the stockroom after the dust-up with Dad. I couldn't figure out if it was bawling in front of him or his warm hand on my shoulder that altered the balance. When I was getting ready to clock out at noon, he surprised me.

"You wanna have a beer after work?"

"I've got a meeting with a trader this afternoon. He's in town for the day and wants to see me." Carlos knew I sold my carvings to a shop in Albuquerque.

"You taking him that?" He indicated the box I was carrying.

"Yeah. I want see what he thinks about it." I pulled out the carving and showed it to him.

"Hey, man, that's good work. He oughta go ape shit over it. I'm working all day, so I don't get off until five. You know, just in case you finish your meeting."

I didn't really want to have a beer with Carlos or anybody else, but I'd sure would like to hang out with him. Maybe go have a hamburger or something. I hoped he wouldn't think I was blowing him off, but I had to say it like it was.

"I don't know. He might want to take me out to eat."

"Oh, okay. Some other time, maybe."

"Yeah, let's try it another time. I'd really like to go do something with you. I'd do it today if this hadn't come up." I blushed, hoping he didn't misread my words. Or maybe hoping he did.

Van Buren Boulevard was the center of my universe since both the apartment and Arizona Craftsmen were close to the street on opposite sides of town, but the hotel was north of the downtown area. It took a couple of bus transfers, but I got there in time for the one o'clock appointment.

A plump, pleasant woman opened the door when I knocked. "You must be William." She beamed. "I'm Mrs. Gresham. Come on in, we're expecting you."

Mr. Gresham was inside the room talking to a tall man dressed in a suit and tie. For a minute, I about panicked. Had I done something wrong? But this man didn't look like a policeman or a taxman. His clothes cost too much. I wished I'd had time to go home and put on a better pair of jeans. I shifted the box to my left arm and shook hands with Mr. Gresham. He introduced the other man as Ellis Greenby.

The warrior's bust sitting on the table in front of the couch caught my eye. It still looked great after not seeing it for a week, and that's my ultimate test of my own work – looking at it critically after several days.

Mr. Gresham led me to the couch and sat down beside me. I put the box I was carrying on the floor between my boots. The others took chairs nearby.

"Mr. Greenby is a gallery owner in New York," he explained. "He's been a friend and colleague of mine for a long time. He was in the store when I received your latest piece." He indicated the bust on the table.

"It's remarkable work, especially for someone so young" the tall man said in a deep voice. He was probably about fifty, trim, and looked like he was made of money. "Do you mind my asking how old you are, William?"

"Twenty." I stretched it by a few months.

"Remarkable," he repeated. "How long have you been practicing your art?"

Art? My work was art? "Uh ... I've been whittling since I was ten years old, I guess."

He chuckled in a deep, pleasant growl. "Whittling. Well, I guess you could call it that, but all that whittling has produced a work of art."

There was that word again. My pulse picked up. "Never thought of it like that."

Mr. Gresham leaned toward me. "William, it's time you started thinking of your work as just that – art."

"You've gone beyond whittling," Mr. Greenby agreed. "You've gone beyond carving. You're now creating. Creating art." He paused. "Unless, this is just a fluke. Is it? Or do you have more creations like this inside you trying to get out?"

"I don't know, sir. You tell me." I opened the box at my feet and took out the maiden's bust. Mrs. Gresham let out a little gasp when I set it on the table. She reached out and tenderly stroked the tangled walnut tresses.

Greenby didn't subscribe to the Gresham penchant for understatement. "Magnificent!" he exclaimed. Mr. Gresham sat and beamed at me proudly. Greenby turned to him and nodded. "You were right. He may be young, but he's ready. Shall I proceed?"

Mr. Gresham nodded. My head whipped back and forth between them until I was dizzy.

"William, I want to buy these two pieces from you. I'll pay you a thousand dollars for each of them."

My heart stopped beating for a second. I spoke from a dry mouth. "You'll have to talk to Mr. Gresham about that. I always sell my stuff to him."

"No, son," the trader said. "You've outgrown me. These pieces aren't Indian trading post art. They're fine art. That's Mr. Greenby's area. You're lucky he's interested. He's the best in the business, and because he is, he's going to save you about ten years on the way to making your name known in the right circles."

I looked at the tall, elegant man in the chair opposite me. "Can I ask you a question?"

"Shoot."

"Do you operate like an Indian trader? I mean, if you pay me $1,000 apiece are you going to sell them for twice that?"

He chuckled. "Not exactly. Most of the work in my galleries is taken on consignment. I take a fee or a commission when the work sells. Occasionally, when I find a particularly promising artist who isn't well established, I'll buy some pieces to try and set the market value. If you want the truth, I'll offer these pieces to a very good collector of mine at $5,000 for the pair, but I'd be prepared to go down to $4,000."

"Then I won't sell them to you for $2,000. I'll take $1,600 for the two of them, but you'll have to make another check out to Mr. Gresham for $160, because he's my agent."

Greenby glanced at Mr. Gresham. "Why not $1,800 for you and $200 for Gresham?"

"Because you're taking a chance on me. I want you to think about my work as something you can make more money on."

He laughed aloud, and again it was a good sound. "I've been in this business longer than you've been alive. I know my customers, and I know my market. I'm not wrong. I'll pay you what you offered – plus Mr. Gresham's ten percent, and when I sell those pieces, I'm going to split anything I get over $4,000 with you. How's that?"

"That's great." I hoped nobody could hear my heart pounding. "Just remember to take ten percent of my part and send it to Mr. Gresham. A lot of times he paid me more than my work was worth just so I'd keep trying. Now he oughta share in my success." That sounded kind of high-flown, so I added. "Whatever that might be."

"Very well, but I want you to formalize that for me in writing."

Mr. Greenby wrote up an agreement on hotel stationery, and Mr. Gresham and I signed it. I think I was prouder of putting my signature beside his than I was of the rest of it.

I declined their invitation to dinner that night. I wasn't dressed right, and I was afraid I'd pick up the wrong spoon or fork or something. Anyway, I needed to get back and see what was happening at home. If they'd invited me for a quick hamburger, I'd have accepted.

I left the hotel with my head in the clouds and a check for more money than I knew what to do with. My brain almost froze up with all the emotions whirling around in it.

I walked all the way back to Van Buren Avenue trying to sort things out. I stopped long enough to open an account in one of the bank branches near the apartment and deposited Greenby's $1,600. I half heard the teller when she told me I couldn't draw on the funds until they were collected from the New York bank. That was okay with me. I could wait.

Then I wandered on down the street in a daze. All kinds of crazy things rattled around my head. Why did I think of the gallery owner as Greenby, yet I resolutely called the trading post owner Mr. Gresham? All that elegance and money should have made me think of the New Yorker as a "mister." But Greenby fit him. Just as Mr. Gresham fit my friend and mentor.

Oh, Lord! I was a certified artist, not just a wood carver anymore. I halted in the middle of the sidewalk, drawing irritated looks from passing pedestrians. Who could I tell? Who could I share my good fortune with? Nola couldn't keep secrets from Junie, and that sweet little girl would blab whatever she knew. I didn't dare trust Mom because she'd tell the old man. I couldn't share my good fortune with anybody except in little bits and pieces and dribs and dabs – buying clothes and small things for the family. Otherwise, it would cause more problems than it was worth. In the midst of delirious joy, I was suddenly sad.

Then I thought of Jason. Happy again, I went back to the bank and changed a ten-dollar bill into a roll of quarters. When I dialed his Albuquerque number from a nearby pay phone, a deep, male voice answered, sending waves of sexual tremors through my scrotum and up my back. This must be the handsome Indian in the painting on Jason's wall. This was David. His magnetism, his sexuality came five hundred miles over the telephone wires and rattled my cage.

"Is ... is Jason in, please?" Getting those words out wasn't easy. I fought the urge to hang up, but I was desperate to hear that voice again.

"Who's this?"

"Uh ... this is William."

"William? Oh, you must be Wilam," he said pleasantly.

So Jason had told him everything. The thought set my testicles to tingling. I began to harden. "Yeah, that's what they call me."

"Sorry," he went on, "but Jason's not here right now. He'll probably be back about five this afternoon. Can he call you back?"

"No, I don't have a phone, but I'll write him a note. I promised to let him know where I ended up."

"Yes, I know he was looking forward to hearing from you."

What was he wearing? Was David standing at the phone in tight jeans and no shirt? Had he just come out of the shower and was naked?

97

"This ... this must be David." I wanted to let him know Jason had told me about him, too. I wished I were in a closed phone booth, so I could touch myself.

"Yeah, I'm David."

"That's a real good picture he painted of you," I blurted.

'I've seen the one he did of you, too."

"Well, just let him know I touched base like I promised. I'll drop a line as soon as I can."

"He'll be sorry he missed you."

"He told you about me?"

"Yes. He said you helped him over a rough patch."

His deep voice clawed at my vitals. "And ... and you don't mind me calling?"

"I don't mind. Jason likes you a lot. He'll be sorry he missed you. Where are you calling from?"

"Phoenix. Telephone booth. Well, thanks, David. Bye."

I hung up the telephone in a strange frame of mind. The joy of my good fortune had faded. I would have traded all that had happened today to be in Albuquerque with them. That was crazy. What they had was private. There was no place for me. Even so, it would have been great to be friends with those two powerful personalities and just talk about life and the weather and anything else we could think of?

The cheap watch I'd got at the flea market in Albuquerque said it was five o'clock. Would Carlos still be at the store? I plugged quarters into the pay phone and dialed.

CHAPTER 15

Carlos answered the phone at Arizona Craftsmen. "'Lo. Who's this?"

"It's William. My meeting's over. You still want to go do something?"

"Yeah, sure. Jump in your car and swing by here."

"I don't have a car."

"No wheels? Man, how do you get around this place? I'd be lost without my buggy."

"I take the bus where I can and hoof it everywhere else."

"Okay, where are you?"

I told him, and he said he'd pick me up in thirty. I ran all the way home to make sure the girls were all right. Dad had apparently recovered enough to get out of bed and take off somewhere, so I turned around and ran back to stand on the corner until Carlos's vintage Camaro came down the street. With a cherry red body and lime-green fenders, it was hard to miss. The dual pipes burbled as he braked.

"Yo, man." Carlos popped the door lock and waited while I piled into the passenger's seat. Then he gunned the motor and shot out into traffic. "Where to? You got a favorite watering hole?"

"No. I don't know any of the places around here."

"Leave it to me, bro. Leave it to me."

I'd intended to go for a hamburger and maybe splurge on a milkshake, but Carlos chose a green and white painted Mexican bar on the south side. I walked through the door of the place wondering if I'd see my father. He always badmouthed the Spanish people, so this wasn't his kind of place. Of course, if someone offered to buy him booze, then anywhere would be his kind of place. He'd fit in just fine. Woodie Greyhorse was a chameleon drinker – he'd drink with anyone anywhere, regardless of color – and look like a lifelong fixture in the place while he did it.

I was trying to figure a way out of bar hopping when a swarthy man with a heavy, drooping mustache stopped us at the door. "ID?"

"You know me, Guillermo. Been here lots of times, and I can vouch for him," Carlos said. "Hey, you're both Williams. William, meet Guillermo. That means William in Spanish."

"ID," the man repeated. His blank features said little, and his body language added nothing to the conversation.

"Shit." Carlos dug for his billfold and pulled out his driver's license.

Guillermo eyeballed it and handed it back. He took my New Mexico ID, scanned it, and shook his head. "Quintana, you're okay. Your buddy ain't. He's not legal."

Carlos looked at me bug-eyed. "You're not twenty-one?" He turned back to the bouncer. "Aw, come on, Guillermo, let us in."

"You can go in." The doorman stuck a stubby thumb in my direction. "He can't."

Carlos wheedled, but it did no good. We ended up back in the cherry and green Camero.

I apologized and suggested we just go get a burger, but Carlos was in the mood for drinking. He bought a six-pack and found a neighborhood park. Ignoring a prominent sign that read, "Public Park, No Alcohol or Firearms Allowed" in both English and Spanish, he pulled into the rear of the parking lot and backed into a space shaded by an overhanging desert willow.

He rolled down all the windows and slid his seat back as far as it would go. Flipping a lever, he moved the steering wheel up out of his way and pulled two tall boys from the six-pack between his feet. He handed one to me and popped the lid on the other. The sharp tangy odor of alcohol and hops overpowered the brilliant Bird of Paradise outside my window.

After a long swig, he let out an "ahhh" and spread his legs as far as they would go. I couldn't help noticing the big lump in his britches. I think he caught me staring, but I quickly grabbed the pull-tab and opened my beer, grateful when it fizzed a little, causing a diversion.

"So tell me your story." He reclined his seatback slightly, making his groin even more prominent.

"Not much to tell." I fiddled with my seat, lowering it a little. Did I pooch out like that, too? I took a look. I did. My ears went red from what I was thinking.

Between nervous gulps of beer, I told him a little about myself. I'd never had more than a sip of beer before, so I hadn't learned to like the stuff – and it takes some learning. Still, it felt good to sit beside Carlos – even with a beer in my hand. It was like … well, like being men together. By the time he handed over the second can, I was pretty relaxed.

"I got *sangre del* Indio in me, too," he said. "My people are from up near Copper Canyon. You ever hear of the Tarahumaras?"

"Guess not."

"They're called the ghost runners of the Sierra Madres. They live in this really high altitude, so their lungs get real big, and they can run for days and days at top speed. They used to wear white capes that flapped when they ran, and that's how they got that name. You know, the ghost runners."

I took a slug of my second can. "You never heard of the Pinoans, and I never heard of the Tara … Tara …."

"Tarahumaras."

"So that makes us even." I hiccuped.

"Huh?"

"Nothing." I snatched a look at his crotch again. He was swinging his left leg back and forth, and that made the lump behind his fly move like it was

100

crawling around in there. It wasn't ... but it looked like it. I took another drink and started moving my right leg. Maybe he'd think mine was crawling, too.

He kept talking about how his grandparents – *mis abuelos* he called them – came over the border to work the chili fields in southern New Mexico, but I didn't catch much of it. I was totally fixed on his fly. When I upended my second can, and he handed me a third, our hands touched. The can was cold. His fingers were hot. Mine were hotter. Hell, I was hot all over. I felt movement. My cock was crawling down my leg.

Afraid he'd see it – hoping he'd see it – I twisted toward him. My left wrist flopped on the armrest between us, and my hand sagged down, almost touching his leg. I chugged a quarter of the can and looked again. My hand was even closer.

When he reached for the last can in the pack after finishing off his second, his arm brushed mine off the armrest, and I woke up. What the hell was I doing? I felt flushed. Giddy. Foolish.

"Hey, man, you look funny. You all right?"

"I don't drink," I blurted.

"You don't drink?" His eyebrows climbed. "Then how come you're swigging beer like there's no tomorrow?"

I shrugged. My shoulders felt so loose I shrugged again. "Dunno. Being friendly, I guess."

He laughed aloud and swigged his can. "I better get you home before you pass out on me. Can you believe it? Drunk on three beers."

"Two and a half." I giggled and shook my can. "I got half a beer left." Feeling adventurous, I drained my can and burped.

# # # # #

My euphoria evaporated as soon as Carlos dropped me off. I still had half a mile to hike because I was ashamed for him to see where I lived. Hell, he probably lived in a dump just as bad, but I was too sick at my stomach to reason things out. Something – the beer, most likely – collected at the base of my throat and clamored to get out. I needed to throw up. Bad. Oh Lord, was I becoming one of them? Mom and Dad spewed vomit without making a big deal out of it, but it was a whale of a deal to me. My muscles ached, my skin crawled, and my craw was clogged with something sour. I started looking for a trash bin or somewhere to toss my cookies.

Cookies! That was all I needed. I turned away from the sidewalk and emptied my stomach on a neat, pristine patch of grass in front of a fancy motel. Passers-by stared at me in disgust. I could read their faces – another drunken Indian. Well, I couldn't argue with them right at the moment.

I finally made it home, staggering up the sidewalk, hating the thought of going inside the apartment in this condition. But my body demanded the comfort of the sofa or better yet, my bedroll. I took a deep breath before fumbling with the doorknob and reeling inside. I threw out a "hi," to anyone who wanted one. Nola gave me a queer look, and Junie barreled into me, almost bowling me over. When I bent down to kiss her, she turned away.

"You smell like Daddy, Wilam."

Shocked, I fell back on the sofa and sat there without moving until Nola brought me a sandwich and chips sometime after nightfall.

"Mom?" I muttered.

"Bedroom. Passed out." Nola spoke through thin lips.

That sounded like a good idea to me, but I laid aside the sandwich and forced myself off the divan to go clean up in the bathroom before falling into my bedroll and doing a little passing out of my own.

# # # # #

I woke the next morning in the cold, hard clasp of the Grim Reaper. Or that's the way it felt, anyway. My mouth was so dry everything was stuck together, lip to lip, tongue to palate … everything. My eyeballs burned from somewhere inside my head clear out to the front, and they didn't focus very well until I gouged crusts of dried matter out of them. That cleared things up – a little.

It was my belly that was really killing me. It roiled beneath my skin like it was trying to figure out which way to run. There was a blowtorch burning my insides to a crisp. Then the nausea hit, sapping my will to move at a time I couldn't afford not to.

I rolled out of my blankets and crawled on my hands and knees into the bathroom. I made it to the stool before green, sour bile erupted out of my mouth and nose and dribbled down my chin. My gagging and gasping and choking brought Nola to the door.

"Wilam, you all right?" she asked through the plywood.

"All … right." It was more a sigh than an answer. She came inside. It didn't even bother me I was in my underwear. Modesty was at the bottom of my priority list right then.

"You've been drinking." She sounded maternal. I hadn't heard a peep out of my real mother yet, and frankly I didn't care to.

"Yeah. Little." I swiped my mouth and nose and chin with sheets of toilet paper. Then I expended the effort required to turn my head. The expression on her face cut like a knife. Fear twisted her features into an ugly mask. I fell over on my butt and faced her. "It's not like that, Nola. I swear. I'm not turning into Dad. I won't do it again, I promise."

The hollow words hung in the air between us like an impenetrable curtain. Fear shot through me. I'd betrayed the only two people in this world I loved … and who loved me. My connection to them stood in jeopardy. How many times had Nola heard Mom and Dad utter those same words? I labored to my knees and levered myself to a standing position.

"Don't worry, Nola. I'll never do this again. Three beers. Three beers, and I'm sick as a dog. Some people may consider this having a good time, but not me."

The quick hope in her eyes clouded into suspicion. "Wilam, I don't think I can make it if I can't rely on you."

"It's the same for me, Nola. If I didn't have you to help me with little Junie, I'd be lost. We're all that count, you know. Junie and you and me."

"I know."

The words were so forlorn, the fear in her black eyes so desperate, I'd have hugged her if I hadn't been naked except for my shorts. Instead, I rested a hand on her shoulder. "I swear to you Nola Greyhorse. I swear I won't let you down. I'm no drunk, and I won't ever be. You'll never see me in this condition again."

Eyes unreadable, she touched my cheek and spun on her heel. When she was gone, I knew I'd have to earn her trust again. I slipped out of my shorts and stood under the cold shower until I could feel the human me stirring under the miserable me. Sapped of strength, I climbed out of the tub, toweled off, and worked on my teeth for five minutes. No matter what I did, I couldn't get that foul taste out of my mouth. I had a quick panic attack until I remembered it was Sunday and I wasn't scheduled to work today.

I didn't want anything to eat; my stomach threatened to rebel at the thought, but Nola forced a glass of milk and a piece of dry toast on me. It helped some. I tried whittling, but my hands acted like Mexican jumping beans, skittering this way and shooting that way when I wasn't expecting it. So I put away my knives before I sliced up my fingers and watched Nola work on the necklace she was making – her first.

She was doing a twelve-inch strand made of gold and silver wire twisted around one another with a turquoise bevel as a pendant. I'd given her the turquoise from my supplies. It was a good first effort. My little sister had talent, too.

When I felt stronger, I took the girls to the park. After Junie took another sniff she warmed up. Apparently I didn't smell like the old man any more. I pushed Junie on the swing set; Nola pumped herself. When they tired of that, we took a seat at one of the picnic tables.

"Here comes Mom," Junie said, looking back up the sidewalk.

I watched her come. She'd been passed out longer than I had been, but here she was walking a straight line. There was a smile painted on her mouth, even though it didn't look like it came from the inside.

"Wilam," she said when she got close. "Did you get paid yesterday?"

"Yes."

"We need some groceries. You don't look too good, son. I heard tell you came in drunk last night. Just give me the money. I'll go get us something to eat."

I glanced at Nola; she shook her head. Little Junie, bless her heart, told everything she knew. "We'll all go to the store together."

"That's all right. Just give me the money." A frown line appeared between her eyes, and I knew she'd begun to feel the bottle she craved slipping away from her.

"We'll go," I said firmly. "But we're not buying a bottle, Mom."

"Just a pint, son."

"We're not buying a bottle."

She tuned up like she was going to cry. She held out a hand to me that shook so badly she looked as if she was flapping a wing. The composure she'd mustered to wheedle me out of drinking money evaporated. She demanded my paycheck as if she had a right to it. Then she begged for it, saying she just needed a good drink to steady her nerves. Was there ever a drunk in the world who didn't try that old line? Then she did cry, and I got embarrassed.

"I put my arms around her thin shoulders. "Come on, let's go grocery shopping."

She wasn't over five-four, so she had to glance up to seek out my eyes. Her tears were dried, but she still snuffled. "Did you see Woodie while you was out last night?"

"No, Mom. I didn't see him."

"I hope he's all right. He was sick, you know?"

"Sick how?"

"Got a cold, and it went down in his chest."

"Then why'd he go out?"

"He had a thirst. A bad thirst."

What does it say about a man when his children are grateful he's not around? Mom was the only one who missed him. I shook my head. Why? Why would she pine for a miserable bastard who abused her whenever he felt like it? I guess I had a lot to learn about life.

CHAPTER 16

It was all I could do to make it through my work down at Arizona Craftsmen, and that was only a half-shift. I didn't dare pick up a knife for four days, and Mom sulking because I wouldn't buy her a bottle of whiskey didn't help any. She got the shakes so bad I wanted to take her down to the Public Health Hospital, but she went stubborn. She probably wanted me to see her suffer, hoping I'd relent and buy her booze – her ultimate treatment for the condition. I didn't; I just hardened my heart.

Didn't do much good. Wednesday afternoon, the old man came home and upset everyone's routine. He seemed to have recovered from his bout of bronchitis, or whatever it was. He'd hit a minor jackpot somewhere because he had several bottles of hooch. Mom wheedled a pint of Old Crow from him, which transformed her. She got in a better mood – not happy, mind you – but better. Happy was beyond her now. She'd turned sneaky and sly. I know for a fact she filched another pint from the truck when Dad was sleeping.

One day, as she sat at the kitchen table nursing a bottle, I pulled out a big block of wood and started carving. Cora Greyhorse emerged from that cottonwood root in no time flat. It was like she was really in there, and my knife simply freed her from the wood. I caught her wizened, half-out-of-it look, but she just appeared downtrodden, not drunk. Sitting in a rocker in a traditional dress with feet crossed, head lowered, she seemed to be studying something on the floor in front of her.

I stowed it away for two days before taking another look. My heart stuttered in my chest when I studied it again. It wasn't my mother; it was some ancient crone at the end of a hard life. It depressed me so much I boxed it up and sent it to Mr. Gresham to get it out of my sight.

# # # # #

Nola was getting pretty good at her jewelry making. I sent some of it to Mr. Gresham without her knowing. If she missed it, she never let on. She probably figured Dad had taken it to sell for booze. She'd met a boy at school who apparently didn't know she was alive, so she might not even have realized it was gone.

Her melancholy mood was too rich to waste. Suffering a momentary twinge of guilt for exploiting her imagined tragedy, I convinced her to sit sideways on her hip, torso supported on her right arm, head lowered while she picked at a thread in the frayed living room carpet. I made two or three rough sketches – the only kind I was capable of – before releasing her to go about the business of mooning over what's-his-name.

I worked hard on the piece for a couple of weeks, turning her into a pensive Indian maiden of the nineteenth century lazily dragging her finger through the water of a pond or stream. All of the flesh was stone; everything else was made from different types of wood. I used bits of coral, gold, and silver as porcupine quill embroidery on her buckskin dress. The ornaments in her hair were mostly turquoise. I had Nola make a fancy pair of red coral earrings for the tiny earlobes and beat a couple of strands of silver so thin I could almost see through them to represent the water. It was a good piece of work.

Right about the time I finished it, I got a letter from Mr. Gresham with a check made out to Nola. He'd bought all of the stuff I'd sent him. He didn't pay much, but it was more than the cost of the materials that went into the jewelry, so Nola benefited from the efforts of her labor. More valuable than the money, he made some suggestions about improving her work and named a couple of specific items he'd be interested in for the future. My sis was as proud as a peacock when I took her down to the bank and helped her cash her first check.

Then she faced the same problem I did – how to hang onto it. Some of her stuff had already disappeared – besides the pieces I'd sent to Mr. Gresham. Both Mom and Dad recognized the marketability of gold and silver and semi-precious stones. I'd had some of them disappear, too.

# # # # #

The old man must have been laying low from the law or some other kind of trouble because he was hanging around the apartment, hitting me up for money – mostly out of habit, I think. I gave him a couple of bucks to avoid a fight and busting up my work. I finished the maiden at the stream and shipped it off without my customary second look. This time, I sent it directly to Greenby. It was more in the style he wanted.

Dad had figured out my game by now, and that brought up another problem. Some of my carving knives vanished. Then a head I'd almost finished went missing. Some small animals and figures I'd made for Mom and the girls were gone, too. The son of a bitch had sold them. That must be how he came home flush a couple of times.

How had my father had sunk so low? There'd been a time back on the rez when he'd hunted and fished for the family's food. He'd done some trading – collecting junk and swapping it in Mapleton for cash. I don't recall exactly when he quit trying to support the family and started rooting around for drinking money, instead.

Ever since Albuquerque, he'd popped in and out of our lives without giving a clue to how he got his money. He probably stole from someone else like he stole from us. Now that he'd caught on my carvings had value, he was going to be a problem for the rest of my life – or as long as I lived under the same roof. That thought held a powerful attraction, but it was just daydreaming. I couldn't leave because of the girls, but I sure as hell could take my tools and my work somewhere else.

I scouted around the neighborhood until I found a converted garage behind a house around the corner. The owner agreed to rent it to me for fifty dollars a month. I salvaged a couple of sagging chairs and a rickety table from a dumpster near a big apartment house, put in some time repairing them, and ended up with a halfway comfortable place. I built a sturdy worktable in the corner where Nola could study and work at making jewelry. I found some small cigar boxes to store her findings and other supplies. I bought some toys, so Junie could play and blankets for her nap.

Right after my shift at Arizona Craftsmen, I'd pick up Junie and take her to my "studio." She got a bang out of going with me later to walk Nola back after her last class. There weren't any sanitary facilities in the shack, so we bought a slop jar and carried in a supply of water and anything else we needed. I bought an ice chest, so we could store cold drinks and lunches. One day, I'd get us one of those little refrigerators. Mom never asked where I took the girls every day.

Both of my sisters earned a little money by helping me out in the studio. Nola was good at blocking out pieces from the soapstone when I could pry her away from her earrings and necklaces. That got a little more difficult when she got her second check from Mr. Gresham – this one a bit stouter than the first.

Little Junie liked to play house and keep the place clean. I cut a broom handle in half so she could manage the thing, but she still made Nola and me giggle as she swept the floor on her short, stubby legs with a broom that was still too big for her. I made a place on the wall for every tool I owned, even going so far as to paint a black silhouette of each one, so Junie knew where it belonged when I wasn't using it. Every day, she'd put them away … sometimes before I was finished with them. Each time I gave her a little something for her efforts, she put it in a cigar box and called it her "household money."

When my birthday rolled around, they bought me a nice shirt with the little bit of cash they had stored away. I loved them even more for thinking of me.

In the privacy of that one-room shack, I finally came to grips with the fact I was an artist now. Well, maybe an artisan, although I'm not sure what the difference was. Except for the hours spent at Arizona Craftsmen, I worked constantly at my craft.

Climate control was the biggest problem with my new set-up. It's always hot in Phoenix, and as the months marched on, the little shack turned into an oven. I spent almost four hundred dollars on a window air conditioner, but even so, the place was unbearable by the shank of the afternoon. I saved those hours for doing my running around … buying supplies, banking, and things like that. Junie got a bang out of climbing on an air-conditioned bus and going with Nola and me on our trips.

Sometimes I worried the girls weren't associating with kids their own age, and I knew from my stunted social skills how important that was. Nola got some of it at school, but Junie was with me almost all the time. It couldn't be helped, because for a month after I set up my studio, Dad was on the prod, trying to find out where my work tools and my carvings had gone. He even tried to shadow me once, but he wasn't hard to spot – or to give the slip. Nola got off the hook, when he faced her down about that "gold stuff," and she claimed she'd quit making it because nobody wanted to buy it. It was a school project, anyway, she said, and she'd had to return all the unused material to them.

It wasn't so easy for me. One day, he threatened me with a frying pan. Holding it bottom side up, so I'd know he wasn't figuring on cooking something, he gave me a dirty look. "Where them tools you always cluttering the place up with? And your whittling. You know, those animals and things?"

"I don't do that anymore."

"Good. Then give me the knives. I'll get rid of them. Might as well bring me whatever carving you got left, too."

"Already sold them. All of them."

He tapped the pan against the palm of his left hand. "Then gimme the money."

"Already spent it on food. And the rent. It has to get paid some way, you know."

"So where you go ever day?"

"I'm working full time down at AZC now." That was what we'd started calling Arizona Craftsmen. Oops. I'd stepped into a pile with that lie. Now he'd want me to hand over my check. So I went cheeky. "Had to. It takes all my check to cover the rent on this place. How about it, Dad? Can you give me some money to help out this month?"

I took a step backward in case he decided to use the frying pan, but he just snarled at me and went back to the kitchen. I took a shaky breath and got out of there.

# # # # #

I got a check in the mail from Greenby Galleries for a thousand dollars for the figurine of Nola. I'd worked a lot harder on it than on the busts I'd done before, but I decided the price was more than fair. After I sold two more pieces, I quit my part time job and started concentrating on my art full time. I felt good about it, except I missed seeing Carlos. I liked the way he still joshed me about getting soused on three beers.

He came over to see my studio one afternoon while Nola was taking Mom and Junie to the thrift store for some summer clothes. He took one look at the place, wiped the sweat from his neck, and took off, returning with a boxful of tools. Without asking me anything about it, he set to work making the place airtight. What it really needed, he said, was more insulation – lots more. When he finished, the window unit started working more efficiently. The place was bearable even during the hottest part of the afternoon. Not comfortable, mind you. Just bearable.

He wouldn't accept any money, except for the supplies he'd bought, but he took to coming over occasionally after work to hang for a while. Of course, Nola fell in love with him right off the bat. He was manly and handsome, and he had an easy way about him, so it was natural. But he treated her like a little sister, which irritated the hell out of her.

One evening, when Mom was behaving herself and the old man was nowhere in sight, I went back to the studio to finish up some work. Five minutes after I got there, Carlos showed up with a six-pack. He tore it open and handed a bottle to me.

"You wanna try it again?"

"No way. Not ever, man. I learned my lesson."

"Okay, leaves more for me."

"Go ahead ... poison yourself."

We joshed around for a bit while he tugged on his bottles. I was close to completing the largest soapstone piece I'd ever attempted, a standing warrior in a breech clout looking off in the distance, a coup stick grasped in his left hand with the haft resting on the ground. It stood about four-feet high.

"Hey, man, that's good." Carlos squatted down in front of the sculpture to study it closely.

"Thanks."

"You always do that?" he asked.

"Do what?"

He gestured. "Put a cock behind the breech cloth?"

"I just try to make it look realistic." I glanced at the carton of beer and saw he was on his last bottle. "As a matter of fact, I modeled it after you."

"Me? I don't stick out like that." He checked and looked up, red-faced. "Well, yeah, I do. Causes me a problem sometimes."

I swallowed hard. "I've never seen any evidence of it."

"Naw, you were too drunk to notice."

"Huh?"

"Hell, I had a hard-on in the Camaro the night you got plastered."

"You ... you did?"

"Yep. Getting one right now, too." He grinned. "Does that door have a lock on it?"

"Yeah, why?"

"Privacy." He made sure the lock was engaged before turning to face me. He stood there with his legs spread and his hands on his hips. Waiting for me to make a move, I guess. I wanted to but didn't know how. My mouth went dry. He was so good looking and sexy. Finally, I licked my lips and walked over to him.

"I been thinking about this a long time." His voice was husky.

109

"Why didn't you let me know?"

"We worked together. That's dangerous, man. You know, we might act different, and people would catch on. Now, you don' work at AZC anymore. So what are you going to do about it?"

"Me?" I mumbled. "I don't know what to do. I don't have much experience."

"Me neither. You know us Latin types, we chase women, not guys." He winked. "But every once in a while, we let some hunky dude catch us." He turned serious. "You can't ever let on to anybody, you hear? Promise?"

I nodded and clasped his shoulders. I let my hands slide down over his arms. I liked the feel of his hard muscles and silky skin. I moved to his waist, and after a moment of indecision, I cupped my hand over his fly. He throbbed behind the denim. He pulled me to him, and we stood groin to groin. He was taller than I was, so his cock was poking against my belly.

"You game?" His voice was almost a growl.

I nodded. "But what are we gonna do?"

"We'll figure something out."

His palms cupped my ass, making it tingle. After that, we ended up naked on the blankets where Nola and Junie took naps. Carlos was built strong but slender, and he was brown all over. His flesh was tight and smooth.

He lay back with one hand behind his head, exposing a bit of dark hair in his armpit. I put my mouth to his left nipple and sucked. When it was standing up, I did the same thing to the other one. Then I licked his chest and moved down to his navel. I had to hold his hard cock out of the way, so I could poke my tongue into his belly button. After that, I was stumped.

"I … I don't know what to do?"

"You could always blow me."

My disastrous experience with Enrique leapt to mind. "I don't do that. Do you?

"Hell, no. I'm no queer."

"M … me neither. I guess we could always … you know, jerk one another off."

He stirred restlessly, moving his leg against my groin. It felt good. "Naw. I need more than that."

I examined his cock. It was big … lots bigger than mine. Long and straight and cut and hard as a rock. There was a pearl of pre-cum in the slit.

Despite what he'd said, I took it in my hand and gently stroked it. He wiggled his butt and let out a sigh. Bolder now, I began to pump him.

"How does that feel?" I asked.

"Okay. But …."

I held my breath, afraid he was going to say forget it; he could jack off without my help.

He lifted his head and looked at me. There was a bright shine in his dark eyes. "I heard about something else. Maybe we can try it?"

"What?" Was he talking about what James did that night on the Beaver? A little shiver of ran down my back. Fear ... or anticipation?

"Lay down on top of me."

"What?"

"Just do it, okay? Get up on top of me. On your belly."

I straddled his long, slender legs and spread my body over his. It felt good; better than I thought it would. His hot, hard cock lay right next to mine, pulsing against my belly. I hoped he could feel mine throbbing hungrily.

"Now," he said. "Start hunching."

So I did. In a minute, it started to feel great. I watched his handsome face as I fucked his belly. After he caught my rhythm, he started thrusting back at me, and I liked the feel of his big cock sliding up and down my stomach.

"You ever kissed a guy?" He was panting slightly. There was a wild look about him.

"N ... no," I lied.

"Me neither. Let's try it."

He placed a hand behind my head and drew me to him. Neither of us missed a beat as our lips touched. I don't know what his reaction was, but it was an epiphany for me. When I'd kissed Karen Sue, it was a meeting of mouths. With Carlos, it was more ... much more. Even better than with Jason. The nerve endings on my lips sent an exciting message down my back to my scrotum and the hard cock rubbing against his smooth, hairless stomach. His lips parted, and I pushed my tongue into his mouth. He sucked on it a moment and then thrust his into mine.

My ears rang. Or maybe it was bells far off somewhere. My mind sought to embrace his. To understand what he was feeling. The intensity of the act intensified, soared, took on meaning.

When I sensed he was becoming uncomfortable, I reluctantly pulled my lips away. He started to say something, but checked himself as he ground his hips against me more urgently. His time was approaching. Mine wasn't far behind. His eyes went out of focus. He wrapped his long legs around me and drove himself against me as if he were trying to penetrate my belly button. His excitement heightened my own. Then he let out a loud gasp. His semen splashed against my belly, lubricating my frantic movements.

"Ohhhh," he moaned. His lids slipped over his eyes. He had long, sable lashes. Rapture claimed his fine features. The erotic image sent me over the edge. My testicles drew up, my hips pumped, and my cock swam in his slick sperm. I exploded in a long, intense orgasm. Finally, it slowed and ended. I held myself tight against his chest and buried my head in the crook of his shoulder. His cheek was smooth against my ear. Our hearts beat in unison.

"Wow," he said. "That was something."

I raised my head and met his eyes. They slid away. Like Enrique's had done.

"Yeah," I panted. "Intense."

"That's the word. Intense."

"How'd you come up with that idea, anyway?"

He grinned. "I got with this girl once. Woman, really. She was lots older than me. She got buck naked, but wouldn't let me put it in. So I just fucked her belly. She said the old Greeks used to do it. She called it some French name that sounded like frontage. I don't know how to pronounce it, so I just call it belly fucking."

"That's what you call it, huh? With all the guys you do it with?"

I was teasing, but it was a mistake. His lips tightened. "Never done it with anybody else. Just you. And her."

"Well, I'm glad it was me. It … it was as good as the real thing."

"You think so?" He tipped me off him. I lay as close as I could at his side. "It's awful messy down there." I said it for something to say.

"Yeah, it's two buckets of cum instead of one."

"Right, like I come a bucketful." I glanced at his belly. His navel, an innie, was full of cum. "You might, though." I touched the milky pool in his belly button. "I wonder how much of that is you, and how much is me?"

"Don't go weird on me, Greyhorse." He gave an embarrassed laugh and got to his feet.

I admired the graceful way he moved. Manly. Or as they say around here, macho. *Muy, muy macho.*

"You got anything to clean up with?"

"Yeah." I brought over a small washbasin and a rag. He reached for it, but I evaded his hand and started cleaning him off. He flinched but permitted my touch. I put a hand on his ass cheek to steady us as I worked. My fingers burned.

"That's good enough," he said, moving away from me. He collected his clothing as I cleaned myself. He was dressed by the time I finished.

When he made as if to leave, I spoke. "Carlos. That was really great."

"Yeah, it was okay."

"Best I've ever got it."

"No shit? Including girls?"

"Yeah, you're better than any of the girls I've ever had." I tried to make the truth sound like a joke.

"Don't say that in polite society. In fact, don't say it at all, Indio."

I tried to match his playful tone. "Indio's okay, but I don't want to hear any of that *maricón* shit."

"Not from me."

It took me a minute to realize we were joshing around because he was ashamed. He was embarrassed and mortified and didn't know how to handle it. If I was lucky, he'd be back. Maybe not often, but once in a while. That was more hope than I'd had before he showed up tonight.

CHAPTER 17

"Is he all right?" Mom clutched a tattered robe to her skinny frame and leaned against the doorjamb. The porch light made her skin look yellow.

I'd been so deep into sleep, I hadn't even heard the knock, but her voice woke me. I pulled on a pair of pants and got to the door in time to see a vaguely familiar man walk down the sidewalk and disappear into the night.

"What is it?" Nola asked. Little Junie, still in their sofa bed, started whimpering.

I took Mom's arm and closed the door. She said nothing as I led her to the kitchen table. Nola got Junie and sat across from her, bouncing the baby on her lap. I handed Mom a glass of water and took a chair.

"That was Aaron, a friend of your father's." Her voice was hollow. "He's in jail. They've got your father down at the jailhouse."

"Big deal," I snapped. "He's been there before."

She slapped my arm. "This isn't like the other times. It's different. He got in a fight down at the bar. Somebody called the cops, and they took him to jail."

"What's the charge?" Nola asked.

"I don't know. Aaron said something about assault."

Dad's troubles here in Phoenix had been limited to drunk and disorderly up until now. All he'd got for those was probation. This time, maybe they'd see the error of their ways and lock him up.

Mom clutched my arm. "We have to get him out, Wilam. What will we do without him?"

My mouth got away from me. "What we've always done when he's gone to jail."

"He's never gone to jail for hurting somebody."

"What about Brewster Whitetail? He should have gone to jail for that. That's why we had to leave home."

"That's ... different."

I didn't see how, except this time he got caught. I was wasting my time arguing with her. She wasn't going to listen to me, anyway. "He's never around, Mom. We'll be just fine."

Fear made her eyes look sunken. "Hush up! He's your father. He's head of this family."

I ground my teeth but kept my lips closed.

"You always have money, son. Go down there are bail him out."

"Right now? Mom, I don't have any money. I give it all to Nola for food and clothing and rent. I've got nothing left for bail money."

"I heard him say you had a lot of money in a bank. For emergencies. Well, this is an emergency."

"Not the kind I had in mind. Anyway, the bond people won't touch him. He's got no job, no roots here. They'll figure he'll run away as soon as he clears the jailhouse door."

"You have a job."

I hadn't told her I'd quit because it avoided having to explain where I went every day. So far Junie hadn't given away our secret.

"I might have one, but it's not me they'd be bonding out. He has to have one. Besides, he got himself into this mess, so he can get himself out of it."

It was two o'clock in the morning when I made that judgment call, but it was another two hours before Mom gave up mewling, so we could all get some sleep.

When I dragged out of bed later that morning to walk Nola down to the school bus, Mom was all puffed up at me. She wouldn't say anything, beyond begging me to go down and get my dad out of jail.

Since my beloved father was safely locked behind bars at the moment, I went straight to my studio after the bus picked up Nola and her classmates. When I showed up at the apartment for lunch, I found Junie abandoned and sitting on the sofa crying. Mom wasn't anywhere around, She'd probably gone to try and see Dad. It tore at my soul that she could run off and leave the baby for that miserable SOB.

I fixed us something to eat and then took Junie to the studio. She immediately went into her housewifey mode and started sweeping out the place with her cut-down broom. Pretty soon, she was singing a little song.

We went down to pick up Nola at the school bus stop that afternoon and swung by the apartment afterward. There was still no sign of Mom. Nola worried she might manage to find a bottle. If she did, she might not come back at all – she'd probably end up behind bars right beside Woodie.

She showed up later that night, acting hurt and put on. I didn't mind that so much because she was sober.

"You see him?" I asked.

"They wouldn't let me. Said I had to come during the visiting time. Son, how can you desert him? He's your father."

"You heard him say I wasn't the seed of his loins. Said there was no way I could have come from his blood, and he's right. We're not anything like one another. The only way I know he's my father is because you say so. Other than that, I've never seen any evidence of it."

# # # # #

The next few days were a trial. I spent as much time as possible in the little shack I called a studio. The girls and I even slept there a couple of times. I'd have moved in permanently, but even though she was on my back at the moment, I was worried about Mom. She wasn't the woman she was before Dad put her in an Albuquerque hospital with a busted head.

114

Woodrow Greyhorse was convicted of simple assault and got forty days in the hoosegow. That probably meant he'd do around thirty. At least, I hoped so. Now that it was a done deal, Mom came off her high horse and acted as if she'd never been mad at me.

As soon as I knew he was safely behind bars, I went out and rented a better place for the family. I paid six months' rent on a two-bedroom apartment and got some better furniture at the thrift stores. I found a used color TV and even had a telephone installed. Mom had her own bedroom. The girls shared one, and I slept on a daybed in the living room, something a lot more comfortable than the floor.

The new place was in a little nicer part of town, which meant it was a longer walk to the studio. After Mom settled down, Nola and Junie started spending more time with her in the apartment. Things were looking up, even though Mom tried to sneak a bottle now and then. Still, she was handling things well enough, so I wasn't afraid for the girls to stay with her now.

Since I had a longer hike each morning, I started my workday a little earlier before it got too hot. I was laboring hard to finish some pieces in order to build up my savings after spending all that money on the new place. I missed having the girls with me, but I put out some pretty ambitious pieces. Greenby accepted them all. Carlos showed up a couple of times, and that always picked up my day. We did the frontage thing, and each time was just as awesome as the last.

I took to wandering through some of the art galleries during the hottest time of day and discovered alabaster. It was totally different from the soapstone, but I bought some of the gypsum rock plus the tools to work it, setting aside a couple of hours each day to experiment with this new medium. The first thing I produced was disappointing, as was the second and fourth and dozenth, but I discovered a local trader who bought those things I didn't feel were up to the quality either Greenby or Mr. Gresham required. Of course, I didn't sign those pieces. Nevertheless, I couldn't help but feel this beautiful stone held something important for my future.

If my professional – I liked the sound of that – life was pleasing and challenging, my personal life lacked something. It was great when Carlos came around, but I wished he'd do it more often. I even asked him to go places with me after work. He gave me a look that said he knew I was trying to date him, and that wasn't who he was. He never treated me shabby or bad-mouthed me, he just kept his distance … except when he needed something.

That was better than nothing, but sometimes working alone in the evenings, I'd find myself thinking about Jason and David and wondering what it would be like to be with them. I fantasized about watching David make love to Jason while I touched his powerful body. Sometimes, in my daydreams, it would be me he was making love to. At times like that, I'd turn out the lights, lay back in one of my old stuffed chairs and jack off. Afterward, I always felt depressed.

I found the section of town where the gay prostitutes hung out and walked through the area a time or two, but the bold glances embarrassed me. There was a little park in the neighborhood where I started playing football with some other guys on the weekends. When I stayed late one night, I discovered it was a hangout for lonely men looking for other lonely men.

One morning, I went over before it got too hot, but there wasn't a game going on. A couple of people hung around, and one was a guy about my age who looked as if he took an interest in me. Whenever I glanced in his direction, he'd look away. As I left the park, I sensed rather than saw him following along behind me. Sure enough, when I got to the bus stop, he walked up and stood waiting. He smiled; but my courage failed, and I didn't smile back. He got off at the same stop I did and was right behind me when I headed into the public library.

I had to take a leak, and I was curious about what he'd do. I was halfway finished pissing when he moved up to the urinal beside me. As soon as he looked at me, I got hard. He smiled and pulled himself out of his trousers. He was already stiff. People were coming in and out of the place, and when someone took the urinal to my left, I stuffed myself into my trousers, gave my hands a quick wash, and fled the restroom. He was right behind me.

I wandered around not knowing what to do or where to go. I hadn't seen Carlos in a week, and this was a decent looking guy. Despite the fact this had a cheap, tawdry feel about it, when he motioned with his head, I followed him into a room filled with row after row of book stacks.

He found a little cul-de-sac, I guess you'd call it, and smiled encouragingly as I slowly came up to him. He squatted down like he was looking for a book on one of the lower shelves, but as soon as I was close enough, he reached out and felt my cock. It sprang to life. He fumbled with the zipper and freed me from my trousers. It was hard and throbbing and eager.

"Oh, sweetie, look at that lovely thing," he said in a mincing, falsetto voice. He took the end into his mouth, and I deflated a little. His tongue did a little dance on the end, and it came back again.

He took me out of his mouth and looked at it greedily. "Honey, this girl likes what you've got." And he did sound like a girl. Like a cheap streetwalker.

I pulled away and hid my cock back in my britches. "I think I made a mistake." My skin crawled on my back.

"What are you, sugar, a cock tease?" He reached for my zipper and tugged it back down. "You don't want to be that. Not a hunky man like you."

I grabbed his hand and twisted it. "I said I made a mistake. Now don't you make one, too."

"All right. You don't have to be a jerk about it," he said in a man's voice. His eyes flashed angrily as he jerked free and walked away. If he'd talked like that in the first place, I would have let him do it. I left the stacks and watched him walk out the library.

Since I didn't want to run into him outside, I went into the reference area and looked up some books on sculpture. I got a bang out of looking at photos of statues and urns and columns. I had discovered Michelangelo here, and I took out a book of his works and pored over every photograph I could find. This guy was great. Even his unfinished stuff was magnificent. He worked in pure white Carrara marble. I decided right then and there I'd try that someday.

Then I found a book on alabaster, the stone I'd recently discovered. I learned there were two types. One was the kind I'd already carved called gypsum alabaster. That kind was so soft I could score it with my fingernail. The ancients used another kind called a calcite. It was harder, more durable, but you could still carve it with a knife. I studied photographs of a really ornate alabaster vase and a cosmetic jar with a lioness on top, both taken from the tomb of that old Egyptian pharaoh they called Tutankhamen. Was there still some of that Oriental alabaster to work with? Oriental – that was what the book called the calcite type.

Excited over what I'd learned, I caught a bus home, but by the time I got there, I remembered the guy who'd acted like a gal had had my thing in his mouth, so I took a long, hot shower with lots of soap.

That night Carlos showed up while I was working at the studio, and I surprised him by my aggressiveness. He usually took the lead, but this time, I tore off his clothes, pushed him down on the pallet, and rubbed myself all over him. My cock was leaking and left smears on his tits. He let me have my way until I finished fucking his belly, shooting off like I'd never come before. Then he rolled me over on my back, crawled on, and returned the favor. Once, when he was rubbing my chest with his hard dick, I came close to pulling him up and taking him into my mouth, but I didn't. I wouldn't have minded trying it with him, but I wasn't sure how he'd react because I knew how he felt about queers ... despite what we did.

He slid down on me and gave me a deep kiss, really working with his tongue. When he erupted, he seemed to get as much of a bang out of it as I had. At least, his eyes rolled up into his head for a minute. His orgasm over, he lay as he was, his torso atop me, his legs between mine, and I knew something was coming. I probably shouldn't have been so pushy with him, but that couldn't be undone now.

"Wilam," he said. He'd started using my pet name as soon as he heard Nola call me that. "I can't do this anymore."

My heart froze up inside my chest. "I'm sorry. I won't act like I did tonight again. You can be the one to make the first move."

"No, you don't understand. It wasn't anything you did. Hell, I like it when I get you so turned on you go crazy." He gave a lazy smile. "Makes me feel good. But I met this girl, and we're getting kinda serious. We promised one another we wouldn't get with anyone else until we figure things out."

"You told her about me?"

His eyebrows climbed. "No! It's just that we promised not to get with anybody."

"Oh. So why did you come over tonight?"

"To tell you, and to be with you one last time. I like you, Wilam. You're kind of weird sometimes, but I like you. I dig what we do … did. So I wanted to do it again … you know, to remember it by."

Tears threatened my eyes, but I blinked them back, hoping he hadn't seen them. "So this is it, huh?"

"Yeah. I'd like to keep coming over. Just as a friend, but …."

"That's okay, you can come over anytime you want. I understand the situation, and we can just shoot the shit. I'd like to be friends even if we can't do the other. Heck, I'll even have three beers with you again."

He laughed and gave my arm a squeeze. Then he gazed into my eyes a long time before he spoke again. "I don't think so. I don't believe I could keep my hands off you. I remember what you said to me the first time we did this. You said it was better than doing it with girls. I was beginning to think so, too. Until I met Lydia. That's the girl I told you about. Before her, I was beginning to think I was turning … well, queer."

"Is that what you think I am?"

"I don't know. Maybe. You really dig it, but you're the guy who has to answer that question. Are you?"

I shrugged helplessly. "I don't know. All I know is I'm willing to do things with you I wouldn't do with anyone else. Even things we haven't tried yet." He looked startled. Maybe there was hope. "One time before I left the reservation, a friend – a guy – told me he loved me. It made me feel funny inside. But you know what? I could say that right now to you. Without any trouble at all."

"Don't!" He had a panicked look on his face. "It'll just make things more complicated. I want to remember you as a friend. Who knows, maybe someday I can handle it, and we can bud around some."

"I'd like that. I'll always remember you as a friend."

He dressed and hugged me to him, but it was more like a Mexican *abrazo* than a lover's embrace. Then he was gone.

I sat down and stared into the dark for an hour. It took a long time to realize I was still naked. Calling up the image of his beautiful face hovering above me, I took myself in hand and masturbated. The ejaculation, when it came, was almost as good as it had been with him. In a way, it was with him. He was still here, a fading ephemeral presence. I sobbed while cum dried on my chest and belly. He was gone now. Forever.

# # # # #

Summer arrived while I grieved. Dad got out of jail, and Mom brought him home. To our new home. That put an end to a bittersweet phase of my life. He came through the door pissed I hadn't helped him out, especially when he saw the new furniture. He started getting on my back so much, I had to take the girls to the studio again. If he was there when I got home late at night, he'd start right in on me. One night, it came to a head.

"You fucking little queer," He towered over me in the living room. "I want some money out of you, and I want it now. You're not going to leech off me all your miserable life."

"Who's a leech? I pay for this, you don't."

"Watch your tongue. I'm the man in this family."

"Some man you are. You may have the equipment, but you're no man. You're nothing but a sot. An alcohol soaked bum."

He came for me, but I was ready. I was standing with my hand on a little rocker I'd made for Junie, and I grabbed it and swung as hard as I could. He caught the brunt of the blow on his shoulder, but one of the rocker arms slammed him in the head. He went down ... and stayed there.

With a screech, Mom ran over and put herself between the two of us. She crouched over him like a guardian angel. Did she think I was going to hit him while he was out? I turned away to calm down the girls. Junie was heartbroken because her special rocker was lying on the carpet in pieces. It said something about the Greyhorse family when the baby was worried about a stick of furniture instead of her father lying unconscious on the floor.

After she satisfied herself Dad was just stunned, Mom urged me to run away before he got up again. I couldn't leave her and my sisters with him. Not when he was in this kind of a temper. So I sat down and waited until he came to his senses – if he had any left in that rum soaked brain, that is.

Why had he called me a fucking little queer? Did he know about Carlos? No, if he knew where the studio was, he'd have wrecked it by now. Did I act queer ... you know, prance around, not quite a man or a woman either, for that matter? I wasn't as much of a stud as Carlos, but I wasn't swishy either. It must be because I never had girls around. When Matthew was growing up, he was always with a girl. Dad had never even seen me with one.

Should I go find a woman and pretend to be interested? Hell no. Who gave a damn what he thought. If a woman came along, that was okay. If she didn't, that was okay, too. Screw him and what he thought.

He started stirring quicker than I wanted. "You cold-cocked me, you bastard," he mumbled.

"What? I was supposed to just stand there and let you beat on me? No way. Not anymore. Those days are over."

"Didn't think you had it in you." That sounded halfway like a complement.

"I got that and more," I said in a worked-up voice. I hoped it sounded mean enough.

He made some threats, but his heart wasn't in it anymore. He kept his hands to himself all right, but he kept ordering everyone around and making

119

plans for things that would never happen. I wished with all my heart Mom hadn't brought him to our new apartment.

I didn't trust him not to club me to death while I slept, so I stayed in the studio the next few nights until he went off on another binge. The unintended result of sleeping there was that I got a lot of work done. Greenby took four more of my pieces, a couple of them in alabaster. I also sent Mr. Gresham a few small pieces out of the gypsum rock. He must have liked them fine because he paid more for them than anything else I'd ever sent him.

CHAPTER 18

Maricopa Stone supplied me with soapstone, so that's where I went to get my alabaster, as well. They found a source for the calcite kind, and I liked working with it better. Still intrigued by the Michelangelo marbles, I bought a good-sized slab of that material to experiment on. The task turned out to be a bigger deal than I expected; not only was marble heavier and clumsier to move – not to mention get through the door of the studio – but also I needed a different set of tools for working it. If I ever got serious about marble, I'd need a pneumatic chisel, but first, I wanted to work the stone the way the old master had done – with muscle and hard labor. Even so, I had to buy some tools: a subbia for the rough work, a three-tooth chisel for shaping curved surfaces, a couple of flat chisels, and a rasp. I made do with the hammer I used for the other materials for the time being.

Marble was hard and unforgiving. Mistakes were difficult, if not impossible, to correct. A chisel applied at the wrong angle could crack a block or even shatter it. I ended up with lots of broken pieces the first time I tried anything, but I used these scraps to master the techniques of smoothing and polishing the stone. It would take a long time before I was capable of producing anything of value from it – if ever.

# # # # #

Self-release wasn't doing the job anymore, so I pretty much kept my hands off myself except when things became unbearable. I got brave enough to go to one of the dirty book stores in a downtown neighborhood once, but I was embarrassed by the naked men and women on the magazine covers and uncomfortable with the stares of people in the store. I put some quarters in one of the video machines and watched some film, but there was a hole in one wall of my booth, and some guy stuck his hard cock through it. I got up and left while the film was still running and his thing was waving in the air.

Let's face it. I wasn't a predator. I didn't know how to go out and look for what I wanted. I started going to a nearby church and met a nice girl. I started a relationship with her, but that wasn't very satisfying. After a couple of months I even took her to bed, and while it was better than giving myself a hand job, it wasn't as good as with Carlos. Within minutes, I was hungering for something different. Nonetheless, I kept on seeing her.

Carey, that was the girl's name, sensed something was amiss, but I don't believe she figured out what it was. The relationship staggered on for six months before we called it quits. The night we made the decision to stop seeing one another, I took her home from the diner where we'd been eating. That's not quite right, she took herself home in her own car, but I rode along with her to make sure she got in the door safely. I usually did that and rode the bus back home. I think she would have let me come inside and make love one last time, but it was over, so it was time to cut it off. I wasn't as considerate to her as Carlos had been to me.

After I said goodbye at the door, I strolled back to a bus stop uncertain if public transportation was still available because it was later than usual. If the buses weren't running, it was a long hike home. Deciding to wait and see if one came along, I sat down on a bench and thought about things while I waited. My cock kept getting hard and going soft as my thoughts alternated between Carlos and Carey.

After thirty minutes, I decided to call a cab from the first phone booth I came across instead of walking. I was moving down the sidewalk looking for a telephone when a late model Ford Taurus pulled to a stop beside me.

"Miss the last bus?" a pleasant-faced man asked.

"Looks like it." I thought about another time a guy had stopped for me on the street.

"I'm going straight down Van Buren on the way to Mesa, if you want a lift. I'd be grateful for the company."

I took a good look at him, and he didn't seem weird or dangerous or anything. "Okay."

"Walter," he said as I slid into the passenger's seat with my arm stuck out. He pumped my hand twice and let it go.

"William." Since he didn't' give a second name, I didn't either.

He kept up the chatter for the first couple of miles, trying to make me relax, I guess. We learned a little about one another. I told him how long I'd been in Phoenix and that I wasn't married. I said I worked, but didn't explain what I did.

Walter was probably in his forties, a divorced white man who worked in a local insurance company. He was almost good-looking, but not quite. Pleasant, was more like it. He carried no real fat but was a little soft around the edges. He seemed like a pretty decent guy. Then I caught him glancing over at me a couple of times and knew what was coming.

"How come a good-looking guy like you hasn't been snapped up by some girl yet?"

"Broke up. Tonight as a matter of fact."

"Sorry."

I shrugged. "The breaks."

"Anything in the wings?"

"Nope."

"Look, I don't want to be offensive, but if you're feeling down or lonely or anything, we can spend some time together. I'm a good listener."

"Thanks. I'll be all right."

He let a few more blocks go by. "Again, I'm not trying to be pushy, but well, you're a really good-looking guy and I'd be happy to … spend some time with you."

Walter wasn't any better at chasing what he wanted than I was.

"Thanks for the offer, but I'll be all right. It wasn't a messy breakup or anything. It just sort of petered out."

"Oh." More silence. "Look, William, I'll level with you. You're one handsome son of a gun, and I'm really attracted to you. Oh shit, I said that out loud, didn't I? Please don't get mad or anything ...."

I almost laughed. "I'm not mad. I'm just not interested."

"I know I'm older than you and a little out of shape, but I could really take your mind off of your troubles."

Despite myself, I grinned. "It's not that. You seem like an all right guy, but I'm not used to being picked up off the street."

"I'll pick you up anywhere. Just tell me where."

I did laugh then, but he didn't mean it as a joke. He was sincere.

"I can make it worth your while." He was beginning to sound a little desperate. He looked at my crotch again. I had on tight jeans, and my fly pooched out like Carlos and I used to joke about. Sort of like that painting of me Jason had done.

"Thanks, but I don't need the money."

"I'm glad you're not getting pissed at me, but geez, I wish there was something I could say or do to make it interesting for you."

I didn't answer him, and he fell silent. After a half a mile, I thought of something. "Is it hard to learn to drive?"

"What? No, not hard at all. Why?"

"I never learned, but I'd like to. I don't have anybody to teach me or a car to learn on, and I don't want to go to one of those driving schools."

He straightened up in his seat. "I can teach you. Maybe we can make a deal." He gave sad sigh. "Hell, I'll teach you even if we can't. Just as an excuse to be around you."

"No. If you take your time and gas to teach me, you ought to get something in return. Maybe we can work something out, but it depends on what you want."

"I want to get my hands on you," he blurted.

"You don't expect me to do anything back?"

"You just turn me loose on you, that's all."

"There's more than one way you can mean that." I probably blushed. "What I mean is, I've gotta understand exactly what the deal is."

"You want me to spell it out?" He braked for a red light and cleared his throat nervously. "Okay, what about this. I take you home with me and strip you naked. I feel everything you've got. Then I suck on that big cock of yours until you come."

"How do you know it's big?"

He motioned toward my fly. I just hoped he wasn't disappointed when he saw the real thing. It looked bigger hiding behind the denim than it did in the flesh. Or that's the way it seemed to me, anyway.

"And that's all you'd expect?"

123

"That's enough. There's lots more I'd like to do, but that would be enough. If we decide on something else later, that'd be frosting on the cake."

"I won't," I warned him.

"Okay, it's enough. Deal?"

"I guess so.

"Can I feel it now?"

I started to protest, but my legs spread involuntarily. That was all the invitation he required. His warm hand pressed down on my fly. My thing responded immediately.

"Look," I said as he fondled me, "how are we going to do this? I mean, when will you teach me to drive? Where will we practice? How long will it take? And how many times do you want to do me?"

"Every day. Twice a day."

I laughed and closed my legs, imprisoning his hand. "Come on, that's not reasonable. You teach me to drive and help me get my driver's license, then I'll let you suck me."

"Aw, man, that's no good. It's going to take at least two weeks to learn to drive properly ... maybe longer. I'd go crazy before then."

"Okay, then once a week."

He eyed my basket. "Tell you what. After your first lesson, we'll go to my place, and you let me suck you. Then after next Friday's lesson we'll do it again. I'll blow you on Monday, and then the following Friday we'll go down to Motor Vehicles and get your license. You need a vehicle to take your driving test. You can use mine. Then we'll go home and do it again."

I decided not to try and whittle him down. What he proposed seemed fair. "All right, when do we start the lesson?"

"How about right now?"

I laughed again. "No, it's too late. You tell me what time to meet you tomorrow. How much time will we need?"

"About an hour for the lesson. And maybe another for the other. I'll buy us a steak or burger or something before we go to my place."

"What time?"

"Tomorrow at afternoon at six. We'll do a lesson a day except for the weekend. One more thing. I get to touch you anytime I want to. Except when there are people around, of course."

"I don't know ...."

"Come on, William. It's going to be hard to keep my hands off you. I'll try not to overdo it."

"Okay." I offered him a hand on it, and we decided on a place to meet the next evening. He wanted to pick me up at the apartment, but I didn't want him knowing where I lived. Besides, my dad might be home.

He felt and rubbed my crotch and my legs and my belly all the way down Van Buren. To tell the truth, I enjoyed it, except it left me standing on the street corner with a hard-on that wouldn't quit. I'd been tempted to tell him to get rid of it for me, but I'd made a bargain, and I like to stick to my bargains. Besides, I was afraid to let him know I needed it as much as he did.

CHAPTER 19

Junie started turning into a little Indian girl in buckskin and beaded moccasins the next morning as I made sketches to guide me in my work. Sketch was too strong a word for it, since I can't draw worth a damn. I just put enough lines on a piece of paper to guide me in what I was trying to do when the real subject can't sit still longer than two seconds at a stretch. I was tempted to try her in alabaster, but I wasn't confident enough in that medium yet, so I stayed with soapstone and wood and a little gold wire, coral, and bits of things to create a few highlights. Nola made a tiny turquoise necklace and some earrings to match for the piece. She was really getting good. Mr. Gresham took everything she sent him now.

I left the studio early to take a good long shower and scrape off the few bristles I had on my chin and upper lip. Dressed in my best clothes, I knew I'd look pretty good to Walter. I hoped he was a good teacher. Even though I was ten minutes early, he was already waiting in the parking lot where we'd agreed to meet. The relieved look he gave me said he'd been afraid I wouldn't show. If he only knew how reliable old William was, he would have been spared an anxious day.

"You didn't think I'd show up, did you?"

He ducked his head. "I wasn't sure. Sometimes …."

"Not me. My word's good."

He let loose a smile, and I realized that showing up wasn't the only thing worrying him. He'd been afraid I'd cheat on my promise even if I did keep the appointment.

Walter gave me a bunch of booklets he'd picked up at Motor Vehicle on traffic laws and the procedure for obtaining a license. Although I was eager to get started with the driving part, he insisted on reviewing everything thoroughly. When he was satisfied I understood the booklets, he drove to a big flat area south of town where we could drive without getting in anybody's way. He had me watch everything he did carefully before he put me behind the wheel. The actual driving wasn't very hard. His car had an automatic shift, so it just seemed like stop and go ... stop and go ... stop and go. Well, except for parking the way he wanted.

The hour seemed to whiz by in no time, but as soon as it did, Walter turned from a hard taskmaster into a shy guy wanting in my britches. He was dying to take off home and collect his payment, but he tried not to act too eager. After a while, I took pity on him.

"That was a pretty good lesson, Walter. You're a good teacher. I learned a lot." I hesitated, teasing him a bit, I guess. "How about a hamburger before we go to your place?"

He agreed, even insisting on paying for the hamburgers although I tried to buy my own. I found out he liked Miracle Whip on his burgers rather than Mayo, and preferred sweet pickles to dill. He told me a little about his insurance business, and I let him know I was a sculptor. That was the first time I'd ever described myself like that.

"Really? Have I seen any of your work?"

I took a bite of my burger and chewed a minute. "Don't think so. This Indian trader in Albuquerque takes my small stuff. A fellow in New York buys the bigger pieces."

"Hey, that sounds great. I'd like to see some of your work."

"It usually goes right to UPS as soon as I finish it, but I can hold one out to show you."

"Great. Maybe I can buy it."

I didn't know how I felt about that. I mean, it was okay he wanted to buy my work, but would it obligate me in any way?

"We'll see."

Walter lived in a house just before you got to Mesa. It wasn't a real big house, but it was neat and well-trimmed. I liked it, and I was beginning to like Walter, although I was nervous about what was coming up. This was different from the other times. I didn't have a real yen for him – not physically – and when you came right down to it, I was trading him something for teaching me to drive. It made me feel funny, but a bargain's a bargain.

He offered me a bathroom and a flannel robe. I took a piss, rinsed off my private parts in the sink, and then walked out to the bedroom in the robe. Poor Walter wasn't sure what to do, either. He'd taken off his shirt but kept on his pants. He didn't look bad for a guy his age. In fact, he'd kept himself in shape better than most. No real flab, just a little puffiness here and there.

When I stood in front of where he was sitting on his bed, he reached out and undid the belt to the robe. I shrugged my shoulders and it fell in a heap at my feet. Walter's eyes roved over my chest and belly and groin, but he seemed incapable of touching me. He stared at my cock so hard it moved a little.

After an awkward minute, he came awake and put his hands on my thighs, pulling me closer until his forehead rested on my abdomen. He moved slightly, and his nose pressed into my pubic hair. His lips touched my cock, and not much happened. Afraid I wasn't going to be able to go through with this, I closed my eyes and conjured an image of Carlos. I thought of Jason and David together, and the damned thing got rock hard.

Walter lost his shyness and took me into his mouth, bobbing up and down on me eagerly. I leaned into him, rolling him back onto the bed. I lay atop him now, my hard prick shoved all the way down his throat, my legs straddling his bare chest. Then we lost contact as I rolled sideways until I was lying on my back. He sat up to look at me.

"William," he said through a tight throat. "I can't believe it."

"Believe what?"

"That someone who looks like you would be here with someone who looks like me. I know we made a deal, but still …."

Some of my own vulnerability showed then. "I don't get with many people, and I sure don't get with anybody I don't like. So that makes it all right, doesn't it?"

"Does that mean you like me? At least a little."

"More and more as I get to know you. Now you woke the little guy up, are you going to put him back to sleep?"

He giggled. "I am, but I'm going to take my own sweet time doing it."

Walter turned me on my stomach and felt every inch of my skin, including between my buttocks. I clenched at first, but then relaxed and let him feel his way to my sphincter. He turned me on my back and explored me from head to toe. He felt me with his hands and then he did it all over again with his mouth and tongue.

When he spread my legs and took my balls into his mouth, I thought I would lose it right then. I almost said something, but he came up and gently took my glans into his mouth. He sucked me down his throat and then came out to the end to wash me with his tongue. I grabbed a handful of sheets and hung onto the bed as he started to work on me for real.

He had a little trouble taking all of me. It wasn't my length, but my cock was thick enough to make him work at it. He went at it patiently, and soon his lips were in my bush. Then he did something with his throat. He hummed and made it vibrate. It felt different in a good and exciting way.

While he bobbed up and down on my shaft, he caressed my testicles and explored my chest and belly with his hands. I tried to make it last, but it had been a while, so I came before I wanted. My balls drew up, and a little electrical tingle built up behind them. When it discharged, I shivered and shook like I was having a fit. My cum poured out of me – hot and thick and eager.

When my balls stopped delivering their load, he stayed down on me for a while longer, keeping up a slight sucking until I softened. Then he came up and looked at me.

"You were sensational." His face glowed.

"Thanks. That was great."

He looked down at the bed. He'd gone shy again. Still, he managed to ask a question. "I wasn't your first, was I?"

"No, but just about."

He gently rubbed my torso; I guess to extract the last bit of pleasure out of it for himself. "You probably want to go home now."

I took pity on him. "Let me clean up and get dressed, and then you can show me your house if you want."

He beamed. "I'd like to."

I spent almost another hour with Walter; probably trying to keep both of us from feeling like this was a flat trade-off, even though it was. He showed me a red Nissan Titan pickup he had in the garage and said we'd finish my driving lessons in the truck because it was a stick shift. I needed to know how to drive those, too, he insisted. It was one of those small trucks. It wasn't new, but it was 2005 model and seemed to have everything on it.

We were comfortable together by the time he took me back to the parking lot. I hiked home from there. Everything was calm when I arrived, so I read the driving brochures for a while and then went to bed where I mulled over what Walter and I had done together this evening. I decided I felt all right about it. Then I thought about Carlos and Jason and David. That called up recollections of Enrique and James. It took a little time to drop off to sleep, but it was an easy slipover for a change. I wasn't tensed up from wanting something and not knowing what it was.

# # # # #

I got a lot of work done that week even though I quit at five every day to get ready for my lessons. Walter was thorough. I learned how to drive on pavement and on dirt, and on dry roads and wet roads. We worked on controlling spins and braking too hard and the dynamics of taking curves. Sometimes he would get into the teaching and forget to touch me, and other times his hands were on me so much they got in the way of driving. When I complained about that, he just laughed and said I needed to learn how to drive that way, too.

Friday night, he got a little bolder. When I came out of his bathroom in the robe he'd laid out for me, he was sitting on the bed dressed just in his shorts and socks. Once again, he took me standing up, but I pushed him over on his back with me on top. This time, I didn't roll off. I stayed where I was and fucked his mouth. His hands roamed my thighs and buttocks and the back of my legs until I shuddered and came. It wasn't dramatic and intense like it had been with Carlos, but the ejaculation was pleasant, filled with sensations of warmth and release, heightened by the moist mouth encasing me. Finally I rolled over onto the bed.

He drew a deep breath, probably the first easy one since I rammed my cock down his throat. "No one's ever done it to me like that before," he said. "It was ... it was great."

"I liked it, too. I was afraid I was being too rough."

"No. Well, it was a little rougher than the other way, but I liked the difference. I don't know if I can explain it right, but when you lie on your back and I lean over you. It's just me doing it to you. Just now, you were participating instead of just letting me have my way."

"I guess I participate either way. At least, I do when I come."

"Yes, but there's a difference." He paused. "Can I ask about the men you've been with?"

I looked at him. He was propped on an elbow, studying my naked body, probably afraid to reach out for fear he'd chase me off.

"It's okay, you can touch me." His hand moved to my chest. "I was with one guy for three weekends. We sort of did what we just did." I hedged because I was only willing to share a little of my time with Jason. "He was my first time, and he knew it, so he took it easy. He was a great guy."

"Why did you stop seeing him?"

"We moved here." I didn't feel like telling him about David.

"Anybody else?"

"Well, this one guy and I fucked a couple of girls together and got curious about who had the biggest cock. Typical kid stuff, I guess." I didn't tell him I was nineteen at the time. "Anyway, when we measured, we got carried away and made each other come. You know, with the hand." I also wasn't about to admit how Enrique had conned me into blowing him.

"Just that once?"

"Yeah. We weren't friends after that. Embarrassed ourselves, I guess."

"Who won the contest?"

"What? Oh, you mean who was bigger? He was longer, but I was bigger around, so we never figured it out."

"Is that all?"

I paused to consider my answer. The subject of Carlos was still tender to the touch. "No, there's been one guy since I came to Phoenix. I saw him a couple of times."

He could probably tell from something in my voice he was on thin ice, so he started telling me about himself. He hadn't known he was gay when he married at eighteen, but things went wrong almost from the start when his wife's brother seduced him. Tears came to his eyes, but his marriage was long over, and he had come to terms with the fact he liked men, not women. He told me about a few of the men he had been with, and as I suspected, there hadn't been very many. I believe he was sincere when he said I was the best one he'd ever been with.

On the way back to the parking lot, he told me he was doing some remodeling on his house over the weekend. Figuring I could learn something, I volunteered to help out. He picked me up Saturday morning to help rewire and insulate his garage. I stripped to the waist and waded in to help. By the afternoon his hands spent more time on me than on the work, but the job was done. I was right; I had learned a lot, enough to insulate the studio and make it a lot more comfortable both in winter and summer.

When we finished, Walter wanted to go to bed, and I wouldn't have minded, but I kept to our original agreement because when I make a deal, I try to stick to it. I did let him put his mouth on me and suck at me through the denim of my pants just before we piled in the car to take me home.

131

I thought my plans were going to derail that next week because my dad went on a tear and was hanging around the apartment a lot. In fact, I was so worried I had Walter cut the lesson by fifteen minutes on Monday, which was a shame since we were in the truck – and driving a stick shift was a whole other ball game. I also put off our session in bed until the next day.

Dad was drunk and raising hell when I rushed home from the shortened driving lesson, but I stood up to him. This time he backed down. The girls went to the studio with me the next morning. He had disappeared when I checked on Mom at noon. He hadn't shown up by five-thirty, so I figured he was in some bar or the other, which meant he'd be gone for the night. So I went to my lesson – and my session – with Walter.

# # # # #

The rest of the week was a nervous but productive time. I shipped off two good pieces to Greenby, mastered a stick shift, and was ready for my driving test by Friday afternoon. Walter took off from work after lunch to take me to Motor Vehicle. Since he was in insurance, he had a contact at MVD who'd given him an application. We filled out the form before we went down to keep the appointment he'd made for me. I was comfortable enough with Walter now, so I didn't mind him seeing my address and last name on the application.

After we completed the form, he reared back and looked at me down his long nose. We were sitting at a picnic table in a little park not far from MVD.

"What are you going to do for a car when you get your license?"

"I'll buy me an old clunker somewhere."

"How much do you figure you can afford to spend?"

"Three ... thirty five hundred, somewhere in there."

"Can you go four?"

"If I had to. For the right car, that is."

"Would you need financing?"

"No. I sold a couple of good-sized pieces the other day. I can handle it."

"How about insurance. You're gonna need two ... three hundred down."

"I can handle it."

"Okay, here's the deal." He pulled some papers from the bottom of the pile he'd weighed down on the table with a rock. "The truck's yours for thirty two fifty. You need three hundred or better to register it and a couple of hundred for insurance."

I shook my head. "Walter, the truck's worth a lot more than that."

"I know, but I don't need it. There's nobody I'd rather have it than you."

"I'd like to have it, but I can pay what it's worth."

"Good. Then you can handle the thirty two fifty easy. The paper work's all done. You just need to sign it and go down to get your license and register your truck. I've got an insurance card already made out for you. As soon as you get your license, I can give it to you."

I would have argued some more, but he was so proud of helping me out that I gave in. But I had to be square with him, too.

"You know, that after tonight …."

His face fell. "I know. It's over. That doesn't mean we can't be friends."

"If you want to forget about the truck, I'll understand."

"No way. That truck is yours. Don't try to welsh on me."

I laughed. "Okay, you hooked me fair and square."

We went to the Motor Vehicle Department, and while the driving test was a little hard because I was nervous, the rest of it didn't take long. I hadn't expected to buy a truck on the spot, so I wasn't carrying enough cash to pay for registering the car. Walter had that covered, too. He paid the tab, and after that I drove my new truck to the studio where I kept my checkbook. He came inside with me, and I was sort of ashamed of the run-down shack until he spotted the piece I was working on. Then everything was all right.

"That's your work?"

I nodded as I looked at the almost finished bust. Carlos's face was straight out of my memory, but I'd managed to render his features in alabaster. It was Carlos staring back at the viewer, all right. It was the way he looked right after an orgasm, relaxed and with a lazy cast to his eyes. I was already torn between keeping it for myself or sending it to Greenby.

Walter caught on right away. "This is one of them. One of the guys you said you'd been with." He looked over at me, his eyes wide. "It's the guy you got with here in Phoenix, isn't it?"

I nodded again, still not saying anything.

"Sorry. Didn't mean to pry, but he's so beautiful, it just came out."

"It's okay. Yes, this is the man I met here. We got together more than I let on." I swallowed. "I'd probably still be seeing him if he hadn't met a girl."

"Oh, man, I'm sorry."

I believe he meant it. That was the kind of guy he was. I got my checkbook, and we went to the bank for a cashier's check so he'd know he had his money.

When we got to his place I phoned to make sure everything was all right at home, and then settled in to pay the rest of my debt to Walter. When I came out of the bathroom, he was standing at the edge of the bed, naked this time. His cock was long and kind of thin.

"I hope you don't mind." He was blushing.

"It's okay." I shrugged out of the robe.

He put his arms completely around my waist and pulled me to him. Then he tumbled me on the bed, twisting so that I landed on my back. He went a lot slower, this time, trying to draw everything out of it. He suckled my nipples and moved slowly down my body. He went around my cock, which was hard and hungry by now, and played with my testicles. He parted my legs and lifted them, exposing my backside. His tongue worked on all of my sensitive places.

Releasing me, he shyly asked me to turn over. I complied and felt his lips on my back. He tasted everything I had at least twice before he turned me back over and drew my cock into his mouth. After a few moments, he pulled me over on top of him. Everything I had was crammed down his throat.

Wanting this last time to be good for him, I took it easy, grinding my hips against him slowly, and withdrawing languidly. I froze once when he began that strange vibration of his throat muscles. Just like the first time, I think my cock got stiffer and bigger. Finally, I experienced the tingling in my sac that let me know things were becoming more urgent. I stopped caressing him with my tool and began fucking him with it.

When I came, the orgasm lasted for a long time, and I kept up my movements even beyond that. At last, I withdrew and sprawled back on the bed. He was up on his elbow in an instant.

"Oh, William ...." He choked off the words like he was suffering a loss. I reached out and drew him into the crook of my arm. He settled there with a soft sigh. We lay without talking for a few minutes.

"I ... love you." He whispered so low the words were but a shadow in the room. I gave him a slight squeeze to let him know I'd heard. His hand lay motionless on my chest.

After thirty minutes, I recovered enough to give Walter the surprise I had planned for him.

"Hand me the robe, please."

He was slow to hand it over, and I knew he thought I was about to get up and go. Instead, I took a small foil packet and a little plastic tube from one of the pockets and handed it to him. At the same time I rose and straddled his chest.

"Put that on me, will you? But first, you've got to get it hard for me again." I thrust my hips forward until my flaccid cock rested on his lips.

He looked at the condom without comprehension for second, and then the meaning of what I intended struck him. A big grin split his face. He happily sucked me into his mouth. He combined tongue action with that humming thing, and I reared up as hard as ever. He rolled on the lubricated rubber with nervous, clumsy fingers.

Then I moved back down his body and lifted his legs. His butt rose toward me. I squeezed the plastic tube of lube on his sphincter, and as I placed my sheathed penis against his ass, I caught his eye. He nodded, and I pressed into him. He parted and accepted me easily. I fucked him slowly, keeping a gentle rhythm going. His eyes closed and his mouth opened. He panted aloud.

After fifteen minutes of steady but leisurely thrusting, he reached for his own cock. I pushed his hand away, and increased my pace and my power. I drilled into him. I slapped against his flesh. I thrust so hard I penetrated a deeper place, causing him to open his eyes and gasp. I drove into him again and again until I could no longer hold back. I groaned as my sperm shot through me and into him. When I finally worked my way through my orgasm, I took him in my hand.

Walter gave a start of surprise as I began pumping him. He was circumcised, and I found it more difficult to jack off a cut penis, but he was so far gone he came almost immediately. He rolled his hips and arched his back and shot into the air. His internal muscles clenched and clasped and massaged, and I kept beating his butt with my cock until his climax was spent.

"William …." Again his words failed him. "I never expected anything so wonderful. I never expected you to be so much man."

I patted his cheek fondly and withdrew. "Can I use your shower?"

"You can use anything I've got." He was still on the bed panting.

I took my time, and when I finally emerged Walter was lying on his stomach crossways on the bed, his head handing over the edge. I remembered Jason lying on his stomach. Before Walter could rise, I knelt on the bed and donned a second condom. I parted his legs and took him from behind. Without speaking, I fed him my cock, faster and rougher than the first time. He lifted his ass to meet me, driving me deeper into him.

He stuffed a pillow beneath his groin and fucked it while I fucked him. It was pure, raw sex. He was a receptacle for my cock and my lust. I drove into him. I pounded him. I speared him. And I came in him. My sac poured cum in hard little spurts, and still I pounded his ass. Then I felt his muscles grab hold and work my exhausted cock as he had his own orgasm. For his sake, I kept at it until I fell exhausted against him. We lay that way for a few minutes, neither of us moving except to struggle for breath.

I dozed for a bit while lying beside him on the bed. I woke with a start, wondering where I was. Then it all came back, and I glanced over at him. He was staring at me. I don't believe he'd closed his eyes.

"You're even handsome when you sleep," he said in a serious tone. "Me, I go all slack and wake up with a dry mouth. That probably means I snore."

"I can't swear I don't," I said.

"You don't. You just lie there and look peaceful and serene and … sexy."

"Walter, you're a bullshitter."

"Oh, no. Every word's true, I swear."

"Well, I guess I need the shower again. Hope I don't send your water bill out of sight."

"You can send my water bill out of sight any time you want."

When I emerged naked from the bath, he watched silently as I dressed. When I was ready to leave, he put on a robe and walked me to the door. The tears in his eyes made me uncomfortable.

"William," he almost whispered. "I don't know how to thank you. You were more than I ever expected. You gave me something, not just took something from me. Nobody's ever done that for me before."

"Walter," I said before he went totally maudlin. "You were one hell of a lot more than I expected. Don't you understand? It was you. You drove me to give more than I intended. And it was good. Every minute of it."

He mustered a wan smile. "Liar. William, is there any possibility ...."

"Who knows? Maybe someday I'll get hot and bothered and give you a call."

"I hope so. I won't ever forget you. I meant what I said. I love you."

I swallowed hard and left quickly before I said something I didn't mean. As I drove home in my new truck – well, new to me – I thought back over the last few hours. Walter was a decent guy, and he wasn't girlish or embarrassing to be around. The sex was nice. Hell, the sex was good, but it wasn't the same as with Carlos. Or Even Jason. I wanted Carlos to last forever, and with Jason, I would have kept coming back until he told me to stop. Why couldn't I do the same with Walter? I didn't know. Maybe I'd call him one day when I was really horny. No, that would just be using him. I shrugged in the dark cab. We were using one another.

Deciding I was a stranger to myself, I tried to turn my thoughts elsewhere. It occurred to me I was driving a vehicle on my own for the first time. There wasn't anyone in the cab with me. It was me and the Titan and my new driver's license against the world.

I mentally hauled myself up short. Where was I going to keep my new truck so the old man wouldn't find it?

CHAPTER 20

I had continued to buy some of my supplies at AZC, so I ran into Carlos Quintana a couple of times over there. I looked forward to those casual meetings even though they cost more than they paid: thirty seconds of camaraderie followed by a long down-slide and a stone ache afterward. He wasn't there when I went in this morning. I asked about him, and was told he'd quit last week to follow his girl to Tucson. No one had heard from him since.

His sudden disappearance, plus missing Walter just a little bit drove me to work harder. It was tough on my personal life, but helpful to the professional. Pretty soon, it seemed like that was all I had. The personal Wilam didn't exist any more.

My father had virtually taken over the apartment I'd rented for the girls and my Mom, but there was nothing I could do about it as long as she refused to leave him. I kept my sisters with me at the studio most of the time. That meant I had to invest more money to make the place halfway habitable for the girls. I used what I'd learned at Walter's place to do a better job of insulating. I bought more comfortable furniture and made one corner of the big room into a living area.

Unwilling to go to the expense of installing a telephone in the studio, I bought one of those cellular phones and carried it around with me. I also got the property owner's permission to park my truck at the studio. So far, I'd managed to keep the Titan a secret from Mom and Dad. It was only a matter of time; however, since little Junie eventually told everything she knew. It was a miracle she hadn't blabbed about the studio yet.

In between working on pieces I could sell, I continued to experiment with the marble. It was the most difficult and exasperating of all the mediums, but I was determined to master it.

# # # # #

Greenby called me at the apartment one evening right after I'd almost got in another dust-up with my dad over roughing up my mom. I was a little breathless when I answered.

"Did I interrupt something?"

"Just me running for the phone."

"Well, I'm glad I caught you. I've got some wonderful news."

"What's that?"

"I have a commission for you."

"Commission?"

"An order for a particular piece a collector wants you to do for him. When you start getting commissions, you know you've arrived."

"What if I can't do what he wants me to?"

"Have a little faith in yourself, William. You can do it, okay."

"What does he want me to do?"

"He wants to meet you here in the gallery, so he can tell you face-to-face exactly what he wants."

"He wants me to come to New York?" My voice went up an octave.

"That's right. He's willing to stand the entire cost of the trip just to meet you."

"Can't you just tell me what he wants? You know, over the telephone?"

"Yes, but he wants to tell you, himself. So you have to act like you're hearing it for the first time from him. He wants a large figure of a warrior in his middle age ... a chief, maybe, sitting with a blanket around him sort of like he's smoking and speaking to someone opposite him. He wants it to be about half-size."

"You mean about half the size of an actual man?"

"Exactly."

"You just told me all I need to know. Why do I have to come to New York?"

"Because he wants to meet the artist he's commissioning. It's no big thing, William."

"I'm sorry, Mr. Greenby, but I can't come right now. I've got ... well, I've got family reasons why I can't come."

Greenby sounded disappointed. "It's a very generous commission. This is something you have to expect as you get to be known in the art world, son."

"Maybe later, but not right now."

"Would $10,000 change your mind?"

I hesitated before I answered. "No, sir. Please believe me. I'm not being stubborn. I just can't do it. Not right now. Like I say, it's a family thing. My father's causing some trouble, and I've got to stick around to see it doesn't get out of hand."

He sighed. "All right, let me see what I can do."

Before hanging up, I gave Greenby my new cell phone number and suggested he dial it from now on. Having to refuse his request left me depressed and ashamed. I would have liked to go to New York. I'd never been to the East Coast. My dislike of my father almost crystallized into hatred. I worked even harder for a couple of days.

Thursday, I let the girls go home after school because the old man had disappeared again. A little before four, my cell phone rang for the very first time.

"Good news," Greenby boomed in my ear. "Mr. Hartrand, our client, has agreed to come to Phoenix to meet you. He really likes your work. He must like it a lot to take time out of his busy schedule to meet you. He's flying back to New York from Los Angeles Friday evening. He'll layover in Phoenix and meet you at the Camelback Inn Saturday morning. I presume you can manage that okay."

It wasn't sarcasm, he was merely seeking confirmation I'd go meet the man. He was probably worried because he wasn't going to be there to make sure things went okay.

"Yes sir, I can do that. He's not going to expect to come see my studio, is he? It's just an old garage out behind somebody's house."

"I don't know the answer to that question. You'll have to handle that with him. He's a wealthy, powerful man, William, but he's also a reasonable one. Just talk to him the way you did to Gresham and me, and you'll get along fine."

"Something else. How will he want me to dress? I just have jeans and things like that. He's not going to expect me to show up in an Indian ribbon shirt and fringed buckskin trousers, is he?"

There was a noise on the other end of the wire that could have been a muffled laugh. "Dress like you did when you came to meet me. Don't worry yourself into a tizzy over this. Everything will be all right. Nobody expects a flamboyant, colorful artist like you see in the movies."

I let out a sigh. "Okay, I'll try. But if my work can't stand on its own, I sure as hell can't carry it off any other way."

# # # # #

Things stayed peaceful until Saturday, so I was able to go to the hotel without fretting too much about the girls or Mom. Dad was growing more violent, but Mom always refused to call the police – or allow us to do it. I was going to have to do something about the situation one day, but short of kidnapping Mom and running off in the middle of the night, I couldn't figure out what.

My heart was in my throat as I rapped on the door to Room 1215 at the Camelback. A hard-eyed, handsome blond man about thirty or so answered the knock, giving me a surprise. I figured he'd be older.

"Mr. Hartrand?" I asked uncertainly.

Blue eyes measured me in a single sweep. "No, I'm John Savage Davis, his aide. Who are you?"

"My name is William Greyhorse."

Surprise replaced suspicion in his eyes, and I would have bet money that didn't happen very often.

"You're Greyhorse? Hmmm, I expected someone older." I thought for a minute he was going to ask for an ID; instead he gave me the once over more slowly. He eyed the box I was carrying, and then stood aside, opening the door wider. "Come in; I'll let him know you're here."

Room 1215 turned out to be a suite, and I was left standing in the living room while Davis disappeared. A minute later, he trailed another man into the room.

Mr. Hartrand was just as I had pictured him. Not too tall, but not short. Broad-shouldered, silver-haired, and reeking of power and money. He gave me a genuine smile as he shook my hand.

"Mr. Greyhorse, it's a pleasure to meet you. Sorry you couldn't come to New York and spend some time tossing around a few ideas, but I understand prior commitments."

So that's what Greenby had told him. "Thank you, sir. And, my name's William."

He waited until we were seated to pick up the conversation: "Well, William, Greenby told me you were young, but I didn't realize just how young."

"Twenty-one," I answered the unasked question.

"Only twenty-one and putting out such fabulous work." He shook his head as if he couldn't believe it; then he got down to business. "I understand Greenby told you what I'm interested in."

"Yes, sir, but it would help if I could hear it from you and understand where the piece is going to be, the surroundings, I guess you'd say."

We spent three hours talking about the piece he wanted. He had a very firm idea of the work, but he was careful not to tie things down so tight I couldn't offer my own suggestions. When he said he wanted a chieftain, I was afraid he'd want one of those full headdresses like you see in John Wayne movies, but when I asked about it, he just said I knew more about those things than he did.

Since I don't draw very well, I had brought three small statuettes and a book with Polaroid pictures of all the things I'd done since my work had become art instead of whittling. He examined the pieces and looked at every picture carefully, pointing out things he particularly liked. He offered to buy the three statuettes, but when he sent his aide for a checkbook, I told him to work it out with Greenby Galleries when he got back to New York.

Davis interrupted us several times, twice to tell him they had to leave for the airport, but Mr. Hartrand waved him away and said to notify the pilots of a change in plans. I guess that meant he had his own airplane.

After he sent Davis packing, I asked a question. "I think I'll do the piece in alabaster, Mr. Hartrand. Have you given any thought as to the color you'd like?"

His eyebrows climbed. "I thought it was white? You know, like the alabaster skin you're always hearing about."

"A lot of it is white. When alabaster's found near iron oxide, it has a brown shade. Then there black alabaster. It's rare, but there's a place in Oklahoma where they mine it."

"What do you recommend?"

"Snow white."

"Go with it."

I hemmed and hawed when he asked me to have dinner with them. Mr. Hartrand was sharp; he caught on to the fact I didn't have the right clothes for most of the places Davis suggested. He steered us to a decent place where I didn't have to wear a suit and tie. Mentally, I resolved to do something about the clothes situation come Monday morning.

Right at the end of the dinner, Mr. Hartrand left the table for a private telephone call, leaving his aide and me alone at the table. Davis was looking at me through different eyes ... in a couple of ways. His high-powered boss spending hours with me, and even staying over another night, altered things in his eyes. I wasn't just another Indian punk hanging around rooting for scraps. We were peers, and he was having trouble dealing with that.

Especially with the other thing I saw in him. He wanted me. The desire was naked in his eyes. There's no doubt he would have been crude about approaching me, if the power structure hadn't changed. Now, he decided to be suave.

"You're awfully young to have cracked the New York art scene."

"Thanks."

He looked at me through cold, blue eyes. "Somebody like Mr. Hartrand could push you over the top."

"You think so?"

"I know so." He let a little silence grow. "I can see that he does."

"Why would you do that?"

"You get right to the point, don't you?"

"Seems to me you're the one who started this."

"Yes, I guess I did, at that. Okay, I'll answer your question. You're a handsome, sexy guy. I've seen enough of them – including movie stars – to know what I'm talking about. Some of them are better looking, I guess, but none of them are as sensual as you. You're a package of raw sex."

"Thanks ... I think."

He looked at me for a minute. "You think? That's it? Thanks ... you think?"

"Actually, I should have said, no thanks."

"What?"

"No, thanks. I'm not interested."

"Why not? Don't tell me you've never made it with another man."

"That's a personal question and none of your business."

"I'll take that as a yes. Well, you've never been with a man like me. I'll suck you like you've never been sucked. I've got the best tongue in the business. I'll give you a fuck like you've never been fucked. I'll rim you and ream you and leave you quivering."

So help me, he was beginning to get to me, but I instinctively knew it would be a terrible mistake to let him see it. "Like I said, not interested, but thanks all the same."

141

He wasn't deterred. "Have you ever had a man and a woman at the same time? I'll suck your cock while she sucks your ass. Then I'll fuck her with my big cock at the same time you fuck me with yours."

"Kind of a confusing picture, isn't it?"

Davis laughed harshly. I don't think he got turned down very often. At any rate, he wasn't very gracious about it. "You're probably right. I'd ruin it for you with everyone else."

Angered by his arrogance, I leaned forward and whispered savagely. "You got it backwards, pal. By the time I got through pounding your white ass with my red cock, you'd be a whimpering pile of yellow-haired shit."

His mouth hung open, his eyes went out of focus, and I realized I'd played into his game. I didn't understand it, but somehow he liked the rough stuff, the humiliation. It probably took that for him to get it off. In spite of the insight, I kept it up.

"I'll bet you've never had Indian cock, so you've never had a real man before. You don't want me in your bedroom, asshole, because after I whipped you with my cock, I'm just liable to beat all the cum I've left inside you out of your miserable body with my fists."

He gave a little moan, his eyelids drooped, and he hitched forward in his seat. Damned if I didn't think he'd creamed his pants.

"But you'll never know, because I'm not interested."

Suddenly his eyes came back into focus and shifted to the distance. "Here comes the boss," he said in a normal voice. He licked dry lips and gave me a pleased smile. "Maybe we'll do this again some other time."

"No, thanks. Don't worry, I'm not going to say anything to Mr. Hartrand."

He smiled easily. "Of course, not. What would he think of you bringing up something like that at the dinner table?"

The rest of the evening went fine. The commission was given. There was even a suggestion there might be follow-up work if he liked what I produced. We hit a glitch when he said Greenby Galleries needn't be involved in future work. I had to set that one straight.

"No, sir. Mr. Greenby set this up, and he's my gallery. Anything else we do ought to go through him, too."

A slight smile told me I'd just passed a test of some sort. "Then that's the way it will be. Thanks for taking the time to meet me. I like the concept we've come up with. I'm glad you made your own suggestions for the piece. You handle yourself well for someone your age."

And for an Indian, I mentally added, but even if he'd said it aloud, it wouldn't have been mean-spirited. He was paying me a compliment, so I accepted it. "Thank you, sir. I hope we meet again."

"Count on it, William. Count on it."

I stopped in the lobby to call home and make sure everything was all right. As I closed the cell phone, Davis exited the elevator and gave me a nasty grin.

"Waiting for me?" he asked.

"Nope, making a phone call."

"Setting up your date for the night since I turned you on?" His eyes played down my body and lingered on my crotch. I prayed I wouldn't get hard. He looked up and smiled again. "We'll see one another again, Billy Boy."

"If we do, I'll know the game you're playing. Tell me, how did you keep from soiling your britches?"

"You caught on, did you? It's called planning. You put on a rubber beforehand. That way if we play with words, I'm ready. Or if we play physically, I'm ready for that, too. Pretty impressive, don't you think. Not many men can shoot the moon just talking with a sexy hunk."

"If it wouldn't turn you on, I'd tell you how disgusting you are."

"I'm all ears ... well, almost," he said as I walked away. He was staring at my butt so hard my sphincter itched. I didn't relax until I passed safely through the doors and out of his line of sight.

CHAPTER 21

Greenby had already spoken to Hartrand when I phoned him Monday morning. Our client was pleased with the meeting, which meant Greenby was, too. I told him my supplier, Maricopa Stone, said it would take about ten days to deliver a block of alabaster big enough for the job. I promised to get started as soon as it arrived.

Later, as I walked to the studio with one eye behind me watching for my father, I reviewed our conversation and decided Greenby knew about Mr. Hartrand's offer to deal directly with me. He probably set up the thing to see if I had the same kind of loyalty to him I had to Mr. Gresham.

After planning the commission piece, I went downtown to the fanciest men's store I could find and bought the kind of clothing I'd need if Mr. Hartrand ever came back to town. Of course, I had to buy shoes, too, so I ended up spending a lot more money than I'd intended, but next time – if there was one – I could go to any swanky restaurant in town. Just as soon as I learned how to handle the knives and forks and spoons, that is. My only social skills at the moment were chewing with my mouth closed and using a napkin when my lips got greasy.

I decided to attempt to carve a mortar and pestle out of marble while waiting for delivery of the alabaster. The book on working with the stone said a mortar was the usual first piece for a beginner. Everything I'd done up to that point with the rock was simply trying out cutting and carving techniques. Even so, I'd already learned working marble was physically exhausting. That Michelangelo dude must have been one strong sucker. My mortar would be a bowl about eight inches high buttressed by some fancy scroll work on three sides, sort of like a baptismal font.

Before I'd made much progress, Maricopa delivered the alabaster block, and I had another problem. My studio was a converted garage with sealed double doors fronting onto an alley. When we couldn't get the stone through the regular door, I got the owner's permission to open them up again, so long as I kept the place pretty well airtight.

Even though Mr. Hartrand's commission was my first serious attempt at something that large in alabaster, the work took shape quickly. Or maybe that was merely by comparison with the marble I'd been laboring over. That was good, because I wanted to spend a lot of time on the details of Hartrand's chieftain.

Within a month, there was a forty-year-old Plains Indian sitting in my studio wrapped in a blanket, naked torso partially exposed as he held out a long ornamental calumet to the invisible person opposite him. One moccasin-clad foot and bare ankle protruded from the bottom of the blanket. All the details of the man were finished, and I had rubbed in oils to provide flesh tones in the otherwise beautiful white gypsum.

Only the intricate patterns of the blanket shrouding him and the decorations and quill work of the pipe remained to be done. These were the most difficult. If I made a mistake now, an expensive hunk of rock and a lot of hard work went down the drain.

I put in eighteen-hour days for a week to accomplish them, and that made me testy. Irritable. Even with Mom and the girls. My father showed up again, and in my mood, I was more than ready for a showdown. Fortunately, he left me alone.

After making a small but potentially bad mistake on the pattern of the blanket, which I corrected by creating a new fold in the material, I decided to take a break rather than risk ruining it with another mishap. I put away my tools and went home for a long, hot shower.

When the water cascading over my body gave me a roaring hard-on, I knew it was time to take care of other needs. My tired mind figured out that it was around mid-day on Saturday. Dad would be safely in a bar somewhere and probably wouldn't show up at the apartment until Sunday night or Monday morning. I got dressed and dialed my cell phone. Walter answered on the third ring.

"Walter, this is William. I need you."

"Tell me where to meet you."

"I'll come to you, if that's all right."

# # # # #

He couldn't hide his pleasure when I got out of the truck and walked up to the porch. He had the door open and his hand outstretched while I was ten yards away.

"God, it's good to see you, William. But you look terrible. Worn out."

"I am." I didn't explain, and he didn't press me.

"You need some sleep." He closed the door behind us.

"Yes, I do, but first I need to fuck you until your eyeballs rattle."

His face lit up. He took my hand and led me into the bedroom without saying another word. I'd forgotten to bring condoms, but he had some, admitting he bought them in the hope I'd come back someday. Now someday had arrived.

I screwed him on the bed, and when he shot off with me still inside him, I did it again, this time pounding him mercilessly. Afterward, he brought water and a warm towel and washed me as I lay exhausted. I was asleep before he finished.

I slept until around ten o'clock Saturday night. Then I stumbled out of bed, took a piss, and blundered into his living room naked. He looked up at me from the chair where he was reading and followed me back to the bedroom. This time, I took it easy and made it last a long time.

When it was over, he insisted on cleaning me up again. I sort of liked having him tend my needs while I relaxed on the bed. When he brought me a tray of food, I tried to cover up, but he pulled the sheet off me, so I ate on top of the covers. He inspected my naked limbs while I discovered how hungry I was.

"You know," he said at last. "I don't know which I like better."

I paused, a spoonful of soup halfway to my mouth. "What do you mean?"

"You went on a rampage, and I thought you were going to tear me a new asshole. I loved it. I thought nothing could be greater than the way you just grabbed hold of me and ripped it off."

I chuckled at that, spilling some of the soup on my chest. He wiped it off with a finger.

"But just now, you were so gentle I wanted to cry while you were doing it to me. I didn't want it to ever end, but when it did, it was like you were giving me your seed, giving me ... no, loving me with your cum. And that seemed better."

"Maybe each was what we needed at the time."

"Thank you for coming to me for relief."

His emotional response embarrassed me. I didn't say anything. After I finished eating, I called home to check on the situation there. Everything was okay, so I went right back to sleep. I vaguely heard Walter come to bed but didn't really wake up. At four in the morning, I woke with a hard-on. Blinking into the darkness, I saw the gleam of Walter's eyes. I pulled him to me, and he gently worked his way down to my groin and sucked the sperm out of my cock and balls. He didn't want to come, himself, but asked to sleep in my arms.

I didn't get dressed until I left Sunday evening. I'd fucked him two more times, once from behind and once with his legs resting on my shoulders, and he blew me once, although it was more like fucking because I was on top of him pounding his mouth brutally. The rest of the time, I slept in his bed or dozed in his chair while I tried to wade through the Sunday paper. When I prepared to leave that night, I was refreshed and rejuvenated; Walter looked like a wreck.

An attack of conscience struck before I stepped through his front door. "Walter, I'm sorry."

"For what?" he asked through bruised lips and a sore throat.

"I took advantage of you. I needed my sac drained and to get away from everything, so I came over here and imposed on you when ... when ...."

"When it isn't going to grow into anything more. I know that. You've always made that clear. Listen to me. I love you so much I'll take whatever part of you I can get. You can come over here and beat me with that big cock of yours anytime." He paused. "I'd like to ask you for one thing, and if you can't do it, I'll understand."

"What?"

He looked down at the floor and over at the TV and at my groin, and finally into my eyes. "Can I have a kiss? You've never kissed me. I've never wanted to kiss a man before, but then I've never known a man like you."

I moved into his arms. He kissed bashfully, lips half-open and barely touching mine. After a moment I drove my tongue into his mouth as far as it would go. When I released him, he seemed dizzy.

"Talk about rattling eyeballs. Thank you, William."

On the way home, I considered my relationship with Walter. He was a good man. He was decent looking. He was good sex. He liked me. Hell, he loved me. Why couldn't I muster some feelings? Something beyond just wanting my balls drained? What was wrong with me?

# # # # #

Two more weeks passed before I was satisfied with Mr. Hartrand's piece. When it was finished, I levered it onto a sturdy pallet mounted on four rubber wheels and moved it to a corner. I covered the statue with canvas and left it for another week.

After that, I took things easier for a while, spending some time with Mom and the girls, taking them places after school and spending a little money on them. Mom was doing better. She hardly ever drank around the house – which was the only place she ever drank – and looked healthier, even though the headaches still came and went occasionally. I couldn't remember the last time she'd passed out from drinking. As a result, the girls were prospering.

The old man must have been working some kind of deal because he came and went during the middle of the week, sometimes just stopping by to clean up or pick up clothes and sometimes to stay for a few days. He was close-mouthed, but his eyes took in everything. I saw him mentally calculating the cost of everything in the apartment. Thank God he didn't know about the red Nissan pickup yet.

Occasionally, I caught his dark, fathomless eyes studying me, and that made me nervous. Maybe he was thinking about selling me as a sex slave. Get serious, William. Nonetheless, perhaps I should take a little more interest in what he was doing. If we were lucky, it might be something that would get him put away behind bars for a long time.

I sucked in my breath. Was I the kind of man who'd go looking for a way to put his own father in jail? No, but I was the kind of man who'd do anything to protect his sisters – and his mom.

I took to watching him closer after that, and what I saw made me sad. Sometimes, I could still see the handsome man he'd been before the drink took over. If I stretched my memory, I could recall times as a child when he was good to be around. I could remember Matthew and him hunting and fishing

MARK WILDYR

together before the stories turned to them drinking together. Fearful of what I might someday have to do, I tried to ease things between us. I hinted about going with him to a bar one night. That got me nowhere.

"You a drinker? Shit, Wilam, you got drunk one time and figure you can drink with men?" So Mom had told him about my lapse. "You don't have the balls to stand at a bar tossing down liquor with real men. You're nothing but a fucking queer, and I don't want you in any bar I go to."

There it was again – queer. It was as big a surprise as the first time. I was shocked to find my fists balled. "Why did you say that?"

He laughed in my face. "Have you even fucked a girl yet? None of them ever come around here. You whittle and play mommy to your sisters. Nothing but a pussy does that."

I felt my face go red. "Or a father. I look after my sisters because nobody else does. That's what a man does. He takes care of his family. He doesn't go running around drinking up the grocery money and come back begging his son for more. If that's what you call a man, then you're right. I'm no man."

I turned around and left the apartment before we went for one another's throats. Within ten steps, I was more sad than angry. If he ever had feelings for me, they were gone, washed away in envy and jealousy and alcohol. He hated me because I was trying to make something better for myself and because I was stepping on his toes by taking care of his family. One day, he would hurt me for that. In my heart and in my mind, I knew he would kill me or cripple me one day. If I hung around, that is. The realization didn't frighten me; it just depressed me.

# # # # #

The following week, I uncovered the commissioned piece, and it still looked good to my critical eye. I did a couple of minor adjustments in the folds of the blanket around the chief's shoulders and then made arrangements with a trucking company to pick up the sculpture and ship it in accordance with Mr. Hartrand's instructions. I sent pictures of the finished product to Greenby with a copy of the shipping receipt together with three smaller works I'd finished while waiting to take the critical second look at Hartrand's chief.

The truck had no sooner left than there was a knock on the studio door. It was a hard knock, and that put me on my guard. Had the old man finally tracked me down? But when I opened the door, someone far more welcome stood there with a grin on his face.

"Carlos!" I almost gave him a hug but restrained myself. He was standing out there in the open, even if that was the back yard of a neighbor's house. Instead, I grabbed his outstretched hand and pulled him inside.

"Hey, Indio. How they hanging?"

"Not so low since I got a look at you." Afraid I'd blundered, I rambled on. "I thought you were in Tucson or somewhere."

149

That earned me a frown. "Yeah, I was." The sunny side of him surfaced again. "But I'm here now."

"I thought …." I was talking too much about the wrong things.

"You thought I was down there living in bliss with my girlfriend."

"Lydia. Wasn't her name Lydia?"

"Yeah, but that didn't work out."

"So you moved back to Phoenix?" My heart took off.

"Just visiting my folks, looking up a few buds. Thinking about what to do next."

"How about moving back here permanently?"

He shrugged, a sexy gesture. "Thinking about it. How about you? You still making sculpture?"

"Yeah. That's my gig for the rest of my life, I guess."

"You got any more hunky dudes with cocks behind their granite buckskins?"

"Shipped off my last one," I said. "But I can start another one right now. You want to strip and pose for me?"

"Don't mind stripping, but I don't know about posing."

We met in the middle of the room. It more was more of a collision than a hug. His mouth sought mine so desperately it took me by surprise. He stripped off my shirt and had my fly undone almost before I moved. In moments, we both stood nude, frankly examining one another as if it were the first time. His cock throbbed in the air before him. Mine was rapidly rising. He reached down and retrieved a small bottle from his shirt pocket and then led me to the pallet in the corner.

As we lay down, it was clear he considered himself in charge. That was all right with me. At that moment, I'd have done anything he asked. Anything.

"Wanna try something new?"

"Yeah, sure."

He got up on his elbow, opened the bottle, and poured a small amount of liquid into his palm. Then he smeared some kind of clear oil with a subtle, musky odor all over my body. He turned me over and kneaded it into my back, down to my waist, and over my buttocks and legs. I almost came just lying there. Somebody was making cooing noises. I was surprised to discover it was me.

He lay atop my back, and I felt the warm throb of his long cock against my crack. I thought for a minute he was going to take me, but he merely moved his hips so that he rode the length of my buns.

"Mmm," he sighed. "Feels good." He rolled over onto his back and handed me the bottle. "Do me, will you?"

Lubricating him with that warm, slick oil was as erotic as almost anything I'd ever done. I felt the strength of his muscles, the resilience of his skin. His warmth. His overt sensuality. His essence.

150

When I finished, he pulled me atop him and began moving his hips. He drove his cock up my belly on a slippery film of oil. He hooked his legs over mine and drew my head to him. He ground his lips against mine, forced open my mouth, and fucked me with his tongue. Caught up in his passion, I began hunching against him, countering his thrusts with mine. We were both breathless when I pulled my lips away. The little studio echoed with the sound of our gasps and the slap of one oiled body against another.

I didn't want it to end, but I needed the explosion of a climax. His eyes closed, and his mouth opened to emit a little moan. We came in simultaneous orgasms so powerful we sounded like we were in pain. I collapsed, spent and exhausted, my head resting in the crook of his neck. No one spoke in the long minutes before our breathing became less labored.

Finally, he laughed and tipped me off him. "I was afraid of that."

"Afraid of what?"

"Afraid it was that good. I was halfway hoping I'd remembered it wrong."

"Why?"

He turned over on his side and leveled his eyes at me. They were mostly brown with little green and orange flecks. "Because I don't want to be queer."

I blinked. "How … how …."

"How could I not be?" He touched my cheek and traced my jaw line. "If I squint my eyes, I can almost imagine you're a girl, you know that? You're pretty like one. When I open them up wide, I see you're not. You've got too much man in your face to be a girl." He moved his hand over my chest and down my belly. His fist closed around my cock. "And when I get here, there's no way I can pretend you're one. What bothers me the most is I don't want you to be a girl. I like it you're a man. So answer me, am I queer?"

"You'll have to answer that for yourself. I've struggled with that question for a long time."

"Have your reached any conclusion?" He stroked my testicles.

"Yes, I have. Accepted it, you know. I'm gay. I dream of you, not some girl. Nothing I've ever done with a girl compares with what we just did."

A sad, frightened look came over him. He drew a shaky breath. "You know, if we went any further – you know what I mean – I think I'd be lost."

"You mean if I sucked you or if you fucked me." I used the terms deliberately.

His eyes flicked to mine. "Yeah, that's what I mean. I almost did, you know. When I got on your back and was rubbing you with my cock, I almost went for it."

"I'd have let you."

He shuddered and closed his eyes. "I'm glad I didn't know. I don't want to be queer, Wilam. I want to be a normal guy with a wife and two and a half kids and …."

151

"I know. I fought that battle."

"I gotta go, man." He jumped up and started grabbing his clothes. "I gotta go or I'm going to fuck you and …." He stopped and turned to face me. "I'm going to make love to you, and I'm not ready for that."

He left then, without telling me his plans, without providing a way to contact him, without giving me any reason to hope. He did take the cell phone number I scribbled on a piece of paper while he put on his boots.

Still naked, I sprawled atop the pallet and fucked the pillow until I came, trying desperately to recapture his warmth, his musk, and his touch. My orgasm was disappointing.

CHAPTER 22

I tried to keep busy as I waited for Carlos to contact me again. By the end of the week, I drove over to AZC to see if anybody knew how to get in touch with him. A couple of guys said he was still in town, but nobody had any contact information. I considered getting in the truck and haunting the area where his parents lived. No, that wouldn't be right. It was his decision to make. Every time my cell phone rang, my fingers grew clumsy, and I damned near dropped the thing before I could flip it open. It was never Carlos.

Greenby called to say he'd talked with Hartrand, who was pleased with the sculpture of the chieftain. A week ago, that would have meant something, but now it was only mildly exciting. So was the $10,000 he was sending to my bank.

School ended, which meant my sisters would be home all day. The old man had been getting wilder and more outrageous in his behavior. I'd have to keep the girls with me this summer.

And then, my world shifted – again.

I came home from the studio Saturday night around eight. Saturday is one of the safe days because my dad is at a bar pretty much full time over the weekends. This was the one Saturday when I should have been home. I heard screaming before I even got to the front door. As I rushed into the apartment, I saw Junie crouched in a corner hiding her eyes behind little fists and wailing like the furies were after her. Mom was half-lying, half-sitting on the sofa, holding her right eye with one hand. She was trying to get up, but wasn't having much luck. Terrified cries came from the bedroom.

Ignoring Mom, I raced down the hall and halted in my tracks. My father held Nola pinned to the bed with one hand. He had ripped off her clothes and was fumbling with his fly. Before I could move, he pulled out his thick cock and drunkenly offered it to his daughter.

"Suck me, baby," he slurred.

I rushed forward, putting everything I had into a blow to the back of his head. He staggered and almost fell on top of Nola. He recovered his balance, shook his head, and turned to see what had happened. His eyes went flat when he saw me.

"Matter?" he mumbled. "Jealous. 'Kay, you can have it."

I went in low. My rush carried us clear across the mattress and dumped us into the narrow space between the bed frame and the wall. I landed on top and punched at him in a killing rage. My dad was a bar brawler, and like a lot of them, he's hard to hurt when he's really drunk. He absorbed the heaviest blows I could deliver almost without a grunt.

Then he threw me off him, and when I fell against the mattress, he began doing what he'd done a thousand times, tossing his fists. He was too unsteady to be accurate, but he hit me enough so I felt it. Getting desperate, I kicked the cock still hanging out of his fly. Hurt, he doubled over, allowing me time to get to my feet in the middle of the room. He straightened up and staggered around the end of the bed.

I had to find more room so I could maneuver. Or maybe less, so he couldn't. Nola cowered naked in a corner as I started backing out of the bedroom. I tried making a stand in the narrow hallway. His head was too hard, so I worked on his belly. It might have looked soft, but he took a lot of punishment without seeming to flag. Then he got past my defenses and rocked me with a solid punch to the jaw. I reeled backwards but managed to stay on my feet.

When I looked into his eyes, my blood almost stopped flowing. He had come out of his stupor. He knew who he was fighting even if he didn't know why. But he liked it. His time had come. He grinned through the blood staining his lips. He was going to kill me unless I could stop him.

He backed me into the living room. I got in some telling punches when he tried to get close for a bear hug. If he ever got his arms around me, it was all over. I changed tactics; dancing and bobbing like a boxer, but my wind was going. This wheezy, alcoholic wreck was going to outlast me. I got desperate, and that was dangerous.

I watched his eyes. Suddenly, he lunged, but I was ready. I sidestepped him, clasped both fists together, and pivoted like a baseball player swinging a bat. My knuckles caught him on the right temple. He faltered. Then he dropped. So did I. If he had anything left, I was a dead man. But he lay like a felled tree.

Mom ran to him crying his name. Why him? Why not me? I was her son, and he'd tried to kill me. Nola, now covered with a robe, and Little Junie rushed to my side, fussing over me and trying to get me to my feet. I gave each of them a pat with a hand that weighed a hundred pounds. Then my vision went blurry. I probably slipped into unconsciousness for a few seconds, because the next thing I remember was Nola pressing a cold, wet cloth to my forehead. The girls helped me get up onto the couch where I sprawled like a boneless rubber chicken until I began to get a little control over my muscles.

Suddenly Mom was at my side, making caring noises. If I could have spoken in anything other than a wheeze, I'd have told her to go back to the drunken brute she cared about. Then I realized she'd checked him to see if I had done any permanent damage – the kind the law might be interested in.

"Son." She patted my cheek to get my attention. "You got to get outa here. When he wakes up one of you's gonna get killed. He's got a gun."

"Yeah … hunting …." I gave up.

"Not his rifle. A pistol. He brought it home with him. You have to leave."

"Can't. Girls. You, too."

"You take the girls. Go somewhere safe. Hurry and get out."

"Sorry ... can't ... hurry."

Thank God the old man was really out of it because it took me fifteen minutes before I got my legs to working. When I staggered over to the phone to call the cops, Mom jerked the instrument out of my hand.

"Get away and leave me alone." I yelled in a voice I didn't recognize. "I'm going to call the cops. He gave you a black eye, and he was trying to rape his own daughter. Your daughter. I'm calling them."

"You can't do that. He's your father. He didn't know what he was doing. He won't even remember it when he sobers up."

"No, but Nola will. For the rest of her life."

I got mad. I ranted and raved, but she was adamant. I felt less of a man because I wasn't able to do it in spite of her objections. That meant we had to get out of there.

I started collecting all of my personal possessions and sent Nola to pack hers and little Junie's stuff. I wasn't about to leave either of them in this house of degradation.

We begged Mom to come with us, but she said somebody had to be here to take care of Woodie. I seriously considered removing her by force, but her headache was coming back, and I was afraid to add any more stress. Frankly, at that moment, I wasn't up for another row. She could have put me down all by herself.

The girls were crying and hugging their mother when I staggered the half-mile to my studio. I drove the Titan back to the apartment and threw our things in the truck bed. As we started to leave, Mom stopped me with a kiss – the first one I could ever remember – and told me how proud she was of me. I started to argue about going with us again, but she laid her hand across my lips.

Surrendering to the inevitable, I gave her my cell phone number, which I hadn't shared until now, and asked her to call as soon as she knew Dad was all right. I didn't want to be responsible for killing him – no matter that I'd tried doing just that a few minutes ago.

Both girls were still bawling when I bundled them into the pickup and drove across town to a motel that didn't look like it cost too much. We took a big room with two queen-sized beds to wait out the call from Mom.

When I finally got Nola to talk about it, she said Dad had tried to get to her before, but she'd always stopped him by getting loud and getting physical. This time, it didn't faze him. When Mom had tried to get between them, he'd backhanded her and dragged Nola into the bedroom. If I had come home five minutes later .... Well, I shuddered to think about that. Poor Nola was more mortified by me seeing her naked than by anything else. I told her I'd been too busy to notice. I finally got them to bed that night, but nobody got much sleep. I think we were all waiting for the phone to ring, but it never did.

# # # # #

It would be a miracle if Woodie didn't have a pretty good idea where my studio was, so Sunday afternoon, I went over to clean it out. I scrunched down in the seat as I drove by the apartment. The Dodge was sitting at the curb; Woodie was home. Everything was quiet; however, as I turned down the alley and parked beside the shack. I sat in the truck a few minutes, trying to see if there was any sign he'd been here. The door was still locked, and when I slipped inside, everything was as I'd left it.

I had to abandon a lot of my unworked stone, but I managed to load the unfinished mortar and everything else into the bed of my truck. It was beyond the capacity of the springs by the time I finished. Then I knocked on the door of the house in front of the studio and gave the keys to the woman who came to the door. I told her I was leaving my $400 air conditioner in payment for the short notice and the fact I hadn't cleaned up the place.

I spent Monday in the motel room waiting for Mom's call. The phone didn't ring until later that afternoon, and by that time, I was about to go crazy with worry.

Mom claimed she was all right. From the sound of her voice, she was worried but probably not hurt. Woodie had gotten up off the floor about an hour after we left with a hell of a headache. After waving around his pistol and ranting a little, it dawned on him the girls and I were gone. He ran outside and emptied the revolver into the air before collapsing in bed to sleep off the liquor and the effects of the fight. She said it was a miracle the cops didn't show up at the door after all that shooting. It wasn't a miracle – it was damned bad luck.

Sunday, he'd gone on a rampage again. He dragged her with him and ran around the neighborhood until he found my studio – probably right after I left. He knew I had a truck, too, but Mom claimed she told him the wrong color. I wasn't sure that was true; she was putty in his hands. He'd take it out on her when he wasn't able to lay his hands on me, so she'd do what she had to. The fact I'd caught him trying to rape his own daughter was the last straw. The family was now torn in half, and nothing would ever put it right again.

Since Woodie was gone from the apartment, I took a chance and drove over as soon as Mom hung up the telephone. She about panicked when I came through the door, but I told her we had to make some plans. She was afraid for me to stay in the house, so we drove back to the motel. The girls went off on another crying jag as soon as they saw her, but she sat on the edge of the bed and settled them down. They hung onto her while we talked.

"Son, you have to take the girls and get out of town. Someday he'll run across you if you don't. If he does, something bad will happen. Can't neither one of you afford that."

"I'll go if you'll come with us. You don't even have to go back to the apartment for anything. I'll buy you a new wardrobe. Whatever you need." Desperate, I added something I shouldn't have. "I'll buy you a bottle. A case even. How about that, a case of Old Crow."

The look in her eyes was like a slap in the face. "I don't have time for that right now." She drew a breath, fighting demon rum with everything she had. "I have to make sure you're safe, and then I have to go take care of your father."

After an hour of arguing, I was convinced she meant what she said. She was not going to leave the man she had married, no matter what. At my urging, she phoned Aunt Aurora back in Rolling Hills and halfway explained the situation. I took the phone out of her hand and told it like it was. My aunt's response surprised me.

"We've been expecting this call for years, Wilam. A long time ago we decided Clara would take Cora's children when the time came."

"How did you know?"

"It was coming. It was just a matter of when. It's a shame, son. I wish you could have seen your mother and father when they were young. She was so pretty, and he was so handsome. You look an awful lot like he did. I don't know when it went wrong. Woodie always liked his whiskey, but he handled it okay. And he made a good husband for Cora and father for you kids – at first. I've seen lots of men take to drink before, but I've never seen them surrender to it all of a sudden like he did. It probably had something to do with his experiences in the army."

"Woodie was in the army?"

She paused. "Yes, but only for a little while. He got sent home for some reason. Had to do with some kind of assault charge. When he came back, his drinking changed. He got Cora hooked on it, too. Anyway, I'll call Clara in Denver and let her know you're on your way. How will you be coming? Do you need traveling money?"

"No, ma'am. We're all right for money. I'll drive up in my truck. I'm going through Albuquerque and spend a day or so there. There's just one thing."

"What is it, honey?"

"Mom. She says she won't come. She's going to stay with him."

"Yes, I expect she will. I'll try talking to her, but you remember those little girls. That's who we have to think of first. You sound like you can take care of yourself."

"Yes, ma'am. And I can take care of the girls, too. I might need some help now and then – you know, sitting Junie sometimes. Things like that."

"William," she abandoned the pet name, "I know you've done the bulk of caring for your sisters ever since you were in short pants. They need a mother, and you need your life. No, the girls have to go to Clara in Denver."

"She's married to a white man."

"Darin Holiday may be a white man, but he works for the BIA and he's married to an Indian and he's got two blood children. He chooses to live his life around us, Wilam. He's a good man, and he'll treat Nola and Junie like they're his own."

My heart underwent another wrench. I'd been pacing the room, but now I sat down. "I don't know if I can."

"Of course, you can. Stay in Denver with them, if you want. Get your own place and be near the girls."

"I'd planned on coming back to the reservation."

"Then do it. Come on up. You can stay with us until you decide what you want to do. Or your old house is vacant. Uncle Dulce will see if he can get it turned over to you. Of course, it's in pretty bad shape."

"I'll try to figure it out. Can you talk to Mom? If you tell her we can have our old place back, maybe she'll change her mind."

They talked for fifteen minutes, most of the time in our native tongue, which I didn't understand very well. At the end of that, Mom handed the phone back to me.

"I'm sorry, Wilam. She won't budge."

"I could force her."

"She'd just run back to him the first chance she had."

"I don't understand it. He treats her like crap." I sighed and gave up. "When you call Aunt Clara, tell her it'll just be the girls staying with her. I'll hang around a couple of days till they're settled, and then I'm coming home."

"We have a room you can use."

"Thank you, ma'am, but I'll be on my own. If Uncle Dulce can get our old house for me, I'll move in right away."

We took care of some housekeeping things like telephone numbers, vital statistics on the girls and the like. Fifteen minutes after we closed the conversation the telephone rang again. It was Aunt Clara – whom I hardly remembered – saying she was looking forward to seeing us. She had a talk with mom, but with no better results.

I left Nola to look after Junie while I dropped mom off near the apartment. On the way, I asked her what Woodie had done to get himself thrown out of the army. She went real quiet, but eventually, she answered.

"He wouldn't talk about it much, but there was this other man, somebody over him – you know, outranking him – in his outfit. Anyway, the man wanted to do things with him."

"What kind of things?"

She looked away from me and stared out the window. "Things you don't talk about."

"Abuse him, you mean? Sexually abuse him?"

"That's what I figure."

Stunned, I shut up to consider what I'd learned. It might explain things. A lot of things. When I let her off a couple of blocks from the apartment, I promised to pay the rent for the next six months and prepay the utilities, telephone, and cable. She thanked me and said not to worry about her. She'd be all right.

Just before she walked away, she looked at me through hooded eyes. "Son, about that case of Old Crow."

"Only if you come with us, Mom."

"I can't do that, but it sure would help me."

"Only if you come with us."

She sighed aloud. "Take good care of your sisters."

Something tugged at my guts as I watched her walk slowly back toward whatever fate had in store for her.

# # # # #

Surprisingly, little Junie didn't put up a fuss when she found we were leaving without Mom. In truth, Nola and I had been more of a mother and father than either of her real parents. The problem would come when I left for the reservation.

The next morning was spent closing my bank account, calling Greenby to let him know I was relocating, and informing Mr. Gresham we would be in Albuquerque sometime tomorrow. He promised to reserve us a room at the Classic since I was a man of means nowadays.

The pickup handled well on the highway, and I was looking forward to an uneventful trip. Nola got awfully quiet as we cleared the Phoenix metropolitan area and breezed down I-40. She was finally coming to grips with the fact she was leaving her mother ... maybe forever. Junie, taking her cue from her sister, began to droop. I tried to get them interested in some road games like finding all the letters of the alphabet on roadside signs and counting license plates from different states, but my attempts flopped.

My phone rang, and the girls perked up, probably hoping it was Mom telling us to come back. I whipped off the upcoming exit ramp and pulled to a halt on a dirt road before answering.

"Hey, Indio, where are you? I'm at your studio. The door's broke down, and the place is trashed. You okay?"

"Carlos?" My mouth went dry. I told the girls to get out and stretch their legs but to stay off the roadway. As soon as they left, I spoke into the phone again. "Yeah, that's no surprise. My old man went crazy, and we got into it. I had to clear out the studio. It was bad, man."

"No shit? If you don't have the studio any more, where are we going to do it?"

My heart actually hurt as it tried to go in two different directions – soaring for the moon and dropping into the pit. He was back. Carlos was back.

"I'm ready to do it, man," he said. "Go all the way. No turning back, like they say. You ready for that?"

I swallowed and glanced at the girls strolling hand in hand ahead of me at the edge of the dirt road. "More than ready, man. I want you. I want you every way I can have you."

"Then get that hunky ass on over here. We'll rent a motel room or something. I want you, too, Wilam. More'n I ever wanted anybody. Does that sound like I made up my mind, bro?"

"Yes. It does. But …."

"But?"

I glanced at the girls strolling back toward the truck. Responsibility was a heartless bitch.

"I'm on the road, Carlos. It got so bad I hurt my old man. I had to leave."

"Aw, shit! Well, turn around, and come on back. I went through a lot to get up the nerve to call you. But I'm ready man. I'm ready to come all the way over. Translation: I want to fuck your ass. It's a hell of a nice ass, by the way."

My head throbbed. My lungs burned. The air was so thick I could hardly inhale. "Man, you don't know how good that sounds, but … but I'm committed. I've got the girls with me. I'm dropping them off in Denver with an aunt and uncle. Then I'm going on to the reservation. You come on up, and there won't be anybody to get in between us. I've got a place of my own up there."

"I don't know, man."

"I'll pay your way. Tell me where to send the money. I'll cover everything, Carlos. Please. I need you, man."

I held my breath while the phone went silent for thirty seconds.

"It's a sign, Wilam."

"What?"

"It's a sign. I've been wrestling over this thing. I mean, really fighting it. Then when I make up my mind, you're gone. It's a sign. A warning I was about to make a big mistake."

"No, it's not. That's not it at all. It'll be better up there, you'll see. Look, when I drop the girls off in Denver, I'll drive back and pick you up. We'll have a hell of a trip, and when we get there we'll have our own place."

"Sorry, man. It wasn't meant to be." The phone went dead.

Numb, I sat for a minute with my forehead on the steering wheel, feeling hollow all over. I pulled air into my lungs in shallow gasps.

"Wilam, are you all right?"

I swiped the moisture from my eyes and looked around. Half blind, I had trouble finding Nola standing right beside my open window. When I could finally see, she looked so solemn and wise, I wondered who she really was … down deep inside. I lifted a hand that weighed a ton to the door handle. Nola moved back as I practically fell out of the cab. She grabbed my arm when I stumbled.

"I'm okay, sis. Really."

"No, you're not. That was Carlos, wasn't it?" I nodded. "Do you love him?"

160

Stunned, I looked at my little sister. She wasn't so little any more. She was beginning to develop into a young woman. Her question shook me, but I owed her honesty.

"Yes."

"And now you have to leave him. Because of us."

"Don't go taking that load on yourself. It's because of Woodie that we have to run away." I met her eyes briefly. "When did you figure it out? About Carlos, I mean?"

"You always brightened up when you heard his name. You'd get all happy when he came to visit at the studio. I wondered if it would ever happen to me."

I had trouble speaking. "Don't you brighten up when you hear your friends' names?"

Her answer tugged at my heart. "I don't have any friends, Wilam."

I hugged her to me. "You will, honey. You will. When you get to Uncle Darin's and Aunt Clara's, you'll have a normal life. You'll have friends and boyfriends and a family that loves you. It'll be all right."

"I already have a family that loves me. You and Junie. You won't have anyone, not up there on the reservation."

"There's Uncle Dulce and Aunt Aurora."

"That's not enough, is it?"

I had no answer, so I held onto her in silence.

"Wilam, I don't think any less of you."

I gulped. "About what?"

"About loving another man."

CHAPTER 23

I drove like crazy all night. I had to, or I'd have turned around to go hunt for Carlos. The thing that kept me heading east was the gut knowledge he wouldn't go through with it. He took that sign business seriously. So I kept my foot on the accelerator hard enough to earn a whole bunch of speeding tickets. I didn't even see a cop, much less collect a traffic fine. It was hard on the girls doing it this way, but they didn't complain.

When we dragged into Albuquerque, I checked us into the hotel and fell into the bed without even cleaning up. I heard Nola cajoling a sleepy Junie through her nighttime routine, but I was out of it before they came back to claim the other queen-sized bed.

# # # # #

Nola apologized for waking me at noon, but Junie was hungry. I crawled out of bed and took a shower, finishing it off with icy pellets of water. That helped some.

I made a big deal out of our nice hotel room and eating lunch in a fancy restaurant, but that didn't buck up their spirits very much. Then I called the Greshams and explained the situation. They both came over to the hotel, and the girls responded to Mrs. Gresham. It was hard not to, she was such a nice lady. By the middle of the afternoon, they were laughing and talking like old friends. Mr. Gresham praised Nola for her jewelry-making skill, and Mrs. Gresham showed her a bracelet she was wearing. It was one of Nola's.

We had dinner at their home that night. Junie fell asleep in Mrs. Gresham's lap, and Nola sat in a chair fighting to stay awake as Mr. Gresham and I talked over my family situation. Both of them made no bones about it – they agreed with Aunt Aurora and Aunt Clara. My sisters needed a mother.

The following morning, I made the call I had been thinking about since I knew I was coming to Albuquerque. Jason answered. He was pleased to hear from me and happy when he learned I was in town. An hour later, I took advantage of an offer by Mrs. Gresham to leave the girls with her and drove to Jason's house. He met me at the door, pulled me inside, and gave me a bear hug. It felt good, and so did sitting in his den bringing one another up to date in our lives.

"I always thought there was something you weren't telling me about your family," Jason said when I reached the end of my tale.

"It's something you don't talk about too much."

"I guess not, but you should have put the son of a bitch in jail for what he did."

"I would have if it wouldn't stress out my mom too much."

"In the short run, but she might have come with you if he was in jail. Or better yet, prison. Attempted rape and incest are felonies, Wilam. They earn you a lot of time."

I shook my head. "No, Mom will stand by her man even if he kills her. She would have stayed right there until he got out of jail or prison."

"Why?"

"I wish I knew. Maybe she feels she made a bargain and has to keep to it no matter what. She loves him, I guess. Or more likely, she loves what he was."

As someone entered the house through the garage, Jason looked at me and pointed toward the kitchen. "Maybe I do understand. That man would have to kill me to get rid of me. David knows you're here, by the way. He had to run out for some tubes of paint. He's turning into a very good artist. He's sold several of his canvases."

When David entered the room, it felt like he sucked all of the air out of the place. I was drawn to him, not just as a person, but almost as if he were the source of my oxygen and light. In that instant, I knew I needed my own David. In fact, realized I'd been subconsciously searching for him. Had that been Carlos? A pain knifed through me but vanished as David smiled and stepped forward to be introduced. He had an easy way about him.

I managed to bring myself back to reality and make a good visit of it. They insisted I share a lunch of cold cuts and salad. I envied the comfort of their relationship. I basked in their friendship, even though David's goodwill was merely an extension of Jason's. But it was enough; I would take it on any terms.

Not wishing to overstay my welcome, I went to the pickup for a box I had brought with me. It was a small alabaster piece of a Plains warrior, kneeling to examine the tracks of a bear in the path before him, reins to his pony in one hand, rifle in the other. The pinto behind him held his its head high, nostrils flaring, so you knew the bear was close.

"It's marvelous," Jason exclaimed. "My God, Wilam, you're great."

David took the piece from him and examined it closely, paying particular attention to the decorations on the pony. He glanced up at me. "Cheyenne?" I nodded. He gave a half smile. "It's good. You got all the markings right."

I about burst the buttons on my shirt.

Jason had his own surprise. When I unwrapped his gift, I saw myself as I was three years ago in the little park behind Presbyterian Hospital. After all this time, he'd finished and framed the painting. His timing was perfect. Now it was safe to take it with me.

I spoke around a big lump in my throat. "Thanks, Jason. This brings back memories."

He walked me to the pickup as I took my leave. "Why the reservation? Why not Albuquerque?"

I answered him honestly. "Because Albuquerque is too close. I couldn't handle it."

He understood I meant too close to him. He laid a hand on my arm. "Wilam, how did you get to be so smart?"

"I'm not smart. I just do what my gut tells me ... even if my head is screaming something else."

"Keep in touch?"

"You bet. Thank you, Jason. You don't know it, but you made my life a lot better than it was before. I don't mean just showing me who I really am. I mean giving me a glimpse of a different kind of life ... a standard of living. I decided that's what I wanted for myself, so I worked hard." I shrugged. "I guess I've done all right."

"That you have, my friend. Three years ago, you left here a little boy. Now you've come back a man. Mind you, you were a little boy with a big cock and a nice set of balls, but inside, you were immature. Not anymore." He gave an impish grin. "Makes me wonder what the man's cock and balls are like now."

I laughed. "If things weren't so good between you and David, I'd show you."

"You like him, don't you?"

"He knocks me for a loop. But he's your David, and I'm glad for you. One of these days...." My voice stuck in my throat for a second. "One of these days I'll find my own."

"Maybe you're someone else's David, did you ever think of that?"

"No, but I like the idea."

My stomach felt hollow on the drive back to the Greshams'. Nola caught my down mood when I picked them up, but I was all right by the time we went to have dinner with Matthew and his wife and baby daughter that night.

It was good to see my brother. I liked being called Pissant again. I was relieved at how clear his eyes and skin were. He wasn't drinking, or at least, he wasn't overdoing it. Myra had matured in to a pretty woman, and my tiny niece was something else. Both of the girls immediately played with her like she was a doll. She reminded me of Junie a few years back. Matthew was still working at the construction company, doing supervisory work now. We stayed far too late since he had to be on the job site early the next day, but we had a lot of catching up to do. It relieved my mind a bunch when he told me I'd done the right thing getting our sisters out of the apartment.

The girls and I made Denver by late evening the next day. Aunt Clara and Uncle Darin were waiting and made us welcome. They had a son about my age and a girl a little older than Nola. I hadn't seen my aunt and uncle in

165

fourteen years. Nola had been an infant then, and little Junie had never set eyes on them.

Despite Aunt Aurora's assurances, I'd been a little worried about how Uncle Darin would take all of this, him not being of the tribe and all. But he was as comfortable as an old moccasin with the sides worn down. The girls would be all right there. They wouldn't be exposed to alcoholic parents or be run all over the country every few years. Little Junie wouldn't fail a grade as Nola and I had because we were never in a place long enough to get settled in and keep up with our schoolwork.

I stayed for a week, sleeping in the house for a couple of nights, and then moving to a motel to put a little distance between the girls and me ... especially Junie. I found where the gays hung out around the capitol building when Wilbert, that's my cousin, made some kind of disparaging remark one day.

The night before I left for the rez, I got antsy and drove down there. There were so many people circling the big, stone building it felt like a circus. I went back to the room without making any real effort. Walter sure would have been nice to have around right then.

The morning I pulled out for the reservation, Nola gave me a gold chain necklace and a pair of turquoise and coral earrings for Aunt Aurora and a silver money clip with an onyx stone on it for Uncle Dulce. She couldn't hold back the tears as I got into the truck, and that set little Junie off. Until then, the baby figured I was just going away for the day as I'd been doing. It broke my heart leaving with her crying like that, but the sooner I got out of sight, the quicker Aunt Clara and Nola could get her settled down.

I took things easy, stretching out the drive and making it an overnight trip. That might have been because I picked up a hitchhiker or two. I was missing Carlos so much my gut actually ached. Starved for human contact of any kind must have made me a little more foolhardy than usual. I had a good deal of money on me as well as some expensive tools in the back of the truck.

One of the hitchers was a hunky Arapaho youth who really appealed to me. He set me on fire so much I was desperate to approach him. But he talked nonstop about his girlfriend, so there wasn't an opportunity to bring up anything else. I watched him for a few minutes as he walked down a country lane after I let him out. He turned around once and hesitated when he saw I was still there. Then he lifted an arm in farewell and kept on walking. I felt like going after him, thinking maybe he did understand, but I chickened out and headed on down the highway. My eyesight got blurry for a couple of miles.

I reached Mapleton without incident and without relief. I stayed the night at a motel right outside the reservation, but that didn't turn out very well. The couple in the room next to me went at it all night. Their bed was right up against the wall, so I felt like a participant. I heard him – it sounded like a young voice – groaning and moaning and carrying on every time he shot his balls. She laughed and "oohed" and "aahed" a lot, too.

When I heard them up and moving early the next morning I peeked out the window as they left. He was a skinny Indian kid in blue jeans and black cowboy hat; she was a plump little gal who looked juicy and ready. The car tags were from South Dakota. Sioux, probably. I hoped they got some rest between here and there.

# # # # #

Aunt Aurora was plumper than I remembered, and while we were not demonstrative people, she pulled me to her breast and hugged me warmly. She insisted I stay with them until I could get the house in livable condition. I stowed my bag in the spare bedroom and gave them Nola's gifts. Aunt Aurora carried on over hers like it was something from Tiffany's. Uncle Dulce was a little more restrained, but I think he appreciated the clip. After my aunt donned the necklace and earrings, we piled into the pickup and went down to the tribal headquarters where I was granted permission to occupy our old house.

One look at the place sent my spirits plummeting. It needed a hell of a lot of work, but I figured I could do a lot of it myself. The first week I got a contractor out to re-shingle the whole place, including the large barn out back, which was going to be my studio. He also put in a septic tank plus a bathroom in each building. I called in a well driller to sink a new well with a submersible pump.

I had an electrical contractor put in the circuit boxes, but I wired the house and barn as I'd learned to do from working on Walter's place. Then I set about laying insulation right on top of the existing walls and covering that over with sheet rock. Working alone had its drawbacks. I missed Nola and Junie like crazy, and I still ached for Carlos. There were times I sat down on the floor and wondered why I kept trying.

I called the girls almost every day until I figured that was getting in the way of Junie settling into her new home. She ended up crying every time we talked. I let Mom know I'd arrived okay and told her the girls were doing fine. She'd already called her sister and talked to them a couple of times. She wouldn't say much about Woodie, so I figured he might be back in jail. Of course, I couldn't telephone the man I really wanted to talk to. I didn't have a number for Carlos. He'd called from a payphone when he caught me on the road to Albuquerque.

# # # # #

I'd been back on the rez about two weeks when I drove into Mapleton to arrange for the installation of a land line telephone and to change my cell number to a local area code. As I drove down the street on the way out of town, I spotted the two Tallboy brothers sitting on a concrete wall outside a bar. They waved me over, so I parked, got out of the cab, and stood jawing for a minute. They'd heard I was back and was fixing up the old place.

167

Just as I was turning to leave, I noticed another guy sitting on the same half-wall in front of the bar a little way down and apart from the Tallboys. I did a double take. It was James Longhunter.

I walked over, gave him a big grin, and offered my hand. He shook it half-hardheartedly, not bothering to stand up. Mystified by his greeting, I let him know I was back in the old place and invited him to stop by sometime. I puzzled over James's reaction all the way back to the house.

He was probably embarrassed by what he'd said the day we left for Albuquerque. There was something about his appearance that bothered me, too. He was still a handsome man, but there was something about him that puzzled me. My cock didn't have a problem with his appearance; it got hard when I remembered the night I'd pretended to be asleep on the Big Beaver.

I was working too hard on the house to worry about things like that, although my labor didn't keep Carlos from intruding on my concentration. The job had come down to the point where another pair of hands would make things go a lot faster. At mid-morning the next day, I went to the tribal headquarters to see if anybody was hanging around looking for a temporary job. Nobody was, so I went back to the house. When I pulled into the driveway, James was leaning against the wall near the front door.

I greeted him and invited him inside for a cold drink. When I handed him a cola, he hesitated a minute before accepting it. He'd probably expected me to bring out a beer. We spent a few minutes talking over the last few years. His life sounded about like it was when I left three years ago. He still wasn't married, wasn't working, and wasn't going with anyone.

"James, I was just down at the tribal headquarters looking for somebody to give me a hand fixing this place up. You interested?"

"Sure."

"I can pay ten dollars an hour."

He shrugged. "That's okay."

The work went a lot faster with two extra hands. Mostly I had him hold sheet rock while I hammered it in place. Pretty soon we both shed our shirts, and I noticed James wasn't as skinny as he looked; his muscles were just long instead of bulky. I saw him studying my torso and got hard, but I don't think he could tell because I was wearing a carpenter's belt that covered my groin.

He came back every day for the rest of that week, and on Friday, I paid him in cash. He suggested we go into town for a couple of brews, but I begged off. I wanted to start clearing out the barn, line up some paint, and do a whole bunch of other things to get ready for next week. He promised to be back Monday morning and took off.

When he was gone, I thought back over the week and decided we'd acted like strangers thrown together on a construction crew – amiable, companionable even, but not old friends. Certainly not like guys who'd once said they loved one another. Well, he had, anyway.

The moment I was alone again, Carlos came back strong. His memory did, anyway. I went into the bedroom, shut the door, and tried to take care of it. It only gave me partial relief.

# # # # #

James didn't show up on Monday. He didn't come back Tuesday, and by the time he showed up Wednesday morning, still shaking from a bad hangover, I was so pissed I considered sending him packing. Instead, I just gave him the cold shoulder, refusing to talk to him beyond "go get that" or "hold this." The relationship was strained for the rest of the week, and when I paid him the next Friday, there was a lot less money because of the days he'd missed.

He made it by Tuesday of the next week, but he was shaking so badly he wasn't of much use. I paid him for it anyway on Friday, and told him if he wasn't here Monday morning, he didn't need to come back at all.

He was there all right, about an hour late and still drunk but coming down fast into a hangover. He tried to work even though he was suffering. He had to go outside and throw up a couple of times, and some of the boards ended up crooked because he couldn't hold them straight. We took them out and did them again. That set the pattern for the next three weeks. After that, we were finished.

The old place was unrecognizable. It looked great. It wouldn't be much of an exaggeration to say it was the showplace of the rez. I'd put in gray and brown native stone siding about halfway up the four outside walls and painted the wood above that stark white. The trim around the windows and doors was bright green. The house had three comfortable bedrooms, a sizable living area that was combination den, kitchen, and dining room, and a big bathroom with both a shower and a tub. The barn out back was now a huge, airy studio with big double doors at the back I could throw open to enjoy the breeze. It had lots of light, good insulation, an office, a supply room, and a bathroom of its own. There was plenty of room for storage of my rock and woods and a separate place for finished pieces.

Alongside the barn, I built a carport open on two sides that was big enough for my Nissan pickup with room for another vehicle beside it. I'd hooked the barn and the house together with a breezeway, so I could go back and forth between the two and stay out of the rain and snow. The last thing I did was bring in several loads of gravel to extend the driveway around to the back of the studio, since some of my pieces were apt to be big enough to require a hauling company.

James and I were more comfortable with one another by this time. He always came in with a hangover on Monday, but he worked, sweating the alcohol out and the shakes away. It should have put me off him, but I reasoned when the time was right, I'd get him to AA or some other place like that. I

169

intended to keep him on as a helper and hoped he'd get so involved with the work he'd forget about drinking.

I told myself I kept James on after the remodel work because I needed someone to shape the bigger pieces of stone for me. He couldn't handle the chisel until Tuesday afternoon at the earliest. He would have ruined too much material right after a weekend drunk. Still, he turned out to be a natural at it. He could read grain and only messed up two or three pieces before he understood what the stone would or would not tolerate. The real reason I kept him on, of course, was that having him around tended to put off Carlos's shade until the uneasy night.

I continued to experiment with marble, and finished the mortar I'd started in Phoenix. It didn't turn out like I'd planned. Instead of being eight inches high, it was more like six, and the ornately scrolled buttresses turned into simple graceful forms. As I said, marble was an unforgiving medium. Working the stone was nothing more than taking some of it away with a chisel, but every time I took away too much or scored it in the wrong place, I had to change the design.

Nonetheless, I was halfway proud of the results. I polished and sealed the bowl, but left the base rough for contrast. The buttresses were smooth except where they joined the body of the bowl. I left those places textured by the chisel marks. As I viewed the ten-pound result of my efforts, I decided to tackle a more complicated piece for my next project ... after I invested in a wet saw and a pneumatic chisel.

Alabaster remained my principal medium, supplemented by soapstone, and occasionally a wooden piece. James had an affinity for the stones and quickly learned to shape the blocks down to the marks I'd draw on them as a guide. In the three months after we completed the remodel of the house and studio, I made more money than I had in all my life up to that point. Mr. Hartrand ordered a couple more pieces, and I did two other commissions. In addition, I sent several small pieces directly to Greenby Galleries.

Despite working like crazy, memories of Carlos became so vivid that I was beginning to hurt. My need was getting harder to ignore, regardless of twelve-hour days. That was foolish. James was right here in the studio, and he had made it clear he wanted to get together with me before I left. Did he still feel that way? I needed to know.

Sounded simple. Just reach out to him. But I wasn't able to do it. I had rejected him before leaving for New Mexico, and besides, I didn't know if he still did things like that. Beyond looking at my naked torso from time to time, he gave no sign, no hint of feeling anything for me. If there was no feeling, then it wouldn't be any good. If we'd done something together before I left, maybe it would have been easier to try and revive it.

Given my train of thought, I began to take closer notice of James and caught him studying me more than I'd realized. As he left one Wednesday evening – his first decent day that week – I decided to approach him the next day.

Thursday morning found me nervous ... and crabby. I barked at him once over something so trite I was ashamed of myself. I tried to ease off, but it was difficult, mostly because I hadn't figured out what to say. By the end of the day, I was morose because I had failed. There was no way I could ask him right out for relief. And that's all it amounted to.

I'd have knocked the block off any clown who walked up and said, "Hey, how about helping me get my nuts off," and that was the only thing that came to mind. Then I remembered how Jason had approached me when he reached the limits of his frustration. I lifted my head. Was he still here? I'd heard him in the studio bathroom taking a shower a few minutes ago, but I didn't know if he'd left. Shirtless and sweat covered, I stood in the studio, looking out of a window, nursing my thoughts and resentments.

"What is it, Wilam?" I jumped at the sound of his voice. I hadn't heard him come up behind me. "I'm sorry, man, I didn't mean to scare you." His hands touched my bare arms. I grabbed them and held onto him.

"Not your fault." I gave a shaky laugh. "I was just thinking."

"What about?"

I turned to face him. The light bathed his open face. He was as handsome as ever, except there were smudges beneath his eyes that never seemed to go away. They faded somewhat along toward Friday, but they were back again on Monday.

"I was remembering us talking behind the store the day I left. Do you remember what we talked about?"

"I remember."

"I was thinking about what you said. You know, how you felt about me. I've thought about that a lot of times since then."

"How come you didn't write and tell me so?"

"Scared, I guess. I don't know why it scared me so."

He shrugged. "Because that was something everybody said was bad."

I swallowed hard. "Do you ever think about...."

"Just every day. I think about you fucking me every day, Wilam. Do you think about it?"

"J ... James." I faltered.

"I know. You don't want me talking like that. I've tried not to since you got back. I wouldn't have said anything now if you hadn't brought it up."

I swayed and reached out to him for support. "You don't understand. I've been acting like a bastard today because I was trying to get up the nerve to ask you if you still felt the same way."

He looked me straight in the eye. "Sure I do. I never stopped feeling it. Never will."

His warm hands felt good on my naked back. He moved forward and rested his head on my shoulder. His breath was hot on my flesh.

"I need a shower. I'm dirty and sweaty," I said.

"You're just the way I want you."

"At least let's go to the house. We're standing in front of a big window here."

He drew back and looked at me. "I'm afraid I'll lose you between here and the house."

I laughed aloud. "I need you, James Longhunter. I need you to do everything you told me you wanted to do to me that day almost four years ago."

He gave a half-grin and touched my groin for the first time. "Sounds – and feels – like you're serious."

"I am. I'm serious about you sucking my cock and then using it to make love to you."

It was almost as if I had never done it before. I was awkward and clumsy, so he took charge. He undressed me, even stooping down to untie my sneakers. Then he put me on my back on the bed, undressed himself, and got between my legs with his body halfway up my chest. He licked a nipple. He rubbed my arms and shoulders and belly, finally taking my hard cock in his hands. He looked up.

"I've wondered all these years what it would feel like. You've grown some." He shook my thing for emphasis.

"How do you know? You've never seen it before. Not in this condition."

"That's what you think. I watched you jack off over at the creek one day."

"When?"

"Hell, we couldn't have been more'n fourteen."

"If you wanted me back then, why didn't you come over when you saw me doing it?"

"Afraid I'd scare you off, but I jerked off while I watched you doing the same thing. That's when I knew I was in love with you."

I started to say something, but he lowered his head and took me in his mouth. Whatever I'd been going to say came out as "oooh!"

His tongue on the underside of my penis reminded me of the first time Jason had done this to me, and the feeling was just as intense. Finally, he took me all the way down his throat. I had to hold his head motionless for a moment or I would have lost it. What did they call that? Premature ejaculation?

James understood, and simply remained quiet, holding me in his warm, moist mouth. When I released him, he began to work on me. He took everything I had without any trouble. I sighed and lay back on the pillows as his mouth and tongue loved me. He was in no hurry. He clasped one of my hands in his, and toyed with my belly with his other. I expected my orgasm to be harsh and explosive since it had been such a long time, but it was smooth and long and intense as my muscles delivered cum down his throat. He took it all. Then he went still, allowing me to grow soft in his mouth where it felt warm and safe.

At length, he moved up beside me. I opened my eyes. He was studying me closely. Looking for something. My reactions, I suppose. But I hid them … at least one of them. For a brief second I felt I'd betrayed Carlos.

"That was great, James." I laid a hand on his cheek and gently touched the bruise beneath his eye. "Thank you. I really needed that."

"So did I. It's been hard keeping my hands off you while we worked. You're so beautiful. A man's not supposed to be beautiful, but you are. You've always been prettier than any girl I ever saw, even when you were little. But you look like a real man."

"Don't talk like that." I fell back into my old ways.

He ignored me. "Did you know all the girls used to be jealous of you? They said you had the best eyes in the whole school – bar none."

"Come on." I felt my cheeks grow hot. "James, I've gotta ask. Have you been with many men?"

He put his head down on my shoulder so I couldn't see his eyes. "I won't lie to you. I've been with lots of the guys around here."

"That's ridiculous. Not everybody around here's gay."

"Hardly any of them. Maybe one or two. But most of them like to play around sometimes. There wasn't anybody I really wanted to do it with except this skinny kid who ran away to New Mexico. How about you?"

"No, not many. Three, if you don't count this kid in high school I jacked off with once. He got so embarrassed we never even spoke to one another again." I almost believed that version of the story by now.

"That painting of you in the living room. The artist. He was one of them, wasn't he?"

I nodded. "The first." I told him all about Jason and Walter. I told him about Carlos, too, but for some reason I went through that one in a hurry. He listened carefully but said nothing.

"Are you okay with this?" he asked when I finished talking.

"Yeah. I'm okay with it."

"Me, too. Real okay with it."

I pulled him over on top of me and kissed him. He looked surprised, then pleased. We kissed again, more intensely.

He looked at me when we parted. "Nobody's ever kissed me on the lips."

"Nobody?"

"Nobody. Not a girl. Not a boy. I liked it."

We kissed again, longer, wetter, and more passionate. Then I told him he'd have to work to get me hard. After that, I'd do all the work.

He sucked me until I was hot and heavy again. I watched his face as I entered him. I went slowly, allowing him to adjust to my bulk. By the time I was completely seated, he had little beads of sweat on his forehead.

"Wilam, I never liked it this way very much. I think it was because I was waiting for you."

"Shut up, James. We're going to fuck now."

"Right on! Do it, man."

I moved my hips; he groaned with pleasure. I grew bolder, and thrust harder. He gasped, and then smiled, locking his ankles around me – like Carlos used to do when we belly-fucked. My thrusts grew longer and harder. I came almost all the way out of him, and then lunged back. He squirmed, he groaned, he panted. This time there was nothing gentle about my orgasm. It exploded, electrifying every cell of my being and spewing my seed into his hot ass. I cried out and ground my hips against him, sending more cum deep inside him. He crooned as I kept hunching to drive out the last of my jism.

When I finally finished, I reached for his big cock, He was longer than I was, but not as thick around. He was leaking a lot of pre-cum. I lunged against him, reinserting myself fully, and began pumping the foreskin back and forth over his glans. With a look of surprise, he grabbed onto the bedding and hung on, his mouth gaping, his hips twitching. In just a few moments, he came all over both of us. I could actually see his heart pounding against his rib cage.

"Would ... would you believe nobody's ever done that for me before?"

"What? Nobody ever made you come?" I looked at him in astonishment.

"Nobody. The only time I ever came, I made myself do it. Thank you, Wilam. Now I know what it feels like. It was great."

I shook my head. "I can't believe no one ever gave you anything back."

"Now I'm glad they didn't. I'm glad you're first one who did it for me."

Still thinking about what he'd said, I rose and went into the shower. He followed me, insisting on washing me with lots of soapsuds. As I dried off, I wondered why I'd felt submissive with Carlos, but with James, I needed to be the man. Weird.

CHAPTER 24

James moved into the house, taking the bedroom next to mine. That arrangement made the situation clear to me. Had it been Carlos, I would have wanted him in my room and in my bed constantly. I adored James, yet I wanted him near and available, not in my immediate space. With Carlos, it was love. With James, it was infatuation. Would it blossom into love? Perhaps.

Remembering he had confessed a liaison with a number of men, I belatedly grew alarmed, so we both went to the Public Health hospital for a blood test. The only thing I knew about AIDS was I didn't want to become intimate with it. On the first Friday after he moved his things into the house, I halfway expected him to leave, but he stuck close. We took the weekend to drive all over the countryside, visiting places and things I hadn't seen in years. He had a few beers on the way, but he didn't overdo it by getting drunk.

As soon as our blood tests came back negative, I put him on his stomach and entered him roughly. The next day, he sat atop me and did all the work. That same night, he was still horny, but I was sated, so I introduced him to the frontage thing. I was almost sorry I did so because memories of Carlos haunted me as James enthusiastically fucked my belly.

#

I worked hard for the next six months; both of us did. I put out a number of soapstone and alabaster pieces, and I spent a part of everyday learning to handle the marble. I was beginning to get the hang of it by now and was learning something new every time I worked with the stone.

James behaved himself for those for six months. He still drank, but he came home every night. On weekends, he usually showed up tipsy, if not outright drunk, but his behavior was tolerable. Then one Saturday night, he didn't come home. I fretted over it, more irritated than worried. By Sunday night, I was considering going to look for him. Exercising a great deal of self-restraint, I got a rein on my imagination and stayed put.

When he showed up on Monday, reeking of alcohol, I let him know I was pissed but otherwise let it go.

#

Aunt Clara put Nola and Junie on the bus for a visit during Christmas holidays. I couldn't believe how much they'd grown. Nola had obvious breasts, which embarrassed her, but it was clear she was thriving. The changes in Junie – excuse me, she insisted on being called June now – were even more remarkable. She'd gone from a jabbering toddler to a chattering child. The girls were happy and excited, and their visit was something I needed badly.

We opened presents on Christmas day, and I made sure James had as many under the tree as the rest of us. Nola's gift to me almost struck me speechless. She'd made me a ring out of pure silver set with a large fire opal in one corner and my initials, WG, in the other.

James spent the morning with us before heading out to his mother's place. Despite everything I could do, and no matter how much Nola treated him like a brother, it was obvious he felt like an outsider. He moved out of the house while the girls were there, sleeping over at Mrs. Longhunter's. It was his decision, but I was grateful for it. I wasn't comfortable with him living in the house while the girls were here.

On their final weekend in Rolling Hills, he disappeared. He'd promised to go with me to drive my sisters to the bus station in Mapleton, but he didn't show.

After watching their bus out of sight, I made a circle of the town's bars until I found him sitting alone at a table full of empty beer cans. He was barely able to focus on me when I spoke to him.

"I thought you were coming to say goodbye to the girls."

"They're your sisters, not mine."

"Maybe so, but they liked you. They were disappointed you didn't show up."

"Wasn't in no shape." He emptied a can and set it down on the table with a metallic thump.

"Well, let's start getting in shape. We've got work to do." I held out a hand to help him up.

He struck my arm away. "I'm not through drinking. Sit down and have a beer."

"No thanks."

"Didn't think so."

"What's your problem, James?"

"Right now, you're my problem. Buy me a drink or fuck off."

I ended up hauling him out of the bar with his arm twisted behind his back and trying to ignore sniggering remarks about never seeing a guy so desperate for a blow job. When I shoved him in the driver's side of the pickup, he headed out the other door. I grabbed his shirt collar and held on. He tried to jump out twice before we got home.

I threw him, clothes and all, into a cold shower. He yelped and danced and tried to fight, but he was no match for me. After he was clean, I made him eat some soup and put him to bed. He stayed there for the rest of the afternoon and night.

I quit giving him a full paycheck. Instead, I sent his mother a portion of it every week and gave him the rest as pocket money. Without letting him know, I set up a joint bank account in both our names and made deposits to it each week. That way, he didn't have as much to throw away on drinking, but his mom had a decent income. When he whipped this liquor thing, he'd have some savings in the joint account.

James never got over resenting me for hauling him out of the bar. Things improved between us, but they never got back to the way they were. Every time I analyzed our relationship, I came to the same conclusion. James wasn't my David. Hell, he wasn't even my Carlos. I probably loved him a little, but there were too many dark spots in the relationship.

I kept making unwanted comparisons between James and Woodie. When James wasn't drunk – or resenting me because he wasn't drunk – I knew he loved me. He was a year older than I was ... that made him twenty-three; yet sometimes I felt like a man raising a little boy.

He went on a real bender over New Year's. I sat at home with a bag full of fireworks we'd planned on setting off, waiting for him, fearing for him, and trying to keep from going to root him out of some bar. Hell, he probably wasn't in a bar. He was out in the boondocks with a bunch of people at some party. I prayed he survived it.

He did, and I took him back even though I didn't get much work out of him for the next week. Or much loving, either. Things were going to hell; I had to go chase him out of bars a couple of times before spring came around.

# # # # #

Prying James out of Mapleton's watering holes exposed me to something I hadn't fully faced up to. The the minute something happened on the rez, everyone knew about it. I'd closed my eyes to people figuring out James was more than just rooming with me. What would Uncle Dulce and Aunt Aurora think about it?

I started a campaign to inoculate myself, and hopefully them, by becoming involved in local activities. I attended powwows, even going to the trouble of making and wearing the proper regalia. I donated money and a few small sculptures for prizes. I contributed funds to build a playground on the grade school and to improve a track at the high school over in Mapleton where our older kids went. I bought basketball and football uniforms for the teams. Although I never let anyone publicly announce these donations as mine, everyone knew it before the ink was dry on my checks.

I also attended a few tribal council meetings and argued issues of the moment. When I had cuts and scrapes – something that happened regularly working with knives and chisels and stone – I went to the local shaman for ointments and salves. The short-haul trucker over in Mapleton was making too much money carting my pieces to the depot, so I found a couple of reliable guys on the reservation who had a decent truck with a Tommy Gate on the back and hired them to do the hauling for me.

Spreading money around, getting involved in civic activities, and giving lip service to some of the Old Ways worked reasonably well. As added damage control, I joined a local softball team and did pretty well at the game. At least, they didn't harass me or bad mouth me in public because I wasn't dating girls or getting married. Everybody knew I was an artist, and artists were crazy anyway, weren't they? Of course, there was some jealousy because I was doing better than most, but that happens everywhere.

Still, I heard enough comments; some given in honest warning and others in cynical asides, to understand James was still considered the reservation queer. Nothing but time and staying away from the local boys would overcome that. But since he was drinking again, how did I know he wasn't still chasing guys? Maybe pinching his money supply was backfiring.

Then James started missing work on Mondays. A couple of times, he didn't show up on Tuesdays, either. Finally, I'd had enough. I told him the next time he missed work he didn't need to bother coming back.

The next Monday he didn't show up. I made mental excuses for him and worked out how I'd manage to forgive him again when he dragged in looking hangdog and contrite. When I hadn't heard from him by the following Monday, I was about crazy. I made the round of the bars without success. His mom hadn't seen him. After two weeks, I was worried sick. When I got over my anger; I was simply concerned for my friend. Where the hell could a guy hide on a small reservation like this? Plenty of places when you stop to think about it.

By the third week, I knew I had to find him somehow, even if it meant swallowing my pride and asking around about him. Somebody knew where he was. Hell, everyone probably knew except me. Rounds of the bars failed to turn up any sign of him. I even had a couple of drinks with some people I knew and asked about him, but nobody would admit to knowing anything.

On the return home, I drove past his mom's place and noted a light was still on. After parking the pickup in my carport, I decided to see if she'd heard anything since the last time I checked. To walk off some of my fear and frustration, I got a big flashlight from the studio and set off down the road on foot.

His mother hadn't seen or heard from James and was as worried as I was. After I left her house, I decided to follow Big Beaver and walk back home through the woods. It was longer that way, but I wasn't sleepy and needed the fresh air. At the old swimming hole on the creek, I turned down the path leading to the little clearing where we'd pitched our camp. After I'd come home to the rez, James and I had gone there one night and put down our blankets where the lean-to had been. Then we'd made love under a sky so bright with stars it was nearly like daylight. Lost in memories of a better time, I almost failed to hear the voices drifting on the night breeze.

"Did you guys hear something?" someone asked.

"Shhh, butthead! Keep it down," another voice said.

I snapped off my flashlight and made my way as quietly as I could down the path. At the edge of the clearing, I stood in the shadow of the trees. Someone was moving around on the north side making little muffled noises, but it wasn't until the moon cleared a cloud that I could dimly make out what it was. I had found James.

I snapped on my flashlight. The powerful beam tore through the darkness. James was lying naked on his stomach. His head was at the crotch of one youth as he sucked the boy's big bone. Another husky youngster had mounted him from the rear, his energetic thrusting now halted by the sudden light. A third boy lay back on his elbows, apparently waiting his turn. They were all nude. I yelled the first thing that came into my head.

"Police! Don't anybody move."

The three youngsters – they had to be high school age – scattered to the winds, a couple of them with their clothing, one with only part of it. Poor drunken James curled into a fetal position with one hand in front of his face to block out the light. The other hand grabbed money from a nearby rock – a feral claw snatching at prey.

At first, he was furious when he found out I was the one who'd interrupted them. Then he got sloppily sentimental. I couldn't get him dressed, so I collected his clothes and dragged him across the clearing by an arm. He smelled terrible. He'd been lying on the bare ground, so dirt and twigs clung to him.

So drunk he could hardly walk, he stumbled along behind me. Suddenly he halted and yelled, "Hey, dude, you want a blow job? Good blow. Only ten bucks." Then he ran around in front of me and knelt in the dirt, his head at my groin. "Feels like a big one there. Ten bucks, man. It'll be worth it, okay?" He fumbled with my zipper.

I hit him. I hit him in the jaw, pulling my punch at the last minute. I hit him out of disgust and fear and concern and because I was hurt.

He cried then, long mewling sounds. I dragged him off the ground and brushed away the leaves stuck in his hair. I threw him over my shoulder in a fireman's carry and toted him home. We entered by the back door to keep out of the light I always leave on over the front entrance.

I drew a tub of warm water and put him in it. He kept trying to get out, but I knelt beside the tub and held him down as I washed away the filth. When I finished, he stood still and allowed me to towel him dry. He smelled better on the outside, but the inside was something else. I made him brush his teeth, but that didn't help. The odor of decay remained in my nostrils.

He sat on the living room floor wrapped in a blanket and stared at me balefully. What was he thinking? Hate? Love? Or worse, not thinking of me at all? He mumbled endlessly, and one minute they were tender words, the next, hateful curses.

Suddenly he threw off the blanket, rolled back, and threw up his legs, fingering his ass. "Come here, lover. Put it right here." He spread his cheeks. "Here it is. Put it right here in my asshole."

"You're obscene!" The words were out of my mouth before I could stop them.

179

"Think so? Made thirty bucks tonight being ob ... scene." He laughed. "Didn't take all day slinging a hammer and chisel to do it, neither. Oh wait, that's not right. Made forty bucks. Charged that kid twenty to fuck me in the ass." He sobered. "Where's my money? You take my money? Motherfucker, you stole my money!"

"Your money's in your pockets. This is it, James. We're through."

He flew across the room on his knees and buried his head in my lap, crying for forgiveness. Then he went quiet and slowly lifted his head. He stared at me through unfocused eyes. Pushing himself away, he fell on his butt in the middle of the floor and wrapped himself in the blanket.

"You're fucking right it's over. Don't need you. I can get all the cock I want. Bigger cock than yours. There's some big cock on the rez, you know that? And they pay me for it, too. Got me a new main man. Kid's been sniffing around for a while, and I'm gonna let him in. Good-looking fucker. Big cock. Bigger'n your little thing." He held his hands apart at an impossible length and then cupped them to create an improbable girth. "No lie. I saw it once after he got through running with a hard-on that wouldn't stay in his shorts." James laughed, a harsh, bitter sound. "That's what I'm going for."

He fell silent then and sagged back on the floor. He was out instantly. I couldn't wake him, so I covered him with the blanket and slipped a pillow under his head. I stood and looked at him for a moment. He appeared as innocent as a baby.

James was sick. Hadn't I seen it with my own father? Then I heard a voice in my head spouting my mother's old excuses for Woodie. "He was drunk. He didn't know what he was doing. If he'd been sober, he wouldn't have sold his ass to school kids. Revolted, I vowed to find a local AA chapter and begin putting things right.

Around three in the morning, I finally fell asleep. Then I must have literally passed out because when I woke at mid-morning, James was gone. So was the hundred dollars I'd had in my billfold and the four- or five-hundred I kept in the house for emergencies.

Saturday morning, I stopped by Mrs. Longhunter's to see if he was there. He wasn't, so I headed for the Tribal headquarters, but there was no one around who could tell me much about AA or the tribe-sponsored alcohol recovery programs I was supposedly helping to fund. Then I went to the studio and worked as hard as I could to try and put the events of the past few weeks behind me. I missed Nola and June terribly ... and Carlos.

# # # # #

Late Sunday night, the doorbell rang as I was getting ready for bed. My heart fell when I saw the tribal police chief on the porch.

"Hello, Chief. You want to come inside?"

"No thanks, Wilam. I've got a nasty job for you. Mrs. Longhunter ain't up to it, so she asked me to come see you."

"Oh, no." The words slipped out of me.

"I need you to come identify somebody."

"Is it ... is it ...."

"Yeah. It's him. Law says family or close friend's gotta identify him."

A man in his early sixties, the Chief had probably cut me off, so I wouldn't speak James's name aloud. That meant my friend was dead. Speaking the name of the recently deceased might call up his ghost according to the old way of thinking.

"Where is he?"

"In Mapleton. Local cops saw it was one of ours and called me. Can you come?"

"Sure. Let me get my shoes." I buttoned my shirt with wooden fingers and picked out a pair of moccasins that didn't need laces tied.

The world was unusually silent as I followed the policeman to his unit and got into the passenger's seat. He saved me the pain of asking questions as we headed for town.

"Car hit him. They say it looked like he just walked right out in front of it."

I stifled a groan. Oh, God! Why hadn't I heard him when he sneaked out of the house in the middle of the night? Why had I been so hard on him?

"He was working for you, wasn't he?" The Chief's voice startled me.

"Yeah. He's worked for me ever since I came back."

"Shame. We lose too many of our boys this way." Suddenly he pounded the steering wheel. The car wobbled. "Too goddamn many!"

It was James, all right. They'd cleaned him up before I got there. He looked peaceful except for an ugly cut on his head. Most of the damage must be out of sight underneath the sheet covering him. I confirmed the identification and signed the necessary papers. Then the Chief took me back to Mrs. Longhunter's. There was another lady with her, so I just stayed a few minutes before walking the rest of the way home.

Chapter 25

I wished Nola was here. She could have consoled me. She'd know exactly what to say and what not to say, but Nola was down in Denver, probably sleeping. She'd have understood my relationship with James and withheld judgment for it. At the very least, she'd have sat at the edge of my vision and lent mute support.

I dozed a little in the chair where I sat the rest of the night. When I finally crawled to my feet. I took a long shower and tried to get some food to stay down my craw. It didn't work. Everything came right back up. Still shaky from a bout of nausea, I paused at the front window. A figure stood leaning against the lamppost at the end of the drive staring toward the house. Angry at the morbid interest of a stranger, I threw on some clothes and burst out the door.

The man pushed off from the post and started walking toward the house the moment I crossed the threshold. I came to a halt, struck by how handsome he was. Stunning was the word that came to mind.

"Is James here?"

At first, I thought he was taunting me. The whole reservation would know James was dead, and nobody would call out his name. Not even a youngster like this one. If he didn't believe the nonsense about ghosts, he'd at least consider it bad luck.

I sagged against the door frame and gave him the benefit of the doubt. "I guess you haven't heard. Our friend isn't with us any more."

He stopped dead still, his big black eyes perfect orbs. "He ... he ...."

"A car hit him last night over in Mapleton."

The young man swallowed hard and swiped his mouth with a hand. "Sorry. I didn't know. My family and me just got back this morning from visiting my uncle over in Oklahoma. I bummed a ride and came over to .... Aw, never mind."

"It's okay. What did you need from him?" Vivid images flashed through my mind with my unfortunate choice of words.

"He said there was a box of old tools I could have. I was supposed to pick them up today."

I had asked James to get rid of some tools I no longer used. Apparently he thought they had some life left in them and had offered them to this boy.

"They weren't ... uh, his were they?" I gathered from the question he was superstitious about dead people's possessions.

"No, they're mine, but I asked him to get rid of them. They're in the studio somewhere. I can find them, if you want to come in."

The kid was flustered. He started backpedaling. "No, thanks. I'll come back for them Friday. I can get a truck by then. Uh, if that's okay."

"Sure, but we can take them in my truck if you want."

"No, I'll come back Friday."

"Okay, that's fine." I nodded to the carport. "Look for the pickup. If it's there, I'm either in the house or the studio out back."

"Thanks." He backed away a few steps, turned, and trotted down the driveway.

I watched him out of sight. He was probably about eighteen or so – and on the small side. Small side? I chuckled beneath my breath. He was as tall as my five-nine. He was probably a runner. A lot of our people were runners. He was lean enough for it. He had a certain presence about him. Handsome face, good-looking body. Was this the guy James had been babbling about the other night. Or had that been drunk-talk?

When I returned to the house, my mood lifted somewhat. I still grieved for James, but the young man who'd appeared unexpectedly in my driveway was clear evidence that life went on. I found myself anticipating Friday, despite all that had to be done before then.

# # # # #

Other than James's mother and a few of her friends, I was the only one who turned up at his funeral. It was quick and final. Afterward, I gave Mrs. Longhunter an envelope containing a check for the amount in the joint account I'd set up for James and a little note explaining he had earned and saved the money.

I don't think of myself as an emotional man, but when I got back to the lonely house, I wept real tears for my lifelong friend and … my lover. I guess our relationship had qualified him for that. Some of the tears were for the sense of guilt and culpability I suffered with his death. I couldn't shake the idea that if I'd been smarter about handling things, James would still be alive.

Angered by my weakness and lonely for companionship, I went to the studio and attacked the large slab of beige Galala marble from Egypt I'd had delivered a few days ago. It was planned for a simple statue of a boy or girl. Without any plan or measurements or rational thought I started working the stone.

In time, it turned out to be one of my most spectacular pieces: two three-quarter-sized mountain lions, the male slightly behind the female with his jowls over her back as if he were contemplating mounting her. Her head was turned to him, a vicious snarl of rejection on her countenance.

The vibrations of the pneumatic drill I used for working marble were soothing somehow. Trying to smother sadness and guilt and loneliness, I worked almost around the clock in the days immediately after the funeral.

Late Friday, I realized the young man had not returned for his tools. The realization brought a pang of regret. Damn, was I craving human contact so much that a brief, meaningless interlude with a handsome youth was something to look forward to? The thought brought a sense of betrayal with it.

When I ran out of steam about midnight and went to clean up and get something to eat, the blinking light on the answering machine reminded me I needed to have a telephone extension put in the studio. I punched the answer button, and a young baritone filled the room.

"Uh ... this is Joseph Sixkiller. You know, the guy who came to see you about those tools. I couldn't get my brother's truck today, so if it's all right, I'll stop by tomorrow. Okay? Thanks. Uh ... bye."

I cleaned up, dropped into bed without eating, and slept soundly for the first time in weeks.

The next morning, I was deeply engrossed in the work on the lions, so I don't know how long he had been watching from the doorway before I noticed him.

"Gee, that's really something," Joseph said when I looked his way. "I never saw anybody do that before." The top portion of both cats had emerged from the stone, and I could imagine how dramatic the results were for someone who hadn't seen marble worked before. I knew the hardest part, the delicate legs and long tails, were yet to be done.

"Thanks for leaving a message for me yesterday, Joseph."

"Oh, okay. I still didn't get my brother's truck and Ja ... uh, our friend didn't say how many tools there were or how heavy they were."

"More than you can carry by hand. Let me clean up, and I'll drive you where you need to go."

"You don't have to do that."

"No, I don't. But I'm offering to because I need a break."

"Okay, but before we do, could I watch for a while? Or does it bother you to have somebody look over your shoulder?"

"Naw. My sisters used to do it all the time. And ... our friend did, too. Just stay back, so you don't get marble chips all over you."

He perched on a worktable and watched silently for over an hour. His big black eyes taking everything in gave me shivers up and down my back. I was glad I was working without a shirt. Carving stone had filled me out where I needed it and leaned me down where I didn't. How's that for vanity? Finally, I reached a natural stopping point.

"That's enough for now. Let me see where those tools are."

It took some rummaging around before I found the box. He went through it carefully, making comments about some of the tools and asking the purpose of others. After we loaded the box in the back of my pickup, he followed me inside the house where he nursed a cola while I cleaned up.

I came back into the living area carrying a fresh shirt and still toweling my hair dry. "Sorry it's such a mess out there in the studio." I made conversation to mask my nervousness. Why did this kid make me nervous?

"Our friend used to keep the place up for me, but he's not around now. I don't do a very good job of it by myself."

"You don't have anybody to do that since he's not around?"

"I haven't hired anybody else yet."

"What all did he do?"

"He kept the tools clean and put them away where they belong, and he swept out the place every day after we finished. Working with stone creates a lot of dust. If it's not vacuumed up, it can be a mess. He also helped me crate the bigger pieces and box the smaller ones. The most helpful things he did were to shape the stone and polish it at the end."

"What does that mean?"

"When I get a piece of marble or alabaster, I try to picture what I see in it. When I decide what it wants to be, I mark off a general shape, and Ja ... uh, our friend would chip away the extra stone down to the marks I put on it. Does that make sense?"

"Yeah, sure. And the polishing? Is that what it sounds like?'

"Exactly what it sounds like. I use a square of fine emery paper, you know, sand paper. After that, I mix a polishing powder with oxalic acid and apply the paste with a little elbow grease."

Does a fellow have to know all about the rocks? You know, the marble and whatever?"

"No, that's something I'll teach him."

"I don't have a summer job yet."

"It's not just a summer job. I need help all year."

"Oh." Disappointment clouded his face.

"I can probably work around school hours, if I have to."

"Can I give it a try?"

"Let me think about it while we deliver your tools, okay?"

"Sure." He chugged the remainder of his soda and got up.

We talked as we drove, so I could learn a little more about him. I wanted to give him the job. He was eager, and I had the feeling he'd make a good worker. He was slender, but there were good muscles beneath his T-shirt, so he could probably handle the lifting required. I had hoisting devices and trolleys for the bigger pieces. And I liked him. Those were all the reasons why.

There was only one reason why not. I liked him. Was strongly attracted to him. Could I keep things on an even keel? Keep from creating a situation that might drive me off the reservation if it went wrong? My head said no. My head lost out.

After we finished unloading the tools in front of his family's house, I told him the job paid ten dollars an hour and asked when he could start. We settled on Monday and a forty-hour week until school started next fall. Then we'd probably cut the hours back to twenty and see if he could handle that and his classes, too. All the way back to the studio, I worried over whether I'd made a bad mistake.

CHAPTER 26

By the end of Joseph's first week, things seemed to be working out okay. He came in on time, got the mundane things like cleaning up the place out of the way, and eagerly tackled the chores he had to learn. Both of us worked without a shirt most of the time, and the sight of his naked flesh excited me, although I managed to settle for merely enjoying the view.

He liked working with the stone and quickly learned everything I could teach him. He even went to the library over in Mapleton to read everything he could find on alabaster and marble. Within a month, he was confidently chiseling the smaller stones into shape but was still nervous about the bigger pieces.

One afternoon, he accidentally split off a sizable hunk the first piece of pink Tennessee marble he tackled, which rendered it useless for what was planned. He panicked, probably believing he was going to lose his job. I assured him I had done the same thing more than once and stopped what I was doing to study and re-plan the broken pieces to show him most of the material was salvageable.

Because of the accident, he took far too long shaping the second piece. I didn't worry. That would correct itself in time. He was a good worker, and that made things go faster and smoother in the studio. Besides, he was likeable company, which helped me personally.

Now, if I could only expunge the worm of desire crawling around in my belly, everything would be all right. I was handling it okay so far, although proximity to Joseph prompted many, many desperate thoughts of Carlos and long, lonely nights.

Eventually, a pretty girl whose name I didn't catch started coming around at noontime to bring him lunch. The first time he claimed he forgot to bring it with him, which was nonsense because as often as not I sent him in the truck for hamburgers or sandwiches from the closest diner. When I didn't object, she started coming more regularly. I have to give Joseph credit, he took one hour off to eat and hang around with her, and then he was back at business, although his crotch seemed to be fuller right after she left.

# # # # #

Greenby talked me into doing a one-man show in his New York gallery, which meant I'd have to put in some really long hours to get my existing commissions filled in addition to twelve to fifteen pieces for Greenby's exhibition. He wanted three major works, three to four medium-sized, and half a dozen smaller pieces. Thank goodness Joseph was here to help me.

I decided the lions, an almost life-sized alabaster fletcher – an old man making arrow points – and a soapstone Indian pinto decorated for a powwow rodeo would be my large pieces. The lions were virtually finished, so I started in on the other two major works to get them out of the way first.

Right in the middle of the madhouse, Nola and June came for two weeks before school vacation ended. They were a joy to be around, but thankfully both of them adopted Joseph right away. He ran them into town and hauled them all over the reservation, leaving me free to get some work done. Aunt Aurora also helped to keep them busy. I took a break and spent the last two days of their visit with them while Joseph worked at shaping the rest of the stone for the showpieces.

The weekend my sisters left, we called Mom on the speakerphone, so we could all talk together. She sounded stronger than when I'd spoken to her about a month earlier. None of us asked about Woodie, and Mom didn't volunteer any information. Despite my feelings about the man, it was sad.

Letting the girls go back to Denver was difficult, but they were growing up strong and healthy and happy. My aunt and uncle had good moral compasses they were passing on to my sisters. Both were healthier physically than I'd ever seen them. They were going to be okay.

The girls were no sooner gone than Joseph started back to school. He'd done a good job for me, becoming adept at shaping the stone, including marble. He was so accomplished in sanding and polishing the pieces I gave him a decent raise when we cut his hours to the part-time status we'd agreed on. We scheduled five of his twenty hours a week on Saturday. That wasn't convenient for me, but this gave him time to do his homework during the week and take part in school activities. I knew he gave his mother half his pay and saved a quarter of it, so I wanted to keep his paycheck as healthy as possible.

At first, I thought I'd made a mistake in giving him the raise. The Saturday after school started, he made it to work on time, but he had a hangover. If it hadn't been for my experiences with Woodie and James, I would have laughed it away. He was plainly sick, but he still did yeoman's work. Along about noon, he told me some of his schoolmates had had a party, and he wasn't much of a party person. That rang a bell with me, so I took pity on him and drove him home after work.

I bought a couple of new suits for the New York show and dragged out the two I had bought in Phoenix. I'd only worn them a couple of times, but they were a little snug in the shoulders. All of the showpieces were finished, and I'd had time to put them away for a second look, but now they needed to be crated and shipped.

The freight company was to pick up the crates on Monday morning, which meant they needed to be at the Mapleton depot by Saturday. When the workday ended Friday much later than usual, we still had a considerable amount of crating to do. It was clear we would need to start earlier than usual the next morning, so I offered Joseph the use of one of the spare bedrooms for the night.

After we'd cleaned up and eaten, he noticed a chessboard set up on a table in the corner and asked if I could teach him to play. I'd bought the set almost a year ago when James said he'd like to learn the game. We hadn't used it – not even once. I'd read enough to know the principles of the game and the moves of each of the pieces, so Joseph and I tackled the board and had fun learning about it together.

Since tomorrow was going to be a hard day, we turned in early. As tired as I was, I had trouble dropping off to sleep because of the handsome guy sleeping just on the other side of the wall. Even so, I woke early. After cleaning up and straightening my bedroom, I made coffee. There was no sign of life from his bedroom. He was sleeping the sleep of the innocent, no doubt. I fixed him a cup of coffee the way he liked it and went to wake him. He'd left the door to the bedroom ajar, so I just walked in. I had my mouth open to call him but snapped it shut and stood transfixed.

He was sleeping on his back, head turned to one side. His lips were parted, and his long lashes lay against his cheeks. One arm was thrown above his head on the pillow. The other lay crooked at his side, hand resting on a sheet-covered knee drawn up beside his body. His lean torso, like many of my people's, had no hair except for a little at the armpit. As I stood staring, he straightened his leg, drawing the cover down with it. He was naked.

I felt as if I'd been slugged in the solar plexus. I lost my breath for a moment. His flaccid cock was long and thick, even in repose. He wasn't circumcised, and its general shape reminded me of a spear. The large glans flared out over the thick trunk. The penis lay over his round, full sac.

The sight physically staggered me so much I spilled coffee on the carpet. I now knew why Walter had seemed to be in a trance the first time I stood naked before him. I could have watched Joseph for an hour, but I didn't want him to wake up and find me staring at him. As I stood debating whether to wake him or get the hell out of there, the decision was made for me. The phone in the living room started ringing. He stirred at the sound, but I escaped the bedroom before he opened his eyes.

The call was from the local guys who hauled my stuff to the freight office. I gave instructions to meet us here at noon and hung up the phone with shaking hands. When I turned around, Joseph stood in the middle of the room, wiping sleep from his eyes. He had on his jeans, but no shirt or shoes.

"Sorry," he mumbled. "Overslept. Your bed's too comfortable."

"That's okay. We worked hard yesterday. But we better get it in gear now."

He frowned. "I just stepped in something wet on the floor in the bedroom."

I indicated the coffee mug on the table. "Yeah, I was bringing you a cup to wake up with, but the phone rang. I spilled some when I ran to answer it. You go get ready, and I'll clean up the mess."

"'Kay." He reached for the coffee. Was he blushing?

The crating went well, but we were tired by the time everything was delivered to the freight office in town. We had to use the Titan in addition to my local hauler's truck in order to make it before the depot closed. After that, I dropped Joseph off at home and went back to my place for some much needed rest.

Even though it was only late afternoon, I stripped and went to bed. I kept drifting in and out of sleep, my drowsy mind conjuring images of Joseph spread out on the bed. I woke with a hard-on and masturbated.

# # # # #

A week and a half later, Joseph drove me to the airport in Junction City, a big town seventy-five miles north of the rez. I gave him two days worth of work to do and told him he could have the remainder of the week off with pay in appreciation for the hard work we'd put in preparing for the show. I also told him he could drive my pickup while I was gone but I'd whip his ass if he went drinking in it. He allowed as to how that wouldn't happen.

CHAPTER 27

My mind refused to accept what my eyes were seeing. For the past ten minutes the airliner had been flying over an immense metropolitan complex. Mile after mile of nothing but buildings and houses, concrete and brick. The entire East Coast must be one big, scary, confusing city. I was both excited and lost when we landed. Passengers crowded into the aisles, so they could stand and wait for the stewardesses to open the door. Eventually, the aluminum tube that had carried me to New York expelled me into an air-conditioned terminal filled with a mass of humanity rushing this way and that. They all appeared to know what they were doing and where they were going except me.

Salvation arrived in the form of a man dressed in black holding up a sign with my name on it. I rushed over to him as if he were a long-lost brother or something. I think my eagerness made him uncomfortable. At any rate, he was the driver Greenby had sent to JFK to deliver me to the gallery. Thank goodness the man knew where and how to rescue my luggage.

The block-long black limousine threaded its way unerringly through the heaviest traffic I'd ever seen in my life. It must take a lifetime of experience just to figure out how to exit the airport. I gawked like every other tourist, feeling like a pigmy staring up at concrete and glass trees soaring into the sky ... and there was very little of that visible. Nothing – not Albuquerque nor Phoenix nor Denver nor even pictures of New York City itself – had prepared me for such a cultural shock.

The driver hidden behind the smoked glass partition separating the two of us must have had some way of communicating because when he pulled to a stop at the gallery on Broadway, Greenby was standing on the sidewalk to greet me. He pumped my hand enthusiastically and ushered me into a big, airy building with a second-story balcony running all around the perimeter. I was surprised to find my work took up the entire main floor of the gallery. He allowed me a moment to absorb that fact and then introduced me to a whole raft of people, dismissing my protest that I was in my jeans, pullover shirt, and sneakers, not to mention I was grimy from the trip.

One of the people present was a very handsome woman a little over thirty whom he introduced as Diane Leighton. I don't remember any other names, but they were universally polite and attractive people. I gathered Greenby had turned out some of the city's art elite.

He put me up at the Plaza, and I got a kick out of looking out on the green of Central Park, a startling contrast to all of that concrete and asphalt and steel and glass. Later, we went to a party at someone's penthouse apartment where I met the beautiful Diane again. This time she latched on and remained at my side the rest of the night.

I'd been afraid I would stand around all evening gawking at the city lighting up the night beyond the windows while everyone stared at the red yokel from the sticks. But people seemed genuinely interested in my work. I must have explained about a hundred times how I got started.

Midway through the night, a new couple entered the room. It took me a minute to recognize Mr. and Mrs. Gresham, my friends and mentors from Albuquerque. My natural reserve broke, and I gave each a big bear hug, which didn't seem out of place in New York where everyone was always hugging and air-kissing. The rest of the evening was spent bringing one another up to date on our lives – with Diane Leighton right at my elbow.

She was there later when Greenby took the Greshams and me back to the Plaza. She got out of the car when we did and was still standing at my side as Greenby and his limo pulled away from the curb. Not wanting to seem rude, I agreed to her suggestion of a cocktail in the lounge. I was tired and didn't really want another drink, I'd already had one – something called a gin and tonic – at the party, but I went along. The Greshams begged off and retired for the night.

Diane was still at my elbow when I unlocked the door to my room about two a.m. More than slightly tipsy, I wondered what the hell I was going to do with her. She took care of that. She stripped me before undressing herself. Then she pulled me over on top of her in the bed.

"I've been dying to get my hands on you all evening." She kissed my chin and neck. "Actually, I've wanted you for the last six months. Ever since Ellis showed me a picture of you. You're even better in the flesh."

I guess I was drunker than I thought because what went through my mind was ... all right, lady. I'll show you. You invade old Wilam's privacy, he's gonna fuck you blind.

As if that were possible. She rendered me into that condition – and utter exhaustion, to boot. We did it with me on top. We did it on our sides with our legs scissored between one another. We did it with her on top. I think we might have done it once again after I fell asleep.

My internal clock wasn't set for New York, and I wasn't accustomed to a night like I'd had. Still, I woke early. Deciding on revenge, I managed to get worked up enough to give it to her one more time while she was trying to sleep.

It backfired. By the time we finished, I had smudges under my eyes like James used to have after his hard drunks. Diane wouldn't get up, so I left her in the room while I made a noon meeting with Greenby. Make that Ellis. He now insisted I call him by his first name. Most of the people who had given me commissions over the last year were at the luncheon to meet and greet me. The only one I'd ever set eyes on before was Mr. Hartrand ... and his toady, John Savage Davis.

I managed not to make a fool of either Ellis or myself during the lunch, but I decided this was harder work than carving stone. Inevitably, the first comment out of everyone's mouth upon meeting me was, "You're so young." I almost blurted, "Man, you shoulda seen me before Diane got her hands on me."

She caught up with me at dinnertime, and my eyebrows shot up when someone greeted her as Mrs. Leighton. Ellis noted my reaction and whispered the word "widow" in my ear.

There was a party at the opening of my show at the gallery the next morning … and every night thereafter. I soon accepted the fact Diane was going to accompany me to every one of them, after which we'd go back to the Plaza and fuck. No commitments, she warned me the second night. We were just going to enjoy one another. That was all right with me.

The show was a whopping success. Every single piece sold the first day for outlandish prices. The buyers of each of the three major pieces announced they were being donated to different museums. When this sent Ellis off into orbit, Mr. Gresham explained that was the best of all worlds. The art could be widely viewed and appreciated in museums, whereas, in private collections, viewing was much more restricted. He'd already donated six pieces – the original six heads made of walnut mounted on marble – to the Albuquerque Art Museum.

Ellis later told me there were three steps to the big time: commissioned work from serious collectors, a one-man show on both coasts, and work on display in museums, and that I had accomplished all three while only twenty-three.

When I reminded him I'd only had an event on one coast, he dropped the other shoe. He had two more shows scheduled in the next six months, one in his own gallery in Los Angeles and a second in an associate's place in Santa Fe. He softened the blow by telling me my take from the first showing, and I couldn't honestly refuse him after all he had done for me. If the other two shows were anything like this one, I could live for years in relative comfort.

I had two regrets about the showing. I wished Joseph could have been here to share it with me. I could imagine his eyes popping at the antics of some of these people. I'd never seen so many gay people in my life. Five men and four women propositioned me, not counting Diane who wouldn't let me get away long enough to accept any of the offers, even if I had been so inclined.

The second was letting go of the hit of the show – the two cougars – because the work had been born out of the anguish of my tragic relationship with James. The two lions were us … James and Wilam. I had come perilously close to carving our names in the base. The female's tail curled to the side signifying the body's acceptance of the male's advances, yet her face was twisted in angry rejection. A metaphor for our tangled lives.

Seen in the lights of the gallery, the piece, with its tawny cast, was magnificent. The male's head resting on the back of the female and her reaction to him were subtly sexual. Ellis had priced it higher than anything I had ever done. Even so, a little bidding war broke out over it. The final price apparently broke some invisible barriers for a brand new artist. That didn't matter to me; I wished it were still mine. The fact it was going to a very prestigious New York museum helped me bear the emotional loss.

By my last night in New York, I was completely worn out. I had been able to satisfy Diane thus far, but this evening I was flagging. Even so, she wouldn't give up. I was lying on my back enjoying her warm mouth administering to me when I had a sudden, unbidden image of Joseph lying asleep in my bedroom, hand over his head, his magnificent manhood exposed to my view. I came alive, growing hot and hard in an instant.

Hardly knowing what I was doing, I pulled Diane up off of me, threw her face down on the bed and got between her legs. She arched her back, and I entered her vagina roughly from the rear. She cried out in pleasure.

Thrusting at her with the image of Joseph in my mind should have brought me off quickly. But the image faded as she became more audible and intruded on my thoughts. I lost some of the urgency but continued to pound her while she panted and grunted and moaned. She came and came while I struggled vainly to achieve orgasm.

I was about to fake it or simply quit when the phone rang in my ear. Without thinking, I snatched up the receiver and panted a hello. Realizing what I had done, I tried to control my breathing so that it wasn't obvious what was going on.

"Wilam?" a light baritone inquired. It was Joseph.

"Wai ... wait just a minute, will you?"

I laid the phone on the table beside the bed and turned back to Diane. Totally revived, I gave her the ride of her life. She was panting by the time I exploded inside her. My juices poured. They flowed, drawing grunts and groans and moans from my tortured lungs. After a moment, I leaned back on the pillows and picked up the receiver.

"Are you still there?"

"Yeah," he answered uncertainly.

Diane pecked my cheek and spoke in a loud whisper. "Oh, darling, you're a magnificent animal! I'm going to go clean up in the bath. You're simply running out of me."

She said it deliberately. I'm sure she thought it was a woman on the line.

Joseph gave an excited, "Arright!"

When she was gone and I had recovered enough to speak without wheezing, I asked him what he wanted.

"Thought I better let you know," he got serious, although there was a giggle hidden somewhere in his voice. "Some people were here today trying to take pictures of the studio. I chased them off, but not before they got some shots."

"Who were they?"

"Said they were from some magazine. Geez, Wilam. Who was that?"

"Joseph, that's none of your business."

He did giggle then. "Yeah, I know. I guess I'm just sorta excited."

"I think titillated is the word."

The giggle became a guffaw. "Yeah. Well, anyway, those people got inside the studio before I knew what was going on. I was working on that block of marble you left for me, and I didn't see them until a flashgun started popping. The guy was taking pictures like crazy while the lady started feeding me a line of bull. They got a bunch of shots before I could make them leave."

"Did they say what magazine they were from?"

"Yeah." He hesitated and made me ask.

"Well?"

"One of those trashy ones you buy in the grocery store."

"Did they say why they wanted pictures of my studio?"

"Nope. After I shooed them outside, I locked up and went in the house, but they were still outside taking pictures. I called the tribal police and reported trespassers, but they were gone before anybody got over here."

"It's okay, I don't know what's going on, but it sounds like you did what you could."

"Yeah." He snickered. "It sounds like you're doing what you can up there, too."

"All right, asshole," I said fondly, "back to business. You know what time my plane gets in tomorrow?"

"Right. I'll be at Junction City. Try to get some sleep on the plane, so I don't have to carry your butt to the truck." He was laughing aloud when he hung up.

I sat in the bed grinning until Diane came out of the bathroom wanting some more of what she declared was the best sex ever. My grin turned into a grimace, but I gallantly mounted her again, thinking resolutely of that handsome, virile male back home getting a bang out of me getting a bang. That did the job. She finally gasped she'd had enough of a good thing.

# # # # #

Ellis and his chauffeur came to take me to the airport the next morning. Diane had said goodbye in the room so well that I was going to have to sleep on the plane or else Joseph would have to haul me out of the terminal. She refused to go with us to the airport, saying she didn't like public goodbyes. Secretly, I was glad. I wasn't at all sure she wouldn't try to get in one final round in the limo with Ellis sitting there watching.

When I told him about the trespassers at my studio, he looked at me oddly. "You haven't a clue, have you?"

"About what?"

He shook his head. "I keep forgetting you're so young and inexperienced at dealing with us eastern reprobates. William, I'm sorry. I should have cautioned you. You've just spent the week with one of the

197

wealthiest, most sought after socialites in New York. She makes the gossip columns everywhere she goes. You're someone the tabloids have never seen before. So naturally, they're interested in you because of your connection to her. Your successful show merely adds fuel to the fire. May I speak to you like a Dutch uncle?"

"Sure, go ahead." I wasn't sure what a Dutch uncle was.

"Diane is known as a woman of great sexual appetite ... a nymphomaniac almost. The fact she stayed with you day and night for the entire week is an open secret. And it's unusual. She ordinarily keeps a man around only a day or so. You're apt find yourself labeled a super stud."

I snickered, but I couldn't explain this "super stud" gave a famous nympho the fuck of her life by concentrating on the image of a handsome young man. Then I remembered the other nights. I had handled those all on my own.

"Sorry, but the idea of me as a super stud is laughable. If everyone knew how few women there have been in my life and how long it was between them, that idea would go out the window in a minute."

Ellis chuckled. "Well, we won't tell them, will we? All the publicity will be good for sales."

We talked about the upcoming shows until my plane was ready to board. He relieved my mind by telling me some of the pieces for the next shows could be commissions, which we would deliver afterward. Of course, he also reminded me that we wouldn't make as much money that way.

I finally agreed to do the two shows and said I would try to see that only about a quarter of the showpieces were commissions so most of the work would be available for sale.

CHAPTER 28

Joseph was waiting in the Titan when I walked out of the Junction City commuter airport terminal late that afternoon. I deliberately staggered the last few steps. He howled and beat on the steering wheel in glee, going off into another fit when I said the lady was walking a straight line and prowling the streets of New York for new meat. Without thinking, I reached out and squeezed his knee.

"You're good for a guy's morale, Joseph." After I took my hand away; my palm tingled for five miles.

Joseph drove on the way back home because he claimed I was so worn out from chasing women I couldn't be trusted behind the wheel. On the way, he told me more about the team who showed up taking pictures and asking questions.

"Did you tell them anything?" I asked.

"Just that you weren't there and to leave." His face twisted into a sudden frown.

"What's the matter?"

"When they stood around outside and wouldn't go away, I got mad."

"And?"

"I gave them the finger, and the guy got a picture of it. Sure hope they don't put that one in any magazine."

It was my turn to laugh. After a minute, he joined me, and we flew down the highway laughing our fool heads off. God, it was good to be back among sane people.

# # # # #

We went to work immediately. I had commissions to fill and two shows in less than six months. Perhaps it was my imagination, but there seemed to be a difference in the relationship between Joseph and me. Some sort of bond had been formed. Things were comfortable between us. Lifting the stone and spotting it and crating the work afterward, made physical contact necessary, but now it was easy and natural. Did that mean there had been tension before? If so, I hadn't noticed. Nonetheless, it was different now in some indefinable manner.

Ellis sent a set of photos of my New York trip, and Joseph sobered a little when I pointed out Diane. I think he'd been expecting a bimbo, but what he saw was a beautiful, sophisticated lady.

# # # # #

A week later he came into the studio with a shit-eating grin on his face. He held something behind his back.

"Guess what? You done made a splash in the tabloids. Us pore hick Injuns got us a ce-leb-bre-tee right here on the rez. A real, live super stud." He brought the magazine from behind him and jabbed his finger at it. "It says so right here. Super stud William Greyhorse. And you know them papers don't lie."

"You go to hell."

"Maybe I oughta give those folks a call. I've got some real inside dope. I personally heard the lady say 'you wuz a mag-ni-fi-cent animal and your cum wuz runnin' outa all her pores.'" He almost collapsed from laughter.

"I repeat. You got to hell. Here I was in New York working my butt off ...."

That sent him over the edge. He beat his knee with a fist as he howled.

"Sorry, poor choice of words."

I expected the ribbing I got from Joseph, but everywhere I went on the reservation I drew smirks, or looks, or outright comments. In town, where they didn't know me as well, I simply got a few handshakes and an occasional remark about "them nice articles."

Stories appeared in all the tabloids, as well as the slightly classier magazines that reported on the comings and goings of celebrities. Most of the text had to do with Diane, but there was more than enough verbiage and speculation about me for comfort. I had to admit some of the snaps they printed showed us as a pretty good-looking couple. There was one of me stepping off a curb in front of the hotel that made my crotch look fuller than it really was. It was embarrassing.

The notoriety gradually died away, and the only long-term result was that I started getting invitations to parties and events from as far away as Hong Kong. They all went into the trash.

# # # # #

One day I discovered Joseph had been collecting marble and alabaster dust and chips in big containers. When I asked him why, he shyly showed me how he made small animals by carving a substance he'd created from epoxy impregnated with the particles. He acted as if he'd been caught doing something wrong, but I encouraged his efforts.

I held up one of his carvings. "You know what you have here?"

"Uh. A bear."

"Right, a bear. But that wasn't what I was talking about." I tapped the carving. "This is reconstituted marble."

"Reconstituted?"

"They also call it cultured marble."

"Fake marble, you mean."

"I guess you could call it that, but its basic content is marble. They make counter tops and things like that out of it. Now you're making art."

"I wouldn't call it art."

I showed him how to create some reusable molds, so he could pour the figures instead of whittle them.

But mostly, we worked. Long, hard hours ate up the rest of the year. I took a week off between Christmas and New Year's to enjoy a brief visit from Nola and June. Mom even allowed me to fly her up, but not until she knew I'd sent a round trip ticket so she could return to Phoenix. That probably meant Woodie was spending his Yule season in jail.

I can't begin to describe how much we enjoyed ourselves – even Mom. I caught her laughing and relaxing more than I had ever seen her. I saw some of the attractive woman Aunt Clara had described to me. She made the rounds of her sister's family and all our shirttail relatives, dragging us with her everywhere she went.

Joseph had his own family, of course, but when he was around, he fit right in. I gave him a sizable bonus and a marble bust of an Indian youth for Christmas. If you looked closely, you could probably notice a resemblance to him in the piece. Both of my sisters flirted with Joseph shamelessly, and Mom took to him, too. I'd been apprehensive over her reaction because of the way she had treated James. But Joseph was no James.

It was hard saying goodbye. I made sure they all had enough money and assured Mom I'd go on taking care of her expenses. It bothered me that I was keeping a roof over Woodie's head, too, but it was a price I was willing to pay for her sake.

A year earlier, I had also started sending a check to Aunt Clara every month to help with the girls' upkeep. She put half of the money in a savings account for them and used the rest for clothes and special things. They were getting a good, loving upbringing ... and it showed.

Despite the interruption of the holidays, work was coming along well for the Los Angeles show. Two of the bigger works were figures I called "The Victor" and "The Vanquished." They were two separate statues made from blocks of cedar-red Tennessee marble. The pieces were stand-alone, but they showed much better as companions. One was a life-sized Plains warrior clad in breech clout and moccasins. He had a horsehair roach and a fierce countenance. His naked skull gleamed. Crouched forward with his weight on one foot, he held a broken lance shaft horizontally in his right hand. Viewed alone, he seemed to be engaged in a savage dance.

The companion piece was a second warrior, similarly dressed, but with two upright feathers in his braided hair. He had collapsed onto his legs, one hand in the dirt supporting his weight; the other clutching the broken lance embedded in his chest. His face was incredibly handsome and serene – even as the shock of the lance was killing him.

After "The Victor" was completed, I experienced a little difficulty with "The Vanquished." I was hesitant to use the chisel on one of the collapsed legs because my mental image wasn't too clear. Finally, I called

201

Joseph over. I was so deep into the problem that I forgot to explain. I simply told him to take his pants off.

"What?"

I laughed at the strange look on his face. "I'm having trouble with this leg. I want you to strip to your shorts and get down in the same position he's in. I need a temporary model."

"Okay, but you gotta close the doors first. All I need is my girl walking in on me in my skivvies. You didn't tell me this job involved stripping."

I couldn't avoid staring at his crotch when he got into position, but I tried to keep from being obvious about it. I kept him kneeling in front of me about a half-hour longer than I actually needed because I was enjoying myself too much. When he got up to dress, his cock caught in the fly as he stuffed himself back into his pants. The outline behind the cotton looked as big as I remembered.

Both of us were really taken with the two pieces, but for different reasons. When placed facing one another, "The Victor" no longer seemed to be dancing, but was staring down at his victim to make certain he was finished. Joseph liked them because they stirred the latent warrior in him, but my emotional connection was different. Somehow they reminded me of the triumph and tragedy of my life.

Joseph's snagging of his genitals on his zipper inspired my other large piece. For the first time, I did a nude ... two nudes, actually. A life-sized, naked man stepped toward a maiden, who stood, head lowered modestly, with a proud look on her pretty face. Her hands were folded demurely over her vagina. Her mate reached out with his left hand to cover her with an intricately patterned blanket, which fell in folds from his out flung arm. The other hand clutched the opposite end of the blanket at his groin, shielding his manhood. He was finely muscled, handsome, and dramatic in his movement. She was smooth, beautiful, and absolutely still. Made of a delicate green Mexican alabaster, the contrast between the two works was fantastic.

I liked Joseph's reaction to the pieces. He suffered with "The Vanquished" and exulted with "The Victor." And when he finished his examination of "The Lovers," he simply turned and walked away. It was the greatest compliment he could have paid me. The sculptures had moved my loquacious friend to abject silence.

# # # # #

By laboring long and hard – Joseph far exceeded his scheduled twenty hours – we managed to avoid the last minute rush to get the showpieces sent to California. One night when we were both tired, Joseph attempted to get a thirty pound piece of marble off a high shelf where it had been put out of the way. Normally, he would have used the short stepladder for such work, but he didn't want to take the time go get it. By stretching he was able to scoot the piece to the edge of the shelf and tip it over. Then he lost control and scrambled to push the marble back onto the shelf. He let out a yell and held onto the teetering stone with both hands. If it fell, it would have landed on the silent, naked form of the Indian maiden.

I ran to him and nearly compounded the disaster. In reaching for the piece, my body slammed into his, almost causing him to lose his tenuous grasp. On tiptoes, my body pressed hard against his – groin to butt, my legs between his, my bare chest flush against his naked back – I managed to keep the rock from tipping over. Beneath me, he stretched and found a handhold again. The rock was now steady but still off balance. I jumped three or four times, gradually shoving the rock back onto the shelf. Each time my body rode up between his legs, my cock got harder and harder. By the third or fourth jump, he must have been aware of my excited bone riding the curve of his ass.

When it was over, we each turned away from the other. He found a seat on one of the benches, placed his elbows on his knees, and leaned forward. I sat on another bench, left leg up, so my condition was hidden. Neither of us spoke for a minute.

Finally, he looked at me: "I'm sorry, man. I almost ruined that piece."

"Well, we saved it."

"I'd never forgive myself if I'd broken it. That's your work, man. You put what you are into your art. Not very many people in the whole world can make something like that, but any jerk like me can tear it up."

The vehemence of his outburst took me by surprise. Was this his way of dealing with our unexpected intimacy? When it was safe to get up, I walked over and clapped a hand on his bare shoulder.

"It's my fault as much as yours. I've been driving both of us too hard. We're taking chances we wouldn't ordinarily take. To hell with it. We're going to have plenty of pieces for the show. Let's cut our hours back to normal, okay?"

He took a deep breath, and my hand fell away. "I don't want any more scares like that." He rose and my eyes fell to his groin. I had to turn away or I would have reached for it.

Joseph was subdued for the rest of that week until we finally shipped everything for the show. He perked up Friday afternoon when he took a call in the office and came bouncing into the studio to let me know my own personal nympho was on the line.

Diane wanted me to know she was going to be in Los Angeles for the entire week. Part of me said that was bad news, but another part of me got rock hard. I guess it was more obvious than I thought because when I walked back into the studio, Joseph laughed and asked if I was sure who the nympho really was.

I blushed, but I was perversely glad he'd seen my erection.

CHAPTER 29

When Joseph drove me to the Junction City airport Saturday morning for the Los Angeles trip, he was pensive. I told him to take the week off to work on his own castings, making it clear he was free to use the studio. He was experimenting with different colored stones and dyes in the marble dust-epoxy mix he used. Then he surprised me.

"William, I don't think I ever told you how much this job means to me." He'd never called me William before. As with everyone else around here, I was Wilam to him.

"You're a good worker, Joseph. What's just as important to me is you're good company. We make a great team."

"Yeah, we do. But my life would sure be different if I didn't have the job. My whole family's life would be. My dad's been laid off from work for three months now, and what my brother and I give Mom is about all we have." He'd once told me his father worked off the reservation for some car dealership.

"You're worth your hire, Joseph. You earn every dime you get."

"Anyway, I wanted you to know."

"Thanks."

I puzzled over that exchange all the way to Los Angeles. Had rubbing up against him when we almost had the accident offended him? Was he thinking about leaving? That made no sense. Had he figured out I was hot for him and was saying he'd do whatever was necessary to keep the job? Even if it involved exchanging favors for a paycheck.

# # # # #

By the time I was settled at the hotel, I was in a pretty grim mood. I phoned the house. Nobody answered. Of course not, it was Saturday evening, and I had given Joseph the week off. I contemplated calling him at home, but decided against it. My mood deepened, and Diane paid the price ... or reaped the benefits, as the case may be.

She showed up at the door ready to go to dinner as we had planned during her phone call. Instead, I pulled her inside and fucked her until the topknot in her hair came undone. We ordered room service, ate, shoved the dishes outside the door, and I took her again, this time from the rear. Sometime around three in the morning, she called it quits and retreated to her own room.

Sunday, she was ready for me again, and this time I was the one who begged for mercy. We went sightseeing, but my legs were so rubbery we spent most of the time in a taxi. If she hadn't been so damned demanding, Diane would have been good company. The first part of the week we were pretty free to do what we wanted, aside from a few luncheons with Ellis's clients.

Actually, I guess they were my clients, too. By Wednesday, we were tabloid items again. After the paparazzi started swarming, it ceased to be fun.

By that time, I was also having trouble keeping up with Diane. Images of Jason and David and Carlos and James and Joseph allowed me to keep up the pace until Thursday. There was a party the night before the opening of the show at Greenby Galleries-Los Angeles. I suspected I would probably fail Diane for the first time when we went back to my room this evening, so I had a few more drinks than were good for me. Alcohol always fueled her fires, but it tended to tamper my coals. Surprisingly, there were a number of people I knew from New York at the reception, so I was able to circulate a little and put some distance between the two of us for an hour or so.

Later in the evening, I found an unoccupied office and called the studio on my cell phone even though I knew no one was there. Maybe it was just to put me closer to Joseph by dialing a number where he usually answered the phone. To my surprise someone picked up the receiver. There was a moment of heavy breathing, and then that clear, familiar baritone came over the wire.

"H ... hello?"

I stifled a laugh. "Sounds like the shoe's on the other foot."

"Wilam?"

"Who are you screwing in my studio?"

His breathing softened a little. "Nobody. Why?"

"Either you're screwing the brains out of some little girl, or else you're there alone pretending you're screwing the brains out of some little girl."

"Awww." I heard a muffled noise, and then he whispered, "It's my boss, I gotta take it."

"Well, thank you for using the couch in the office instead of messing up my bed."

He gave a fierce whisper, "Desk."

"Jeez, Joseph. Don't break it."

"I ... uh. I won't."

"Well, I'm interrupting your work, so I'll hang up. Unless you want to lay the receiver down, finish the job, and then talk to me."

So help me, I heard receiver clank down on the desk. Then there were muffled but urgent noises on the other end of the wire. After five minutes, I heard a cry, a female. And then I heard a long groan. Him. Definitely him. That was his baritone.

A minute later, he picked up the receiver. "S ... sorry about that." He took some sharp breaths. "You called at a real crucial time."

I laughed. "Just paying you back."

"Uh, what did you call for?"

"Just wanted to confirm I'll be coming back Sunday."

"Okay. I'll pick you up."

I remained in the office, the dead phone to my ear, with a party going on in the room behind me, wishing I were home with him. I wanted to hear his laugh, see him, talk to him ... be with him. Finally, someone pecked on the door. It was Diane.

I put away the phone, stepped over to her, and pressed my groin against her leg. "Let's go."

She felt my erection. "Oh, my. I hope that's for me. But maybe I should ask who you were talking to?"

"Business. That's not what got me in this state. Come on, I'll show you what did."

I got a key to the gallery from Ellis and told him I was going to give Diane a preview. We slipped out a side door of the hotel and evaded the photographers at the front lobby. A short taxi ride later, we stood in front of "The Lovers." She was entranced by the pale green figures. She ran her hands over the muscular buttocks of the male and the smooth torso of the female. Then she stepped out of her clothes and lay down on the carpet.

"Do to me what he's going to do to her. I want to watch them while you fuck me, William. I want to feel what she's going to feel. Please."

I was naked in seconds. I straddled her body on my knees and pushed my hard, aching cock into her mouth. When she had sucked it until I was even harder, I put it between her breasts and squeezed them together over it. Then I placed her legs on my shoulders and entered her in one long thrust. She was so turned on she was dripping wet.

I beat her with my cock. I fucked her without any thought of her needs or wants. I only thought of Joseph. Joseph in his shorts as he posed for the statue in the other room. Joseph stretched taut against me as we struggled with a thirty pound piece of marble. Joseph as he lay sleeping with his body exposed to my gaze. Joseph as I imagined him atop some girl on my desk – this very evening, perhaps again at this very moment. That last thought sent me over the edge. A cry burst from my lips, and I fell over her, my muscles spewing load after load of hot cum.

Diane was uncharacteristically quiet after we finished. We dressed, and I showed her the other pieces. She fell in love with "The Vanquished," crying at the thought of his impending death. She touched each of the red-brown figures and then turned to me. "I'm going to buy them."

"Which ones?"

"All three! I want 'The Lovers' because they are us. I want 'The Vanquished' because he touches my soul, and I must buy 'The Victor' because I couldn't bear for them to be separated."

"I feel like that, too. Maybe I can get Ellis to drop the price."

"No. I'm going to pay more for these pieces than anyone's ever paid for a Greyhorse."

"Why?"

"Because they're the best work you've ever done." She walked the room again, examining each of the sculptures. Finally, she turned to me.

"William, we have to talk about something. I was going to wait until later, but after what I've just told you, I don't want you to think I'm trying to influence you by buying your art. The two things have nothing to do with one another."

"Sounds serious."

"It is, at least for me. I know we agreed there would be no strings, no attachments when we first met, that we would simply enjoy one another and then go our separate ways." She paused. "But I've fallen in love with you. As ridiculous as that sounds, it's true. I'm almost twenty years older than you are, but no man has ever made me feel like you do. No man has ever satisfied me like you. And I don't mean just sexually."

My heart raced, but I wasn't sure if it was excitement or panic. I touched her cheek. "Diane, this comes as a surprise. I'm probably more in love with you than I've ever been with any woman, but …." I cleared my throat. "But we would eat one another alive."

Tears sprang to her eyes. "I know. Isn't that rich? I know what you're saying is true. It wouldn't last, but for as long as it did, we would have something magnificent."

"That's not enough for me. When I commit, it's for the rest of my life." I shrugged. "It's in my genes, I guess. My mom's still with the worthless drunk who claims to be my father."

We talked for an hour. She acknowledged she wouldn't be happy shut up on the reservation, not after the novelty wore off. The tribal council would probably throw us both off the place within six months she was so outrageous. I would suffocate in New York. My art would shrivel, and I would die.

After she tearfully acknowledged it would not work, I made a more gentle love to her. She sat facing away from me while I entered her from behind. Then she leaned forward to lie with her head in the dying, marble lap of "The Vanquished' while I brought us to a climax of sweet ecstasy.

# # # # #

The show was a total success. Diane kept her word and bought the three pieces, announcing she was donating "The Victor" and "The Vanquished" to a large Los Angeles Museum with the written instructions they were never be separated. "The Lovers" she kept for herself.

On the plane back home Sunday, I did some quick calculations and realized I would have enough to live on for a long time with or without another successful show. My expenses were minimal – except for the donations I made to scholarships and health and alcoholism programs on the rez.

My biggest expenses were for Mom and the girls. I already had enough put away in separate accounts to see my sisters through college. In five short years, I went from poverty to independence – thanks to Mr. Gresham and Ellis Greenby. Of course, I'd made them a great deal of money, too, but what they had done for me transcended economics.

Eventually, I dozed on the plane and dreamed of Joseph.

CHAPTER 30

Joseph wore a cat-caught-the-canary grin as I stepped outside the Junction City terminal. He leaned against the fender of the pickup at the airport holding a sheaf of tabloids. I drank in the sight of him. When I walked up, he shoved the papers at me.

"Did it again, super stud. Except now, you're ... let me see, oh yeah. A 'Native American sculptor, toy boy, super stud.' Tell me, is that better than being just a plain old super stud?" He pounded the fender in glee.

He sobered a bit when two women walked up and asked for my autograph, gushing over how much they enjoyed my work. I was surprised they recognized me and seriously doubted they'd ever seen a piece of mine. Nonetheless, I played it up for Joseph's benefit. It was useless; he just turned it back on me when they left with their signed bits of paper.

"Shit, he's an autograph-signing, Native American sculptor, toy boy, super stud. Tell me, did you sign that as a sculptor, a Native American, a toy boy, or a super stud?"

"Shut up," I snarled good-naturedly. I tossed my bag in the back, barely missing his head.

"Now, now, don't let that artist's temper get out of hand." He laughed us out of the parking lot.

I glanced at the articles as he drove. They were the usual garbage, but there was one new wrinkle. The Society Scene, a particularly nosy tabloid, claimed the "handsome twosome" had broken up. It went on to say:

"The split, while not unexpected given Ms. Leighton's track record with lovers, was not of her making. What – or who – everyone wants to know, could make the handsome Indian sculptor throw over the glamorous millionairess? That is the question on the lips of beautiful people all across the country."

I looked at the handsome, uncomplicated youth who was unknowingly the answer to that question. He glanced over, a grin on his face.

"Who? Who is it?"

"Who is what?"

"The one you'd walk away from all those millions for?"

"You wouldn't believe me if I told you."

"Really? Geez."

"It's nothing like that. You know how those people get everything all screwed up. Besides, where would I hide anyone like that? You're around all the time. Have you seen anybody I'd throw Diane over for?"

His hand reached out and scattered the papers in my lap until he found the one he wanted. He tapped a page opened to another article, inadvertently pressing against my growing cock. "No, but how about this? Did you do that?"

I read it, feeling foolish and sad at the same moment. The article claimed I had taken Diane to the gallery on the night before the show where we made love a final time among the "beautiful, marble and alabaster images created by the talented young sculptor. The following day, the wealthy socialite purchased three of these mute witnesses for well in excess of $100,000 each. Not many of her legions of past suitors have apparently made such an impression on the beautiful lady."

"Did you? Did you?"

"Did I what?"

"You know, screw her with 'The Victor' and 'The Vanquished' and 'The Lovers' looking on?"

I played to my audience. "First, I took her while she was on the floor watching 'The Lovers' as I did it to her."

He squirmed and dropped his elbows to his sides. He was getting excited. Fortunately, the cheesy magazines in my lap hid my condition. I decided to have no mercy.

"And if that gives you a hard-on," I said, "wait until I tell you that after that, she put her head in 'The Vanquished's' lap while I screwed her from behind."

"Behind? You mean ... in ...."

"I mean in the proper place, just with me behind her."

"Oh." He moved his hips again, trying to get comfortable. I almost snickered. That wasn't going to be easy in those tight jeans.

"Did you break it off with her?"

"I don't know. We talked about getting married but didn't come to any conclusion." Why was I hedging? Maybe I was looking for his reaction.

"But the papers say you did."

"Do you believe everything you read in the papers?"

"In the comics, maybe, but these don't have any. Are you going to get married?"

"Do you think I should?"

"Me? Why would what I think matter?"

"You're a part of my life, you know. If we got married, can you see a woman like that living here?"

That deflated his tool quicker than anything. "No, not really."

"Neither can I."

"Does that mean you'd close up the studio and move away?"

"If we married that would be the only thing to do."

He got quiet after that. I allowed five miles to go by before speaking again.

"But I can't see me living in New York any better than I can see her living here."

"Naw, I can't either."

I was surprised at how much I had shaken him. I shouldn't have been; after all, he'd let me know how much his job meant to him just before I left.

"What are you going to do?" he finally asked.

Feeling a little like an ass for worrying him needlessly, I let him know we'd talked it out and agreed it wouldn't work. "That's when I fucked her with her head in 'The Vanquished's' lap."

The big, sunshine grin came back. This time he reached over and pounded my knee. "Arright! Love-'em-and-leave-'em- and-then-love-'em-one-more-time-wild William Greyhorse."

I was back home again, and it was great.

# # # # #

The next day, I started planning the last show of the season coming up in a couple of months in Santa Fe. I told Joseph I knew the general outline of the three major pieces I wanted ... a warrior protecting his pregnant wife, a modern Indian runner, and a powwow dancer.

"I want you to model the runner," I finished up.

"Me? Aw."

"In your running thins."

"Jeez."

"Will you do it?"

"Yeah, sure. If you want me to."

Joseph had become so good at reducing the marble and alabaster blocks to the general shape I wanted that he saved me a great deal of time and increased my productivity. Even so, we had a lot of work to accomplish before the Santa Fe show. I had most of the minor pieces already done, but none of the three major pieces had even been started. That meant we were under the clock again.

I tackled the family piece first in Travertine, a kind of calcite alabaster. The tableau evolved as a loincloth clad warrior, knife in one hand, war shield in the other, leaning forward slightly as if he were preparing to lunge. His pregnant wife, dressed in buckskin, sat collapsed behind him, almost between his legs. One hand gripped his thigh, the tips of the fingers hidden beneath the flowing material of his breech clout. The other hand held the shoulder of a child of around three. She appeared more bewildered than frightened. He looked to be facing furious odds in defending his little family. From what? That was left to the imagination of the viewer.

After that piece was finished and stowed away behind canvas to await my second examination, Joseph donned his skimpy suit, locked the studio doors, and self-consciously posed for me. This time, I worked in Parian marble from Greece. I wanted him to be as eternal as Michelangelo's "David."

As the piece progressed, I released him for other work, but kept him in his thins in case I needed him to "assume the position" again. His handsome

213

face and well-knit form emerged from the stone just as he broke the winner's tape, chest thrust out, hair riding in the wind, and an obvious, but not offensive bulge at the groin. A length of torn tape stretched across his chest and trailed down either side of him. His high school racing number and the name of the team showed clearly on the uniform. His muscled legs lacked only a light dusting of hair to be perfect. The statue's thin nose, high cheekbones and pointed chin mirrored Joseph's own. Veins stood out on his temples and corded arms. In the end, I think he was pleased with the result, but I caught him critically eying the full groin more than once.

The powwow dancer took the longest. He was a young male turned out in all his feathered glory. Only I was aware he was a young descendant of Tarahumara warriors named Carlos. I'd gone on the Internet to get the details of his regalia correct. He had one foot firmly planted on the ground; the other touched the earth at the toe. He was bent forward at the waist, and in the process of turning in a War Dance. His feathered cape was delicate and exacting. I'd done him in white alabaster rather than marble.

A week before we were to ship the last pieces, we found ourselves growing careless from exhaustion again, so we slacked off early one evening. Joseph obviously wanted to discuss something, but he waited until both of us had cleaned up and were sitting in the kitchen nursing sodas before he came out with it.

"Wilam, can I talk to you about something personal?"

"Sure."

"It's really kinda personal. Sure it's okay?"

"Go ahead."

"When you ... you know, do it with a girl. Do you get satisfied?" He rushed ahead before I could react. "That's not exactly what I mean. I really like to do it, and when I zap it's great, but –"

"Zap?"

"You know ... get it ... cum. But as soon as it's over, I want something again. Not again, I guess, but it's ... well, it's like I'm kinda disappointed; like I was looking for something different. Aw, forget it. I don't know how to say it right."

I swallowed a flip remark and tried to answer a serious question seriously. "I think I know what you mean. Despite my reputation of late as a super stud, I've not been with that many women. My brother paid the first one to lay me for my eighteenth birthday. That was a disaster, and I was glad when I never saw her again. The second was a girl at high school in Albuquerque. When we did it, I was left feeling ... well, uneasy comes as close as anything."

"Yeah, uneasy" He leaned forward over the kitchen table, his face screwed into a frown. I had his full attention.

"We moved away not too long after I met her, but our relationship was already on the rocks. To be honest, I really wasn't interested in her. The next one in Phoenix was simply physical relief when I needed it. It just ended,

214

I guess you'd say. We were still friends, but having sex with her wasn't giving me what I needed. Diane's come closest to giving me real satisfaction, but in all honesty, she simply demands sex and then wears me out, so I'm not really sure how I feel about it."

"So?"

"So I guess I'm saying I've never really gotten total satisfaction from having sex ... with a woman." Did I really pause before adding that last? "Maybe I just haven't found the right person. That might be your problem, too. When you do find the person, you'll be satisfied. Does that make sense?"

"Yeah, that makes sense. With the right girl it's bound to be better, right? Because then it's not just physical, it's spiritual, too."

"That's as good a word as any. Or maybe emotional."

"Yeah, emotional." Then his sense of humor surfaced. "That's it, huh? That's all the girls you've done it with?"

"That's the sum total of sex with women in my life."

He grinned. "I've done it with more girls than you have."

"Yeah, but you haven't done it so spectacularly they write about you in half a dozen magazines."

He sobered. "Then maybe there's nothing wrong with me, huh?"

"Joseph, there's nothing wrong with you. You're a normal eighteen-year-old who's making discoveries every day about himself and the great act of sex."

His face cleared, and he got up. "Guess I'd better go. Got a little studying before finals."

"Take the truck home. I'm not going anywhere before you come to work tomorrow afternoon."

"Okay, thanks."

As he left, I ached to run out the door and tell him that's not all there was to it. All I did was watch from the window as he backed down the driveway and out onto the street.

# # # # #

On Thursday, we found ourselves in pretty good shape and knocked off a little early, so he could go home and finish studying. He had finals next week, after which he would graduate. Once again he hesitated before departing after we cleaned up.

"Another Coke?" I asked.

He nodded. I got two cold colas and sat down opposite him at the table. God, he was a beautiful man.

Joseph had to try three times before he got started. After a couple of uhs and ahs he asked if I remembered what we had talked about the other night. I said yes.

"You said ... you said something like not getting total satisfaction from sex with women. Can I ask you something really, really personal?"

"Shoot."

"Did...." He swallowed hard and stalled by taking a sip of cola. Then he shifted gears. "Do you know what everybody said about your friend?"

"What?"

"Well, they said he was, you know ... queer."

"That's a pretty harsh word."

"Well, gay or whatever you want to call it."

"Yes, I know."

"He stayed here with you, didn't he?"

"For about a year." I closed my mouth and made him ask.

"Did you ever do it with him?"

I didn't answer right away. I looked into his eyes until his gaze fell off to the side. He studied his soft drink and then took a nervous gulp. "Did you, Joseph? Did you ever do it with him?"

"No," he said shortly. Then after a moment, he added, "But I talked to him about it once."

"How did that happen?"

He traced a pattern in the moisture ring left by the can. "I ran a race one day, and sometimes after the race is over I ... I get excited. I don't know why, my dink just pumps up and gets hard. I usually walk off by myself. This time, I walked clear over into the trees because it was real bad. So bad, I slipped it out of my jock strap and hoped the fresh air would make it go away."

He ducked his head as if ashamed. "I didn't know he was there until he said something about how he could take care of that for me. Course, I knew who he was and what they said about him. I don't think I really wanted to, but it felt different with him staring at my cock standing up hard like that. So I asked him how he'd take care of it, and he told me."

So James had told the truth that day. "What did he say?"

Joseph blushed but plodded on. "He said he'd give me a blow job I wouldn't ever forget, and if I wanted, he'd do the other thing, too."

"What other thing?"

Joseph gave me a peculiar look. "You know, let me fuck him."

"What did you say?"

"I told him I didn't think so. That was when he told me about the tools. He said to come get them Saturday. After he helped me load them in my brothers truck, we'd park somewhere on the way back. I said I'd like to have the tools, but I didn't know about the other."

"I see." God, he looked young just then. Young and handsome and sensual. "You answered me honestly, so I'll do the same. Yes, I did it with James." He flinched, although I didn't know if it was from my confession or the use of James's name. "It's all right; he's been gone long enough to call him by name."

216

"What? Oh, yeah. What did you do together?" He darted a glance at me and then looked away.

"Just what he described to you."

"Both of them?"

I nodded. "Yes, both of them. And, Joseph, after doing it with James, I wasn't uneasy and didn't feel like I was wanting something an hour later."

His black eyes studied me intently. "Didn't you feel ashamed?"

"No. James was up front with me about what he wanted and what he could do for me. It was a long time before I allowed him to try. When I did, I found I could accept and enjoy the relationship. Of course, it didn't last. He was too far into the bottle by the time I came back to the rez. He stayed sober and kept away from others for about six months. After that, it went downhill fast."

Uncomfortable under his scrutiny, I said, "Joseph, I once heard someone say that most men live their lives in fear. Fear of what might happen or what might not happen. That's the way I've lived most of my life."

He placed his elbow on the table and rested his chin in the palm of his hand. "Fear?"

"Yes, real fear. I didn't really break out of that mold until three things happened. I faced down my father who ruled his family by fear because he wasn't capable of handling it any other way."

"How'd you do that?"

"I stood up to him in Phoenix. He'd beat me all my life, and I was determined he wouldn't do it again. I knocked him silly and left the house before he woke up. I took my sisters and left. Tried to get my mom to come, but she wouldn't leave him."

"What was the second thing?"

"I faced what was probably my biggest fear. I was afraid of who I was, who I might become. I ran away from my feelings, from what I wanted. James helped me face up to that, and I owe him for it."

"I ... I see," he said uncertainly."

"Do you really understand?"

"I think so." But I could see he didn't. A moment later, he stood. "Well, I better get home and finish studying. Unless you have some more work you need me to do."

I sighed in disappointment. Had I revealed too much? Chased him away? He hadn't asked about the third thing.

"No, we're in pretty good shape. Take the truck home again if you want."

"Okay. Wilam, thanks for talking about things with me. For some reason, I needed to know."

CHAPTER 31

Joseph was unusually quiet all the next day as we crated pieces for the Santa Fe show. The work put us in close contact, and although he didn't shun it, I got the feeling he was wary. I regretted answering his questions honestly yesterday. It was poisoning our relationship.

We worked into the night, and because we needed to finish up early Saturday before the local short-haul guys came for the crates, I offered him a bedroom again. I expected him to decline, so I was surprised when he accepted. We cleaned up, ate, played one game of chess, and said our respective good nights. I tossed and turned most of the night. Joseph asleep in the room next to mine was a form of cruel and unusual punishment.

The next morning, I cleaned up and fixed coffee before he appeared. As time wore on, I decided to wake him, but I didn't want a repeat of last time's fiasco. He would really panic if I showed up and found him naked now. Naked, hell. He'd probably slept in all his clothes last night – including his shoes.

I tapped on the door, which was partially closed, and called his name. No answer. I knocked louder; called louder. Nothing. What the hell, had he left in the middle of the night? Puzzled, I stuck my head around the door. What I saw stopped me in my tracks.

Joseph lay propped up on the pillows. He grasped the bedstead with his right hand. His left knee was up. Wide awake and staring right at me, he lowered his leg, taking the sheet with it. He had a huge erection.

"I ... I'm awake, this time," he stuttered.

I don't even remember entering the room. I found myself beside the bed drinking in a stunning array of muscles and organs and rank sexuality. I couldn't move. I couldn't speak.

I saw uncertainty in his eyes, but instead of folding, he made a bold move. He reached up and untied the belt of my robe. The doubt cleared from his eyes when he saw my cock rising up to meet him.

"Gee," was all he said.

Shrugging out of the robe, I sat on the side of the bed. "Are you sure? You have to be sure."

He glanced down at himself. "Doesn't it look like I'm sure?"

I stroked him lightly, gently, as if his flesh were fine silk that would soil or tear if handled too roughly. He did feel like silk. Satiny flesh shrouded his magnificent cock. It was huge, long and as thick around as my own. He moaned as I fingered it. He reached up and pulled me down on the bed beside him. A sudden frown creased his perfect forehead.

"I don't know what to do."

I pulled him close, burying his face in the nape of my neck. "I'll teach you, Joseph. But we have to be patient with one another."

"Why? What do you mean?"

"Think about it for a minute. Think about the role James played for me and offered to play for you."

He understood. "Ohhh." He drew out the word. "I didn't think about that. We're both looking for the same thing."

"Don't worry, we'll find a way to give pleasure to one another."

He moved his hand to my groin. I trembled at his touch. "Maybe like this." He pumped me gently.

"It's not enough. I want it to be better for you than just masturbating."

"Have you ever done the other? You know, given a blow job?"

"No. Well, I tried it, but I'm not sure how well I did."

Determined to make his experience as pleasant as possible, I moved to his chest, tasting his large, brown nipples. He arched his back, pushing himself toward me. I suckled first one and then the other, working my way down his torso, feeling the slabs of muscle padding his ribs. I reamed his navel lavishly, holding his straining cock out of the way in order to reach it. I rubbed his legs slowly, sensuously.

I rose and changed positions, putting my head near his groin and my groin, near his head. I licked his sac. He flinched momentarily before opening his legs to give me access. I felt his fingers on my testicles. Moments later, a warm, damp mouth gently massaged my sac, sending tremors up my spine.

I moved my tongue up the bottom of his long shaft and found a clear, tasteless dewdrop crowning the end. When I sucked him into me, he filled my mouth with just the end of his engorged cock. I gagged before taking half of it. I eased off, and accepted only what was comfortable.

When his lips closed over my glans, the sensation was so intense my cock jumped involuntarily. He came up off of me. Determined to give him all the pleasure I could manage, I tongued the bottom of his shaft as I moved slowly up and down. His mouth took me again. His hands began a tentative exploration of my lower belly and legs. I played with his big balls, rubbed the base of his cock, and struggled to take more of it.

I worked steadily at him; he worked sporadically on me. Before long, he gasped and came up off of me. "Ohhh, Wilam," he crooned. "I'm ... oh!"

His entire body convulsed. His legs thrummed against the bed. His hands found my head and held me tight. His hips thrust against me, driving more of him into my mouth. I gagged. He delivered. His cum spewed, going down my throat, escaping down the side of his big cock. He came for a full minute, while I struggled to take him.

In his excitement, his hand found me and began pumping rapidly. Moments later, I shot, taking him by surprise. My sperm spurted over both of us. He pumped until I was through my orgasm. I collapsed across his legs, his warm manhood pressed against my chest. He released my cock and rested his hand on my leg. No one spoke.

After a few minutes, he grew restless. I rose, recovered my robe, and tousled his hair. He covered himself, glanced up at me a moment before looking away ... as Enrique had done.

Crestfallen, I went to my room and dressed for work. After a silent breakfast of cold cereal, we went to the studio, crated the balance of the showpieces, and turned them over to the haulers. We spoke only when necessary. The atmosphere was not hostile, merely cool. After work, I took him home. He waved thanks and disappeared into his house.

# # # # #

The next week was less hectic, but difficult for both of us. He took some time off to finish studying for finals, and I sat at home, fearful I had ruined a precious relationship.

Friday, I attended his graduation and afterward joined his family for a celebration. That was when I learned his father was Sioux. Our tribe, like many others, traced lineage through the mother, so he was enrolled as a Pinoan. I was warmly received and treated as an honored guest.

Just before I left, I gave him my present, the title to the Nissan Titan and a check covering six months of insurance and the registration costs and taxes. That meant he had to drive me home, and it was almost like the old relationship, but I knew that was only because he was excited about graduating and having a vehicle of his own. He and some of his classmates had dates and were going to a dance later that night. He was up about that, too.

After another restless night, I got ready to go to the airport too early and then had to wait for him to show up. The truck turned into the driveway about five minutes late, which was unusual for him. I was disappointed to see two people in the cab. It was probably his date from the night before. He said he hoped I didn't mind, but she'd be company on the drive back from Junction City. We talked inanities for seventy-five miles. The girl, probably the one he'd screwed on my desk, did most of the talking. She certainly wasn't the shy little Indian maiden of popular legend. I wondered if she was along because he wanted company or as a message to me. Probably a little of both.

221

CHAPTER 32

I had expected the show in Santa Fe to be smaller and less well attended, but I was wrong. There were the usual parties beforehand with an amazing swarm of celebrities for a town of less than 100,000 sitting at the base of the Sangre de Cristos Mountains in north central New Mexico. I managed to find a day to visit the Greshams and Matthew in Albuquerque. While I was there, I called Jason, who invited me over.

David greeted me at the door. As usual, his physical presence left me mumbling like an idiot. He sat with us in the den for ten minutes before leaving Jason and me alone.

"I'm looking forward to your show," Jason said when his friend had left.

"Glad you're going to be able to come. Will David be with you?"

"I couldn't keep him away. He admires your work a lot. As a matter of fact, if things weren't so good between us, he'd probably be interested in you."

My eyebrows shot up. "Don't tell me that. I can hardly utter an intelligent sentence in his presence now."

Jason laughed. "You're looking good, Wilam. We're both proud of what you've accomplished. Who would have thought that shy, skinny, Indian kid I picked up in a park and about scared out of his wits would make such a big splash in the art world? What was it I said? Something about screwing me cross-eyed."

"Now be accurate, Jason. You said you wanted me to crawl on top of you and fuck you until I couldn't fuck anymore."

"So you remember? And you did it. For the next two weeks every orifice I possessed was sore. I'll never forget the sight of you limping down the alley that second weekend. You acted like your 'thing,' as you called it, was going to fall off."

We both chuckled at the memory.

"So how are things with you? With William Greyhorse, I mean, not the artist."

"Not so hot." I was glad he'd made it easy for me.

"Want to tell me about it?"

I described the tragic affair with James and the abortive experience with Joseph. After a few well-chosen questions, he leaned back in his chair.

"Maybe your imagination is getting out of hand. After all, he initiated it. He started talking about sex; you didn't. He seduced you, if you come right down to it. Not that you were hard to get, but he's the one who made every move."

"That's true, but when it came to performance, I let him down. I was such a disappointment he hasn't acted the same since. I'm sure he fucked the girl he took to the party Friday night, and bringing her along on the ride to the airport was a message."

"Perhaps. Wilam, you only have a couple of options. You can do nothing and let the situation wobble on down the road with him in control and not really knowing what he wants. Or you can take control. Face him down and tell him how you feel. Tell him you want to try again. If you wait for him to come to that conclusion, it's liable to be another year ... or never. Tell him you'll try to make it better. Then take your time and deliver on your promises."

"Then there's the other problem."

He looked me squarely in the eye. "The problem of who plays what role in the relationship, right?" I nodded. "Wilam, do you want this young man, or do you want this young man on certain terms and conditions?"

"I want him."

"Unconditionally?"

"Yes. I want him however I can have him."

"Then you don't have a problem. You'll do whatever it takes, play whatever role that's required."

I absorbed his words. "It really is that simple, isn't it?"

"When I first met David, he was just like you. He'd never had an experience with a man before. I honestly believe the idea had never crossed his mind. But when circumstances put him in a position where he was receptive to me, I didn't worry about who was going to do what. I just knew this beautiful man had a need and I was going to fill it. When I saw the size of his equipment, I about went into shock, but I did what I set out to do. I only made one condition, and I did this up front. I told him sex was a two way street, and a fellow's partner had to achieve orgasm, too. I left it up to him how to achieve that.

"Candidly, for a long time I had to be satisfied with him masturbating me. But it was enough, given the pleasure I got from giving him pleasure. When it became more than that, it raised things from the best relationship I'd ever had to the best one I could ever expect. For whatever it's worth, my second best relationship was with you. If I had met you first? Well, who knows?"

"Thanks. I dreamed about you for a long time." I hesitated, wanting to pick up on a point he had made, but uncertain about asking such personal questions.

He saw my dilemma and took me off it. "Go ahead. Ask away."

"Am I so obvious? It's kind of personal, but ... well, you mentioned the size of the equipment. This kid is one hell of a lot better endowed than I am."

"And you're no slouch as I recall."

224

"Joseph is a lot longer and as thick as I am or more."

He smiled. "I can see why you would hesitate. Well, don't let David know I told you, but he's eight inches and as big around as a tree trunk."

"Damn!"

"Exactly. But I accommodated him just fine once I learned to relax and he learned to go slow until I adjusted to him. Do you understand what I'm saying?"

"Yes, I think so."

"It's important, because if Joseph is anything like David, when he gets into it, he sort of goes ballistic. Then it's Katie bar the door."

"You're scaring me."

"But not scaring you off?"

"No. Only Joseph can do that."

"Now you've come to the real point. You're about to allow him to do precisely that without really understanding how he feels. You've observed some things and assigned your own interpretation to them. We all do that. It's human nature. What you have to realize is you're basically very shy. So you err on the side of caution. Let me ask you a question. Have you ever had a sexual partner where you actually initiated the events which led to the act?"

I thought over his question. "Only one. A woman in Phoenix I met at church."

"Wilam, you're an introspective person. Think about your problem, and you'll do the right thing."

As I left, David came out to say goodbye, and I couldn't help but check out his basket. Jason caught my eye and smiled. David didn't notice.

# # # # #

As with the other shows, my work sold out the first day. The gossip writers were swarming as thick as in the big cities, but Diane wasn't there, so they concentrated on other unfortunates. Greenby had flown in from New York, which I took as a compliment. This show, I actually enjoyed. It was a rush having the Greshams and Jason and David and my brother and his family – people I knew and cared about – viewing the art I had put so much of myself into. Even better, they all liked what they saw.

Matthew, done up in his best jeans, a sport coat, and a turquoise bolo tie, didn't know what to make of it. I believe he was a little in awe of his baby brother. I hoped not. I wanted to hear him call me "Pissant" a whole bunch more times.

Friday, I found time to call Joseph at the studio. He answered and asked if that lady had showed up to jump my bones.

"No, did your girl show up for a hump on my desk?"

He laughed. "Nope. Your desk doesn't have any butt imprints in the dust."

225

"Dust? You're supposed to keep things dusted. And I don't mean for you to use Tootsie as a dust mop, either." Now was a good time to clear up the problem of Diane once and for all. "No, I'm afraid the lady you referred to is history."

"So no more headlines, huh?"

"Probably not. What have you been doing to keep busy?"

"I'm trying something new with my stuff. I hope that's okay."

"You know it is. I told you that a long time ago. Will you show it to me when I get back?"

"It's not good enough."

"Nonsense. I want to see it. I'm interested."

"Okay, I guess."

"I just called to confirm I'll be back on the Sunday flight. Can you pick me up?"

"Sure thing. By the way, they delivered your new car today. I didn't even know you ordered one. It's neat. Bitching color."

Before I'd given Joseph the truck as a graduation present, I'd ordered a new, bright red Nissan Altima four-door sedan. "You want to pick me up in it?"

"Can I? You know it doesn't have a keyhole, right? Just a push button."

"Yes, I know. Yeah, pick me up in the new car. See you Sunday afternoon."

A black mood descended on me when I hung up. Events soon closed in on me, so I was able to shake off the malaise.

Saturday afternoon shortly before closing time at the gallery, a slender young Hispanic about twenty or so entered and began making the rounds. As he studied the runner, his back was to me, and for a moment I thought it was Carlos. No, this kid was only about five-seven, and Carlos was taller than I was. His shoulders were broad, his waist very narrow, and his hips slender. He moved with a grace that attracted my attention. It was neither effeminate nor macho, but had elements of both.

I answered a question for a lady about one of the minor pieces, and when she moved away, he was standing nearby, waiting to talk to me. He introduced himself as an art student at the University of New Mexico in Albuquerque. His ambition was to be a sculptor, so he asked a host of questions about techniques, tools, quality of stones, and the like. We talked for almost thirty minutes.

There was no doubt this youth would have followed me to my hotel if I permitted it. He was not obvious, but he was eager and vulnerable. If I took him, it would not be me fucking him; it would be the sculptor he admired. Some artists used the mystique of their craft to seduce admirers, but I wasn't sure I was capable of doing that.

Nonetheless, I checked out the interesting bulge at his fly, and he caught me at it. He looked pleased as his eyes dropped to my groin for a long instant. All I had to do was nod. I wanted to. I needed to. But I couldn't. I was standing there getting a hard-on unable to even nod my head. His body language changed as he saw what was happening. His eyes stared into mine, and then slowly moved down my body.

Ellis called to me from across the room wanting to know if I would join him in a drink. I yelled over my shoulder that I was going to my hotel and rest; I didn't dare face him in the state I was in. He waved acknowledgment and left the gallery.

"They're closing, so we'll have to leave." I said.

"I'll leave with you if that's all right. I wanted to tell you, Mr. Greyhorse ... uh, William, how much I enjoy your work. This isn't the first time I've seen it. I was in Los Angeles about a month ago and saw your 'Victor and Vanquished' at a museum there. I think they're wonderful. I got mad at 'The Victor' for killing such a handsome warrior." We were outside the shop on the sidewalk now. "Did you use yourself as a model for 'Vanquished'?"

"No, afraid not. But thank you.... "

"Luis. Luis Chavrez."

"Thank you, Luis. Well, I'd better be off."

"I'll walk with you part of the way. Are you staying at the La Fonda?" He stole another look at my basket.

"No, the Hilton."

Hell, I didn't even have to nod. He would follow me right into my room. Just outside the hotel I turned to him. "It was nice meeting you, Luis."

"Thank you. It was wonderful meeting you, too. I can come up if you want. You said you wanted to rest, and I give a good massage."

I looked at the attractive young man. "I'm sure you give a hell of a blow job, too. My cock probably would fit in your ass like they were made for one another. I appreciate the offer, but no thanks."

He licked his lips. Oh, hell, was he another John Savage Davis, getting off on talk? "I sure would like to take care of that erection you're having trouble with."

"Look, you seem like a nice guy, but I'm not interested. There's someone else I save all of that for."

"Lucky guy."

"Or woman."

"Uh ... yeah. Okay, I just thought you might need company in a strange town."

After that, I could hardly wait to get back home. That's not fair, I enjoyed the dinner that night. Ellis had invited the Greshams, and they were always good company. Nonetheless, I was glad when the plane touched down

Sunday afternoon only seventy-five miles from my front door. I wondered if
Joseph would show up alone or with company.

Chapter 33

Joseph leaned against the grill of my shiny new Altima and grinned broadly. He was alone. As he walked over to the passenger side, I motioned him behind the wheel. He didn't argue.

"How does it handle?" I asked as we pulled out.

"Like a dream. It's fantastic. Haven't you driven it?"

"Not yet. I bought it over the phone."

"Jeez, nobody does that."

"William Greyhorse did."

He asked questions about Santa Fe – the show and the town – on the drive back to Rolling Hills. As I watched him out of the corner of my eye, I was glad I hadn't taken the art student to my room in Santa Fe. Win or lose ... this was the man I wanted. Remembering what Jason had said, I opened my mouth twice to make my move. Twice, I closed it without uttering a word.

# # # # #

Monday morning, Joseph seemed okay, but some of the easy companionship was gone as we worked shoulder to shoulder picking out marble pieces and chiseling them down to size. After a successful show, I usually get right to work on commissions I'd brought back with me. Consequently, I didn't remember to ask him about the experiments with his own work until Wednesday.

He ducked his head like a shy little boy. "I'm not sure they're good enough for anybody to see."

"Come on. You see my work when it's only scratches on a block of stone. Why can't I look at yours at whatever stage it's in?"

With a show of reluctance, he went to the storage area and brought back a large box. Then he stalled. "You're not going to like them."

"Why? You've shown me the animals you've made before. Why is this so different?"

"It just is. I'm not even sure it's art."

When he finally drew out the first piece, I understood. His other work had been castings or carvings of trinkets. What he had here was a whole other genre. The first piece he showed me was an open bowl about sixteen inches across, but it was not pottery; it was cast. White from the marble dust, with dramatic black and red and yellow swirls created by other materials, it was terrific. I told him so.

"You're not just saying that?"

"No. This is great, Joseph. How long have you been working on this?"

"Since you went to Los Angeles."

"Why didn't you show it to me before?" He shrugged as I turned the piece over. "You forgot to sign it."

"Aw."

"It's an early Sixkiller. Someday it might be worth more than a current piece."

"It's not good enough for that."

"Have you ever seen anything like it before?"

"Well, not exactly like it."

"My friend, you've stumbled onto something."

"You think so?"

"I know so. Can I see the rest?"

Eagerly now, he took out the other pieces. One was a tall vase painted with geometric Plains Indian designs in a mixture of paint and marble dust. It was better than the first one. He had six pieces in all, each a little different, and each in its own way more interesting than the last.

"Joseph, these are definitely works of art, but they're also utilitarian. Some of them are made to contain food. You need to test the material to make sure it's a suitable eating surface. You know, how well it will hold liquids, whether or not it absorbs foodstuffs. Those kinds of details. Is it fire resistant or fire proof?"

Some of the questions he could answer, but others required research and testing. He had several of what he considered failures in the storeroom that we filled with milk and Coke and orange juice and anything else we had in the house. We put scraps of food in others and stored them away in the refrigerator.

He was so pumped by my reaction I couldn't bring myself to broach the subject I so desperately needed to bring to a head. We labored side by side, sometimes on my work, sometimes on his for the rest of the week. An easier companionship returned to our workday.

I knew Joseph was seeing his girlfriend after work, but he never talked about it. Occasionally, she would walk up from the rec center for a ride home at quitting time. That association further discouraged me from talking to him about our relationship, so time dragged on with no resolution to my problem.

Our experiments showed he needed to find a way to seal the surface of his bowls and vases. We spent time researching the library over in Mapleton and talking to West Coast arts and crafts suppliers. Based on this, we tried a few of the more likely options, finally settling on one that seemed to work best. I had been back from Santa Fe a couple of months before this process was completed.

# # # # #

Joseph wouldn't even talk about enrolling in college. His grades were good enough, but he was the main breadwinner of the family, and he argued that taking time off for college would be a hardship. I encouraged him to sign up for a class or two at the community college in Mapleton, but again he shrugged it off.

Because we were both physically and intellectually challenged while perfecting his sealing process, I was able to ignore my other needs. But before long, my frustration over the unresolved issue returned. I went to sleep with a hard-on and woke with one. The sight of Joseph across the studio working at something would stiffen me instantly. One day while he was shaping a piece of marble with his shirt off and his jeans riding low on his hips, the motion of his body as he swung the hammer against a chisel brought me to the boiling point. I resolved to settle things by the end of the day.

Wrong. His girlfriend arrived before he finished cleaning up, and then they left together leaving me in total frustration. I came close to bringing myself off that night but managed to avoid it by reading until three o'clock. The next day was the same. She needed a ride home this time. Apparently, she lived out in the boonies somewhere.

Around nine o'clock that night, a vehicle came to a halt in the driveway. I was in my robe trying to struggle through a news magazine, but having to re-read almost every line because my mind was elsewhere. A knock drew to my feet. It had to be Joseph; he never used the doorbell.

"Hi," he said when I opened the door. "What're you doing?"

"Trying to read a magazine I'm not every interested in."

"Can I come in, or is it too late?"

"Sure, come on in. I haven't been going to bed before midnight lately."

"What's the matter?"

I shrugged. "Can't sleep."

He grabbed a glass of milk, and we sat down. His glance took in my robe as I faced him across the kitchen table. My nipples tingled.

"What's up?" I drew the lapels closed.

"Oh, had a date with Lucy. Just took her home and saw your light was on. Thought I'd see what you were doing. Hoped we could talk a little."

"Lucy, so that's her name. Tell me, has Lucy been on my desk?"

He grinned. "Yeah, once."

He talked about his work a little, trying out a couple of ideas on me, but I could tell this wasn't what was really on his mind. Nonetheless, when he finished that subject and made short shrift of a huge baloney sandwich he'd made for himself, he seemed about ready to leave.

I cleared my throat. "Joseph, I've been wanting to talk to you about something, but the time never seemed right."

He glanced at me and absently rubbed a finger around the rim of his empty glass. "Yeah, I know. I mean, I could tell you wanted to say something. But you don't have to say it. I know the gallery shows are over for the year."

Comprehension dawned. The guy thought I was going to let him go. I shook my head. My hand snaked across the table and touched his arm briefly. "Don't even think about it. I've got enough work to keep us both busy for the next six months. Ellis will scrounge up enough commissions to take care of the next six."

He sank back in his chair. "Man, that's a relief. You've been acting funny ever since you got back from Santa Fe, and I just thought. Well, you know." He glanced at me. "Then what did you want to talk about?"

Now that the moment was at hand, I was at a loss how to say it. "Before I went to Santa Fe ... something happened."

He frowned and swallowed hard. "Yeah, I remember."

"I guess it didn't turn out too well. I'm sorry you were disappointed. I really wanted to make it good for you, but I failed miserably."

His jaw dropped. "You got it all wrong, Wilam. I wasn't disappointed. I thought it was great."

I blinked. "Then why have you been so standoffish? After we finished that morning, you wouldn't even look at me."

He licked his lips. "I was ashamed."

"That happens sometimes, I guess."

His eyes gleamed. "No, not like that. I mean I wasn't ashamed of what we did. It was just because I let you down."

"What do you mean?"

"Gee, Wilam. You did this great thing for me, and I didn't give it back to you. I was going to, honest, but I got so wrapped up when I zapped that I grabbed onto you, and you zapped before I knew it."

I covered both of his hands with mine. "You mean we've both been agonizing over nothing?"

"It's not nothing. I messed up. I wanted to ask you to give me another chance, but I didn't know how. I'm sorry."

I shook my head. "We've wasted so much time. But I don't understand a couple of things. Do you remember when the rock tipped over?"

"Yeah, I got embarrassed because I got a big boner and was afraid you'd see."

I laughed aloud. "Hell, Joseph, what did you think was jabbing you in the butt every time I jumped."

"Your keys. You carry around this big bunch of keys sometimes. I didn't think anybody's prick could be as hard as that."

I shook my head. "The girlfriend? You kept bringing her around and rubbing her in my face."

"No, I didn't. I got a date for the party after graduation 'cause all the guys had one. I've been trying to get rid of her ever since. I thought when I told you about how I felt after doing it to girls you'd figure it out. Especially, when you said it was because it wasn't with the right person. You didn't say right girl, you said right person. I decided right then I was going to do it with

232

you. I didn't know how, but I was going to figure a way. Then when we talked about you doing it with James, I thought for sure you'd ask me to stay over for the night or something, but you didn't."

He paused and took a breath. "Then I worried maybe you'd fire me because you didn't want to be bothered like that. That's why I told you how much my job meant to me on the way to the airport. Then I got scared when you started talking about marrying that lady because there wouldn't be any place for me."

I squeezed his hands. "I've been a blind fool. Do you remember when you asked if you could work for me? I had to think about it because I didn't know if I could keep my hands off you, and I didn't want to find myself facing sexual assault charges."

"I wouldn't of." He smiled ruefully. "I guess we've both been kinda stupid"

"Me more than you. I didn't want to make a mistake because I wanted you around even if I couldn't lay a hand on you."

"You can lay a lot more than that on me right now." He ducked his head shyly. "First you gotta tell me the third thing."

"What third thing?"

"You said you lived your life in fear until you found three things. You never told me the third one.

I smiled. "The third thing was finding that person. The right one."

"You figured that's me?"

I stood as he came around the table. I clasped his shoulders and brushed a lock of hair back from his eyes. My lips on his took him by surprise, but after a moment, he relaxed. My tongue invaded his mouth. He pulled me to him and thrust back. He ground his lips and his hips against me. He was breathless when we parted.

"Wow! That was different. You know what? I liked it," he said.

We went to my bedroom, strewing discarded clothing behind us. When we were naked, he fell to his knees and pulled my erection into his mouth. He went slowly, without rushing and without fighting it. Afraid I'd explode too soon, I withdrew.

"I'm not doing it right?" He frowned up at me.

"You're doing it great, but in another minute, I was going to zap, as you call it, and I want a lot more out of this before that happens."

I pushed him onto the bed and hovered over him. I took my time. I touched and tasted every inch of his finely muscled runner's body. Boldly, he told me what felt good, what was great, and what didn't do anything for him. I wanted to learn his body's pleasure spots so well I could read them like a map. When I had felt him all over twice, I slipped my lips over his huge, throbbing cock, sucking away a clear string of pre-cum.

He pulled me up. "Please, not yet. I want to do it for you first."

While he explored, I kept a hand on some part of him. When he finished with his hands and mouth, he sat astride my waist and rubbed his hungry cock all over me, head to toe. Nothing had ever been more stimulating. Then he stopped and took my dripping cock in his hand.

"I want to suck you before you do me. I couldn't stand it if I let you down again."

I drew him up to me, so he was lying full-length atop me. He felt so good there, so natural, so right. I kissed him again. "I love you, Joseph."

He reared back and looked at me with those huge black eyes. It was difficult to see where the pupil ended and the cornea began. "You can't."

"Why not?"

He shrugged. "I don't know. But you can't, can you?"

"Oh, yes. I do love you."

"What if I can't say it back?"

"Tough luck, I still love you."

Joseph frowned. "I don't know if I love you. I don't know what love feels like."

I laughed. "Then you're the only teenager alive who doesn't. They're always falling in love."

He refused to be diverted from what was to him a serious matter. "I know I want you really, really bad. Like, I could zap just lying here on top of you. And I want to be with you all the time. When I'm not, I wonder what you're doing. I feel comfortable with you. And I don't want you doing this with anybody else. Is that love?"

"It's a start, but you'll know it when it arrives. I don't require that you love me, Joseph. But you're entitled to know how I feel."

I kissed him again, to stop him from talking. Then I began to slither down the torso atop me, biting and licking until I was at his groin. I sucked him into my mouth, and heard him gasp. He forgot about doing me first, and began to move his hips. His legs rode down either side of my chest. He hooked his feet on the inside of my thighs and began to get serious.

I was in trouble. He was only halfway down me, but each time he thrust, more of his cock entered my throat. I almost panicked. I couldn't breathe. What was it Jason had said? He learned to relax and everything was okay. I lost my tenseness, and the panic magically disappeared. A little more of him slipped into me. I began to notice things: his weight atop me, the slight musk of his groin. The warmth of his body. The feel of my nose in his soft bush. He drew out almost to the glans, and I took a breath.

Very deliberately, he shoved his hips forward and rode down my tongue into my throat. He repeated that, establishing a rhythm. I lost my fear and concentrated on what I was doing for him. Before I knew it, the root of his big cock was striking my lips; his curly pubic hair tickled my nose. I had him. All of him. I had done it.

I rubbed his legs and buttocks, pulling him into me as he fucked my face. He grew more agitated, more determined, and more powerful in his hunching. My hand found the sweet spot between his buttocks and stroked him each time he withdrew. The first time my finger touched his sphincter, he cried aloud.

He came, flooding my mouth. His big cock expanded as the fluid rushed through it and into my throat. After what seemed minutes, he stopped grinding himself against me, and wiggled his butt. His legs gripped my chest. His feet and ankles spasmed against my inner thighs. Just when I thought I would suffocate, he slowly withdrew and rolled onto the bed beside me. His eyes were round and full of wonder.

"William!" William, not Wilam. "That was ... that was ... stupendacular."

I burst out laughing. "Stupendacular!"

He wasn't willing to laugh it off. "Spectacular. Whatever you want to call it. I've never come like that in my life. That was the best I've ever got it."

He put his head on my chest and gently caressed me with the tips of his fingers. It was almost sexless, but it was wonderful. He turned his head and looked at me, spearing my chest with his sharp chin. "Do you think I can make you come that good?"

"Joseph, even if you don't make me come at all, it's been worth it to hear how good it was for you. If you just want to do it with you hand, I guarantee I'll get it better than with anyone else."

"No way. I'm going to suck you like you sucked me. Give you a blow job. How does that sound? Joseph Sixkiller's going to give a blow job." Abruptly, he turned serious. "You know what? I understand what you mean. It's that right person thing. You said it'd be good if it was with the right person."

I nodded and pushed the stubborn lock of hair back from his forehead again.

"So I'm the right person?" he asked.

"You are for me."

He thought a minute. "You are for me, too. The right person. The only one I want."

"What about Lucy or whatever her name is?"

"Her mouth's not as pretty as yours." He gave a wicked grin and slid up to deliver a wet kiss. Then he worked his way down my torso with his tongue. My nipples ended up sore. My navel was tender. He washed my balls, one at a time. Then he licked his way up the bottom of my shaft, and for the second, incredible time, his broad, handsome mouth closed over the end of my penis. This time I watched it happen, which made it even better.

His tongue did something to me that was wonderful. Then he tried to take all of me and ended up gagging and in danger of heaving. He glanced up at me with frantic eyes.

"It's all right, Joseph. Don't rush it. Take only what you can handle, no more. It feels great."

He worked on me for fifteen minutes, slowly learning to take more of my length and driving me crazy with his hands. He felt all of my secret places while he bobbed up and down on my rigid pole. Finally, I could stall no longer.

"Joseph, I'm about to come. Come up and finish me with your hand. Don't try …."

My muscles contracted. My body went crazy. I flopped on the bed like a fish out of water. I cried his name and spilled my seed. He stayed with me, gagging and fighting the heaves as I poured out into his mouth. Then it was over, and we both lay still. I stroked his back and ran my fingers through his damp hair as my orgasm faded into memory. It had been incomparable.

"Was it all right?" He spoke around my softening penis.

"Never in my life have I had as good or as long an orgasm."

He released me and grinned. "Really? It was that good for you, too?"

I nodded, and he sat astride my groin to pump a fist in the air.

"Arrright! I did it." He sobered. "But I didn't swallow your stuff." He wiggled his butt again. "I'm sitting in most it."

CHAPTER 34

I hadn't realized how tense Joseph and I had been until I heard his carefree laughter the next day. He tarried after work.

"Can we try it again?" He sounded like a shy little boy ... a shy little boy with a sexy baritone voice.

"Again and again," I replied.

"I dreamed about you last night. About us, I mean."

"So did I."

So we told one another about our dreams, getting hotter and hotter was we talked. Suddenly, he stood.

"I can beat you to the bedroom."

I grabbed the belt loops of his jeans and jerked them down around his knees. "No you can't!"

Thanks to my sneakiness, I beat him to the bedroom okay, but he tumbled me onto the mattress and crawled on top of me. Somehow, he'd managed to lose every stitch of his clothing during the mad dash.

I looked at the handsome, virile young man sitting atop me and wanted more of him. I grasped his semi-erect penis. It hardened to my touch.

I lifted my arms as he stripped the shirt over my head. Then I raised my hips, so he could tear off my trousers. "Now, put your legs between mine," I said.

He obeyed. I lifted my knees and placed my legs atop his shoulders. He understood but hesitated. "Are you sure, Wilam? I don't want to hurt you."

"I expect it will hurt at first. Just take it slow and easy."

I handed him a jar of KY jelly, and he lubricated himself before getting into position. The tip of his swollen cock rubbed the sensitive flesh of my butt. He pushed ... gently. Even so, the pain was almost more than I could bear. He saw my expression, and drew away.

"Go on," I urged. "Give it to me little by little. Take your time."

I'd never seen "eager reluctance" on anyone's face before, but that was what I read on his. He slowly pressed himself against me, gradually pushing his shaft deeper and deeper. He steadied himself with one hand on my chest and wiped away the sweat popping out on my brow with the other. At one point he made to withdraw, but I locked my heels around his waist and pulled him into me. He cooed and crooned and studied my face as he rested a moment. His frown cleared as I told him the pain had eased. Slowly, tentatively, he thrust with his hips.

"Is that the best you can do?"

That unleashed him. He pulled halfway out and drove back into me. Instantly, I was lost in the wonder of his lovingly brutal assault. He shed his gentle ways, throwing himself against me as hard as his strong thighs would permit. I watched him as he performed. His black, arched brows frowned in concentration. His wide mouth parted. His chest muscles worked sensuously as he found his rhythm. His flesh slapped against mine.

I noticed a hundred things about him as he fucked me: a brown mole above the right tit, a small scar on his right shoulder, how his torso had developed since he had been working with the stone. I marveled at the clarity of his skin and how utterly and fascinatingly beautiful he was. He was masculine – manly. He mounted me as he had his women, giving me what he had given them. He was sex. He was love. And he was mine ... at least for now.

His hands gripped my shoulders. His eyes went out of focus. His mouth dropped open. "Ohhhh, Williammm!" he moaned. In the next instant, he gave a mighty thrust and froze hard against my butt. His cock throbbed; it twitched; it exploded with his seed.

He withdrew and slammed back into me. I felt another surge of sperm. He ground his hips against my flesh. Then slowly, leisurely, he began humping again, drawing out the last of his orgasm. Still buried deep inside me, he sat back on his heels and fought for breath.

"Take me in your hand, Joseph."

He opened his eyes. Slowly, they shifted to my hard cock dripping pre-cum onto my belly. Almost as if he were regaining consciousness, a smile built on his lips and touched his eyes. He grasped me in a warm hand. I almost came at his touch.

He masturbated me slowly and leisurely. Yet it only took a minute before I gave my own gasp of awe. I saw his look of astonishment when my muscles clasped his softening cock as my ejaculation struck. He firmed up and gave little experimental thrusts with his hips as I continued to pour out over his hand and my belly.

Joseph fucked me again as I cradled his head in my hands. He twisted his neck back and forth, caressing himself against my palms while he pounded me. As he neared orgasm, he fell forward against my chest, his mouth eagerly seeking mine. His tongue fucked my mouth while his cock beat my ass.

Finally it was over. He struggled upright and reached for me again. I stayed his hand. "You wore me out."

"Me, too." He fell forward again, causing his flaccid cock to slowly slip out of my channel. It was a pleasant, goosey feeling.

We showered together, but it was all I could do to stand there while he washed us both. When we were back in bed, he lay with his leg over mine, groin pressed against my hip, arm across my chest. His long lashes tickled my shoulder. It was quiet in the room for a few minutes.

"Did I do all right?" he finally asked.

"You did yourself proud. It was super."

"It was the same for me. I didn't know it got that good. It made ... it made all the other times seem ordinary. But this was for real." He went silent for a minute. "Wilam, are you going to do that to me?"

I patted his smooth butt. "Is that virgin?"

He got indignant. "Course it is."

"Then that's the way I want you to keep it ... at least for now. We're going at a pretty fast pace. We need to be comfortable with one another. Really comfortable. Then we'll see what happens."

He shifted his body against me. "I liked it when you zapped while I was inside you, I could feel it. Awesome!"

"Stupendacular."

He was silent so long I thought he had dropped off to sleep. Then he poked my hip with his warm groin and giggled.

"I told every girl I was with that she was the best. Now I have to go tell them you are."

"Only if you want to stir up a hornet's nest."

After a while he hugged my chest, a warning he was about to speak. "Did you ever tell James you loved him?"

I considered the question. "I wanted to love him, but he wouldn't let me. He didn't believe he was worth loving. That's probably what drove him back to drinking. By the way, he told me about you the day before he died."

Joseph came up on his elbow. "He did?"

"Not by name, but he told me he'd met a runner who was going to be his new main man."

He lay back down on my shoulder, his head touching my cheek. "I wouldn't of got that close to him. Maybe I was curious, but ...."

"I know, Joseph. I know." I patted him on the flank. He gave another little shove with his groin in return.

He hooked his foot around my leg. "Do you really ... love me?"

When I assured him I did, he asked how I knew.

"Because I want to spend the rest of my life with you. I want you to make love to me every day. I want to be with you and do things with you – ordinary things. Share my thoughts and ideas and work with you. Share my successes and failures. See your work grow until you're an artist in your own right. But I really know because my heart aches when I'm not with you."

"Wow." He thought that over for a minute. "Will you promise me something?" He touched my lips and then my cock. "Promise you'll never use those on anybody else. At least until I get this figured out in my own head."

I smiled. "I promise."

"I promise, too. Not even girls."

"Don't make rash promises."

"It's not rash. It's a real promise. Uh ... am I supposed to move in with you?"

"You're supposed to do whatever's most comfortable for you. I'd like you here with me, but I don't want to mess things up for you at home."

"Naw, they like you. They won't think anything if I move over here to be closer to work."

"Then do it. But Joseph, if you think nobody's going to figure things out, you're kidding yourself."

"Maybe, but I've got a reputation with a few girls. And you ... hell, you're a certified woman fucker. I have the trashy papers to prove it. That ought to buy us some time."

Five minutes went by. His groin jabbed me again. "Can we sleep like this tonight?"

"Yes."

Within a minute his breathing told me he was finally asleep. I lay there a few minutes longer reliving the wonder of the evening. Then I, too, slipped over the edge.

CHAPTER 35

I woke at dawn. I was on my side, and Joseph was pressed against my back. When he hunched gently against me, I realized he was inside me, filling me up. I clasped the hand he had around my chest.

"I ... I couldn't wait,' he panted. "I woke up wanting you so bad."

"Ummm. I like waking up this way."

He was as gentle this morning as he had been savage last night. He grasped me and began to pump lazily. The tempo of his thrusts against my back increased, and before long he slipped over the edge. I heard his moan, felt the spurt of his seed, and then I shot off all over the bedclothes.

I swiped ineffectually at the lenin with tissues while he went into the bathroom to clean up. We were both asleep almost instantly when he hit the bed again, me on my stomach, Joseph half atop me from head to foot.

# # # # #

My fear Joseph would have second thoughts about our new relationship in the cold light of day proved unfounded. When I took a bathroom break in the studio about ten o'clock, I discovered dusty hand prints on my chest and belly and all over my trousers. Laughing aloud, I washed my hands and then went out to show them to him.

"Yeah, I know. I like the marble dust. It lets me know if I missed a spot."

He turned to me with an impish grin. Before I knew it, he'd locked the studio doors, and I was flat of my back on the desk in the office with a very hard and very sizable amount of him sliding in and out of me.

# # # # #

I ceded total control of our personal lives to Joseph within a week. We had sex when and how he wanted, but he was always careful to make certain I was satisfied. I was the boss in the studio, but he ran things after hours. We shared the household chores because he didn't want strangers coming over to clean up while we were at work.

"If we did," he said, rolling one of my nipples between his fingers. "I couldn't do this."

His point was made. We started sharing the clean up and stone shaping duties in the studio as well, so he could devote more time to casting his vessels. He was getting much better at it. He resurfaced our patio table with a mosaic of cultured marble made from multi-hued Jerusalem Stone chips and epoxy.

He had learned how to alter the properties of his reconstituted marble medium to get different textures. He could produce a glossy vase that looked like glazed ceramic or finish a bowl with a grainy, dull exterior. He could do the inside in one mode, and the exterior in a different one. Some pretty good pieces were stacking up in the storage area, but I couldn't convince him to do anything with them except to offer them for sale at local powwows and flea markets. They sold well, but at nowhere near their true value.

# # # # #

Late in the summer, I caught up on my commissions and gave him two weeks' warning we were going on a vacation. I arranged for us to fly to Los Angeles, rent a car and drive back to Denver via Phoenix and Albuquerque. From Denver we would fly back home. Joseph hadn't strayed much farther than Junction City, so the idea appealed to him. A week before we left, I packed three-dozen of his best pieces in boxes and shipped them off to Mr. Gresham without his knowledge. When he discovered they were gone, I refused tell him what I'd done with them. He fussed a little, but I held my tongue.

When the day arrived for us to leave, we left the car in the Junction City Airport parking lot. Joseph reminded me of a schoolboy off to his first summer camp. I was almost as excited because I was determined to make this a good trip for him – for both of us. Also, there were four things in addition to having a good time I wanted to accomplish.

# # # # #

He liked the plane ride, but the crowded metropolitan area of Los Angeles turned him off, as did the downtown skyscrapers. He complained he couldn't see the sky. We spent half a day in the art museum where he studied "The Victor" and "The Vanquished" for an hour as if he had never seen them before. While we were standing there, three women walked up. One explained to the others the technique the sculptor had used and the message he was trying to convey. Joseph had his mouth open to make some comment when I jabbed him with my elbow. He glared at me and rubbed his rib cage.

When they were gone, he turned to me. "Why'd you do that?"

"I like my privacy. What's with you, anyway? You were there when those two pieces were born. You started giving them life with your chisel and hammer."

"I know, but it's different seeing them like this instead of in the workshop. Everyone can see them here." He shrugged. "Whenever we sent one of these pieces off, I got jealous because someone else was going to see it. Now I know that's the way it's supposed to be."

He liked the ocean – there was plenty of sky there. He insisted on buying suits, so we could go swimming. One day, when we were lying on our towels, suits still wet and molded to our bodies, three young women came over and joined us. They helped us drink our colas and finish up the snacks we'd brought, and asked all sorts of questions. I suspect they'd been speculating on our ethnicity and were here to satisfy their curiosity. When they learned we were Indians, they asked a bunch more questions, revealing both interest and ignorance.

All in all, it was a pleasant way to spend the afternoon. When it started getting late, one of them, who obviously had her eye on Joseph – she'd had him smear sunscreen all over her body twice – invited us to a party. I held my tongue to see what his response would be.

"Gee, sorry." He managed to look disappointed. "We already have a gig this evening."

"Oh? Maybe we'd like yours better. How about it?"

"Sorry, it's stag. Bunch of old school buddies getting together. That's why we're here."

The girl's face fell. "How about tomorrow?"

"Tonight's our last night here."

Within minutes, the girls departed, disappointed we wouldn't play their game. When they were almost out of earshot, I heard one of them say all of the good ones were either married or gay.

Joseph shot me an evil grin and yelled, "I ain't married, lady!"

Then he curled up in laughter and snaked an arm around my waist, tumbling me in what I hoped looked to be innocent horseplay.

CHAPTER 36

We flew into Phoenix where I rented a new Audi and headed straight for Mom's apartment. She looked pretty good. She hadn't gained any weight, but she wasn't swollen up from alcohol, either. After spending most of the next day with her, I went downtown to take care of the first of my four goals. I looked up the real estate broker I'd been working with by telephone and closed on a house for my mom, taking title to it in a trust my lawyer had drawn up. That way, Woodie couldn't get his hooks on it.

Then Joseph and I spent the next day buying new furniture and moving her into the house. It was a neat red brick with white trim. I'd made sure it had three bedrooms, so she'd have a place for visitors in case Matthew or my sisters wanted to visit. She was living better than she ever had, and it showed. Her skin was clear and her hair glistened like it used to. But she still wouldn't talk of leaving Woodie, who happened to be on one of his occasional misdemeanor vacations in the county detention center. To make Mom happy, I went to see him in jail.

He looked like hell. His whole body was swollen – not fat, just bloated from the booze. His liver and kidneys weren't handling the alcohol too well. These periodic stays behind bars with their enforced abstinence were probably prolonging his life. I told him about the new house and let him know if he tore it up, there'd be hell to pay – with lawyers involved. Beyond that, I got nothing from the visit. Nor did he. He didn't even bother to vent his spleen.

# # # # #

We left the next day after spending a night in Mom's new home. On the way to Albuquerque, we visited the Grand Canyon. I expected Joseph to lap it up like a big kid, but he didn't. He stood for a long time without saying a word. When he turned to each of the cardinal directions, I figured he was praying.

"Unbelievable," he finally said. "It took Him a long time to do this." He turned to me. "Wilam, do you think He'll punish us for what we do?"

That took me by surprise. "I have trouble believing what I feel for you displeases the Creator."

"Everybody says it's wrong."

"Yes, some do. Bouncing from one person to the other probably is a sin. Whether it's with a man or a woman. But finding somebody and being true to him and loving him? I can't believe that's wrong."

# # # # #

We spent our first evening in Albuquerque visiting with Matthew and his family. My brother had done all right. He was working steadily and had bought himself a small, attractive house. There was no sign of alcohol in his face or manner, and he obviously doted on his wife and two kids.

He held up his new son to show him off. "Pissant, this is exactly the way you used to look when you were crawling around and eating dirt."

Joseph soon ingratiated himself with Matthew's wife and kids. He got down on the floor and played with the babies, laughing with them and letting them crawl all over him. He helped Matthew's wife clean up the kitchen after we ate. When it was time to leave for the motel, my brother took me aside for a few minutes of family talk.

I brought him up to date on mom and Woodie and told him about the house and how there was room for them if they wanted to visit her. I let him know our sisters were all set up. In fact, Nola would start this next fall at Denver University. That's when I handed him two bankbooks and a legal paper.

"What's this?"

"That's a trust document that assures there will be enough money to see my niece and nephew through just about any college they want to go to when they get older."

"Man, you didn't have to do that."

"I know. Matthew, you're working your ass off for your family. You're not drinking up every dime of it like Woodie did. I know you'll provide for them, but this will make it just a little bit easier. Is it okay?"

"Hell, yes, it's okay. It's for my kids, right? But if you ever need it back, let me know."

"The way it's been done through lawyers and all, I can't take it back. Besides, I wouldn't if I could. You can tell Myra about it or not. However, you want to handle it."

"Of course, I'll tell her. Thank you, bro. Thanks a lot." He cleared his throat. "Pissant, when are you going to settle down and have your own kids to take care of?"

I met his steady gaze. "I'm not."

"Aw, you'll meet …." His voice died as he glanced at Joseph talking to Myra while they waited by the car.

"Yes." I answered his unasked question.

"No way! He seems like a regular guy. You sure?"

"I'm positive. He's made me happier than anybody ever has."

"That'll wear off. Sooner or later, you'll want your own family."

"That's what nephews and nieces are for." I turned serious. "It's not a case of arrested development, Matthew. It won't wear off. I'm gay."

"Was it James? Did that son of a bitch do this?"

"No. If you want the truth, I got curious about it that night I watched you fuck him in the lean-to." He flushed and glanced away. "That wasn't what caused it, Matthew. I don't even know exactly what it was. Maybe because Woodie and I had a fucked up relationship. Maybe I never grew up."

He snorted. "Never grew up? You were never a kid, Wilam. I used to watch you go home every day and take care of those two little girls. Hell, it's probably my fault because I didn't help out with Nola and Junie."

I grinned. "Don't let her hear you call her that. She insists on being called June now. But don't talk nonsense. Besides, I don't consider it a fault. Everybody thinks I live this fabulous life ... big artist making lots of money and meeting famous people. It didn't mean a thing except I could make a living doing what I liked. If you really want to know, I started experimenting right here in Albuquerque. Yes, after I went back to the reservation, I tried it with James, but he was as bad an alcoholic as Woodie. He tried his best to straighten out, but it was too much for him. One day he went out and walked in front of a car."

"Christ!"

"Then Joseph showed up and started working for me. Nothing happened between us for over a year, even though I wanted him the first time I laid eyes on him. We became good friends, and then ... then it happened. Matthew, I meant what I said. I've never been so happy in my life. If you think less of me, then I'm sorry, but it won't change a thing."

"You're my little brother, Pissant. Nothing's gonna change the way I feel about you," he said through a rough throat.

"Good, I'd hate to think I was never going to be called Pissant again." We both laughed. "And Joseph?" I asked.

"Hell, I like him."

"I hope you won't act differently toward him."

"I'll act like he's my brother. I can't do any better than that."

"Thank you." I stuck out a hand. He grasped it, and pulled me into a bear hug. My second task was now accomplished.

That night at the motel, Joseph got ready for bed slowly. When he crawled in beside me, he turned on his side and shoved his butt at me. As he knew I would, I spooned up against him.

"Matthew seems like he's doing good," he said. "He doesn't look like a drinker."

"No, I believe he's quit."

"I like Myra and the kids."

"They like you, too."

"What did he say when you told him?"

"How do you know I told him?"

"Because I know you."

"He understands. Says it won't make any difference."

"He's a straight shooter. If he says it, he means it." He was quiet for a minute. "Wilam, how long are you going to go on cheating me?"

"What do you mean, cheating you?"

"Do I fuck you good?"

"Tremendous."

"Do you get it good when I'm inside you?"

"Like I've never felt before?"

"So how come you won't let me see how it feels?"

I rose up on my elbow and tried to see his face, but it was in shadow. "You want me to fuck you?"

He arched his back, digging his butt into my groin. "No, I want you to make love to me."

"Joseph, I will do anything you want me to, you know that. I wasn't trying to cheat you out of anything. I was afraid it would chase you off."

That made him angry. "What kind of lover do you think I am? You think you can run me off so easy?"

He'd never referred to himself as my lover before, and it sent a warm feeling throughout me. "The best," I said. "The very best."

"You know what I figure? Once we do that together, we'll have done it all. Nobody else in the whole world ... man or woman ... can say that about you and me."

Incapable of speaking, I pressed my hips against him.

"I want to do it on my back with the light on. I want to watch you make love to me."

"We need some lubrication."

He was ready. He reached over his shoulder and handed me a tube of jelly. Then he kicked off the covers and lay on his back.

Wordlessly, I got between his legs and kneaded his body from torso to groin to release the tenseness from his muscles and to excite his nerve ends. He rose rampant and ready. I lifted his legs and pressed against him. He gasped as he opened to me. As he had done for me, I wiped away the perspiration and soothed him with gentle words as I slowly fed my eager cock to him. When I was completely inside. I paused to allow him to adjust to my invasion.

"It stopped hurting. It feels kind of good."

Slowly, I withdrew and then eased back into him. He shivered, but not from pain. I moved languidly, finding a rhythm, building the tempo. His big black eyes stayed on me, almost without blinking. He studied my face, my chest, and my belly as if he'd never seen them before. He lifted his head to watch the cock that was impaling him. His legs went around me, pulling me into him. My tempo changed, strengthening and speeding up. Such beauty, such manliness, such raw male power ... and he was all mine. He was taking my cock, my physical love, and preparing to accept my seed.

It came so quickly, it caught me by surprise. My orgasm almost overpowered me. My nerves crackled and popped. It started in the pit of my stomach and swept through my body, consuming me. I poured out into him as if I had not come for months. His eyes widened as he experienced the force of my ejaculation.

While I was still in the dying throes of it, I stayed inside him and grasped his huge cock. It was already dripping, and it took only a few moments before he crossed over. He almost squeezed me breathless with his legs when the tremors took him. He arched his back, driving me even deeper into him. His cum shot into the air, striking him on the chin. His hands gripped my shoulders. At the end, while I was still driving into him with long thrusts of my thighs, he pulled me forward and kissed me deeply. I made as if to withdraw, but he clasped me firmly with his legs, holding me inside him.

Nose to nose, lips brushing lightly, he murmured. "William ... oh, my William. I love you." It came out as a soft sigh.

I remained as I was until our breathing eased and his muscles expelled my now limp cock. "Are you sure?"

"Yes. Now I understand. It's all those things you said, but it's more, too. Like I want to tell the whole world." His gaze focused on me. "But it's enough that you know," he added contentedly.

We slept then. I woke several times during the night, and each time I found his hand loosely clasping my penis. It was a good feeling.

EPILOGUE

The next day I took Joseph to the Indian trading post and introduced him to Mr. Gresham. My mentor pulled out a box holding the pieces of Joseph's work I'd sent weeks ago. The trader talked to him for a long time, asking questions about the process he used. I knew from experience, he was getting a measure of the kind of man Joseph was. I heard some of the same questions he'd asked me six years ago about dependability and dedication. When I left them to go run errands, the discussion had progressed to the point where Joseph had a check in his pocket, and they were discussing the pieces Mr. Gresham would like to have over the next three months. My third task was finished.

# # # # #

At noon, I parked the rental car at the Cooperage and went inside to accomplish the last of my chores. This one was different. This was a test that I, alone, had to pass. I was barely seated when Jason and David arrived. I watched in amusement as heads turned. Every man and woman in the place wanted a better look at this striking couple, especially the tall, handsome Indian.

They greeted me warmly. My heart gave a lurch as David clasped my hand briefly. He was so damned good looking.

"You look better than last time we saw you," Jason observed. "Everything worked out okay?"

"Your advice was good."

"Are we going to meet him?" David asked in his deep voice.

I glanced at Jason. He nodded. "Yes, I told him. I usually tell him everything. I even told him I described his dimensions to you."

David turned dark, but he gave his partner a bemused look. "Damn you." There was no anger behind the words.

"*Are* we going to meet him?" Jason asked.

"Mr. Gresham's dropping him off when they finish their business. You were right, Jason, we were talking past one another, but it took me two months to get up the nerve to talk to him."

"William ... William," he chided. And then his eyes shifted. I glanced at David. He was also looking across the room.

I turned just as Joseph signaled the maitre'd he'd spotted me. Now he strode purposefully toward us, threading his way through the tables. Again I saw heads turn as people watched his progress and wondered who this incredible young man was.

I shifted my gaze to David, the standard by whom I measured all men. David was handsome. It was exciting just to be near him, but his mere presence no longer rendered me senseless.

My fourth task – the test – had been met and passed. I watched Joseph move gracefully toward us, a grin beginning to light his face. He seemed to gather the air and draw the light to him ... at least for me. Jason caught my eye and winked slowly. David gave a nod of approval.

I looked back at my own David, who bore the white man's name of Joseph Sixkiller. At that moment, he looked more like the Indian persona his grandfather had spotted as he watched the child toddle among his playmates. That wise old man had named him He-Who-Walks-Unafraid-Among-His-Enemies.

THE AUTHOR

A native Oklahoman, Mark Wildyr has had a lifelong interest in history, Native American cultures, and mythology. After taking an undergraduate degree in history, Mr. Wildyr served in the United States Army before pursuing a career as a businessman. He presently resides in New Mexico, the setting of many of his stories, which explore developing sexual awareness and intercultural relationships.

Over fifty of his short stories and novellas have been acquired by such houses as Alyson Publications, Arsenal Pulp, Cleis Press, Companion Press, Green Candy Press, Haworth Press, STARbooks Press, and *Freshmen* and *Men*'s magazines. His fiction covers many genres, including mystery, adventure, fantasy, sci-fi, military, police, and sports.

The Hawk Takes Flight, a Novela (STARbooks Press) follows the adventures of two Native American trackers on the trail of drug runners along the Arizona-Mexico border.

In *Cut Hand*, his first published novel (STARbooks Press), the author indulges his passion for both history and First Nations in a 19th Century setting.

His second, *The Victor and The Vanquished* (STARbooks Press), examines the delicate path a young Native American gay man must travel in today's world.

Mr. Wildyr welcomes comments on his work through www.markwildyr.com. His philosophy is that he learns from the reactions of readers.